"Vikings?" Gil whispered. "They're Vikings?"

"Don't be absurd. Vikings don't exist." Rachel stared out the narrow window. The ship was closer, still, and through streamers of mist Gil could see the tall curving prow slicing the water. He glimpsed shadowy figures half-hidden by the sail, and, at the high stern, a man; standing.

"Tell them," he muttered queasily.

"They're not real," Rachel snapped. "It's a film set, or they're re-enactors, or something."

Gil shook his head. His eyes searched the dim interior. There was nowhere to hide, no other door; the windows far too narrow to permit escape. The building was a trap. "We've got to get out of here. Now, before it's too late."

Danni blocked his path. "Sit down," she whispered. "And be quiet."

"They're Vikings, Danni." He cast another furtive glance outside. The mist had closed in, but within it, the grim silhouette loomed huge. "There's no more time! Run!" he cried. "All of you!"

He bolted for the door, slammed it open, and was free, running for his life up the steep path into the wood of white trees, panting to a halt in their leafy shade. A twig snapped behind him. A hand closed on his shoulder. He glimpsed a glittering silver bracelet and skin bristling with coarse blond hair. He wrenched himself around, looked up, and gasped.

A huge man towered over him, his bearded face glowing like a ruddy moon. Fierce blue eyes squinted beneath bushy red brows, and a white scar curled his mouth into a ferocious grin.

"Let me go!" Gil shouted. The man growled a sharp, alien word. Gil shouted again. The man's big, hairy face came close to his.

"Be still," he said in English. _____ _____ ____." His free hand flashed before Gil's eyes and su⟨ ⟩lt of an enormous sword.

THE UNDERWATER BRIDGE

THE WARRIORS OF TIR NAN OG

1

By Alison Scott

Pro Christo Domino

APOLOGIA

To the good people of Orkney, Alba, and the Kingdom of the Isles: I have re-arranged your landscape. My apologies to anyone I may have offended, and I promise to put everything back where I found it when I'm done.

That night,
She came to my father's house,
A lass from a far land.
Eyes, nut brown and bold,
Won this warrior's heart.
I plough sea-furrows;
With Saxon blood,
Slake ravens' thirst.
My sword wins amber treasure,
Welsh gold to speak my love.

from *The Saga of Floki Magnusson*
circa 900 (?) AD

...a thousand years
Are like yesterday, come and gone,
No more than a watch in the night.

- Kethuvim

CHAPTER ONE

The day the Stone-Pecker came, Gil Lake was fourteen years, one month, and twenty-six days old. Danni Gross was fourteen years, one month, and three days old. Whatever happened afterwards, Gil started out the oldest. So, he didn't need his mother shouting after him, "Don't...."

"I heard you," Gil shouted back. "I won't go near the river." He slammed the screen door on anything else she had to say.

"Yes, you will," Percy said. Percy was Danni's little brother. He was twelve, but you couldn't punch him for being a wise-ass like someone else who was twelve, because he had Down's syndrome, and he didn't know he was being a wise-ass. Most of the time, Gil didn't want to punch Percy, anyhow. Percy wasn't that smart, but he was nicer than most smart people ever manage.

"Yeah, Perce." He patted Percy, a little hard. "Thanks."

"Percy's right," Danni said. "You shouldn't lie to your mother." Danni pulled herself up straight so she could look down at him from her whole extra inch of height. "You're not allowed near the river in high water. You should do what she says."

There wasn't anything stopping him punching Danni. So, he punched her, and got three sharp thumps back.

"Ow."

"You started it."

"*You* started it."

Percy looked bewildered. He tugged at Danni's tee-shirt sleeve. "Why are you hitting Gil?"

"Because he's a dork and I hate him."

"No, you don't. You like him." Percy blinked. "You do."

Danni put her neat fist under Percy's nose. "If you know the answer, don't ask the question, Slanty-Eyes."

Danni walked away ahead of them and when she reached the big pine at the fork in the path, she glanced back at the house. Immediately, she turned right.

"You're going to the river," Percy squealed.

Danni stopped and faced him. "So? What's the problem, Slanty-Eyes? It's Gil who isn't allowed. Stay with Gil if you don't want to come."

Percy's lip trembled. "Don't call me that," he said.

Gil put his arm around Percy, glad to be talking about something besides the river. He said, "Don't call him that. He can't help the way he was born."

"So? Neither can I. And I'm stuck with him. Hey, you want him? Keep him. The Last Will and Testament of Danni Gross. I hereby bequeath you my beloved brother Percy." She turned sharply and walked off.

"You only have a will when you're going to die, stupid," Gil said.

"I am going to die. I'm going down to the river and fall in. And die. Just like your Dad."

"You're sick."

"Sick of you."

"Why are you always fighting?" Percy said. He scrunched his eyes up; made a bewildered moon face. "You never used to fight."

Danni and Gil stared at Percy, then at each other. It was true. A year ago, they were best friends. Now they couldn't go out for a walk without it turning into a fight.

But, a year ago, Gil's father was still alive, and everything was different.

"Will you stop asking questions?" Danni said fiercely. She shoved Percy out of her way and ran down the path to where the river glinted through the trees. Percy trotted quickly after her and Gil followed. He didn't hurry because he knew exactly where she was going: back to the Indian Kettle pool. Even now, it was where they always wanted to be.

It was their perfect place. The pool was deep and black, beneath a tumbling waterfall, sheltered by boulders from the fast river current. Big trees shaded it, and above the waterfall, where the path came out, was the broad flat Lookout Rock, where you could lie in the sun after swimming until you were warm again, and dry.

But, at the foot of the waterfall was the best thing, the Indian Kettle, itself. It was a perfectly round hole in the riverbed, a smooth, hollow cylinder into which the river water swirled in a black, foaming whirlpool. It was wide enough to fit even a grown person, and deep enough for Gil or Danni to go in right over their heads without touching bottom. The rock walls were so polished that you were sure it had to be man-made. Which was why Gil had actually believed Danni when she told him that the Indians had carved it out, long ago, by Indian magic.

It was Gil's father who had showed him how it was really made; not by Indians, but by little stones tumbling around and around in the water, for ages and ages and ages. Gil found that even more magical than Danni's story. Either way, it was a wonderful place to play on a summer day. Once you trusted it not to drown you.

It took Gil a whole summer to build up the courage to trust it. All that time, he endured Danni's reckless delight as she slithered and tumbled down the smooth rock slides of the waterfall, disappearing with shrieks of glee into the whirlpool and emerging, as always, triumphant and safe.

"Come on, Gil. It's the best thing ever! You haven't lived!"

But it was easy for Danni. She'd always played here because she was born in Greene Mountain Falls. Gil and his parents had only moved up from the City the winter before, so his father, Laurent, could run an outdoor center with Danni's father, Brian Gross.

Gil's first day at his new school was in January. He struggled into his new down parka, stuffed his lunch money into his pocket, and, bracing himself for a bunch of country kids who were going to hate him, went out the door.

But there, waiting on the porch steps, was a girl. Her cheeks glowed pink in the freezing air, her dark eyes shone, and though she dressed as much like a boy as she could, she was pretty.

She flipped back her dark brown braids like they annoyed her, and shook Gil's hand. "I'm Danni," she said, in a made-up voice, "Your Guide for the Day." Then she grinned, and from that moment, she was his best friend.

Because of Danni, the kids at school decided not to hate Gil. She was tough and good at everything, except maybe studying, and no one ever teased her, even when she had Percy with her. But sometimes she could be pretty rough, too.

Like, when, in the end, she got fed up waiting for Gil to get brave, and just pushed him into the Indian Kettle. He remembered his own horrified scream, as he scrabbled desperately at the sun-warmed rocks of the waterfall, and the terror of losing his grip and plunging into the whirlpool's depths. The icy darkness closed over his head. The pummeling currents swirled him around like clothes in a washing machine, and then, just when he knew he was going to die, the tumbling waters welled up beneath him and he popped like a cork to the surface.

And there was Danni, freckled and sun-tanned, hair in pigtails, grinning down from the Lookout Rock. Mad as he was, he couldn't stop grinning back his own sheepish delight. What Danni had been telling him all summer was true. He couldn't drown in the Indian Kettle, not even if he tried. The stronger the current flowed in, the stronger it pushed him safely back out. It wouldn't let him drown. It wouldn't let anyone drown. Or so he thought.

Gil came out of the woods, picked his way through the clumps of poison ivy and looked down from the high Lookout Rock. He breathed in the shadowy river smell, and frowned, puzzled. In his dreams, the river was always dark and foreboding, with huge, foaming rapids. The whirlpool of the Indian Kettle shone like a black, cruel eye.

But the real river below sparkled and splashed, bright blue in the June sunlight, innocent as the summer's day. *June twenty-first*, Gil thought. It hardly seemed a whole year had passed. He felt like he was locked somehow in the same awful moment in time.

Everything was exactly the same. Even the freaky weather. Like this year, it had rained for a whole week and the river roared like a spring thaw. It was too high for tourists' rafts, or classes of kayak beginners, So Gil's father and Brian tossed a coin, and while Brian sat at his workbench mending fiberglass kayak hulls, Laurent went out on the river to play.

At suppertime, he hadn't come home. Then it began to get dark. Brian went out on the wild river, looking for him, and found the empty yellow kayak, spinning like a playful puppy, in the eddies of the Indian Kettle whirlpool.

The rescue people searched the river for days and days. Even after they'd given up, Brian scoured the brush-tangled banks for weeks, and then months, until at last, he gave up, too. That was the worst part for Gil; that his father was in that river somewhere, even now. That part, he wouldn't talk about, not even with Dr. Fairchild.

Danni was standing a few feet away on the Lookout Rock, throwing pebbles into the water. Percy copied her, like a shadow. She skipped a stone, three skips, before it sank.

Gil shouted, "Hey, cool." Danni smiled, like the old Danni again. Gil shrugged at the whirlpool and said, "It always looks littler than I remember it. The Indian Kettle. It looks little."

She skipped another stone. "It's bottomless," she said.

A chill went through Gil's heart, even though he knew this was just another one of Danni's stories, like her Indians. "It's not," he protested. "I touched the bottom. Once."

"You didn't," Danni said. "Nobody has. It's bottomless."

"If it was bottomless, the river would run out," Gil said. "Like a bathtub." He grinned.

Percy squealed. "A bathtub? A bathtub?" He giggled hysterically. Some things did that to Percy. Gil grinned a wider grin.

"Okay, wise-ass," Danni said. "Not bottomless. But really, really deep. So deep that it may as well be bottomless." Danni threw a rock right into the whirlpool. "That rock's never coming out. Everything that goes to the bottom stays at the bottom."

Gil stared at her. Then he lunged forward. "Shut up!" He

grabbed her by one arm and shoved his hand over her mouth. "Shut up! Shut up! Shut up!"

Danni jerked her head free. Her dark brown eyes were wide and scared. Gil grabbed her other arm and shook her. He squeezed his own eyes shut, but the horrible picture rose up behind his lids...*the bones, like old cooked chicken bones...sinews bare, flesh rotting...circling around and around in the sunless murk....*

"Stop it, Gil. That hurts!"

"I hate you!" Gil shouted. "I hate you all! I hate everybody!" He opened his eyes. Percy was crying, big round tears rolling down his cheeks. He pulled Gil's arm.

"I love you, Gil."

Gil sighed. He let go of Danni. She rubbed her arm. "No wonder they got you a shrink," she said. She backed away from him.

"I'm sorry, Danni," Gil said. "I'm sorry. It's the day. It's June twenty-first again."

"Like, I don't know that?"

"I can't keep myself from thinking about it," Gil said. He looked at the river and shrugged miserably.

Danni turned away. "Well, I can't keep being your friend. You're too weird." Then she turned back and grabbed him and shook him, like he'd done to her. "It wasn't your fault! It wasn't your fault! What's it going to take?"

Gil said, "I should have been with him."

"You sound like my dad."

"No," Gil said. He looked at Percy, watching them fearfully. Then he took a deep breath and made a decision. "Perce," he said, "Find us some stones to throw, okay?"

Percy looked at Danni. She nodded. He put on a serious face and went off to gather pebbles into a careful heap.

"That was different," Gil whispered. "They tossed a coin. But Dad wanted me to come. He asked me."

"But you said you never saw him."

"Well, it's true. I didn't see him because I was hiding. He came to my room. I had that new kayak," he muttered, "And he'd been talking about trying it out. I knew that's what he wanted, so I hid in the closet." Danni was staring, mouth open, like a stupid fish. "So I was scared, okay?" he said angrily.

She backed away again. "Okay. It's cool. Okay."

"So, it was my fault," he said. Danni didn't say anything.

"And, even if the rest of my life, I'm punished for it, it still won't ever be right." He flopped down on the smooth, warm stone.

Danni sat down beside him. He could see her thinking this new thing over. Everything going on in Danni's head showed on her face. "Even if it's true," she said in her practical voice, "Who's going to punish you?"

He shrugged, and said, as casually as he could, "Maybe God?"

"For being scared? What kind of dumb God is that?"

Gil threw his hands in the air. "I don't know. I didn't invent the world." In spite of himself, he giggled.

He was glad he had Danni. He couldn't talk to his mother about any of this. Danni's dad, Brian, didn't even believe in God. And Dr. Fairchild just looked at the ceiling and said, "Why do people teach children these things?" before he explained for the zillionth time that Gil's father had had an accident and an accident wasn't anybody's fault.

That left Sophia, Danni's mom. Sophia believed in a Goddess called Gaia. At the Memorial Service they had for Gil's dad, by the river, she threw green leaves in the water and told Gil and Danni that everything that died went back to Gaia. Then she told them to bury a mouse Percy's cat had killed, so it could turn into flowers. Which might have helped if they were, like, six.

Of course, Percy *was* sort of like six and believed everything you told him, so a couple of months later, he dug it up, looking for flowers, and just found bones. It wasn't a big deal. It was almost funny. But that's when Gil's nightmares began.

It was really the same nightmare, over and over again. All he ever dreamed about was bones. Sometimes it was a tree branch in the river that turned into bones. Once the bones were in the cellar of the house. But almost always the bones were in the Indian Kettle, spinning around and around in the watery dark. Whenever he dreamed the bone dreams, he woke up screaming. That was the real reason he needed a shrink.

Still, there was no way he would have had one, if it weren't for Dr. Fairchild. Gil's mother could never have afforded to pay for a psychiatrist. But Dr. Fairchild didn't want money. He'd read about Gil's family in the paper, and he wanted to help. Gil's mother told him he was incredibly lucky to talk to Jason Fairchild, even once. He was famous and wrote books about children's problems and had his own clinic near the City.

Gil expected an old man, about fifty, with a white coat, and maybe a beard. Dr. Fairchild showed up wearing jeans and a fleece. He had wavy blond hair, and brilliant blue eyes, though most of the time he wore sunglasses. Gil talked to Dr. Fairchild every other week, about anything Dr. Fairchild wanted, even the Indian Kettle. But the dreams kept happening, anyhow, right up to the day the Stone-Pecker came.

It was Percy who saw it first. Danni had gone back to skipping stones and Gil was sitting cross-legged, staring at the river. Percy shouted, "Hello, bird!" They ignored him. Percy was always saying hello to things; animals, trees, even rocks. "Hello!" Percy said again.

Gil looked up. Percy was standing off by himself, smiling up at a branch of an old pine tree. On the branch was a huge grey and black bird. It had yellow eyes and an enormous black beak and it was looking right at Percy with a human kind of stare, as if it understood "Hello" perfectly. Then it spread its wings and Gil scrambled to his feet.

"Danni...." he called.

She looked up and stared. "Get away from it, Percy," she cried.

Gil lunged forward as the bird launched itself from the branch, straight at Percy. "Duck!" he shouted. But Percy just stood there, mouth open.

"Get away!" Danni screamed at the bird. She ran at it, waving her arms, as it swooped down on Percy with huge black wings. Gil saw, then, that its beak was half-open, like it held something, and then the beak snapped shut as it soared over Percy's head. There was a sharp click, as the thing from the bird's beak hit the ground.

The bird flew across the pool and landed on a rock above the waterfall. Gil and Danni both turned from Percy to watch. It looked back with its yellow eyes at the thing it had dropped at Percy's feet. He crouched down, and Danni turned quickly and cried, "Don't touch it!"

But he was already holding it in his pudgy hands, smiling his happiest smile. Danni lunged to take it, but Gil saw it more closely then, and laughed. "It's just a stone," he said, relieved. "What a weird bird."

The bird made a throaty, rasping, "Caw," ruffled its feathers, and then sat still. Gil and Danni gathered around Percy. He held up his stone. It was white, circular, flat, a perfect smooth disc, and right in the middle was a smooth round hole.

"What a weird stone," said Gil.

Percy sat the stone in the middle of his palm and pushed his middle finger through the hole. "Look!" He wiggled the finger and beamed.

"Let me see," said Danni.

Percy pulled the finger out and, with both hands, clasped the stone against his chest. "It's mine."

"We know it's yours," said Gil. "We just want to see it." He held out his hand and smiled. "I won't keep it, Percy."

"Come on, Perce," Danni said. "Just a look."

"You called me Slanty-Eyes," he said.

Danni clutched handfuls of her hair and pretended to pull it out. Percy watched, then turned back to his stone. Danni looked across the pool. "That bird's creepy," she said. She crouched down and picked up a dead branch. "I'm getting rid of it."

"Don't!" Gil said.

She raised her arm to throw the branch, but suddenly Percy shrieked. Gil whirled around. Percy was holding the stone flat against his face, the center hole over his right eye.

"What's happened?" Danni dropped the branch. Percy shrieked again. Gil rushed forward and grabbed the stone, snatching it from Percy's fingers.

"Is his eye all right?" Danni cried.

Percy was blinking and rubbing his closed lids. Then he opened his eyes, blinked again, and smiled. "I saw people," he said.

Danni tilted her head, puzzled. "You mean us?" she said.

"You saw us through the stone?"

"No, people."

Gil looked at Percy and then at the stone in his hand. He turned it over, then raised it in front of his face and looked through the hole. He saw the rocks and the river in a circular frame. He shrugged and said to Danni, "Is he making it up?"

"He doesn't make things up," she said, and added quietly, "I don't think he can."

"Well," Gil said, looking back through the stone, "I don't see any people." He lowered it and turned it in his fingers. "It is weird, though. How'd it get that hole in it?"

He handed it to Danni. She looked through it over the river, squinted at the bird, then abruptly tossed it back to Percy. "Who knows? Who cares?"

"Maybe the bird made it." Percy balanced the stone on his finger.

"Made the hole?" Danni said.

"He could peck it. Like a...like a...." he waved his hands, thinking hard.

"Like a woodpecker?" Gil smiled.

"Like a woodpecker!" Percy crowed happily. "A woodpecker! A woodpecker!"

"It's a stone, dummy." Danni put her hands on her hips and glared at Percy. "Birds can't peck stones."

There was a great rush of wings from across the water. "Watch it!" Gil cried. "It's coming back!"

The grey and black bird swept over his head, splayed its wings and landed with a thud at Danni's feet. It fixed its yellow eyes on her face, then lowered its shiny black head and struck the rock, fast and furious, like a miniature drill. The air rang with a loud, staccato rattle. Then the sound stopped. The bird raised its head, made one loud "Caw!" and flapped vigorously into the sky. Before them, in the solid, weathered surface of the Lookout Rock, was a small, perfect, round hole.

Gil and Danni stared at it, open-mouthed. Gil knelt down slowly. He ran his finger around the rim of the hole and felt the smooth inside. Then he looked up at Danni. "That's not possible," he said.

Danni looked scared. "Maybe the hole was there before?" she said.

"It wasn't there before. We just saw it happen."

Danni wrapped her arms around herself and shivered. "I don't like this," she said. She stepped closer to Percy who was playing again with his stone. "I want out of here."

Percy pointed to the bird, back on its perch across the river. "It's a stone-pecker!" he said, gleefully. "Stone-Pecker! Stone-Pecker!" Percy held the white stone up to his eye again. "There's the people," he said, matter-of-factly.

"Give me that!" Gil grabbed the stone and stared through it. He saw river and trees.

Percy patiently waited, then took his stone back. "It's a boy and a girl," he said.

"Don't listen to him!" Danni shouted. "Percy! There's no one there!"

Percy was moving the stone around for a better look. "The boy's face is brown!" He shifted the stone sideways. "The girl has a long, long, *long* braid!" he cried. "Like, like—"

"Lara Croft," Danni said sharply.

"Lara Croft! Lara Croft!" Percy crowed. He looked back into the stone. "Hello, Lara Croft."

Danni smiled at Gil and shook her head. She looked relieved. "It's my DVD. That's where he's getting it from Gil."

But Gil had taken the stone back from Percy again, and was staring through it, transfixed. The girl he was seeing wasn't Lara Croft. She didn't have a long braid, or if she did, he couldn't see it, because over her head was a piece of white cloth. But he could see her face and it was the most beautiful face he had seen in all his life.

"Danni," he said, very softly, "I see someone, too."

"*What?*"

Gil couldn't bear to take his eye from the beautiful girl. He beckoned Danni closer. When she was right beside him, he made himself draw back from the vision, and carefully, he handed Danni the stone. Danni gave him an odd look, but raised the stone and peered through it. She shrugged.

"Can you see her?" Gil said eagerly. "Isn't she…?"

"There's nothing there, Gil," Danni said. He snatched the stone back, so roughly that Danni shouted "Ow!"

Gil held the stone up and then sighed with relief. She was still there, bending over something in her hands. Then she raised her head and looked straight into his eyes. Gil gasped, clutching Danni's sleeve. "Danni, she can see *me*. It's real. It works both ways."

"Let me see!" Percy cried. "Let me see Lara Croft."

"It's not Lara Croft!" Gil said. "She's real. She's a real person." He stared back, meeting her soft green-eyed gaze. "She's so beautiful."

Danni's hand came out of nowhere, and whipped the stone away. "It's Percy's," she said angrily. "And it's Percy's game. He can't help acting stupid. You can."

"No game," Gil whispered, wonderingly. But he let Percy keep the stone. It was Percy's. The Stone-Pecker had given it to Percy. Cautiously, Gil said, "You can see her, can't you, Perce?"

Percy stared into the stone. He smiled happily and chortled to himself. "I see—I see—I see...."

"The girl! Right, Percy? My girl."

"Your girl?" Danni's mouth fell open.

"A cup!" Percy exploded in giggles. "I see a cup! A cup!" He clutched the stone and waved it around, then looked through it again. His voice went soft and hoarse. "I see a beautiful cup!"

"See what you started?" Danni said.

But Gil pounced on Percy, wrestled the stone away from him, and peered through it desperately. He spun it around, turned himself in every direction, but saw nothing but river and trees. Percy was clamoring for his stone back, shouting, "My cup! My cup!" like a little echo. Reluctantly, Gil handed him the stone. Percy stared through it silently. "My cup's gone," he said. He looked as sad as Gil felt, losing the green-eyed girl.

Across the pool, there was a sudden loud "Caw!" and the Stone-Pecker rose up and flew back over their heads, its wings spread wide.

"Oh, you!" Danni cried. "I'm sick of you!" She snatched the stone from Percy's hand, and ignoring his squeal of protest, raised her arm and hurled the stone at the flying bird.

"No!" Gil cried in dismay, watching the white stone arc out across the water, graze the tip of the Stone-Pecker's wing, and plummet straight into the Indian Kettle's swirling black heart. Gil stared at its fading splash. "Oh, Danni," he cried, "You and your stupid temper." He wasn't surprised, only miserable. Danni did things like that. But he'd never have foreseen in a million years, what Percy did next.

"My stone!" Percy wailed. "My Stone-Pecker stone!"

He ran to the very edge of the Lookout Rock, staring into the turbulent water and waving his hands in frantic agitation. And then he just leapt, in all his clothes, right into the river.

"Percy!" Danni screamed.

In a moment, Percy was tumbling down the waterfall. Weighed down by wet garments, he splashed wildly in the deep water below. Then the whirlpool of the Indian Kettle swallowed him in an explosion of froth.

"Percy!" Gil shouted, to where Percy's brown head should instantly emerge. But there was no brown head. Nothing but foam and a downward swirl of black water.

"Ohmygod!" Danni shrieked. "Where is he?"

She stared at the whirlpool, one second longer, then hurtled into the waterfall, skidding down the wet slide on the seat of her jeans. She crossed the pool in two strokes, and dove head first into the circling water. It closed over her kicking feet as Gil watched in horror. It wasn't possible. It couldn't hold two people. It wasn't big enough.

Then, suddenly, he saw the whirlpool of his dreams, enormous and menacing, with hidden terror at its depths. *It's bottomless.* Gil ran to the edge of the Lookout Rock and stopped. He teetered on the wet stone, arching his body out over the waterfall and the Indian Kettle, willing himself to jump. Danni and Percy were in there! He had to—but the nightmare rose up before him; the awful murk, the circling bones…. His feet gripped the stone against his will. His whole body shook. Then he heard Danni's voice, as clear as if she stood beside him: *I'm going to fall in and die. Just like your dad.*

"No!" Gil cried. "No!" He launched himself into the waterfall, skidding and sliding. Then the river took him and he had no more choice. Floundering in his wet jeans, he dog-paddled for a second, took a huge breath, and forced his face downwards into the whirlpool's foaming depths. Arms outstretched, kicking with all his strength, he plunged into darkness, down and down, deeper and deeper, his hands flailing in the circling murk.

His fingers struck something solid and he gasped in terror. But it was not bone. It was something rough and rubbery. A sneaker! Danni's sneaker! He flailed again, and his hand closed around her ankle. "Danni!" he cried and instantly swallowed water. But he hung on, dimly aware he was still descending, faster and faster, into an unimaginable depth.

The strength of the water grew, became unbearable, tearing at his grip on Danni's ankle. He clung desperately, but felt her foot slipping relentlessly through his fingers. The darkness grew, and in the instant before total black consumed him, he lost his grip, and she was gone.

CHAPTER TWO

I'm dead, Gil thought. *This is what it's like.* Darkness pressed against his face. Cold enveloped him. Blackness forever. Cold and blackness. This was the punishment. Terror caught in his throat. *But I'm breathing.* He breathed in and out for reassurance. *I have to be alive.*

But then, the blackness, the cold? He pressed his eyes hard. They didn't hurt. Why couldn't he see? He slid his hands off his face and felt for the shape of his own body in the blackness. His fingers plucked at his tee shirt and jeans, the skin of his forearm. They were normal. But something was strange. Wrong. His clothes were dry. He was in the whirlpool, a moment ago, but his clothes were dry.

Gil looked up, into the blackness, for an answer, and then, with a start of joy, he saw a tiny point of white light. Then another. And another. A star. Stars. He wasn't dead. He was outside and it was night. He had another start of happiness as logic flooded in.

It was night because he'd been unconscious. He'd almost drowned in the Indian Kettle, but it had released him, the way it always did, in the end, and he'd reached the riverbank. So, maybe Percy and Danni did too! Maybe they were waking up, too, nearby.

Gil struggled to sit up, forcing his cold limbs to respond. He reached out his left hand to brace himself. His fingers, seeking sand or stone, sunk into something soft as velvet and bitterly cold. Cold as ice. As—"Snow!" Gil cried aloud, astonished. "There's snow!"

The shock sent a surge of energy through his body. He sat

up and felt all around himself, with his palm. A thin layer of fresh snow-covered rocks and grass and low, wiry plants that felt like nothing he'd seen by the river. Maybe he'd washed way downstream somewhere and maybe there'd been really freaky weather down there, and it snowed, even though it was June. But, how were his clothes dry, on a night that was cold enough for it to snow? Huddled in the darkness, he wrapped his arms around his body, tucking his freezing hands under his armpits. Then, as he sat there, he realized there was one good thing about the weird snow. In the starlight reflecting off it, he could see. Though what he saw made no more sense of anything.

First of all, there weren't any trees. There were rocks and low hills and against the horizon, now fiercely starry, higher hills. Off to the left, something glinted, like water, but it was far too big for even the widest part of the river. Too big for any of the mountain lakes. He peered into the distance at the far glimmering horizon, and his mind refused to accept what his eyes kept seeing: *It's the ocean.*

He shook his head. Slowly he got to his feet and stepped toward the silvery horizon. There was a loud splash and a sudden rush of colder cold enveloped his right foot. Startled, he jumped back. His sneaker and sock were soaking. Right at his feet was a small dark pool. He touched his sneaker toe lightly on the surface; then stepped right in, soaking his foot again. Whatever had happened in the whirlpool, this was real water that made you really wet. He felt strangely relieved. The little pool seemed like a friend.

Reluctant to leave its security, Gil turned around to view the scene behind him. His gaze followed the dim horizon, then came to a brutal halt. A bare ten feet away, an enormous black form rose up and blotted out a huge rectangle of sky. Heart racing, he shrank back, staring at the black thing. Gradually, his breath slowed. Whatever it was, it wasn't alive. Stepping warily through the snow, Gil approached it, with blindly outstretched hands. Its shadow fell over him, just as he touched the vertical surface. Stone. It was stone. A huge block of stone, fifteen, maybe twenty feet tall.

And beyond, there was another. Gradually his vision opened and he picked out the outlines of a receding line of great, rough, rectangular pillars, curving into the night. Cautiously, he worked his way around the dark mass of the first. From its far side, he could make out another curving line of stones extending in the opposite direction. Far off, almost obscured by the night, the two arcs joined, making one vast, snow-filled circle.

Gil stared in wonder. He had seen nothing like it in all his life and his mind could not begin to grasp how such a place could exist, undiscovered, so close to all his familiar world. Maybe he was still unconscious. Maybe it was a dream. He laid both hands against the cold, rough stone, then leaned close and pressed his face against it. He put out his tongue and licked the wet surface. It tasted of salt, and smelled of earth. *This is real*, he thought. *I'm not going to wake up out of this.* And in that moment, he saw a light.

It wasn't starlight. Or a flashlight. It was red; the orange-red flickering light of fire. And it was moving, jerking up and down, and, with each jerk, growing larger as it came closer and closer to where he stood. It was fire, and someone was carrying it. Gil turned and ran, stumbling past the first huge stone. He skidded down the snowy hillside the way he came. The little pool glowed softly in the starlight. At its edge, buoyed by its tiny comfort, he turned to face whatever approached.

The flame was big now, flickering, sending orange tongues of light over the snowy ground, lighting the great black stones and casting their huge moving shadows over the hill. He saw the shape that carried the flame. It looked small amidst the stones. With one arm it held the flame high, on a stick; a burning torch. It stopped, peering, shading its eyes with its other hand, and called out, "Who's there?" The voice, even quavering with uncertainty, was unmistakable.

"Danni!" Gil shouted. "Danni! It's me! It's Gil!"

"Gil!" Her response was joyous. "You've come!" She lowered the torch slightly, extending its light toward him. "You've come at last!"

Then she ran forward, stumbling recklessly down the snowy hillside, the flame bobbing wildly. She opened her arms wide, as if she would hug him, oblivious of the flaming torch in her hand. But just as she reached him, she stopped, as some new caution overcame her. "It is really you, isn't it? Not some Change-Thing?"

"Some what?" he muttered in a voice made small by astonishment. There wasn't any reason for her not to know him. He hadn't changed. But the only things the same about Danni were her voice and her dark, shining eyes.

Everything else was different. She was wearing some kind of dress that covered her, almost to her ankles. There were boots on her feet, with fur on the outside, and a kind of cape with a hood over her shoulders, clasped at the front with shining metal. Her hair was longer, and tied in two bunches with strips of cloth and her face was tanned like she'd been in the sun a whole summer. But she wasn't dressed for summer, and it wasn't summer here.

"Why did you let go?" she cried suddenly. "We've lost so much time!"

"Danni, where is this?" Gil said. "How did we get here? And your clothes—where—?"

"Look out!" she shouted. She waved the flaming torch and pointed, and out of the blackness something dark swept by his face. It gave a loud "Caw!"

"That bird! The Stone-Pecker bird!"

But Danni wasn't pointing at the bird, but at the little pool behind his feet. Gil looked over his shoulder. It was bubbling and swirling; suddenly alive in the torchlight. He stumbled backwards in shock, his heel dipping into the water, and out of the pool that was his friend, something arose like a jaw and gripped his ankle with tremendous force. In an instant, he was jerked backwards, into the swirling foam. "Danni!" he cried, but in another instant he was plunging downwards, into the darkness, the waters closing over his head.

Gil fought back wildly. He struck out with both hands and kicked with his free foot, but the thing that held him had the fierce water on its side. Together, they were impossible to combat. But then he felt the water slacken and then turn, like a tide, changing direction as if it would draw him back up to

Danni. He seized his chance, renewed his efforts, and swam with it, clawing frantically upwards with all his strength. But the thing holding him grasped his other leg, and then his knee. It was stronger even than the water, and merciless, dragging him deeper and deeper, without remorse. *I'm going to die,* he thought. *I wasn't dead at all, but now I will be.* An image flashed before his eyes. It wasn't his whole past life, like was supposed to happen when you drowned, or his mother, or home, or anything. Bewilderingly, all he saw as the darkness closed in was a circle of white stone, and, at its center, a beautiful green-eyed girl.

And then, suddenly, he burst up out of the water, feet first, and then his head, into blinding white sunlight and the river's deafening roar. But the thing still held him. He shut his eyes against the unbearable light, but gasped fresh air in one huge gulp, and with strength returned, fought and kicked for freedom. Over the river's roar, he heard another sound, a loud, male voice, close-up, right in his ears, shouting his name.

"Gil! Gil! Stop fighting! You're safe now! You're safe!"

"*Safe?*"

"Gil?"

He opened his eyes. Brian Gross was holding his shoulders in both big, rough hands, shaking him gently, "You're safe." His face and beard were dripping wet, and water ran from his bright orange dry suit. He smiled a big relieved smile and then said, kindly, "Hey, Gil, now what did I tell you about high water?"

Gil squinted against the sun and looked around. They were sitting on a bare flat rock at the river's edge, downstream of the Indian Kettle pool. Brian's red kayak turned gently, beside them, in an eddy. Two more kayaks were drawn up on the riverbank and their owners, Dave and Ivan, were watching. Gil waved feebly and said "Hi."

Ivan waved back, and grinned, but Dave said solemnly "That was one close call, Gil. If Brian hadn't seen you go in as we came over the fall, you'd be dead. How many times have we told you to stay out of the water when the river's up?"

Gil didn't say anything. He shielded his eyes and stared across the river. The old pine where the Stone-Pecker had perched looked the same, but there was no black bird. The Lookout Rock was the same, but there was no Danni, no Percy. A puff of wind rippled the pool and Gil shivered in his wet clothes. *Wet clothes.* He touched his sodden jeans.

"My clothes are wet," he said.

Brian and Dave stared at him. Ivan gave another of his slow crooked grins. "Occupational hazard of falling in the river, Gil," he said. He raised one bushy eyebrow, and winked.

"And it's daylight again!" Gil looked around, astonished. "And there's no snow!"

"Snow?" Ivan's eyebrows went higher.

But Dave and Brian exchanged a quick look. "Hypothermic," Brian said. Dave dove for his kayak and was back in an instant with a space blanket. He wrapped it quickly around Gil's shoulders and said, "Hospital."

Brian swept an arm around Gil and lifted him to his feet. "Can you walk?"

"Of course I can walk," Gil said, embarrassed. He pulled away from Brian's arm and pointed urgently at the Indian Kettle. "We have to get Danni, first!" he said. "And Percy! Percy must be there, too!"

"Be where?" Dave asked, puzzled.

But Brian's face went white. He grabbed Gil by the shoulders so hard it hurt. "Gil! Were they in the river, too?"

Gil nodded vigorously. "They were first," he said. "Percy went after the Stone-Pecker stone and Danni went—"

"He's hallucinating, Brian," Dave said. "He's not making sense."

"I *am* making sense. Percy went in the Indian Kettle and Danni went in and then I went in. They're still there!"

"Downriver!" Brian shouted. He leapt for his kayak and was in it in seconds. He raised his paddle and called out, "Dave, get Gil to the hospital. Ivan, call 9-1-1, and follow me!" He plunged his paddle deep into the water and shot out into the rapids. "I'm going after them."

"No!" Gil called, but Brian was already a flash of orange, midstream, disappearing around the first bend.

Dave put his arm around Gil and said gently, "Come on.

We'll get you looked after." He turned him away from the river. Gil looked over his shoulder. Ivan was talking rapidly into his cell phone. Gil wrenched himself out of Dave's grasp.

"Don't you understand!" he cried. "They're not downriver. They're in there." He pulled away from Dave and looked desperately at Ivan.

Ivan was Gil's favorite of all of his father's friends. He wore his hair in a ponytail, and a headband with an eagle feather and they called him Crazy Ivan because he did crazy, dangerous stuff on the river and on the mountain. But he talked to kids exactly the same way he talked to adults, and he understood things. The day after the Memorial Service, Ivan sneaked Gil away from his mother and all the grownups, and took him on the wildest white-water he could find. He called it, "getting back on the horse that's thrown you."

"They're in the Indian Kettle, Ivan," Gil said.

Ivan didn't smile this time, but he didn't argue. He leaned over, almost casually, and pulled a paddle from his kayak and jumped into the river. Gil gasped as Ivan slipped into the current and dipped feet first into the whirlpool. But Ivan didn't disappear. He splashed into the foam and remained there, chest-deep. The waters that had closed over Percy and Danni bubbled like a hot tub around him. He waved the paddle at Gil and thrust it down into the water. Gil saw it vibrate as one end thudded against solid rock.

"I'm standing on the bottom, Gil. Nothing in here but me."

Gil stared. For a moment he felt his lip trembling, but he stopped it with his teeth. Then he said, looking straight into Ivan's narrowed eyes, "Not in the Indian Kettle, Ivan. Through it. They went through it." He paused and then said hoarsely, "And so did I."

Ivan stood in the foaming water and met Gil's eyes with his own for what seemed like an hour. Then he said, "Well, Gil, nobody's going through it now." He threw the paddle ashore, pushed off with his feet and surged back out of the whirlpool. Two powerful strokes brought him to the water's edge. He climbed out and looked solemnly down at Gil.

"Do you believe me?" Gil said.

Ivan smiled. "You tell me it happened, Gil, and you're the guy who was there." He put his hand on Gil's shoulder and looked up to a sudden thunderous noise. A big rescue helicopter burst into view over the river, shutting out the sun. Gil thought suddenly of the Stone-Pecker that started it all. He leaned his forehead against Ivan's dripping dry suit and stupidly began to cry.

CHAPTER THREE

Gil sat in the front seat of Dave's pick-up, still wrapped in the space blanket. He didn't want to go to the hospital at all, but if he had to go, he wished he could have gone with Ivan. While he drove, Dave kept making calls on his cell phone. "Your mom's on the way," he said to Gil.

"She doesn't have to come. There's nothing wrong with me." But Dave was on another call. He turned back to Gil and said, "Brian's down at Cedar Bends. All the river guys are out." He paused. "They'll find them. They're probably sitting, miserable, on the riverbank, waiting to be found, right now."

Gil tried once more saying, "They're not in the river," but Dave ignored him. Gil gave up and sat pondering all the unbelievable things that, somehow, he had to make everyone believe.

At least, at the hospital, they believed that he wasn't hypothermic. But then he saw Dave talking quietly with the doctors, and after that, everything changed. A nurse gave him hospital clothes and took him to a room, and made him get into a bed. It was still the middle of the afternoon. He sat in the bed staring in frustration at the bright daylight outside. He thought of Danni in the snow and the dark.

Then the door opened and his mother came in. She ran across the room and hugged him and started crying. For the first time, Gil felt really bad about going to the river against the rules. He even felt like crying, himself, but he didn't have time. "I'm sorry, Mom. I'm really sorry," he said. "But I have to go back, now. Can you take me home?"

"Of course," she said. "Of course I'll take you home." She

was stroking his hair like he was a little kid. "But the doctors think you should stay here over night."

"No! There isn't time. I have to get back to the river!" Gil shouted.

"The river?" His mother's face scrunched up, like she hated the river more than anything in the world. "You're never going near that river again," she cried. "Never!"

"But I have to!" Gil argued desperately. "Danni's in the Indian Kettle, Mom. And Percy." He paused, and shook his head. "They've gone through it to this—this *place*."

She stopped hugging him and sat back. The look on her face was the same he'd seen on Brian's. "I'll be back in a moment," she said. She got up quickly and went to the door.

"I'm not hypothermic!" Gil shouted. But it was like somebody had pushed the mute button on the TV: nobody heard him anymore.

His mother came back in, kissed his forehead, and said, "It's all going to be fine. Dr Fairchild's coming and then we can go home."

"It'll take him hours to get here!" Gil groaned. He flopped down on the bed in frustration. "And I don't need a shrink!" He closed his eyes and saw Danni in her strange clothes, standing with her flaming torch in the snow. "We've lost so much time already."

It was dark when they got back from the hospital. Down the road from Gil's house, two rescue SUVs, an ambulance, and a police car, were parked in a row. There were no flashing lights, and as they watched, one SUV drove away.

"They must have given up," Gil's mother said, in a sad voice.

Dr. Fairchild glanced back at Gil, and shook his head.

"You can talk about Danni and Percy," Gil shouted. "I'm not going to self-destruct."

"Gil…." his mother sounded even sadder.

"Anger is normal," Dr. Fairchild said. Then he turned to Gil. "All right, Gil," he said. "We'll do that."

Dumbass, Gil said to himself. *Dork-face. Couldn't you keep your big mouth shut?*

Gil's mother studied his face in the porch light. "It's late," she said as they went into the house. Gil looked pointedly at the stairs to his bedroom. "I'm really tired, Mom."

"Dr. Fairchild knows best. I'll make you some cocoa."

"Cocoa? Like when do I do cocoa?" Gil said, but she hurried off to the kitchen. "I'm fourteen, Mom!" He punched the living room wall. "Why doesn't anyone ever listen to me?"

"Do I listen to you?" Dr. Fairchild said, over his shoulder. Gil shrugged and then grudgingly nodded. "Let's talk, Gil." Dr. Fairchild pointed to a chair and then sat down in another, facing it. "Tell me what happened, today," he said. His voice was mild, but his eyes, almost too bright blue to be real, locked on Gil's and did not let go.

Gil slid his gaze away from Fairchild's. "Something really weird happened today at the river," he said. Then he told the whole story: the bird that seemed to understand everything they were saying; the stone you could see people through. His beautiful green-eyed girl and Percy's cup. But the more he talked, the weirder it all sounded.

When he got to the part about going down into the Indian Kettle and catching hold of Danni's foot, his mind kept filling with the image of Ivan standing in the whirlpool, with the water only up to his chest. "It really happened," he said lamely.

Gil's mother came in with the cocoa and sat watching him earnestly. Dr. Fairchild said, "Go on." Gil stared at a pine knot in a floor board and told them about waking at night in the snow and seeing the stars and the hills with no trees and the water that looked like the sea, and the great circle of tall black stones.

"Standing stones?" Gil's mother said. "Like Stonehenge?"

"Let Gil tell it," Dr. Fairchild said.

But Gil looked at his mother. "What's Stonehenge?"

"It's a prehistoric stone circle," Dr. Fairchild said quickly. "It's in England. It's very famous. You'll have seen pictures of it."

"I haven't," Gil said. He ducked his head, then, and muttered in a rush, "Then I saw Danni, wearing this weird dress and boots, and carrying a flame, and she said I was late and we'd lost so much time. But then the Stone-Pecker came and the pool started bubbling and this thing grabbed my foot. Only, it wasn't a thing. It was Brian. And I was back." He grimaced, "But she's still there! And we're losing more time now!"

Dr. Fairchild's voice was soft as velvet. "Time for what, Gil?"

Gil hesitated. He looked back at his pine knot. "I don't know," he said quietly.

"No. Is that all you want to tell me?"

Gil nodded.

"Good," said Dr. Fairchild. "You did very well." There was a long pause. Gil could hear the river outside, rushing in the night. "Okay," Dr Fairchild said. "I'm going to explain to you what happened."

Warily, Gil looked up. The psychiatrist smiled encouragingly. Then he held his fingertips together and, studying Gil over them, he said, "You were playing by the river with your friends, and somehow you all fell in."

"We jumped. Percy. Then Danni. Then me. We all jumped."

Fairchild's smile remained. "Very well. You jumped. Either way, you all ended up in the river. At some point you caught hold of your friend's foot. But you were swept away into the whirlpool, head first. There was no room to turn around and the force of the water kept pushing you down. You struggled to escape, but eventually you ran out of air. And without air our brains stop working properly. Time may seem to slow down. We can see things, even people, who aren't really there."

Fairchild leaned forward. "You lost your grip on Danni's foot. Right?" Gil nodded. "That moment, Gil, was seconds after you entered the water. It had to be. Danni went in, you followed. You caught her foot...."

"But all the other stuff happened before. The Stone-Pecker and the stone...."

"Your mind created them, Gil. They all happened in a split-second, like a dream. You lost your grip, Danni and Percy were swept away down the river, and you were swept into the whirlpool. Your mind created everything in the seconds after that."

"But the place...the hills and the stone circle...."

"You saw something like it somewhere. In the movies, or on TV. The same with the clothes Danni seemed to be wearing."

"I didn't."

"Gil, nothing is in our brains that we haven't put there. They're like computers. You upload and you download. That's all." He sat back and said solemnly, "We both know what happened in the river today. But your brain isn't ready to accept it. So, it's created this place for Danni and Percy to be, instead."

Gil shook his head. "I didn't see Percy."

"Well, Danni then."

"Why would my brain create Danni and not Percy?"

Fairchild's smile weakened. "Gil, what matters is your brain did create the experience. You saw Danni because your brain wanted to see her. He leaned back in his chair and put his fingers together again. "Did you think you were going to die?" he asked suddenly.

Surprised, Gil nodded.

"Dying is the scariest thing we know, Gil," Fairchild said quietly. "And our brains are even more afraid than we are. They make things up to tell themselves it isn't happening. We may see angels. Or people who have died. Pictures of heaven. God. It can seem very real. But our brains create it all."

Gil looked at his mother, but she looked away. "Do they?" he said to Dr. Fairchild.

Dr. Fairchild looked at Gil like his opinion really mattered. "What do you think, Gil?"

Gil shrugged. When he spoke next, his own voice sounded like a little kid's. "What happens when people die?" he said.

"Danni and Percy will live on in our memories," Dr. Fairchild said. "Like your father."

Gil felt tears pushing against his eyelids. He jumped up and ran out of the room and up the stairs. He heard his mother's footsteps and then Dr. Fairchild's firm voice, "Leave him. He's had enough."

Gil flung himself on his bed and buried his wet face in the Spiderman bedspread. "But they're not dead," he whispered into the cloth. "They're in that place. Wherever it is."

Then he sat bolt upright, leapt to his feet and dove for his laptop. Hunched over the screen, he typed "stone circle" and hit search. In seconds, the one called 'Stonehenge' was in front of him. But it was nothing like the place he had seen.

Still, there were more. Stone circles, standing stones, rings and circles of boulders and pillars. He ran his eyes down the text, picking out links with names in languages he couldn't read. Fields with huge grey rocks. Rocks with strange carved patterns. He hit another link with a name he couldn't pronounce and then suddenly spun around in his chair.

A dry, sharp tapping rattled the still air of the room. He jumped up, went to the door, and opened it a crack. "Mom?" The bedroom hallway was empty. His mother's voice and Dr. Fairchild's rose from the living room below. He closed the door and crossed to the window, open, but screened with wire mesh. Placing his hands either side of his face, he peered out into the night. He heard the river, but nothing more. With a weary shrug, he turned back to his desk, and froze.

On the screen was an unmistakable circle of black, rough pillars, silhouetted against a sunset sky, and the far distant glint of the sea. "Yes!" he slapped his desk in triumph, turned and raced for the stairs. Outside the living room, he skidded to a sudden halt, hearing his mother's voice within.

"I'll miss him so much," she said sadly. Gil shook his head. Were they taking him back to the hospital?

"Of course it's hard for you to let him go," Dr. Fairchild said. "But he's going to be fine. Trust me."

"Oh, I do," his mother answered. "In a way," she continued, "It's like he's gone already. He's changed so much."

"We've got the best people in the field at the Clinic. A few months with us and Gil will be the boy you remember."

Warily, Gil turned. He edged silently down the hallway and then bolted up the stairs. Back in his room, he stood with his back pressed against the closed door, breathing in gulps. The Clinic. Dr. Fairchild's clinic. A few months! His eyes flew to the laptop screen and the faraway place where Danni and Percy were trapped.

The stones stood yet, serene against their sunset sky. Gil stared hopelessly at the picture. "You upload and you download," he whispered. He slapped his hand down on the mouse and hit close. Then he sat down on his bed and dropped his head into his hands.

When the tapping came again, his first thought was his nightmare of bones. He pictured a skeletal finger, scratching at the screen, and jumped up, terrified eyes on the window. The tapping stopped. There was a scuffling on the windowsill, and then a loud and familiar "Caw!"

"The Stone-Pecker!" Gil cried. "The Stone-Pecker's back!"

He raced to the window and pressed his face against the dark screen. Seeing nothing, he switched off the light and tried again. But there was no big grey and black bird. Disappointed, he drew back, but suddenly something caught his eye on the sloped roof of the porch beneath his window. He stared down at it. It was white; a soft white gleam of reflected moonlight on a small hollow-centered disc of stone. It glowed, like a tiny angel's halo dropped on the shingled roof.

"Percy's stone!" Gil whispered. The bird had brought it back.

Quickly, Gil unlatched the screen, and slid it up. He swung one leg over the sill, then the other, wriggled around and dropped onto the porch roof. The shingles crackled under his feet as he felt his way down the slope to where the white stone shone in the moonlight, just above the gutter. Cautiously, he knelt, and then stretched out, full-length on the shingles. His fingertips brushed the stone. He drew it nearer, inching it across the rough surface; then clasped it, at last, in his hand. Gripping the stone tightly, he wriggled back from the edge, stood up, and tiptoed up the creaking shingles, to his window.

He thrust the stone into his jeans pocket, grasped the frame with both hands, and jumped. His sneakers bumped against the wall, but he got one elbow onto the sill. Swinging his feet desperately, he pushed off with one toe, got his other elbow up, then his chest, and at last wriggled through the open gap, rolled over, and landed on the floor with a thud.

"Gil?" his mother's alarmed voice called up the stairs. Gil scrambled up and slammed the screen shut. Then he dove for his bed and buried himself under the rumpled bedspread, just as the door clicked open. "You okay, hon?" His mother's voice sounded sweet and sad.

Gil lay holding his breath until her footsteps had retreated down the stairs. He threw off the bedspread and dug in his pocket for the stone, reaching with his other hand for the light. With his fingers on the switch, he stopped. A faint glow shone from the center of the stone, like it held moonlight, still, within it. Numbly, Gil raised the stone, and the glow of light bathed his face. But it wasn't moonlight. It was daylight; daylight that leaked through the stone from the place where day was night and night was day.

Gil breathed deeply and then clamped the stone over his eye. At once, he cried out in shock. "Percy!" The boy was dressed, like Danni, in rough cloth and fur, and riding the back of an animal, a shaggy grey donkey. But he was turned around the wrong way, riding backwards, with his round face toward its swishing tail, his back to its haltered head, his hands clinging to its rump. Figures flitted around the edges of the framed circle, passed as shadows in front, like people spoiling a movie. Hands tugged at the halter rope. Hands pushed at Percy. Hands slapped the donkey. Percy's mouth was open, the tip of his tongue showing in confusion, his eyes wide with fear.

"Percy, look at me! I'm here!" Gil whispered. He waved his hand in the darkness. Tears rolled down Percy's cheeks, but he neither heard nor saw. Vision carried through the stone's heart, but no sound. The donkey turned its head right around, and gently licked Percy's leg. Then it looked directly at Gil with its sad brown eyes and shook its shaggy mane. Gil felt a cry for help form itself from thoughts that had no words, as the vision faded into night.

He switched on the light and leapt out of bed, the stone still clutched in his hand. He knew what he had to do, and he knew he had to do it tonight. By tomorrow morning, he'd be in Dr. Fairchild's big SUV, driving south to the city and the clinic. This was his last night of freedom, his last night in reach of the river.

He went straight to his closet and pulled out a small backpack. He packed a spare fleece, a winter shell, gloves, spare socks and underpants, his headlamp and compass, and his cell phone. Slinging the pack onto his shoulders, he crept downstairs to the kitchen.

By the dim light of the open refrigerator, he made two peanut butter and jelly sandwiches, and put them into a Zip-lock. He found a banana, three Mars bars, and a bag of potato chips; then stuffed all the food into his bulging backpack and pulled the compression straps tight. Closing the refrigerator, he felt his way across the room and opened the back door.

The moon was down and the night was really black. Gil ran his hand along the porch railing, feeling with his foot for the stairs. His left sneaker toe found the edge of the top step. Eagerly, he strode forward. But his right foot snagged on something bulky that skidded across the wooden decking. *The recycling box!* Gil lunged and caught the edge of the crate, just as it tipped, spilling an avalanche of bottles and cans, jingling and crashing, down the steps.

The noise woke the neighbors' five husky dogs and howls rose into the night. The hall lights came on and then the kitchen window glowed yellow. "Gil?" his mother shouted his name.

Gil leapt from the porch, stumbling through broken glass, and ran. At the edge of the lawn, he looked back at the house. The back door was open and Dr. Fairchild stood on the back porch. "Gil, come back!"

Gil lengthened his stride and sprinted for the woods and the river. He knew the river path so well that even in the pitchy dark beneath the trees he found the turn-off by the big pine. He reached the clearing by the riverbank. Starlight filtered down, showing the way. Oblivious of poison ivy, he pressed on, scrambling over rocks and fighting through tangles of brambles. Far away, his mother's voice called his name, but he shut his ears.

Then he was free, out of the brush, and mounting the long, smooth slope of the Lookout Rock. He reached the edge. Before him, dim and mysterious in the starlight, lay the silken slide of the waterfall, and, below, the black of the Indian Kettle pool. Barely visible in the darkness, the whirlpool swirled in a lace of white foam. Everything, even the endless roar of the river, seemed hushed by the depths of the night. Fear wrapped itself around his heart.

He hunched his shoulders, staring miserably into the water. His hand in his pocket closed around the Stone-Pecker's stone and drew it out. In the starlight, even the stone looked faint and insubstantial, as if it would fade and disappear. But it wasn't. He tightened his grip around it. It was solid; real, solid stone, the only solid evidence of the whole fantastical day...but no!

"It's not!" Gil cried. He knelt on the Lookout Rock, sliding his hands over the grainy surface. It was here; he knew it was here. And then he found it; the perfect small, round hole, its edges fresh and sharp as they'd been that afternoon: the Stone-Pecker's extraordinary proof. Gil stood up. He felt faith and courage flow back into his heart.

He looked down again at the Stone-Pecker's stone. Was it the key? If the stone was there, would the locked door of the whirlpool open again, like it had for Percy and Danni, and even for himself?

Gil braced himself to jump. There was only one way to find out, and if he was wrong...? He imagined himself plunged, head down, into the Indian Kettle, jammed by its narrow width, trapped, unable to turn, arms pinned to his sides, drowning in the death trap they all said it was. He approached the edge again, again pulled back. His legs were shaking, and tears rose in his eyes. He shook his head, defeated, and turned away from the river.

"Gil!" Gil looked up. The figure, tall and imposing, silhouetted against the starlight, was barely ten feet away.

"Dr. Fairchild," he whispered.

"All right, Gil," the voice was calm and soothing. "You're all right. You're safe. I'm right here. Just come back up the rocks...."

Gil looked over his shoulder. The whirlpool glinted, just out of reach. Dr. Fairchild took a step closer, and another. Gil waited, like a deer caught in headlights, unable to move. Danni and Percy's faces flitted across his mind, like a fading memory.

They'll live on in our memories....

"No!" Gil shouted. As Fairchild lunged, Gil leapt away and flung himself into the rushing water. The waterfall took him and he tumbled head first into the pool, hands reaching out, one still clutching the Stone-Pecker's stone.

Oh, God, if there is a God, please open the door...if there is a door! Then the whirlpool caught him and he plunged downward, into its merciless heart.

CHAPTER FOUR

Something was wrong. Gil knew it at once. The roaring of the whirlpool was stilled, and he was lying on the ground, just like before. He felt quickly over his arms and legs. His clothes were dry. Just like before. Stillness and cold and black, black night. Night. It shouldn't be night. He left night. It should be daylight. He'd seen it, through the stone.

He stared upward, waiting for his eyes to adjust, waiting for stars. But, this time, no stars came. He pressed his lids, checking he hadn't really gone blind this time. He saw his own inner eye-stars, nothing more. Suddenly, the total stupidity of what he had done swept over him. He'd escaped, and he was safe, and now he'd come back. But was it even the same place?

Panic rose up like a black wave. He reached out one hand, hoping to feel snow. But there was no snow, only cold, damp earth. And one small stone. The Stone-Pecker stone! He closed his fingers around it, and grasped it tight, and drew it close against his chest, the way Percy had done.

He raised it to his eye, but he kept its center covered with his fingers. "Show me Danni," he whispered. "Show me where she is." Then he parted his fingers and saw a figure in a long grey dress, crouching in the shadow of enormous trees, and bending forward over a branch of red berries.

"The girl! My girl!" The white cloth that veiled her hair hid her face, but then she raised her head and stuffed a handful of berries into her mouth. Her eyes sparkled with delight, bright and green as the sea. "Look up, look up," he whispered. "You can see me if…." He stopped. A shadowy shape suddenly appeared at the edge of the picture, like the shapes that had surrounded Percy.

The girl finished her berries and, smiling, sucked the juice from each red-stained finger. The shape moved closer; a man's shape, huge above her. "Watch out!" Gil cried. Oblivious, she reached out to the berry-laden branch. But then she froze and the smile faded. She turned, warily, over her shoulder. The berry-stained fingers flew to her face and her eyes filled with terror.

A shadowy hand came down and wrenched back her white veil. Black, shining hair tumbled free. "Leave her alone!" Gil shouted. But the picture was gone and he was alone, once more, in the dark.

Gil clutched the stone with trembling fingers. He shook it hard; then slapped it twice. "Show me! Show me!" he shouted, peering uselessly into the darkness. Even the white of the stone was invisible. The hollow center was a blackness within blackness. "Stupid thing! Useless stupid thing!" Gil stabbed his finger inside the hole, then, seized with fury, he flung the stone down onto the unseen ground.

An image of Danni on the Lookout Rock flashed into his mind. "Oh, no!" he groaned aloud, "I'm as dumb as she was!"

He dropped down on hands and knees, groping with blind fingers. "Please. I'm sorry." His palm closed over the familiar shape and he cried out with joy. Snatching it up, he leapt to his feet, took one step forward, and splashed, knee-deep, into icy water.

The pool! Gil scrambled frantically backwards, onto dry ground. Remembering the dark water by the Standing Stones, he imagined Dr Fairchild's pursuing hand rising like a snake from the unseen depths. He stood frozen as a statue, afraid to take a single step, lest he stumble into the treacherous water. If only he had some light!

He looked again at the Stone-Pecker's stone in his hand, but no gentle daylight flowed through it. Whatever the weird stone was, it wasn't like a TV or a light, or anything you could switch on, or switch off. And then he remembered his headlamp.

He reached for the shoulder straps of the backpack, but the backpack was gone. The whirlpool had torn it off, as it had torn the Stone-Pecker's stone from his hand.

Still, the stone got here. He put it in his pocket, sank again to his knees, and reached wary hands outward, across the damp earth, patting the ground in a cautious circle. When the circle delivered nothing but bare earth, he crawled to its perimeter, and did the patting thing again, striving to remember where he started, wary always of the pool. Once, his hand did stray, dipping fingers into water. He froze again, rethought, and continued.

On the fifth circle, at its farthest edge, he found a strap. Eagerly, he pulled it close. But it was too light, and as he felt its length, he found only one half of a plastic buckle. He explored it blindly trying to guess which part it had come from. But when his fingers touched the buckle, it felt almost soft, and a little warm.

Then suddenly it collapsed in his grasp, crumbled into splinters, and then into smaller pieces, and then rough grains, until all he was left with was a handful of dust. Gil had the feeling he got from the hole the Stone-Pecker drilled in the Lookout Rock. He grimaced in the darkness, brushing the dust from his hands.

On his sixth circle, he found two more straps and a piece of cloth that all turned to dust. On the seventh he found his compass. He couldn't see it, but the glass wasn't broken and it felt okay. He put it in his pocket with the stone. On the eighth circle he found, in a neat heap: the three Mars bars, the banana, a pile of loose potato chips, and his peanut-butter sandwiches. The Zip-Lock bag had gone, but the sandwiches were dry and felt like he'd just finished making them. He took a bite. They tasted great, and since he had nothing to wrap them with, he ate them both. Then he ate the potato chips, for the same reason.

He sat back and licked his fingers and thought of the green-eyed girl with her berries, and how beautiful her hair had been when the veil came off. But at once, he remembered the fear in her eyes, and his hands balled into fists. Pushing the thought of her from his mind, he reached out one more time to start a new circle, and his fingers closed on something small and smooth and joyously welcome.

"My headlamp!" Quickly, he searched the plastic casing for

the switch, and pressed it down. But as he did, the switch and all the casing crumbled, just like the buckle. It broke into pieces and dissolved into dust. In moments, all he was holding was the little glass bulb.

"*No!*" Gil shouted, anguished. He slapped the bulb down on his knee, and then it, too, crumbled into powder in his hand. "I hate this place!" He flung his hand out to throw the useless dust into the dark, and cried out in pain as his knuckles cracked into cold stone, barely a foot from his face.

Stunned, he drew his injured hand to his mouth and tasted blood. Then, warily, he leaned forward and felt with the other hand for what he had hit. It was a broad, flat rock that extended for a couple of feet in each direction. At each edge was a narrow crack, and beyond, another stone. Slowly, Gil stood, running both hands, now, along the rugged surface, from stone to stone. He traced the gaps between; drawing a picture in the dark.

"It's a wall," he breathed. "They're like bricks or something. It's built!" As he moved, he sensed a curving of the line of stones, in both directions, and when he ran his hands upward, it seemed to curve over him as well. "I'm in a building. I'm not outside at all."

No wonder it was dark. It didn't have windows. But it had to have a door. Eagerly, he felt his way further and further along the stone wall, which curved more and more. When he'd gone a dozen feet, he realized the building was round.

Face pressed against the damp stone, he shuffled for what felt like forever, trying to gauge distance, counting his steps, forgetting, starting again. The place seemed huge. Then suddenly his foot came down on something as soft and yielding as flesh. He screamed, and jumped wildly back.

A sweet, familiar scent drifted up to his nose. He bent, and picked up the soft, squishy thing, and laughed. He'd just scared himself with his own banana. But his laughter died, in the same moment. He was back where he started. He'd been around the entire wall. And he hadn't found a door.

No windows and no door. He was walled in forever in utter, total dark; buried alive in a stone walled tomb. Gil sank to the floor and covered his face, huddled warily back from the pool.

Then suddenly he realized that the thing he was avoiding so carefully was his only hope. He'd plunge back in! Maybe Dr. Fairchild was still there. Maybe he'd pull him back through the Indian Kettle, like Brian had.

Quickly gathering his nerve, Gil stood again and then blundered away from the wall, blindly stumbling; waiting for the icy splash. But somehow, he missed the pool, and ran straight into the opposite wall, instead. He turned, bewildered, and staggered back across the dark circle. Again, he missed it. He set out at a different angle, but only met a new piece of wall. When he'd crossed the black room ten times, he accepted the impossible, terrifying truth. The pool was gone.

Slowly, he sank again to the floor and drew up his knees. His foot brushed something, and it rolled against his hand. Bones; a skull, sharing his burial! But the thing was fleshy and soft and wrinkled. A head. A dead head with the flesh still on! He kicked it away, but it rolled back. Horrified, he grasped it and hurled it far from him. He heard it hit the stone with a sickly soft thud.

"Oh, God, get me out of here," he whimpered. Somewhere, far, far away in his head, he heard Dr. Fairchild's calm, clear voice answer, "Why do they teach children these things?" Gil dropped his head into his hands and quietly wept.

Then suddenly he heard a sound; a faint, sweet ringing. A bell. He strained his ears. The sound came again; then faded away. Slowly, he stood up, and peered into the darkness in the direction from which it had come. And then, just in front of him, he glimpsed a tiny pinprick of light.

He tilted his head, and the light vanished. He tilted it again, and it reappeared. Terrified to lose it, he took one minute step, holding his head rigidly still. The light was still there, and now he saw it was actually a tiny, thin line. He stepped again, and again. The light grew, and as he reached the wall, he saw it was daylight, shining through the slenderest of gaps between two great stones.

He laid his hands on either side of it, and his heart fell. The stones were solid, the size of gravestones. The light that crept through the crack might as well come from another universe. Yearning to see, he pressed his eyes against the gap. It was too narrow to show him anything, but a faint tinge of green glowed between the black of the stones; the beautiful green of outdoors.

"Let me through," he whispered. "Please." But the crack couldn't have let an insect through. He pressed his face closer; imagined he could smell sweet air. And then, through the crack in the stones he heard another sound, as faint and as lovely as the ringing bell: a girl's voice, singing,

"*Hosanna, hosanna, in nominay dominey.*"

Though she sang in a language Gil did not understand, the voice was Danni's voice. A burst of joyous hope swept over him.

"Danni," he gasped and then he shouted, "Danni! Danni! Help!" The voice sang on, growing fainter, as if she were moving away. "Danni!" he screamed. "I'm in here. I'm trapped!"

He punched the rock. His bruised knuckles stung and he punched it again, crying in frustration. He pummeled it with both hands, and then clawed at it like an animal. And then, giving up, he sank down on his knees and rested his head against the unmoving stone. And, then, the unmoving stone moved.

At first it was so gentle, and so impossible, that he thought he'd imagined it. Slowly, he sat up a little straighter, and cautiously prodded the point against which his head had rested. There was the faintest creaking sound as it wobbled the slightest bit, beneath his hand.

The rock was huge, delicately balanced on its edge. At any moment, it could fall, and its weight would crush him. His hands flew off the stone, and he crawled hastily backwards. He sat staring up at the thin line of light, torn between his yearning for it, and his fear of the huge rock. "Danni," he sobbed. But the singing had stopped. In the silence he heard only the distant bell. Then it too faded and died.

Steeling himself, he scuttled across the floor, placed both hands on the wobbling rock, and pushed with all his strength. It creaked, shuddered, and then tipped outwards, opening as smoothly as a door. White sunlight flooded into Gil's black prison, blinding him with joy.

Eyelids squeezed shut, Gil staggered out like a new-born puppy, into the glare. His vision slowly returned, and, still blinking, he stood staring in amazement. It was the most beautiful place he had ever seen; a land of low, dark hills and shining blue sea, of sun and rock and the greenest grass in the world.

In a patch of marshy ground, a girl knelt amid white-tufted grass stalks, plucking cottony seed heads and stuffing them into a leather bag. She wore a plain blue dress and her sun-browned arms were bare. When she rose and stepped delicately through the marsh, he saw her feet were bare, too. Bending to her work, she began again to sing.

"Danni?" Gil's voice rasped, an uncertain croak.

She whirled, staring, shading her eyes against the early sun. She was taller and slimmer and her brown hair was twice as long. For one moment she looked as terrified as the green-eyed girl in her veil. But then she dropped her leather bag, stepped forward and cried, "Gil? Gil! Oh, at last! At last!"

She caught up the hem of her long dress with one hand and ran, splashing through the wet marsh, bounding long-legged as a deer. Gil ran to meet her until suddenly they stood face to face. Then his laughter stilled and the arms he had reached out to her dropped slowly to his sides.

"Gil?" she said. "What's the matter?"

He tilted his head back to meet her eyes. "You're so different."

"Bad different?" Her hand rose uncertainly to her face.

"Good different," he said hastily.

Her cheeks were thinner and her mouth was softer-looking and really nice. He stared at her face to keep his eyes from drifting down to her chest, which had gotten really nice, too. "Grown-up different," he said.

She smiled, still uncertain. "You're just the same," she said happily.

"I should be. You saw me yesterday." Gil laughed, but she slowly shook her head.

"Not since the night at the pool."

"In the snow? That was yesterday."

"That was Candlemas, Gil," she said solemnly. "Today is Lady Day in Harvest. It's seven months."

"It can't be," Gil whispered. But all around him everything

he saw told him it was true. Even washed in rich sunlight, this place was not new to him. When night fell, the stars would fill the sky, the ocean would glimmer and somewhere nearby, the great black stones would stand quiet guard. He turned briefly back to his awful tomb. It seemed innocent now, just a mossy mound of stones, covered in grass, a little hill, among hills. You could walk right over it, if you didn't know.

Beside it, a little circle of water shimmered in the sunlight. Marsh grasses rooted firmly at its edges. A small fish darted in its golden depths. Gil plucked at Danni's bare arm. "Look! The pool!"

She stared at the water. "So?"

"But it was inside...."

Danni's hands flew up and covered her mouth. "Oh, Gil," she pointed at the tomb. "You were in there?" He nodded grimly. She ducked her head. "I should have left the door open. I saw it go in. But the sheep get in, and anyhow, I knew it would come out again. It never stops moving. See?"

The pool crept a foot across the field while she spoke. Gil stared. He picked up a rock and threw it at the shining surface. Real water splashed back over his foot. The pool shuddered and then simply vanished, leaving behind only sun-warmed grass.

"*What?*"

Danni shrugged. "It'll turn up somewhere. It always does. It's been behind every one of the Great Stones. Once, it was even up there," she pointed to the top of a little ridge.

"Danni, *how?*"

She shrugged again. "It's the Wandering Pool. But I go to look for it every day," she added fervently. So, I would have found you real soon."

Gil wrenched his gaze from the empty place in the grass. "I thought I was going to die in there, with all those dead heads."

"Those what?"

"The heads. I touched one. It rolled into me. I threw it against the wall." He felt sick.

She giggled. "I don't think so, Gil." Then she bent over and scuttled into the low entrance and reached out her hand. Reluctantly, Gil followed. It wasn't black, inside, any longer, but dusky grey, with one bar of sunlight reaching in the open door. Then Danni scooped something up from the dim floor and shouted, "Catch!" as she flung it at Gil.

He caught it, by instinct, felt the rubbery, wrinkled flesh, and cried out and dropped it, in disgust. "Danni! It's…."

"A turnip!" she said. She waved another. "An old turnip!" She fell back, giggling, against the curved stone wall. Then suddenly she crouched, peering at something white at her feet. She picked up the white thing and slowly stood. "Oh, Gil, I do not believe you brought underpants. You dork," she said fondly.

He grabbed them out of her hand and shoved them into his pocket. "I did bring other stuff," he said stiffly. "Only…." But Danni was staring at the beaten earth floor.

"Mars bars! You brought Mars bars!" She dropped to her knees, ripping the wrapper off one and stuffing it into her mouth. "Ace!" A chocolate smeared grin lit her face as she tore the wrapper off a second and munched it eagerly.

"Wait, Danni. Save some. That's all the food we've got."

She looked amazed. "There's food, Gil. There's plenty of food." She bit the second bar in half. "But I haven't had chocolate since…."

"Yesterday," he whispered as she unwrapped the third bar. But he didn't even believe it, himself. Cautiously, he said then, "Shouldn't you save some for Percy?"

Danni's fingers stilled on the paper. Her smile faded. "Percy isn't here, Gil," she said solemnly.

Gil stared. "But I saw him, Danni. I saw him through the stone. Dressed in funny stuff, like you, and riding a donkey. He has to be here."

"He was," she said, "But he was gone before I even got here. Men came from a ship and took him away. Men of Alba." He knew from the way she said it, they were something bad. She lowered her hand, the half-eaten Mars bar forgotten, and kicked disconsolately at the strap of his lost backpack, lying in the dirt.

"Danni," he said urgently, "I brought lots of stuff. My phone, my headlamp, my backpack…they're all, like, dust, but *this* got here. Look!" He wormed his fingers around the Y-fronts in his pocket and drew out his compass. It was small and round and made of battered brass, and compared to the high-tech Silva Danni had, it wasn't much. When Gil's father gave it to him last Christmas, he explained it was special because his own father had given it to him when he was a kid. Gil had been secretly a little ashamed of the compass and kept it at the bottom of a drawer. But now its old-fashioned needle swung straight and true to the North.

She prodded it with a finger and shrugged. "Some things don't cross."

"Cross?"

"The Bridge. The Underwater Bridge. The way we crossed." She paused. "From there to...here."

"There...the Indian Kettle, the whirlpool...it's the Underwater Bridge?"

"It's one end."

"And here?"

"The other."

He closed his fingers around the compass. "Danni, where are we?" he said.

She looked away when she answered. "Somewhere on earth. I think." Beyond the stone walls, the bell rang again and Danni seized his arm as if glad of the distraction. "We have to go."

"Where?" he said, but she thrust him before her, through the narrow doorway.

Hurriedly, she rocked the big stone back into place. "Come on."

"Where are we going?" he said again. But then a new sound came, a rasping caw from high above. "The bird!" He squinted up into the sun. A dark shape circled on outstretched wings. Danni looked up.

"It's Feannag."

"But it's the Stone-Pecker! It's back."

"I know. Come on, we're late." She started to turn from him, but shrieked suddenly with laughter.

"What?" She pointed, and he looked down. His fly was wide open, displaying more white cotton. He whipped around, and with his back to her, reached for his zip. He fumbled clumsily, and then desperately. Alarmed, he looked closer. The zip had vanished, leaving not one stray thread behind. He jerked his tee shirt down to his hips.

Danni nodded wisely. "Yeah. Those hooky-button things don't cross." She grinned. "I'll make real buttons for you."

She went to the patch of marshy ground where he had first seen her and crouched down beside her abandoned leather bag. Seeing him watching, she quickly stuffed the last of the cottony fluff inside, stood up, and glared. "It's the woman's plant," she snapped, "*Okay?*" Cheeks reddening, she flung the bag over her shoulder and stalked away toward the grassy ridge.

Warily, he started to follow and then stopped, looking down. At his feet, the old turnip that had so terrified him lay abandoned. He picked it up, and ran after Danni up the hill.

She waited for him, perched on a sunny boulder near the summit, her good nature returned. He tossed the turnip up in the air and caught it, and looked back at the stone mound. "I *am* a dork," he said cheerfully. "Why was I so sure it was a tomb?"

"Because it was," said Danni. "But it was raided for the gold and silver, and they threw the bones away. So now it's just a root cellar." Gil winced and dropped the wrinkled turnip among the rocks.

They scrambled the last few feet to the top of the ridge until suddenly they were looking down on the circle of great stones. They seemed gentle and friendly with sunlight softening the black rock to grey and wild flowers blooming at their feet. Before them, a stream ran in dark pools and white waterfalls down to the sea. Small trees, bright green and bent with clusters of red berries leant over it, casting a lacy shade.

At the foot of the ridge, another pool glistened, solitary and mysterious. Marsh grasses swayed at its edge and purple flowering shrubs over-hung it. There were two fish now in its depths. Gil stared in disbelief.

"I told you it would turn up," Danni said. She stepped past him and dabbled the toes of one dusty foot in the water. Gil lunged forward, hauling her back.

"Get out!" he cried, "Get out!" She stood still, dropped her hands, and looked down at her bare foot, ankle deep in the silken water. "It's the pool, Danni! You'll go through!"

She nodded then, and smiled wryly. "Watch." She stepped forward with her other foot, stood with both firmly planted in the water, then turned, pulled the hem of her skirt up to her knees, and waded around in a circle. The water never reached above her calves. She walked twice, back and forth, from one edge of the pool to the other.

He watched, bewildered, and then suddenly shouted, "Of course! It's locked. The door's locked. But I have the key!" He pulled the white stone from his pocket and held it up.

"Aidan's Seeing Stone," she murmured.

"It's the key, Danni. It opens the door. The Bridge. We can go home!" he said eagerly. "Then we can get help and come back for Percy."

She watched him solemnly for a long while. Then she said, "Take off your shoes."

"What?"

"Take them off. And your socks." With a shrug, he kicked his sneakers loose, peeled off his socks and stood barefoot. She held out her hand. "Now come."

Pushing his jeans up over his knees, Gil stepped into the water. It was shallow and warmed by the sun; the bottom, firm sand. Cautiously he moved out to the center where she stood. The water lapped gently around them both, just below their knees. Danni took the stone from him, slipped her finger through the hole, as Percy had done, and gave the stone a wistful spin. "Oh, Gil," she said. "If only it was all as simple as that." She took the stone off her finger and handed it back. Gil stepped from the pool and pulled socks and sneakers onto his wet feet. The bell rang again, closer now, and Danni turned toward the sound.

They had gone a dozen feet when the sunlit silence was shattered by a young girl's piercing scream. Gil looked around wildly. The scream came again, louder, out of empty air. "Help! Help me! Please!"

"Where are you?" he shouted back. His eyes swept the far hillside, but the scream was right here.

"Oh, please! Please! There's fire everywhere!" The girl's voice dropped to an agonized moan. "Oh, please! Someone! Help the children!"

"What children?" Danni cried.

"We can't see you!" Gil shouted desperately. "Tell us where you are!" He waved his hands as if he could part the air like a curtain.

And then, suddenly, she was there, at the pool. Not in it, but, to Gil's astonishment, about a foot above it. She seemed to run, stumbling, for a moment on air itself, and then her foot touched dry land and, at once, she was as solidly grounded as they.

She slapped at her clothes with frantic hands, as if extinguishing invisible flames. "Fire!" she cried again. But her clothes weren't burned and her creamy skin was without a mark. Gil saw her puzzled awareness grow, like his own when he realized his clothes were dry, that night in the snow.

Her hands stilled. She studied them, turning them this way and that, and shaking her head. Then she looked up, and through her fog of confusion, she saw Gil and Danni. She stared at them silently, for a long while, and then nodded her head slowly. "You got out, too?" Her voice was odd, the words clipped. She kept staring, her eyes growing wide.

"Out of where?" Danni said.

The girl shuddered. "It was all burning." Again she looked down, examining her clothes. She wore skinny, low-rise jeans and a white shirt which she'd tied up to show her tanned middle. A blue and black striped man's necktie was looped loosely around her shirt collar. All were spotless.

Her face was long and narrow and pretty in a serious-looking way. Her eyes were dark blue and her hair, dark red and a little frizzy, was pulled back tightly. When she turned quickly, Gil saw the hair was plaited into a thick braid, so long that its tasseled end brushed the seat of her jeans.

"Ohmygod!" he cried. "It's Lara Croft!"

For a moment, the bafflement on the girl's face cleared completely and she gave him a scathing look. "Oh, so original!" she said. The voice got even more clipped, and sounded pretty mad.

"No, you don't understand. Percy saw you…."

But she wasn't listening. She was looking around, the way he had that winter night that was both two days and a lifetime ago. "Where is this?" she said. "How far did I run?"

Gil took a deep breath and said, "Where should it be?"

She answered immediately, as if the question was a bit dumb. "York," she said. "Of course."

Gil blinked. "Where's York?"

Her eyes narrowed and she studied him more closely. "Are you American?" she said.

"Sure," Gil said, puzzled.

She nodded. "So, are you on holiday...vacation," she corrected quickly. "Are you over here on vacation?"

"Over where?"

"York!" she said. Gil shook his head and she sighed. "York, England? Like, maybe check your plane ticket?"

"You think you're in England?" Danni said.

She looked truly outraged. "I know I'm in England. You two need a geography lesson." But as she spoke, she was again looking around and her confidence suddenly collapsed. "But it doesn't look like York, anymore." She peered into the distance. "What's happened to all the buildings? Where's the Museum? I was in the Museum and there was a fire."

She looked, puzzled, again, at her hands. "Did you see the necklace?" she said suddenly to Danni. "There was this beautiful amber necklace, in that case with all the Viking grave stuff. Sort of Goth, with this big amber cross. I was thinking I'd love one like it. My dad would probably go ballistic." She made a small smile. "We *are* Jewish."

She shrugged. "Anyway, when I looked up, the rest of the class was gone. And then some funny stuff happened." Her forehead wrinkled as she remembered. "I heard a noise, and suddenly there was this big, black bird right in the room. Not like a sparrow or something that gets into a room; but this huge black bird. And then the room looked funny, wavy, like it was underwater, and then I saw the fire." She paused, half-closing her eyes, "And the children. There were these children, trying to get away from the flames."

"School children," Gil said, "Like you."

"No, little children. They were dressed funny. Like in costumes. Maybe the Museum had given them costumes" She shook her head, squeezing her eyes shut, "Their clothes were burning, and they were crying for help, I think, but I couldn't hear them. There wasn't any sound. And I ran toward them," the girl said, "and I started beating out the flames with my hands." Gil caught his breath. "With your hands?"

"I didn't have anything else," she said simply. "And my hands were burning, but...." She turned them back and forth, again, and Gil watched her with new respect. She looked right at him, then. "Why aren't they burned?" she asked quietly.

Gil half raised his palms; then lowered them.

"Things are different here," Danni said.

The girl looked more carefully at Danni. "What on earth are you wearing?" she said. "Is that from the Museum?"

Danni looked blankly down at her dress, but before she could answer, the English girl returned her attention to her own clothes, searching her shirt pockets, and then her jeans. "My phone," she whispered, "I've lost my phone." Panicking, she fell to her knees, patting the grass desperately. "I must have dropped it!"

"It didn't cross," Gil said. "Mine didn't either."

The girl scrabbled among the roots of the wiry, purple flowering plants. "I want to call my Dad. I want my Dad."

Danni watched curiously and then pointed down at the pool. "Is that what you're looking for?" A small, white rectangle lay in the shallows at the edge.

"Oh, no!" The girl wrapped her arms around herself and rocked back and forth, sobbing quietly.

Danni crouched, poking the white rectangle with her finger. Suddenly, her eyes opened wide. "I remember!" She plunged her hands into the pool, greedily clutching the drowned plastic. She brought it into the air, her fingers poking it eagerly, her eyes opening wider, like someone emerging from a dream.

The girl reached for it, but Danni turned her back, holding it close. Then she sighed. "It's fading," she said.

"Well, it's been under water," the girl said bleakly. "I'm surprised you got a signal at all."

"No, dummy." Danni whipped around, "*It's* fading." She held the phone up. Before their eyes, its outlines turned shabby, its color translucent, and in moments, it vanished into dust.

"What's happened to it?" the girl whispered.

Gil gave a resigned shrug. "Things fade. Things that don't cross." Danni sifted the dust through her fingers and let it go.

Squeamishly, the girl prodded the heap of dust that remained of her phone. Danni knelt beside her. "I'm Danni," she said. "And he's Gil." She smiled encouragingly.

"I'm Rachel," the girl whispered dully. Her face was very pale and her eyes big and scared. She rose to her feet, and looked all around fearfully, as if for the first time really seeing where she was. Then her gaze fell on the stones of the great circle, casting long morning shadows in the summer sun, and a wondering smile of recognition lit her face. "I know this place," she said. "I know where we are."

"You do?" Gil whispered. Then he cried out, simultaneously with Danni, "Where? Where are we?"

Rachel turned, looking all around herself, then back at the stones. "It's Orkney," she said. Her voice echoed both certainty and puzzlement. She paused, still puzzled. "I've been here. I know I have."

"Orkney?" Danni said, uncertainly.

But Gil interrupted. "I read that," he said. "I saw it. On...." he stopped. He could see the picture, as clearly as the stones themselves, in front of him. But he couldn't see how he was seeing the picture. That thing. On his desk. In his room. Incredulous, he heard his own voice saying, "I saw it in my picture book."

Rachel's face was incredulous, too. Then Danni said, "Where's Orkney?" and Rachel just rolled her eyes.

"It's an island. A group of islands," she said wearily. "It's part of Scotland."

"Is it near York?" Gil asked.

Rachel looked totally exasperated. "York is in England," she reminded him. "That's like hundreds of miles...."

"So how did you get here?" he said.

Rachel looked back the way they'd come, and then out over the standing stones, and shook her head. "I don't know," she said in a small voice. "But this is Orkney. I know it is. Only... only it's changed. The road's gone. They've taken the road away. And there used to be houses, I think." Her eyes suddenly widened as she pointed toward the nearest of the great stones. "Look! Look!"

"What?" Gil said. He followed her pointing finger with his eyes, stared for a moment, and then laughed softly. Beneath the stone, a pool of water had appeared out of nowhere. He looked down at the empty grassy place at their feet and shrugged. "Don't worry," he said. "It does that. It wanders all over the place."

But Danni was staring at the pool as fixedly as Rachel. "No, Gil, something's happening. Look." She ran toward it and then stopped a dozen feet short and watched, as Gil and Rachel caught up.

The water had begun to stir. A ripple crossed its surface, though the summer air was still. It turned, circled, and began to swirl. Gil remembered the winter night the pool delivered him here and snatched him back. Then the waters erupted, like a fountain, and out of their white, frothing center leapt a living thing. Not a person, but an animal: a deer, slender, long-legged, and as white as sunlit snow.

She sprang from the water, onto the grass, shook dust from her coat, and stood, alert and wary, beside the now quiet pool. She was small, about three feet tall, and had no antlers. Her soft white ears flicked backwards and forwards. Then she flung her head up and stared right at them. Her white tail flicked up and she froze, looking down at the pool. The waters had begun again to swirl.

Run, Gil thought, without knowing why. The deer spun about and bounded away, just as a dark figure sprang from the pool, landed, sure-footed on the green turf, and leapt forward in pursuit.

"A boy!" Rachel cried. "Someone else got through!"

But Gil saw at once this boy came from no English school. His feet were bare and he wore only dusty combat trousers and a tee shirt, over which were slung two heavy munitions belts. His face was dark brown, his hair, thick and frizzy, tied around with a bit of dirty red cloth. In his hand he held a long, pointed stick; a spear.

The boy's face is brown. "It's him," Gil murmured. "It's the boy Percy saw."

Danni stared, transfixed, as the boy raised the spear to launch it at the fleeing deer.

"No!"

Gil turned. Rachel was waving an indignant finger at the boy. "Leave it alone!" she shouted. "Don't you dare!"

The boy whirled and stared at them in astonishment. He lowered the spear and for the first time looked around. His mouth opened, but no sounds came. "It's okay," Gil ventured.

The boy snapped back to full attention. His eyes squinted into the sun, as he assessed them in an instant. Then he dropped the spear and reached for something over his shoulder. He swung it forward and Gil gasped.

"He's got a gun!" Rachel cried.

With surreal horror, Gil watched the boy raise the muzzle of a battered Kalashnikov and point it at his heart.

CHAPTER FIVE

Gil raised both hands, slowly. "Friends! Friends!" The boy did not move.

"Maybe he doesn't speak English," Rachel whispered. The muzzle snapped toward her.

"Don't speak," Gil said.

Danni nudged him and whispered, "Keep him talking. Just a little longer!"

"American?" the boy said. Gil nodded. But the boy suddenly looked confused. He stared down at the gun in his hands, his eyes wide and frightened. Then he cried out, wrenched the shoulder strap over his head, and flung the weapon onto the ground beside his spear.

The gun wavered, grew transparent, and turned to dust. The boy clutched his chest and the crossed munitions belts disintegrated in his hands. He shook his head in disbelief and stared again at the heap of dust on the ground. Then he crouched and caught up his discarded spear. His eyes flicked from one to the other of them. Gripping the spear, he sprang to his feet.

"Friends!" Gil cried again. He jumped backwards, pulling the two girls with him. The boy waved the spear and shook it fiercely. Gil, Danni, and Rachel scuttled backwards, again. He lowered the spear and suddenly grinned, a lopsided, white grin. Then he shrugged and turned his back. Dismissing them completely, he scanned the surrounding landscape with narrowed eyes.

The boy and Danni spotted the deer in the same instant. She had halted her flight beside another of the stones and was sniffing the air in bewilderment. "It's lost," Danni whispered. "Like us." But the boy laughed, softly triumphant, and raised his spear. The deer leapt into the air, and bounded away. With long, lithe strides, the boy ran after it.

"Stop!" Rachel shouted. She waved her fist at him and then broke into a run in pursuit. "Follow him!" she shouted back to Danni and Gil. "He's going to kill it!"

Gil ran, too, with Danni beside him. The deer left the stone circle and dashed left and right in front of the little wood of white trees. Then, with the boy right at her heels, she plunged into the leafy shade. The boy slipped into the trees as swift as her shadow. When Danni and Gil reached the wood, both had vanished, but a distant crackling and snapping of branches told them the hunt was still on. Danni led, onto the narrow path. Rachel pushed by Gil, into the trees.

They broke from the woods, together, looking down again at the sea. Below lay rocks and a beach of shining white sand and, just above it, on a little hill carpeted with yellow flowers, a small square building with a roof covered right over in growing grass; a carved stone cross at one end.

Around it clustered several smaller buildings, each completely round with a round stone roof, and one larger, long and narrow with smoke rising above its thatch. Among them, hens scratched and small brown and white sheep wandered free.

A fishing net was stretched to dry between two oars propped in the sand, and beside it a man worked in a vegetable garden, his back bent over a hoe. He was tall, with stooping shoulders and brown hair cut short at the front and hanging long at the back. He wore a long grey garment, with a hood; its loose sleeves rolled up to his elbows and the hem tucked up over bare legs. A small, striped cat sat watching at his side.

Suddenly the enormous bird, Feannag, swept down from the sky and landed, cawing, on his shoulder. He looked up as the white deer and the dark-skinned boy raced down the hill. At once, he straightened his back and dropped his hoe. The little white deer halted for one desperate moment, seeing him. The boy raised his spear. Then the man held out his arms and the deer bounded down the hill straight to him, and thrust her small body against the folds of his robes. Gently, he lowered his hands, and crossed them around her trembling neck. With a small flick of her ears, she buried her head in his sleeve.

The boy with the spear stood stock still, staring at the robed man and his sheltered prey. The spear in his hands sagged, forgotten. Looking down at his small, slumped shoulders, Gil realized he was no older than themselves.

Rachel shouted, "That horrible boy was trying to kill it!"

The man stroked the deer. Then he nodded gently, and called up to Rachel, "Little daughter, your brother is hungry."

But Danni then shouted, "So? Does that give him the right to kill it? It's not the deer's fault, Aidan."

"You have never been hungry," The man, Aidan, said.

"Yes, I have." Danni balled her fists in indignation.

"No." Rachel said softly, "No. He's right. None of us have." She lowered her head and was silent.

Aidan nodded. "You are wise as well as brave, little daughter." He lifted his hands and released the deer. "Little brother, there is all the food here you need. May the deer have her life?"

The boy stared silently for a long moment, then, slowly and solemnly, he nodded. Aidan smiled and stepped back. The white deer turned her head, her ears flicking. "Run, *Mo'chridhe*," Aidan said, and in an instant she leapt free and bounded away across the green grass, scattering sheep and sunlight in her flight.

Aidan looked down at the boy and smiled. "You will eat, now." The smile made him look young, but there were lines in his face and grey in his hair, and his eyes seemed older still. He raised his gaze to Gil and Rachel. "You have all travelled far," he said. "Come; share my hearth." He laid an arm gently over the boy's shoulders and led him to the long building with the thatched roof.

Danni turned to follow, but both Rachel and Gil hung back. Rachel's eyes swept over the cluster of stone huts and the grass-roofed building with the cross. "It's like a film set." Danni blinked uncertainly. "A movie set," Rachel said quickly. But Danni just shook her head.

"Who *is* he?" Gil said.

"Aidan?" Danni smiled and shrugged. "He's the Ab."

Rachel whirled. "What?"

"He's the Ab." Danni said again. "It means 'father.' That's his church." She pointed to the building with the cross standing on its carpet of yellow flowers, by the sea.

Rachel's dark brows drew together and she studied the round huts and the church in silence. "I know," she said quietly.

Inside the thatched building was a single large room, with an open camp fire burning in the middle of the earth floor. A black pot, like a witches' cauldron, hung by a chain over the low, blue flames. Pale, sweet-smelling smoke swirled around the pot and rose up the sooty, black chain, to the roof. Some of it went out a small hole, there, but most of it spread above their heads, seeping slowly into the thatch. The Stone-Pecker bird perched in the rafters, above hanging strings of grey, smoked fish.

Eyes watering, Gil peered around the dim interior. There were wooden boxes and a long table, with benches, near the fire. At one end of the room stood a tall wooden loom, strung with vertical threads. From somewhere at the other end came a loud indignant bleat.

Gil whirled and stared. Three small brown sheep were clustered in a heap of straw. Aidan knelt among them, milking one, like it was a cow. The striped cat waited patiently on the hem of his robe. When he finished milking, it trotted, tail high, to the table and took up a place on a bench. Aidan filled a bowl with the sheep's milk and set it on the table in front of the cat. He looked up, and met Gil's startled eyes. "Surely you would not ask nobility to eat on the floor?"

"No!" Gil said hurriedly.

"Very wise," said Aidan. He looked at the cat. "For he is a Noble Cat." Then he spoke for a moment in his church language. When he finished, the cat put out its small, pink tongue and began to lap its milk.

The dark-skinned boy crouched on his heels by the fire, warily watching as Danni set out flat rounds of bread and a dish of soft white cheese. Aidan poured the warm sheep's milk into four wooden cups and beckoned them to the table.

The bread was hard and grainy and the cheese smelled of sheep. Still, the more Gil ate, the hungrier he realized he was. Rachel picked at her portion uncertainly, but, in spite of the Mars bars, Danni wolfed hers down. The boy ate in ravenous gulps and clasped his cup of milk in eager hands. But hunger drove him, and once hunger was sated, he withdrew again to the fire. His eyes followed Aidan around the room with the same desperate trust as the deer, and when Aidan rose to leave, the boy hurried to his side.

"Come," Aidan called to Danni, "They must be shown their cells." Gil followed, alarmed, but instead of a prison, the cells proved to be only the little round huts.

"This is yours," Danni led him to one. "Mine's the one next to it." The blank stone walls of the cell curved inward as they rose, making a cone shape. Only the very top needed a roof; a thatch of coarse grey twigs. There was a door, made of woven branches, standing open to the sun, and a small brown sheep with four horns blocking the doorway.

Danni shoved the sheep away and ducked beneath the low lintel, and Gil followed. Sunlight lit the dim interior just enough for him to see its simple furnishings. There was a low wooden bed with a flat mattress covered in a grey and white checked blanket. Furry animal skins, brown, grey, and white, were spread across the bed. A length of beautiful blue cloth lay neatly folded, at one end.

Two wooden boxes sat at angles against the curved walls, and beneath the one window were a small wooden table and a bench. Above the table, a blackened metal bowl hung from a chain. The window itself was a deep slit in the stone. Small wicker doors were set on either side, to keep out the rain.

The floor of the hut was just dirt, packed hard and swept clean. A broom made of a bundle of twigs stood beside the door. On one of the two wooden boxes sat a battered metal bowl and a jug. "That's to wash in," Danni said. "That's your bed. There's another blanket in that kist." She pointed to one of the boxes. "You can put any stuff in the other one." She paused and then her mouth twitched. "Like maybe your underpants."

Gil nodded, only half listening. He looked carefully around

the little room. Even when he teetered on the Lookout Rock, struggling to find the courage to jump, it was here, prepared and waiting for him. He turned to Danni. "Was your hut all ready, like this, too?" She nodded. "It's not an accident," he said, then. "Us being here. It sort of looked like an accident, but it wasn't, Danni."

She turned away, her eyes darting around the room. Her gaze settled on the bright blue cloth on the bed, and she leapt at it eagerly. "I made this cloak for you," she said. "I spun it and wove it, and sewed it." She handed it to him proudly

Shyly he wrapped it around his shoulders and held out his arms, draped in glorious blue. It felt like he was wearing a piece of the sky. "This is awesome," he said, turning slowly. You really made this?"

"Aidan taught me. Making it made me believe you'd really come." She looked down. Tears shone on her dark lashes. "I was so homesick."

Gil reached out a wary hand and patted her cautiously. "But you're, like, really at home here," he said. "You're so good at everything."

"I had to be!" she said fiercely. "Aidan kept saying you would come, but I hardly believed him anymore. And then you did come and you didn't stay!" She choked back a sob. "That's when I started to think maybe I'd never get home." She looked around the barren little hut. "Maybe this was my life. So, I had to learn to spin and weave and milk the sheep and make cheese…."

He shook his head. "*Why?*"

"So I could marry Floki, stupid!" She began to cry.

Gil stared at her. "Marry? You're fourteen! You're a kid. You can't marry anyone." He paused. "And who's *Floki?*"

"I'm fifteen," Danni said. "And we're not kids here." She smeared the tears away with the back of her hand. "Oh, come on," she said wearily. "They're waiting." Gil followed her out of the hut, closing the wickerwork door carefully behind him. A wind had come up, off the sea, and thick fog was rolling in toward the beach. It cloaked the little church so it seemed like the ghost of a building. He was glad of the warmth of Danni's cape and wrapped it snugly around his shoulders.

They found Rachel in her own new cell, examining the hanging bowl above her desk. She dipped a finger into it, sniffed warily, and then wrinkled her nose in disgust.

"Fish oil," Danni said cheerfully. "Look." She reached into a cloth purse hanging from her woven belt and drew out a clump of sheep's wool. Twisting it expertly in her slim, brown fingers, she fashioned it into a fat string and dipped it into the oil. "It's a lamp," she explained. "That's the wick. You can light it from the longhouse fire."

Rachel studied the metal bowl, her brows drawing together again. "I know," she murmured. She shook her head.

Danni looked worried. "Will you be okay in here?" she said. "It gets cold at night."

Rachel tossed her long braid over her shoulder and smiled briskly. "Once a Girl Guide, always a Girl Guide. We'd better see the new boy is alright."

The boy greeted them with a huge grin in the doorway of his own hut. "Come, come," he beckoned. "My home!" He led them inside, dark eyes shining with pleasure. He patted the mattress and swung the wicker shutters back and forth and sat proudly at his desk, looking up at the round thatched roof. "Like Africa," he said. "Like home."

Gil saw himself, Danni, and Rachel through the boy's eyes: rich, white strangers from a world more alien than this. "USA, okay!" The boy said suddenly. He raised his hand in a gesture that Gil knew had to be a high-five. Gil returned it with a sheepish grin.

A rasping cry broke suddenly into the cell, and something thudded into the thatch above their heads. A moment later, a sharp rap came at the door. Danni looked up in alarm and the boy's camaraderie vanished. He reached instinctively for his gun and when his hands grasped air, panic crossed his face. He jumped against the wall, flicked the window shutters closed, and slipped into the shadows as Danni opened the door.

Aidan ducked beneath the lintel, his face calm but his manner urgent. "Now, quickly. Take them to the church."

Danni nodded and at once hastened Gil and the others from the cell. Outside, she looked briefly at the sea and then pushed them in front of her, down toward the beach.

Aidan raced ahead and when he reached the little church, jumped nimbly from a nearby rock up onto the grassy eaves. Scattering two hens and a nibbling sheep, he mounted the steep grass roof with surprising ease and balanced on the roof-tree beside the little stone cross. Eyes narrowed against the glare, long hair blowing in the wind, he peered out to sea.

Gil stopped and shaded his own eyes. A low cloud bank veiled the horizon in luminous grey. As he watched, something emerged momentarily from the mist, a patch of shrouded blue that vanished at once, like a ghost.

"Come on, Gil!" Danni turned angrily. "Move!"

"A sail?" He stared as it re-appeared through shreds of fog.

"*Northmen*, Gil! Run!" She grabbed his arm and jerked him furiously ahead of her.

Aidan jumped down from the turf roof and extending protective arms, shepherded them past a triangular wooden frame, holding a battered bell, to the church door. Made of woven branches, like the doors of the huts, it was tied open with a loop of rope. "In, now, and keep silence. The wind is with her. She will not be long." Danni un-looped the rope and pulled the door closed behind them.

Inside, it was so dark that Gil felt blindly for the stone wall, like in his grass-covered tomb. Then he became aware of daylight sifting through the glassless windows and made out a further point of light at the end of the building; a flickering flame in a black metal bowl, hung by a chain from the roof. The windows were deep-set and narrow, but they had broad stone ledges. On one sat the striped cat, white forepaws solemnly joined, tail twitching.

There were two benches running along the walls and Danni hurried them toward one. Then she stood up on the other and cautiously glanced out one of the windows. Gil joined her, climbing up to peer through another of the narrow slits. Face pressed against the cold stone, he fixed his gaze on a strip of sea and sky and the sail, larger and clearer now, rapidly approaching.

As he watched, the ship broke free, again, of the shifting

cloud bank. He glimpsed a long sleek hull and a tall mast with a single cross piece from which the sail swept down to the deck.

"Get down!" Danni hissed. "They'll see you."

"What happens if they see him," Rachel said sharply.

Danni gave her a bleak look. "If they're just traders, nothing," she said. "But if they're out a'viking?" She nodded uncomfortably towards Gil and the African boy and murmured, "*They'll* be dead. And you and I will be Northmen's wives."

"Vikings?" Gil whispered. "They're *Vikings?*"

"Don't be absurd." Rachel jumped up on the bench. "Vikings don't exist." She wormed in beside him and stared out the narrow window. The ship was closer, still, and through streamers of mist Gil saw the tall curving prow slicing the water. He glimpsed shadowy figures half-hidden by the sail, and, at the high stern, a man; standing.

"Tell *them*," he muttered queasily.

"They're not real," Rachel snapped. "It's a film set, or they're re-enactors, or something. It's all some kind of joke." She glanced at Danni, "A very *unfunny....*"

"You think so?" Danni's eyes flashed. "Then you go out there and take them on, Lara Croft."

Gil shook his head. His eyes searched the dim interior. There were two tables at the far end, one which held two candles, and a smaller one, on which was an open book. Both were covered with white cloths embroidered with birds and animals in colored and gold and silver threads.

Behind the tables, three broad niches were carved into the stone wall. In the first, stood a golden cup, ornamented with silver and jewels, and two gold and silver plates. The second niche held a gold cross standing on a silver base. Golden animals and birds twined and tangled across the silver. Beside the cross was a wooden box, pointed at the top, like a little house, with gold and silver trim. In the third niche were two huge books, their thick covers bound with silver and crusted with jewels.

Gil stared at them with growing unease. The primitive dwellings, the simple food, Aidan's worn rough clothing, all seemed suddenly a sham. Turning abruptly, he surveyed each of the walls. There was nowhere to hide, no other door; the windows far too narrow to permit escape. The building was less a refuge than a trap. "We've got to get out of here," he said urgently. "Now, before it's too late." He turned to the door, but Danni blocked his path.

"Sit down," she whispered, "And be quiet. You heard Aidan."

"They're *Vikings,* Danni." He squinted out the window at the Ab waiting quietly in his garden. "And he's standing there with a hoe? How's he going to stop them?"

"He'll talk to them." She shrugged. "They'll see he's poor. They'll probably settle for a sheep."

"And they won't think about looking in this church?" He waved his arm wildly at the jeweled treasures. "We're trapped in here, Danni. We're sitting ducks."

"He is elder." The African boy's quiet voice startled Gil into silence. "Wise. Perhaps makes peace?"

Gil cast another furtive glance outside. The mist had closed in, as if the ship itself commanded it, but within it, the grim silhouette loomed huge. "There's no more time! Run!" he cried. "All of you!"

Breaking free of Danni's grasp, he bolted for the door, slammed it open, and was free, running for his life up the steep path. Aidan shouted from the shore, but no one followed. Gil ran on, into the wood of white trees, panting at last to a halt in their leafy shade.

Far off, he heard Danni's clear young voice calling his name and guilt swept over him for abandoning her again. Shaking with fear, he turned back toward the church and the sea. A twig snapped behind him, and before he could move, a huge hand closed on his shoulder with an iron grip. Out of the corner of his eye, he glimpsed a glittering silver bracelet and skin bristling with coarse blond hair. He wrenched himself around, looked up, and gasped in terror.

A huge man towered over him, his bearded face glowing like a ruddy moon. Fierce blue eyes squinted beneath bushy red brows, and a white scar curled his mouth into a ferocious grin.

"Let me go!" Gil shouted. The hand, rough as leather, clamped over his mouth. The man growled a sharp, alien word, lifted Gil right off his feet, and slung him under his mighty arm. Kicking and struggling, Gil shouted again, a muffled croak. The hand came away from his mouth and slapped the side of his head. The man's big, hairy face came close to his. "Be still," he said in English. "I do not play." His free hand flashed before Gil's eyes and suddenly it was gripping the hilt of an enormous sword. He brought the blade within an inch of Gil's face and shook it. Then he sheathed the sword, and pinning Gil's arms with both of his, dragged him further into the woods. Gil twisted his head and sank his teeth into his captor's wrist.

The man howled in outrage and flung Gil down on the ground. He sucked blood from his wrist, spat it out, and then drew his sword again, this time with cold, clear purpose. Wincing in terror, Gil shut his eyes.

CHAPTER SIX

"Magnus." The voice came out of nowhere, gentle, but commanding. Gil forced himself to look. Aidan stood before his captor, arms folded, his hands tucked into the long sleeves of his grey robes.

Danni appeared behind him, her face white beneath her tan. "Magnus," she pleaded, "Please, he's my friend. He's Gil."

Magnus kept his eyes on Gil when he answered. "Your friend," he said coldly, "Bites me like a farmyard cur." He smiled without humor and raised the sword, "I find you better friends."

Aidan stepped lightly forward and lifted both arms as if holding Gil and the Northman apart. "Magnus," he said more firmly, "Put away your sword." Then he brought his right hand down gently on Magnus' sword arm and turned the weapon aside.

Magnus gave a sharp, cold laugh. "You sail close to the wind, my friend," he said.

Aidan smiled back. "The boy is my guest, Magnus. Put away your sword."

"The boy may be your guest, Aidan, but you are mine. You, and your god." Magnus' blue eyes blazed and Gil cringed, brutally aware that his new protector's only weapon was his own quiet confidence.

But then a flash of silver light swept from the shade of the little trees and something slapped into Magnus' face, scattering sparkles of silver across his red beard. Danni shrieked and Magnus shouted. Gil stared.

A woman had appeared from nowhere. She was nearly as

tall as the man, but slim and graceful. She wore a long dress, like Danni's, with another sleeveless garment, bright blue, with a many-colored border, over it. Her hair was velvety grey as a cat's fur, but her face was young and beautiful with huge eyes, so dark brown they seemed almost purple.

She was holding a bunch of silvery fish, strung together on a cord. She raised the fish, menacing Magnus again with their shining tails. "You are no better than Floki," she said, looking straight into his eyes. "And he has the excuse of youth. Nor is Cille Aidan your gift, but your father's." She nodded toward the little church below. "You would begrudge the Ab his bit of rock and sand? You, with all Einar's lands, would take back his gift to Aidan?"

Magnus bowed his head and turned his face away. With a quick, angry shrug, he lowered the sword. He looked back at Gil and then turned to Danni who clung to Aidan's arm and watched him fearfully. Magnus laughed. "Hah, Danni, I marry this one to my son, now, not you." His eyes flicked back to Gil, "Since he fights like a girl." Then he sheathed his sword and strode off down the hill, his long, ruddy hair streaming behind him.

Gil climbed warily to his feet. The grey-haired woman watched Magnus go, her string of fish swinging loosely from her clenched fist.

"Ah, Shony, Shony," Aidan said. "I do not know which of you is the fiercer." He smiled. "Come, now. We will have prayers and then we will make better use of these fish than combing your husband's beard."

"He will meet my sword, Mo'Aidan," she said fervently, "Before he drives you from here." Aidan laid a long arm over her shoulders and gestured to the little cluster of stone buildings below.

"My Master had no home at all, Shony," he said with another smile. "Even begrudged by Magnus, I am already too rich." They walked off together, but as Danni started to follow, Gil caught her arm.

"What's happening?" he said. "Where are we going?"

"To greet the ship! It's Floki! Floki's home!" She caught his hand, but frowned, then, her eyes on Magnus' irate back. "You shouldn't have bitten him. That made him really mad."

"I thought he was a Viking. You said if they caught me, I'd be dead."

"Magnus isn't a Viking, now. He's sort of a farmer, now. Anyway," she said brusquely. "He wouldn't have killed you. He'd have kept you to help with the harvest and then maybe let Floki sell you, in the winter."

"Sell me? Like a slave?" Gil stared at her, astounded. She nodded. "And that's all right then?"

"Here, it is," Danni said in a low voice. She ducked her head and walked quickly away. At the edge of the wood, she turned and beckoned him to hurry. Irritation vanquished by excitement, she smiled happily. "Look!" she cried, as they stood side by side above the sea. "It's *Silver Dragon!*"

Gil caught his breath. The concealing mist had parted, like the green-eyed girl's snatched veil, and the great ship surged landward, its beauty, like hers, revealed. The tall prow bore a dragon's head, carved, and painted in silver and black. A curving tail rose at the stern. Sinuous as a serpent, she rode the sea like a living thing, born by nature out of the depths.

Still, Gil could make out shadowy figures aboard and at the stern, a man stood at a tiller, guiding the fantastical beast with a steady hand. He was tall and lean and the sun flashed bright yellow on his long, wind-whipped hair. Shielding his eyes, he scanned the beach.

Danni ran down to the shore and teetered at the edge of the surf, waving. "Floki!" she shouted. "Floki! Gil's here!" The blond Northman waved back, but he held his course. Riding a tumbling bow wave, the ship sailed on, straight at the white beach where she stood.

"Danni, get out of there!" Gil shouted, and the African boy, who had come, with Rachel, from the church, bolted suddenly to her rescue. But then the Northman flung his tiller far out over the side and the longship heaved about, broadside, its blue striped sail slackening as the dragon prow turned again to the sea.

A great wave of water, thrown up by the hull broke on the

shore, splashing Danni's feet. Then the sail slithered down, baring the mast, and revealing ranks of ready oarsmen on either side. Oars dipped and flashed in unison, holding the ship steady into the wind. The blond helmsman released the tiller to a bushy-bearded sailor at his side, sprang up on the ship's rail, and dove into the sea.

Swimming with swift strong strokes, he made shallow water and, jumping to his feet, strode through the surf as if it wasn't there. Danni reached out and he caught her arms and swung her in a giggling circle, her bare feet skimming the waves. Laughing, he pretended to drop her, then scooped her up again, carried her ashore, and set her down lightly on the sand.

Northmen swarmed off the ship, leaping down over both gunwales and wading, chest-deep through the sea. Ashore, they shook themselves like wet dogs, brushing water from their long, bright-colored shirts and tight pants. Some wore leather boots. Others were barefoot. Each had a sword in a dripping scabbard at his side.

Surrounding Magnus, they pummeled and thumped him with rowdy affection. Then, seeing Gil, Rachel, and the African boy watching warily, they fell silent. They were almost all really young. Despite their weapons and their sea-weathered faces, some of them looked like boys. They shoved each other and scuffled, self-consciously, while Floki strode up the beach to his waiting parents.

He bowed gracefully to Shony who acknowledged with a small, proud smile. But Magnus embraced his son in his tree-trunk thick arms and swung him around as Floki had swung Danni. Laughing, they exchanged punches and wrestled until they both tripped each other and sprawled face first in the sand. Amid raucous cheers, they scrambled to their feet.

Danni ran to the young Northman again and tugged at his hand. "Look, Floki!" she cried. "I'm not alone anymore. Gil's here!" She grabbed his arm and dragged him determinedly across the sand. Floki grinned cheerfully and allowed himself to be dragged. He was as tall as his father, but slim, like Shony, and even playfully stumbling after Danni, he moved with Shony's slender grace.

With his free hand he adjusted his sword belt over his dripping red tunic and smoothed his youthful beard. Then, with splayed fingers, he combed out his sea-tangled hair, as yellow as the gold bracelets on his arms, and thick as a lion's mane. He tossed it back over his shoulders, proudly as a girl, and stopped in front of Gil, looking him up and down. Gil saw that for all his preening and his playfulness he had eyes as grey and cold as the sea from which he had come.

"Him?" he said to Danni. "For him you wait since Candlemas?" He looked at the sky as if for an explanation, then shrugged and welcomed Gil with a shoulder-crushing hug. Then he caught sight of the African boy and his eyes narrowed as he walked all around him. "What now?" he said softly. "We befriend the heathen Saracen at Cille Aidan?"

An angry mutter arose among the watching seamen, like the snarls of a dog pack behind its leader. Floki silenced it with a quick wave of his hand. "Great warriors, the Saracen," he said. "I fight one, once. He is fine swordsman. Very brave. Dies well." He grinned and tapped his sword hilt. "Ho, Saracen!" his grin broadened and became almost friendly. "Perhaps we fight. Perhaps I kill you."

The African boy nodded very slightly. "Perhaps." He grinned his own white grin, but Shony stepped hurriedly between him and her son. She laid a hand on the boy's shoulder.

"He is our guest, Floki," she said. "And the guest of the Ab who baptized you. You will show him respect."

Floki stepped back and laughed softly. "I play," he said, "And he knows I play." He nodded to the boy. Then he looked up and around at his ship. "Besides, I bring a Saracen of my own!" He laughed again and shouted cheerfully, "Noble Sir Palamedes! Come show your splendid self to Cille Aidan."

Gil turned also to the ship and saw there what, hidden by the sail and a forest of oars, he had missed. A huge, dark man waited behind the lofty mast, holding the bridle of an enormous black horse. He bowed his head to Floki, handed the animal's reins to a young Northman, jumped into the sea, and waded ashore.

He wore tall, fur-trimmed boots over his trousers and a

dark green tunic that reached almost to his knees. Gleaming chainmail surmounted the tunic, jingling as he walked. Around his waist was a jeweled sword belt bearing a mighty sword with an elaborate curving hilt.

His face was almost as dark as Ismail's and marked with a white scar down one cheek. Black curling hair tumbled wildly down his back and his thick black beard brushed his chest. Even Danni shrank back as he approached. But he smiled then, with a flash of white teeth and his eyes lit up, warm and brown. He bowed before Floki, "Good sir," he said, "I am at your service."

"And I, most certainly, am not at yours," Floki smiled cheerfully. "But come, my friend. This is the holy Ab for whom you cross desolate seas." He turned and held an arm out to Aidan, but as he did, a shadow flickered across his face and his smile slowly faded. "Good father," he said solemnly, "I have done your wish. Let this deed not bring desolation here."

The black-bearded man raised his hands in sad protest. "Surely, it shall not! I am armed with the prayers of the brethren of Alba and the blessing of the Ab of Hy!"

"And this!" Floki smiled again and slapped the jeweled scabbard at the man's side. "For when prayers and blessings fail."

"But it is I who have summoned him," Aidan said, "Thus the deed is mine." He clasped the visitor's hand in both of his. "And swords," he smiled gently at the young Northman, "also fail."

"Not so!" Floki laughed and shook his head. "Here is a sword that never fails!" He bowed suddenly to his father. "Behold Magnus Redbeard, son of Einar, son of Hrolf; Sinker of Ships, Splitter of Helms, Slayer of Saxons, and Lord of Einar's Holm."

Holding one arm out to the Saracen guest, he said with a barely suppressed grin, "Sir Palamedes, Master of Lances, and most noble knight of the vanished King Arthur's vanished kingdom." Magnus clasped forearms with the knight and in spite of his size managed to pull him off balance with his fierce handshake.

"A real knight," Danni whispered and Floki's grin broadened.

"Oh, very real. A knight and a warrior, swift of lance and deadly of sword—who could win by them all a man requires of silver, or land." He paused, having noticed Rachel who stood to one side, watching warily. "Or of women," he finished with a smile. He stepped closer to Rachel and drifted around her, his eyes flitting from the Saracen knight, Palamedes, to the English girl. She jerked her loose shirt down as low as she could over her hips, and moved closer to Danni.

"This is Rachel," Danni said. "My friend."

Floki paused again, his eyes lingering on Rachel's face. She met his gaze. "Yes?"

He laughed and turned to the Saracen knight. "Now here is game worthy of the hunt!" The knight nodded courteous agreement, but Floki looked around his gathered crew and said, "Think! She could be his! But instead, he hunts a phantom!"

"No phantom," the knight protested. "I hunt the Questing Beast, as all men know. The vow of my father, Pellinore, is now my own."

"Have you seen this wondrous animal?" Floki's eyes sparkled mischievously.

"I have heard its mighty voice, questing like the devil's own hounds, shaking the forest with their barks and howls."

"But he has not seen it," Floki addressed his grinning audience. "Nor had his father before him."

"It is said my grandfather glimpsed its black wings and fiery maw."

"One glimpse in three generations? This is an elusive quarry, my friend." Floki smiled and the Northmen laughed, but Shony stepped closer to the knight.

"Is this true?" she whispered. "You are the Knight of the Questing Beast?"

"Hah!" Floki thumped Palamedes' arm with his fist. "Your fame reaches even the Northlands. At least," he added, grinning, "in the gossip of women."

"Enough," Magnus said suddenly. He looked gravely at his son and growled, "Do not mock a guest. Feuds hatch in nests of words."

"I make no mockery!" Floki raised innocent hands. He

smiled at Rachel and Danni and murmured, "Give me sweet fame on the tongues of women and you may keep the praises of men."

"But what *is* the Questing Beast?" Danni said.

"A dragon," Shony answered at once, "The fiercest of all dragons."

"Would that it were!" Palamedes shook his head solemnly. "A mere dragon would cause me little pain. No, the Beast is mightier than a dragon! Fiercer than a lion! Wilier than a griffin! And more enduring than the Immortal Phoenix." Danni cast an awed glance at Gil.

"A phantom," said Floki cheerfully. He leaned over Palamedes' shoulder. "Forsake it, my friend. Come; hunt with me a real quarry. Sleek otters and fine stags on my lands on Hrolf's Isle. Or fine women on the shore of Cille Aidan!"

"Finer women I have never seen," the knight answered graciously. "But a vow to a father cannot be broken. The honor of my knighthood forbids it."

Floki leaned closer as if imparting a precious secret. "This is the Northland, sir, where there are few rules and fewer men that keep them. And the honor of knights is a jest."

"May God preserve me from such a land!" the knight returned fervently, resting his huge hand over his heart.

"And why should he, you pagan Saracen?" Floki flung his arm, teasingly, over the knight's shoulders. Palamedes smiled patiently within his great black beard and gave his young companion a little shake, half warning and half play.

Aidan smiled also. He stretched out his arms, as if embracing them all, but his eyes rested on Floki's face. "Come, now, to Holy Mass, that we may give thanks for your safe return." Shony covered her head with a shawl and, still carrying her string of fish entered the church. Magnus stroked his ruddy beard, and then, with a shrug, unstrapped his sword belt, and, laying the weapon down at the door, followed his wife.

But Floki turned to the sea and pointed to where a thin line of breakers crossed the bay. "Good father, I would rest my keel at Einar's Holm this night. But see there, where the white horses roar and shake their manes? There lies sand that scrapes my

keel at highest tide. And even now, the tide falls. I must set sail."
He smiled, and leaned closer to the Ab, "But bid your Master
hold fast his sea, and I will come."

Aidan's eyes crinkled with laughter. "You place a high price
on your soul, Floki Magnusson."

"Ah," Floki returned at once. "It is the buyer's eagerness
that raises the price. So every trader knows. And I tell you,
again, the prize is not worth the effort." He laughed, and then
turned suddenly to Palamedes. "But here, now, is a prize worth
winning!" He punched the knight's huge arm. "Let the Ab
baptize you and save your black pagan soul."

Palamedes smiled but shook his head solemnly. The laughter
left Aidan's eyes. "Why? To please a Christian whose heart is
forever pagan?" He inclined his head, then, toward the Saracen.
"He will know the Lord's peace before many," he said.

"And me?" said Floki, a light of challenge in his cold eyes.
Aidan was quiet a long while, studying the young Northman.

"You also," he said then. "But you will walk a penitent's
road before you do." He raised the cowl of his robe and walked
away. Floki watched in silence. Abruptly, he turned and ran,
splashing, into the sea and dove beneath the waves. The
watching Northmen swarmed after him, and with a gracious
bow, the knight, Palamedes, waded back to the ship.

When Gil followed the others into the church, the oarsmen
were already bending their backs. He paused in the doorway
and watched as the dragon prow sliced seaward and the sail
rose up the mast. Danni tugged at his arm and he turned
obediently. But throughout the Mass, with its strange language
and strange chants, his eyes drifted toward the open door and
the blue and white sail dwindling to nothing on the misty sea.

When they came out of the church, Shony and Magnus
followed Aidan to the longhouse. But Rachel stopped by the
bell in its wooden frame, stroking the worn metal softly. Her
hand strayed to the hammer resting beside it, as she raised her
eyes to the circle of stone cells. Her gaze drifted from one to the
other. "Cille Aidan," she murmured to herself.

The African boy touched her arm tentatively. "What is
meaning? You know this?"

"It means Aidan's cell." Rachel's attention was still on the stone huts. "It comes from Latin. It can mean 'church,' too. It's the place where a Celtic monk lived. Aidan's a Celtic monk," she said suddenly.

"You know that?" Gil blurted.

"Sure," she said. "He's probably a bishop, too." He stared and she laughed sharply. "Not really, Gil. Celtic monks don't exist anymore." Her eyes swept the little cluster of buildings from the church to the longhouse with its smoking thatched roof. "But it's so *authentic*. You'd really think...." Her face clouded and then lit with sudden delight. "That's it! It *is* a set. It's reality TV! Monks, knights, *Vikings*," she clutched Gil's arms and shook him joyfully. "They're actors!"

Dazed, he nodded. The words meant something. He'd heard them before. But the meaning faded like.... He paused and shook his head. "It doesn't cross," he said. She dropped her hands and turned away in despair.

Within the longhouse, Shony was stirring something in the pot that hung over the fire. In the shadows beyond, Magnus sat on a low bench with a little harp on his knees. "That's mine," Danni whispered to Gil. "But Magnus plays it better." The Northman's huge, rough hands stroked the delicate strings sweetly. He looked up and nodded to Danni. His eyes passed over Gil as if he wasn't there. Still, Gil listened, captivated by the beautiful, unlikely sound, until Aidan called them all to supper.

Magnus rose and put the harp aside and sat down at the table. Gil sat down, too, as far from him as possible, with Danni, Rachel and the African boy in between. Shony served them bowls of smoky tasting fish soup and when the soup was finished Danni brought a bowl of little raspberries and another of cream and honey. She wiped her soup bowl out with some of the bread, and then filled it with berries and cream. Gil did the same and ate his berries, wrinkling his nose at the leftover fishy taste.

After the meal, Magnus took his place in the shadows, playing Danni's harp. Shony built up the fire with driftwood and small brown squares that looked like earth, but burned with a hot blue flame. Aidan lifted the cooking pot down from its chain and hooked the chain up on itself, out of the way. He brushed his sooty hands, and then sat down on a low stool, by the fire.

One little sheep came with a clicking of hooves on the hard floor and lay down beside him like a dog. It rested its chin on his knee and he stroked the flat place between its four horns. The Noble Cat sat down at his other side, washing its ears with a paw. Gil sat beside it and it climbed up onto his knee and began to purr.

Lulled by the sound and the warmth of the fire, Gil felt weariness descend like a soft blanket, and his eyelids tugged downward. When Aidan spoke, his voice sounded far away. "What story will you have, Magnus Redbeard," he said, "Now that we are all friends?" Aidan nodded toward Gil and smiled gently at Magnus, as if the story was a consolation for not having Gil as a slave. To Gil's surprise, Magnus put the harp down readily.

Before he could speak, though, Shony said, "Tell us about Queen Guinevere and Lance'lot."

Aidan turned his thoughtful eyes to her face. "What is there to tell of two sorrowing penitents, making their peace with God?"

"But there is much, Mo'Aidan," she cried innocently. "Floki feasted with an earl on Yula's Isle, and the earl's poet told how Lance'lot rode each night to her convent, that he might see her face."

Aidan smiled gently. "Poets are fine storytellers, and Floki is the finest of all. Such stories will be told yet, when both knight and lady are in their graves, Shony. But not at this hearth."

Shony ducked her head, accepting his admonishment with humility. "Come now," Aidan coaxed gently, "I will tell Child Yesu in the Temple—how our Lord was lost in the great city of Jerusalem for three whole days and three whole nights, while he was still only a boy. A boy alone, among strangers; soldiers and beggars, thieves and merchants; and what happened to him there."

Aidan rested his eyes on Gil's face almost as if he was talking about him. Gil knew he wasn't, though, because he knew that story. He had read it in his Children's Bible when he was little and he could still remember the pictures. He looked warily at Aidan, wondering if he was teasing the Northman. But Magnus nodded his big head and said, "Good. A good tale."

Still, when Aidan began the story, he turned once more and addressed Gil, as if telling it to him alone. "Our Lord, Yesu," he said, "Born into this world, was all things we are in this world. He was a swaddled babe who cried for milk, a little child, who played with toys, a growing boy, like you. He had a mother, Mary, who loved him, as all mothers love their sons." He nodded to Shony, but Gil could only think of his own mother, searching for him still, on the river bank. "And," Aidan continued, "though his true father was God, he had a foster-father, Joseph, and his fosterer loved him as if he was his own son."

He stopped speaking and his eyes swept his circle of listeners. "Why was he fostered?" he asked suddenly, like a teacher. His gaze settled on the Northman. "Magnus?"

"That is simple," Magnus said gravely. "I teach my son, Floki, and also my sister's son, my fosterling, Hakon. And his father teaches my son, as well as his own. Two fathers. Two wisdoms."

Aidan nodded, but Danni burst out, "Why did he need anyone to teach him, if he was supposed to be God?" Her brows drew together with a look of puzzled irritation that Gil remembered from school. But Aidan seemed pleased.

"Well done!" he said. "So asks the great prophet, Isaiah! 'Who has directed the spirit of the Lord, Or as his counsellor has instructed him?'"

Aidan clasped his arms around his knees and tilted his head thoughtfully. "If he did not learn to be a man as all boys do," he said to Danni, "Could he then truly be as all boys are?" She shook her head uncertainly. "And he was as all boys are," Aidan continued. "And a boy, even if he is God, must obey his father. And his fosterer. And, indeed, Our Lord was almost always obedient to Joseph. But a day came when he was not."

He turned abruptly to Magnus. "If it had happened," he said, "That while Floki was with Ragnvald, his foster-father, you had need of him at Einar's Holm, what would you do?"

"I would send word and he would return," said Magnus, "Of course."

"Obedient to his true father," said Aidan. "As a son must be." He nodded solemnly.

"It was the Feast of the Passover," he continued his story, "A great and solemn feast, but a joyful feast, as joyful as Easter. And the boy, Yesu, and his parents went eagerly, with all their kin, from their home to the great city of Jerusalem, to celebrate. And all went well and when it was time to return, the young boys gathered together to travel and Mary and Joseph thought little of it, since this is what young boys do."

Rachel and the African boy both nodded agreement. "And so," said Aidan, "they did not realize when they left the city that the boy, Yesu, had slipped away from his cousins and his friends. For, like Magnus' son, he had heard his Father calling him and could obey his fosterer no longer. And he went alone then, through the crowded city streets, where thieves lurked and soldiers swaggered, seeking the place of his Father's house. And at last, he found it."

"His father's longhouse?" Magnus said.

Aidan smiled. "We will call it that. The holy temple, the place where God dwelt among men. And there he stands now, a slender boy," he nodded toward Gil, "before the great towers and ramparts of the Temple of Jerusalem."

Magnus' bushy brows drew close as he peered at Aidan in the smoky light. "You have seen this place, Aidan?"

Aidan shook his head, "Only in other men's words."

"But if your God lives there," Magnus pursued, puzzled, "Do you not wish to go there, too?"

"Ah, but now my God has gone out into the world," Aidan said, "To live among all men. Now, my God lives even here," he gestured across the low fire, to where the little church lay beyond the wall.

Magnus listened thoughtfully. Then he too waved a big hand, toward the church. "The old gods had finer halls," he said. Aidan smiled, untroubled.

"Indeed they did, Magnus. But they could not dwell in the place my Master alone can dwell."

Magnus rubbed the back of his hand across his moustache. "What place is that?" he asked warily.

"Within the hearts of men," Aidan said. "Within mine and within yours, Magnus, welcomed in your baptism."

Magnus smiled slightly, but his blue eyes were remote. At last, he said in a distant voice, "It was my father's wish. My father, now, is dead." His eyes locked suddenly with Aidan's in a kind of challenge, but then, abruptly, he looked away. "Tell your story, Aidan," he said amiably, "I like your tales."

Aidan bowed his head to Magnus and began again. "Within the courtyards of the Temple were many scholars who sat day by day, studying the scrolls of the Word of God. And they were very wise men."

"As wise as you, Mo'Aidan?" Shony asked, looking up at him shyly.

"Oh, far wiser," Aidan laughed. "Far, far wiser." He shook his head, laughing still. "And so, the boy, Yesu, went in among them, for he had learned the wisdom of his fosterer and now it was time to learn the Wisdom of his Father. And there he remained, among them, questioning and being questioned by the scholars, who delighted in him, because nothing delights men of learning more than young minds seeking knowledge." He smiled suddenly at Rachel, and continued.

"But all the while, his mother and father sought him and sought him, back along the way they had come for all a day's journey, before they had realized he was gone. And they came again to the great city and sought him there, three days and three nights. Until at last, in the longhouse of his true Father, they found their lost son. And all was well."

Shony raised her strange, beautiful eyes to Aidan's face. "But surely, if he was God, he would spare his own mother such grief?"

"Maybe he couldn't" Gil said, suddenly. "Maybe he had to decide very quickly. Maybe there was no time. Or he thought she'd stop him." He looked to Aidan. "He had to go. Didn't he?"

Aidan met Gil's eyes. "He did have to go," he said solemnly. "Even though they did not understand. And a day would come, in his manhood, when he would go again to Jerusalem for the Passover, and again he would be questioned, but these questioners would find no delight in him. And they would mock him and condemn him to death and hang him upon a tree. And once again, for three days, his mother would grieve, thinking him lost. But once more, he would return to her, this time from the dark city of the dead."

Magnus said, "The god, Odin, also hung upon a tree. Six days and six nights he hung there, to bring to men the wisdom of the runes."

Aidan nodded calm agreement. "Odin's tree may give men wisdom," he said then. "But Yesu's tree gives life. What is wisdom to the dead?"

Magnus glowered belligerently for a moment, but then his face broke into a grin, twisting the scar at the corner of his mouth. "Good! You are clever. And your stories are clever, too. But now," he stood up, yawning and ducking his head beneath the sooty rafters, "there are beasts to tend. Nights of story-telling are for Vikings. And I am but a humble Christian farmer, after all." His eyes twinkled teasingly and he slapped Aidan's shoulder, and then gripped his forearm in a hand shake that was at least as fierce as it was friendly. "Good night, my friend," he said, bowing formally. And then, bowing, also, to the others, but ignoring Gil, he strode out the door. When it swung inward, Gil saw the grey mist had rolled in again from the sea.

Shony also bowed to Aidan and went out, her dress and her hair blending at once into the dim light outside. Danni crouched by the fire and raked ashes over the flames with a crackling green branch. She bent her head and said words Gil didn't know. He leaned close and whispered, "Hey, Danni, I sort of need the john. Is there somewhere private, aside from those trees?" He nodded uncomfortably toward the wood where Magnus had caught him.

She led him to the door and pointed into the soft grey mist. Way beyond the shrouded church, Gil saw a small, dark, round-shouldered shape on a rocky ridge on the horizon. It looked like another of the cone-shaped huts, perched at the end of the world. "At least it's low tide," she said, mysteriously. She grinned as he stepped past her, into the mist. But then the grin faded and she caught his arm. "If you see Shony on the shore," she said urgently, "Don't look at her."

He blinked. "Why not?"

"Do what I say!" Danni said. She went into the longhouse and shut the door.

Gil set off up the stony path. Veils of mist obscured his goal. The sea lapped, barely seen, below. He picked his way warily onward, until the hut loomed up suddenly, out of the deceptive fog. He caught at the curved stone wall for balance. The little building sat right on the edge of a cliff. Beyond, was an airy drop into grey nothingness. He edged closer and saw, far below, the misty glint of the sea. Stepping back from the edge, he braced himself for the mountain privy smell, and opened the wicker door.

Fresh, cold air burst out of the dark interior. He peered inside and saw a stone ledge, wide enough for his butt, projecting over an empty space from which rose the sound of the rushing sea. "Brilliant," he said, "indoor plumbing." He dropped his pants, lowered himself onto the ledge and held on for dear life. A wave crashed far below. *At least it's low tide.* "Nice one, Danni."

When he left the hut and closed the wicker door behind him, the longhouse was barely visible in the thickening mist. He strode quickly down the path before it disappeared entirely. Then, just below the church, where the misty track skirted the white sand beach, he heard a soft splash.

Warily, he turned toward the sound. A figure stood at the water's edge; a grey outline against grey sea. Gil peered into the mist, then started back. Shony. *Don't look at her!* He turned away instantly, obedient to Danni's words. But then something within him rebelled against Danni being wise and mysterious about everything, from the cliff-top privy to his underpants in the turnip-head tomb. Shoulders stiffened with resentment, he turned his gaze to the sea.

Shony was still there, her back to him, crouching down to trail fingers in the incoming waves. Like anybody might do. He shrugged, turning away. But then she leaned forward and slipped in one smooth movement, into the sea. Startled, Gil stepped toward her. "Shony, are you okay?" His voice sounded loud in his own ears. With a rippling splash, she twisted around in the water.

She raised her head. "Shony...." The words froze in his mouth. Shony's face had vanished. In its place was a rounded, fur-covered snout, and a dark, whiskered nose. Two huge purple-brown eyes stared out of the silvery fur. They were still Shony's eyes.

Gil's hands flung up to cover his face. There was another great splash and when he forced himself to look again, he saw only a dark, sinuous back plunging under the waves. A finned tail rose for a second, slapped the foam, and disappeared. Then, suddenly, there were dark heads rising everywhere from the grey water. Glistening eyes shone in the mist. The air filled with raucous barking, and one, high-pitched scream, which Gil suddenly realized was coming from his own, terrified throat.

He bolted from the sand beach, up the rocky path, past the round huts, and flung himself against the longhouse door. "Danni! Danni, let me in!" The door jerked inwards and Gil fell inside, landing on his knees in front of her.

"You looked," she said in a furious whisper. "You looked!"

CHAPTER SEVEN

Danni dragged him to his feet and then held up her arm, blocking the doorway. She glanced quickly over her shoulder at Aidan, working his loom at the room's far end, and then shoved Gil back out into the mist. "Please," he begged.

Ignoring him, she beckoned urgently to the African boy and Rachel. In moments they were all together, the longhouse door shut firmly behind them. Danni wrenched Gil's arm behind his back and pushed him down the path. "Danni, no," he moaned. "It's out there."

She stopped at the door of her own cell. "There's no 'it,' Gil."

"You didn't see...."

She kicked the wicker door open. "In." Gil stumbled gratefully beneath the lintel; glad to be anywhere away from the misty grey sea. When they were all gathered inside, Danni released Gil's arm and faced him. "She's a selkie."

"What?"

"Shony. She's a selkie. A seal-wife." She looked him right in the eye. "She's not human."

"*What*?"

Danni paused. "At least," she said thoughtfully, "She's not only human. But we're not supposed to know. So, we never watch. Okay?"

Gil stared. "She turns into some kind of sea monster and we pretend it's not happening?"

Danni looked out the narrow window, at the shore. "People are afraid, Gil," she said quietly. "Selkies aren't really that dangerous. But they're strange. And people are afraid of strange things. Anyhow," she said, "she doesn't turn into a sea monster.

She turns into a seal. Seals are cool."

Gil remembered the sleek watching heads. He reached past her and flicked the shutters closed. "No, they're not," he said. "Or maybe they are if they stay seals...." He shrugged. "Are, like, all of them half human?"

"Most of them stay seals," Danni said. "Most people stay people. Shape-changing is hard."

"No," Rachel suddenly interrupted. "It's not hard. It's impossible. It doesn't happen. People don't turn into seals." She shook her head. "It was foggy and he was scared. He made a mistake."

Danni turned to face her. "He saw it and it was real. Before you can begin to live here, you have to accept that things are different. Everything is different."

Gil huddled against the damp stone wall and clasped his arms around his knees. After a long while he said again, "Where are we, Danni?"

"I told you," Rachel said sharply. "It's Orkney. I've been here before."

Gil studied her bewildered face. Then he stepped back to the window and forced himself to open one shutter. Through the narrow gap, he looked out over the white strand with Aidan's fishing net, the grass-roofed church, the mist-shrouded sea where Floki's ship had sailed away. And then he understood. It came all at once, with the clarity of a dream suddenly remembered. He turned back to Rachel and said, "You haven't been here before."

"I have," she shot back. "I remember it really well. It was the year my mother died. We even have pictures at home. She's standing right in front of one of the big stones. She's got this headscarf she always wore because of her cancer treatment. That's why we came here. She had this idea the stones would make her better." Rachel gave a little shrug.

Danni studied Rachel sorrowfully. "How old were you?"

"Seven." Rachel looked at the floor. "It doesn't matter. It's so long ago. I've completely forgotten about it. I just remembered now because...." she stopped and looked away. "So, I have been here," she said defiantly.

"I know," Gil said. "But not before. After. You've been here after."

"After what?" Rachel said, confused.

"After they built the road you saw," Gil said. Danni was shaking her head, but he continued, "No one's taken the road away. Or the houses. They haven't been built yet."

Danni shook her head harder, but Gil said clearly, "We're in the right place. But we're in the wrong time."

"That's crazy," Danni said angrily. "That can't happen. You can't get from one time to another time."

"People can't turn into seals, either," Gil said, conscious of Rachel's widening eyes flicking between himself and Danni. "Things are different here," he said. "Remember?"

"No!" Danni shouted. "It's not true!"

"It is! Look! It explains everything. Aidan and that weird church. The Northmen with their swords. The ship." He turned and waved his hand at the primitive stone walls. "And this place. They don't have electricity. They don't have toilets, except that thing at the edge of the cliff. They cook over fires!"

"How else would you cook?" Danni said, puzzled.

"They don't even have chimneys!" Gil shouted her down. "It's like the Stone Age! We're hundreds of years ago. Hundreds and hundreds. Maybe thousands. Somewhere where people use swords and sailing ships and look how you're dressed! Rachel's right. It's like a museum! It's not just another place. It's another time!"

"No!" Danni shouted. "It's just a place. It's just a different place."

"Time, Danni. It's a different time. A real place. A different time."

"No! No!" Danni flung herself at him, punching him and kicking him. "I hate you! You're a liar and I hate you!"

Gil struggled with her, grasping her shoulders, fending her blows. She fought desperately, her eyes screwed up, refusing to see; tears blotching her face. Then, suddenly, she stopped struggling. Her hands dropped to her sides and hung there. She lowered her head. Tears ran down her cheeks. Then she looked up, imploringly, into his eyes. "Don't you understand?"

she said. "It means they're all dead."

"Dead? Who's dead?" Gil released his grip and dropped his hands, too. "What are you talking about?"

"My parents. Your mom. All our friends. All the kids at school. Everyone we've ever known. They don't exist anymore. They're dead."

"But they're not dead. They just," he stopped, struggling with the idea, "They just haven't been born yet."

Danni put her face right up to his. "Can't you see?" she said in a hoarse whisper. "It's the same thing! They don't exist in the world we're in. That's what being dead is. There's no way we can ever reach them."

Aware again of Rachel's frightened eyes following him he said softly, "How long have you known?"

"Since the beginning. When I tried to tell Aidan about stuff, ordinary stuff, stuff kids know, and he didn't understand. For about a day I thought he was really stupid, but then I saw he wasn't. He reads huge books and he knows, like the whole Bible by heart, and he speaks about five different languages, and writes them, too. But he'd never heard of a...of a...." she buried her face in her hands and whimpered, "I can't remember anymore."

"A cell phone," Gil said, touching her arm gently. A chill descended on his heart. The cell phone. Yes. And that thing on the desk. And that thing where his mother cooked...it wasn't a fire. But he couldn't see it somehow. "It's happening to me, too," he said dully.

"What's happening?" Rachel looked confused and terrified. "What are you talking about?" Gil turned, to try to explain, but something more urgent flashed through his mind.

"Danni, you said Aidan writes?" She nodded, looking as confused as Rachel. "So, he has paper, pens, something to write with. We have to get it. We have to write down what we're forgetting."

"What are you forgetting?" Rachel demanded.

"The future," Gil said solemnly. "We're forgetting the future. And you will, too."

She stared, uncomprehending, tugging with nervous fingers

at a loose strand of red hair. "How can you forget the future?"

"When you've left it behind," Gil said. He pointed out the window to the strand and the timeless sea. "This place," he said, "has a future, but it hasn't happened yet. Not here. It's happened somewhere else, some place that's another time. That's where we belong. Where you've just come from. Where you saw the standing stones. But here it hasn't happened yet, so we can't remember it."

Rachel listened, as if she was trying to believe, but then she slowly shook her head. "I don't know what's happened to you both. Maybe it's like amnesia, or something. But it's not going to happen to me because the whole thing's not true. There isn't any future you can come and go from. There aren't any time machines or Doctor Who, or...." Her gaze fell suddenly on the little fish-oil lamp hanging above Danni's desk. She touched it lightly, making it sway on its sooty chain.

"It's not real, you see. It's just a very good replica. Like in a museum. My dad would be *so* impressed!" she said brightly. "He's a trustee...of the museum, I mean. In York." Her lip began to tremble and she bit down on it hard. Squeezing her eyes shut, she whispered in a little girl voice, "Will I forget him? Will I forget my dad?"

Danni ran to her and caught both her hands. "No! No!" she said. "Don't worry. You won't forget people. I never forgot Gil, all the months I was waiting. I'm sure I haven't forgotten any people. Or animals. Or trees or rivers. Or anything like that. It's just things. Just some things."

"Things that won't cross," Gil said, suddenly. "Because they don't exist here. People exist here, so we remember people. And trees and rivers and animals. And old things, like plates and cups and books and clothes. But new things, things that no one here has thought of, yet...things without an idea...they can't exist, so we can't remember them."

"A laptop!" Rachel spoke so suddenly that Gil jumped. "You saw the stones on a laptop," she said. "When you said 'picture book' you meant a computer."

Gil hesitated. The words were so familiar, but what they described kept eluding him. An image flickered alive in his head; a kind of book with pictures that moved. "Yes!" he cried. But at once the image vanished.

"It fades," Danni explained eagerly. "Like the things fade. And when you try to remember them, it's like in a dream when you see something written, but you can never read it."

Gil and Rachel nodded. Danni's gaze shifted to the African boy. "Okay?" she said. He blinked his wide dark eyes and said nothing. She turned Gil aside. "How's he going to understand this?" she whispered hopelessly. "He comes from some mud hut village in Africa somewhere."

Gil looked over his shoulder at the boy watching cautiously. Then he turned and put on his friendliest smile. The boy smiled back. They did another high-five, grinning wildly. "Hey," Gil said, then. "My name's Gil. What's yours?" The smile vanished. The boy ducked his head in silence.

"Leave him alone," Danni said. "He doesn't like questions."

Gil faced the boy again, and said slowly, "Okay. That's cool. But there's something you have to try to understand."

He paused, racking his brain. "Okay," he started speaking very slowly. "This place," he made a wide inclusive gesture with both arms, "This place is not our place." He tapped his chest. "This place belongs to our...our ancestors! This is..." he did the arm thing again, "...Ancestor Place. Many, many harvests pass, since this place. Many, many harvests...." The African boy leaned closer, his eyes fixed in amazement on Gil's face. "We travel..." Gil scrunched up his eyes, straining for words, "...we travel like Great Spirit! Into Ancestor Time!"

The African boy nodded gravely. Then he held up his hand, palm outwards, with two pairs of fingers outspread in a neat vee. "Live long and prosper, Captain," he said.

Danni and Rachel collapsed, giggling on each other's shoulders. The boy's white smile re-appeared. "You know *Star Trek*?" Gil winced.

The boy shrugged and looked serious again. "Sure. Before war came, we have cinema. We have Internet café for tourists. We are Global Village!" He grinned a broad white grin. He reached up to offer Gil another high-five, self-consciously pulling his tee-shirt down over his hips.

"You, too!" Gil grinned.

"Those things," Rachel tugged irritably at her own shirt hem. "Those stupid things." Her face screwed up in frustration. Then she cried exultantly, "Zip! It's a zip!" But at once her shoulders sagged and she murmured, "How did I forget anything so stupid?"

Danni grabbed her hand. "Quick, while you're remembering. We can use Aidan's writing place."

She led them to a hut that was larger than the others, standing slightly apart on a little rise. It had two windows and the doorway was tall enough to allow Gil to enter upright. He looked around, his eyes taking in the room. Rachel crowded behind him, eagerly, but the African boy hung back in the doorway.

The stone walls of the hut were coated with a smooth creamy plastering and the interior seemed almost bright. In place of a bed, there were wooden kists and bookshelves and three desks, each with its own hanging black lamp. The shelves were piled with great, heavy books, as imposing as the two in the church, crammed in and layered on top of each other.

Between two of the bookcases was an upright frame on which hung dried animal skins. On a low box beside the frame lay a stack of something like stiff, yellow paper.

"That's where Aidan writes the books. That's where he mixes the colors," Danni pointed to a desk with a slanted top and a row of small pottery jars with wooden stoppers on one of the kists. "That's real gold, in that little box!" She stopped by a second desk, and held up a handful of feathers and a little knife. "Here's where he makes quills. That's what he writes on." She pointed to the paper-thin skins.

"Vellum," Rachel said softly. "Parchment."

Danni nodded, surprised. She stopped proudly at the third desk. "This is where he teaches me." A sheet of the stiff yellow paper lay on Danni's desk, beside a blackened quill.

Rachel circled the room with quick, certain steps, assessing the strange contents with a mix of amazement and familiarity. "I can't believe this," she breathed, "It's a scriptorium. A real medieval scriptorium." She stroked the edge of Aidan's writing desk. "My father would give anything to see this," she said wistfully. She leaned over the desk, studying the oblong piece of paper-like parchment pinned to its surface. Gil stepped closer to see it, too.

Thin, horizontal lines had been drawn across its surface, and between them, rows of black lettering made a beautiful, obscure pattern. Placing a finger beneath the top line, Rachel pronounced clearly,

"*Oh, Lord, You search me and you know me.*"

"You can read it?" Gil murmured.

"Sure. It's Latin." She looked again, "Church Latin, of course. But Latin."

"Brain as big as a planet," Danni muttered under her breath.

Rachel's head came up, her eyes flashing angrily. "My father's an historian, right? It's not like I had any choice about learning this stuff."

"It's okay!" Gil said hurriedly. "We're just, like, impressed." He gave Danni a hard look. "Right, Danni?"

"If I wanted to be hassled by no-brains, I could have stayed at school," Rachel said.

"You have a gift and you fight about it." The voice came so unexpectedly that all three of them jumped. The African boy had stepped into the circular room, at last, and was holding up his hands in a gesture of peace-making. "Is good that Rachel knows what the letters mean. Maybe they will help us understand?"

Danni shrugged and gave Rachel a small apologetic smile. "Tell us about this script-thing," she said.

"Scriptorium. It's where medieval monks copied books." Rachel smiled happily. "Before Gutenberg...." She stopped. "He invented the printing press and then people could print books. But before that," she pointed to the beautiful careful lettering, "you only had this. Books were so valuable that people went to war over them." She stopped suddenly. "I suppose you know all this," she said politely.

"I don't know any of it," Danni said, with an honest grin.

"That explains it!" she said suddenly. "That explains that man! A man came once, on Floki's ship. He wasn't a trader or anything.

He wore stuff like Aidan's, only black. And all he had with him was a book. He'd borrowed it, so he could copy it, I think. They spoke Aidan's church language, so I didn't understand what they were saying. Anyway, he'd come from this far, far place, across the sea and the mountains, just to bring Aidan this book back. Floki says it takes months to get there...he'd come all that way, just to return a book."

"Tell me about this place," Rachel said intently. "What was it called?"

Danni shook her head, trying to remember. "It was a place with a library, Aidan said. Saint-Something. Saint 'G' Something."

"Saint Gall!" Rachel said.

"Yeah!" Danni looked amazed. "How do you know all this stuff?"

"It was a medieval monastery," Rachel explained. "On Lake Constance. So, we must be some time after the year 612, because that's the year Saint Gall founded his monastery. We can't be before that."

"Well, that's cool," Danni said, uncertainly. "I mean, it could have been worse, couldn't it? It could have been like Jurassic Park stuff."

Gil grinned. "Great. Whatever else happens here, at least there's no T-Rex."

Danni glanced out the door at the sky. "We better start," she said. "When the bell rings for prayers, we'll have to stop. You can use the back of that," she indicated the parchment lying in front of him on the desk. Gil picked it up in both hands, turned it over, unstopped the ink jar, and began.

It was a lot harder than he'd thought it would be. The quill scratched itself dry, or dribbled blotches of ink. When he bore down too hard, it split, and Danni had to replace it. As he struggled to scrawl a simple word, Aidan's beautiful script impressed him more and more.

Eventually he managed the words 'cell phone,'" and sat back in triumph. Rachel said, "Say what it's for and how it works."

"I don't know how it works," he said. "It just...works."

"Draw pictures," said a soft voice.

Gil looked up again. The African boy reached, uncertainly, toward the parchment; then drew back his hand. Gil beckoned him closer and held out the quill. "You do it," he said.

Tentatively at first, and then with assurance, the boy began to sketch. His hand was sure and the quill obeyed him, producing a neat clear diagram of a cell phone, and, beside it, two stick figures holding one each and separated by a mountain and a row of trees.

Gil moved over on the bench and beckoned the boy to sit beside him. Danni handed him a quill of his own and a second sheet of vellum. Side by side, they set to work, Gil writing and the boy drawing, while Rachel, brow furrowed, recalled and named the elusive artefacts of their fading world. Danni took some pieces of white bone and brown deer antler from a box, and, with Aidan's quill knife, began whittling buttons.

By the time he'd recorded televisions, computers, and washing machines, Gil had used up the whole of Danni's parchment. Turning to her for another, he brushed the inkpot with his elbow, and tipped it onto its side. Ink stained the desk and flowed onto his parchment. The African boy yanked the red cloth from his hair and blotted it, but still, three lines of Gil's writing and half the African boy's drawing of a car were obscured by a black blob.

Danni looked up, critical, but unsurprised. "Here," she said, "take this." She held out the quill knife to Gil. "Scrape it off. It's okay. That parchment stuff's pretty thick. That's the good news. The bad news is then you've got to write it all again."

Gil looked at the miniature laptop that the African boy had carefully drawn beside his script. For a moment it was just a shape, but then an image of the real thing sprang into his mind and his fingers found their own memory of flying over the keys. He took the knife from Danni and set the blade against the ink-smeared parchment, with a sigh.

He drew the knife down, in one sweeping arc, pleased to see the inky surface peel readily away. Then his fingers, clutching the ink-blackened handle, froze. Slowly he unfolded them and held the knife up in front of his disbelieving eyes. It was a plain, small hunting knife with a bone handle and a steel blade. It looked old and much used, the blade nicked in three places and thin from many sharpenings; the handle worn smooth.

"Danni," he whispered, "Where'd you get this knife?"

"Right here. It was on this desk." She paused. "Aidan said I could use it."

"Aidan," Gil said quickly, "Where did Aidan get it?"

"I don't know." She stopped. "Why does it matter?" Gil drew the knife closer to himself. He stroked the bone handle with shaky fingers. "Because it's my father's," he said.

"Are you crazy?" Danni whispered. But suddenly her hands flew to her face, covering her mouth. "Oh, my God!" she said, "The Underwater Bridge!"

Gil saw in his mind's eye, the yellow kayak turning and turning in the Indian Kettle whirlpool. His senses and his sanity seemed to turn and whirl like the canoe.

He shook his head slowly and then suddenly he slapped the knife down flat on the desk and snatched up a little crescent-shaped blade lying beside the parchment frame. He bent over the bone-handled knife and began to scrape at the join of handle and blade. Soon, bright patches of metal shone through the grime. He scraped harder, then dropped the crescent and rubbed at the metal with his fingers. "There," he turned to Danni. She leant over and with the tip of his nail he traced the tiny lettering:

L.L. Bean
Freeport, Maine

"Ohmygod!" she said again.

Gil's hand closed over the knife. With his eyes closed, too, he savored the warm ache of physical connection, trying to think, trying to hope, and not to hope, trying not to cry.

"Your dad really loved that knife," Danni said. "He used it for, like, everything."

"I gave it to him," Gil scrunched his eyes tighter. Somewhere, a bell began to ring. It took a moment before he realized what it was. The bell for prayers. Aidan's bell. Aidan.

He opened his eyes and his fingers, and looked down once

more, on the knife. Then he grasped it tightly, his hand closing into a fist, turned, and ran out the door. He could hear the others behind him, shouting, calling his name, but their voices seemed foggy and far away. When he reached the church, the bell was still trembling slightly in its wooden frame. Inside, Aidan sat alone on a bench, his head bowed over his book of prayers. He looked up as a muddle of voices announced the arrival of the others, but Gil was already striding up the center of the church, the knife clutched in his fist.

Aidan's hands lay quietly on his book and his expression was of gentle curiosity. His peacefulness, itself, stirred Gil to fury. He shook the knife in front of Aidan's face; then slapped it down hard on the book of prayers. "Where is my father?" he cried.

Amidst the shouts of amazement and alarm from the other children behind him, Gil was truly aware of only one thing: that Aidan had shown not the smallest sign of surprise. When he answered, his voice was quiet and reasoned.

"I cannot tell you that," he said.

"You're lying," said Gil. He pointed at the knife. "You got that from my father. You know where he is."

Aidan shook his head.

"It is my father's," Gil shouted. "I know it is."

"It may well be. But it still was not your father who gave me the knife." Gil drew back, disarmed by Aidan's calm.

"Who did give you the knife," Danni asked from behind his shoulder. Aidan still looked at Gil when he answered. "Magnus Einarsson."

"Magnus," Gil said dully. A chill ran through him.

"Where did Magnus get it?" Danni pursued in her practical voice.

"It was a gift, Daughter. I did not question Magnus' claim."

"What claim?" Gil said.

"That the knife was a gift from the Northmen's god, Odin," Aidan said. He lifted the bone-handled knife gently, and closed his book.

"On the day his son Floki was born," he continued, "Magnus

went to the Great Stones to make an offering...bread, ale, milk, as was his custom. In the moment that he laid down his gifts, he saw a flash of brilliant light, and upon investigating, found this," he lifted the little knife, "the sunlight reflecting on the blade, its point wedged in the stone. He lifted it out and concluded it was meant for himself. A gift from Odin, in return for his own."

Aidan smiled. "A not illogical conclusion," he said.

"Do you believe that?" Rachel said skeptically.

"I believe Magnus believed it," Aidan returned. He turned the knife gently on his palm. "When Magnus came to the way of the One God, he, with great generosity, gave me Odin's gift." He smiled at Gil. "And that is how I have your father's knife."

"That's impossible," Danni said. She looked straight at Aidan, shaking her head. "Floki's twenty years old. So that all happened twenty years ago. We weren't even born! How could the knife Gil gave his father be stuck into a stone back then?"

"You are right, Daughter. You were not yet born. Nor are you born, now. Nor will you be born until the Lord's sun rises on Tir nan Og. Yet, you are here, are you not? Alive, and in the flesh. Very real, very solid flesh, and frequently very hungry, I seem to recall." His eyes twinkled suddenly and Danni giggled.

"We are here," Gil said sharply, "Because you brought us here. You are the reason we're here."

Aidan sat for a long while in silence. Then he said, calmly, "No, Gil. I am not the reason you are here. And I did not bring you here." He turned suddenly to the African boy. "What is your name, little brother?"

Barely audibly, the boy muttered, "John."

"That is not your name," Aidan said. "That is the name they made you take." The boy's head came up, his eyes wide with astonishment. Aidan met his gaze for a long while.

Then the boy said quietly, "Ismail." Two thin tear tracks shone on his brown face. He wiped them with the back of his hand.

"How did you come here, little brother?" Aidan said.

The African boy looked at Gil, and then with painful longing at Aidan. He shook his head slightly as if unwilling to betray his new friend. "Go on," Aidan said. "No harm can ever come from the truth."

The African boy nodded. Then suddenly he crouched down on his heels. When he began to speak his voice was soft and mesmerizing, as if telling a fairy-tale. "It was the fortieth day," he began. "The fortieth day since the Army of the Believers come. The fortieth day since my mother and my father, my aunt and my cousins, die. My father by machete, my mother and my aunts by machete and bush axe, my cousins by fire."

Gil felt his heart constrict, like he'd been wading in shallow water and suddenly stepped over a cliff into icy depths. Behind him the girls both gasped. Aidan nodded gently, without expression.

"The Believers take some of the children with them. My ten-year-old sister, Maryam, my eight-year-old brother, Hassan. Their legs shackled, walking behind, to their camp. They make them soldiers."

"Ten years old and eight years old?" Rachel said.

The African boy shrugged. "I am soldier. I am soldier five years." He held up his hand with five fingers outspread. "I am soldier, nine years old."

"They took you, too?" Danni asked.

The African boy looked at his feet. "I am captive," he said. He looked sadly at Aidan. "I am hunting for food. I make throwing spear and track game." He paused and allowed himself a moment of pride. "My brother and sister, they are not hungry.

"This day, I go out at dawn. In the shadows, is hind. White, like moonlight. So beautiful, I do not want to kill, but we must eat, so I stalk and when she runs, I run. She stops and I raise my spear and she is mine! But suddenly, there is shadow. And I look up and I see great black bird, and the white hind leaps," he demonstrated with leaping hands, "Into a rock." He shrugged in amazement, remembering.

"I go close. The rock is two rocks, very near, and between them, a narrow space. A crevice. Impossible, I think." He gestured with palms barely separated. "But the white hind, she go there, so I go, too. And then," he paused, his face puzzled, "And then all is strange, like under water.

"I am frightened," he whispered, "And I want to go back, but then, there is the hind! The white hind! So I follow, out, into the daylight...." He paused again, pointing at Gil and the others, "And they are there and everything I know, everything I know is gone."

Aidan placed both hands on his shoulders and whispered, "Well done."

But Gil pointed at the crow. "A bird. A big, black bird. Your stone-pecking bird, who you sent to each of us, to bring each of us here."

"He is not my bird," Aidan said, with a smile.

Gil stepped back and looked around the church. His eyes settled on the glittering treasures in their niches in the wall. "Oh, no," he said softly. "The bird's not yours. Nothing's yours. You're not supposed to own anything, right? Except," he shrugged toward the gold and silver vessels, "Maybe all those."

"They are not mine," Aidan said.

"Bullshit," said Gil.

Aidan raised one eyebrow. "They belong to the great *muinntir* from whence I brought them," he said. Then he added gently, "The Northmen may wrap themselves in the cloth I weave, or feast themselves on my sheep, or, if it pleases them, sharpen their swords on my bones. But the treasures of Lindisfarne belong to God." He paused and stroked the striped cat, sitting at his side, washing its small white paws with a small pink tongue. "And here they are safe, until, the same God willing, they may be returned."

Danni watched Aidan twirl the cat's stripy tail through his fingers. "But, then, you didn't send Feannag?" she said sadly. Gil saw, surprised, that the very idea which had enraged him, had brought her comfort.

Aidan shook his head, "I cannot send what is not my servant."

"But you knew we were coming," Gil protested. "The huts were all ready."

"To know a guest is coming is not the same as summoning his presence." Aidan turned again to the African boy, "Ismail, who brought you here?"

"Myself," said Ismail.

Aidan's weathered features softened. "When fear pleaded,

'turn back,'" he said, "Your brother and sister's needs cried out to you and you followed the hind. It is not I who called you, any of you, nor even Feannag. All that called you here was the courage of your own young hearts.

"You are here because you chose to be," he said, to them all. "You came for the sake of what's dearest to your heart." His gaze travelled across their faces and settled on Danni's. "You, for your brother, Percy. You," he turned to the African boy, "For Maryam and Hassan." He smiled when his eyes rested on Rachel's face. "You, for the weak and defenseless."

He leaned back, studying all three together. "To each the treasures of their heart." He turned then, his eyes looking deep into Gil's. Gil suddenly saw himself in his bedroom, the Stone-Pecker's white stone clasped in his hand, his heart filled with yearning for the face of the green-eyed girl.

"But Percy didn't choose," Danni said suddenly. "How could he? He's just like a little kid."

"To each the treasures of his heart," said Aidan. "Percy knew what you did not. You threw the stone away out of spite. And you," Aidan turned to Gil, "You threw it away because it would not obey you."

Gil remembered his moment of idiocy in the Tomb. Then he stopped. "I was alone," he whispered.

"But now," Aidan continued, "I must have it back."

Reluctantly Gil drew the stone from his pocket and handed it to Aidan. "So the stone is yours, anyhow," he said.

Aidan held it between his fingers and smiled. "Yes, Gil, the stone is mine. Also mine: five sheep, seven hens, the cooking pots in the longhouse, the cross of Yesu I wear round my neck, the *bachall* by the altar there," he pointed to a tall staff of wood with a bent handle that leaned against the wall. "This habit," he indicated his grey robes, "Which will serve as my shroud, and the bell at the door, which will ring in the day of my resurrection. These are my possessions in the earthly kingdom. Too many, I know, but I have not yet succeeded in making them less."

Laughing, he held the stone up before his left eye and turned it slowly, this way and that, like a man adjusting a lens.

"What are you doing?" Rachel said, curiously.

"Seeking," he said slowly, "the treasures of your hearts. Look." He held the stone out to her. Gil saw on her face the same compliant condescension with which he'd first taken the stone from Percy.

Rachel raised the stone to her eye. "My father!" she cried. "I can see my father!" She peered into the stone and waved her other hand eagerly. "Dad! Daddy!" Her joy faded. Frantically, she turned the stone, left and right. She shook it, replaced it at her eye, turned it around, and peered again. "He's gone." She said sadly. "But he was there!"

"Please," said Ismail. "You give me stone?" He raised the stone to his own eye. Immediately, he too cried out. "Maryam!" His face lit with delight. "Hassan! Hey, why you sleep so late?" He peered into the stone, and then out the window, and then back into the stone, "Why sun up so late?"

"Let me see," Gil reached for the stone, expecting to see home, too. But the white-framed circle showed him nothing but darkness. Then, slowly, he made out figures, one small and hunched, the other slender and quick moving. Light flared, a candle flame, revealing a round, dirty, tearstained face. "Percy!" Gil cried.

"Let me see!" Danni jostled him for the stone.

"No, wait!" He held it firm as the second figure moved closer. Percy's smudged face lit up with his familiar huge smile. And, as if reflected in its light, the beautiful, half-hidden face of a veiled young girl appeared. She handed a cloth wrapped package to Percy, who stuffed something from it into his mouth. The girl pushed back her veil and the candlelight glistened on black, shining hair. Then she turned and her lips parted with amazement and her green eyes shone with hope.

"It's her!" Gil cried. "It's my girl! And she sees me! She's with Percy and she sees me!"

"Let me see!" Danni cried. "Let me see Percy!" She snatched the stone and held it to her eye. Her face crumpled. "He's gone! You kept it too long."

"Can't you see anything?" Gil said guiltily.

Aidan reached out and quietly took the stone from her fingers.

"I want to see my brother," Danni whimpered. "I want my brother and I want to go home."

Aidan drew her closer and clasped her two arms at the elbow. He looked up into her face. "Your brother, yes. That you will have. But you have left home forever, little daughter."

"No!" Danni cried. She bit her lip and fought tears.

"I will lift my *bachall* and command you in the name of all things holy, to call you home," said Aidan solemnly, "But you will fly from me."

Danni shook her head. "Don't say that Aidan. You're scaring me."

Aidan drew Danni closer and embraced her, enfolding her in the sleeves of his habit, like the deer. "You will have other gifts," he said. Danni wriggled around so she could look up into his eyes without leaving the shelter of his arms. Aidan smiled and took her face between his two rough hands. "What saw your brother through the stone?" he whispered.

"A cup," Gil said suddenly. "He saw a beautiful cup."

Aidan dropped his hands to his knees but still looked deep into Danni's eyes when he answered Gil. "Truly, it is a beautiful cup, little brother, the chalice which heals every ill, Our Lord Yesu's cup of redemption."

Rachel, who had watched in silence, slowly shook her head. Recognition dawned on her face as when she saw the standing stones. "The Holy Grail," she said with a look of hurt disappointment, as if her best friend had told her a lie. "But the Holy Grail's not real," she whispered. "You must know that. It's a story."

Aidan reached out quickly and caught her hands. "The Grail is as real as you and I. It is the cup of Lord Yesu's great Passover, treasured by His Church and carried to these islands by men who had looked upon His face. No more precious relic exists in Christendom. But yes, many stories are told of it, and most are but longhouse tales."

He smiled, and then suddenly he opened his arms wide, and called them all close. Clasping Ismail and Rachel on one side, and Gil and Danni on the other, he said, "But I will tell you a story that is true. And I know this, because I was there, a boy,

no older than you, on my namesake's Holy Isle of Lindisfarne."
He looked up at the altar of his little church. "There was an
old, old monk among my brethren there. He had been a great
scholar, but time had darkened his eyes, and so he put his books
away and was contented feeding the hens and the doves. Thus,
he spent his days, among his flocks, chanting the psalms that a
lifetime had written on his heart.

"He was my *anam cara*, my soul friend and gentle confessor;
and for those things he could not do in darkness, I was his
eyes. I would come, each morning, to his little cell outside the
muinntir wall, and bring him water, and food, though he ate no
more than his doves. Then I would turn him to the east, so that
he might sing lauds toward the dawn he could not see.

"Then one morning, when all was done, he told me he was
soon to make a journey to a far *muinntir*, deep in the Forest of
Caledon, and I was to be his guide. The Northmen were once
more harrying our coast, and there was a certain treasured relic
the Ab had ruled no longer safe within our walls.

"And so, we set out, this old man and I, on two ponies, I
myself leading his, he riding with this precious thing veiled
beneath his habit. When, at last, we came to the Great Forest of
Caledon, my companion warned me to pay closest attention to
our road, because I would return that way alone. I knew then
he would die upon this journey, far from his little cell on Saint
Aidan's Isle, but though it saddened me, he was, as always,
joyful.

"On the fourth day, with our faces to the North, we descended
from a high hill and within the great, dark forest, I saw before
us a mighty keep, and beside it a *muinntir*, whose vespers bell
called us home. And so, I rode on, leading my brother and his
treasure to the castle gates.

"A young man stood waiting there, as dusk fell, and it was
he who found shelter for our tired ponies and food and beds
for ourselves. In the morning, he brought water that we might
wash and led the way to Mass, and after served our breakfast.
Only when our every need was met, did he lead us into the
Great Hall.

And even there, he seated us first, and then each of the

lordly knights, before taking at last a place for himself at a table where all sat in one great circle, with no ordering of rank. And then, lowering the cowl that had covered his head at Mass, he revealed at last the circlet of gold that was his kingly crown.

"He thanked us for the honor we bestowed, and pledged to build a chapel within his hunting forest, thrice-walled, and ever-guarded by his knights. And there the holy relic would remain. All at the table agreed, and they were as noble a band of warriors as could be seen." Aidan paused, looking away over their heads, as if into the past.

"But even in that great company, one stood out—the king's cupbearer at table and standard-bearer in war—robed in Cloth of Gold, his face shining in the firelight as he served the wine, as if he carried light itself within the cup!"

He turned back to them, "How could I, a simple boy, enthralled by garments and weaponry, imagine that this glorious knight would bring all that gracious kingdom to the dust?"

He searched each of their faces as if he would find an answer, there, and then continued. "I returned the next day, alone through the forest, leaving my soul-friend in the care of the *muinntir's* brethren. And, back once more on Aidan's Isle, I addressed myself to my prayers and my books. But the journey I began there was yet within me. And so, many years later, as man and priest, I set out again, to follow where it led, North, to these islands on the edge of the world.

"But by then, the work of the cupbearer was done. For this was Jocelyn Guidbairn, the Golden Knight, the gentle king was Arthur, and the kingdom to which we entrusted the Holy Grail, was Camelot."

"I know story!" the African boy, Ismail, suddenly cried. "I see in cinema. Knights, great warriors—they are Round Table. And king has beautiful queen. But queen is unfaithful and man she loves is king's friend. And so, there is great battle," Ismail said. "And king is wounded and taken far away and beautiful kingdom is ruined by war." He smiled sadly, his childish pleasure fading. "All wars the same," he said. "Everything ruined. Everyone sad."

Aidan studied his face in silence. "You are wise too young," he said softly. "And Camelot is indeed as you say; its Hall and *muinntir* roofless, the great knights leaderless, the gentle brothers driven away. All is now ruled, and ruled brutally, by that splendid cupbearer who dazzled my foolish young eyes."

"But if the Golden Knight rules Camelot," said Gil, "He already has the Holy Grail."

Aidan shook his head. "It lies within his kingdom but not within his grasp. Nothing evil can enter its presence; his own black heart stands ever in his way. This is why he fears you so. Why his men came with sinful treachery; calling me to them on pretense of illness, while others stole the child away."

He looked intently into each of their faces. "You, in innocent youth, can do what he with all his power cannot. You can claim the Grail. And with it, rouse Arthur from his sleep beneath the Eildon Hills, to rise again and win back Camelot. This is why he seeks, even now, to destroy you."

Gil's heart lurched with fear, but Ismail said only, "Where is Eildon Hill?"

"In Scotland," Rachel said, "Alba," she corrected herself to Aidan.

"Yes," Aidan answered. "When Alba lies in Tir nan Og. For that is why you have been called, children of that world, to bring our king back from that world. A call," he said quietly, "From which brave warriors would shrink."

He turned and looked into Gil's eyes. "Your courage has brought you here. But courage alone is not enough. There is much to be learned and much to be suffered. And though you set out as children, it is not as children you will return. Come," he said, "Prayers and supper. It is not good to think without either." He let his gaze sweep over each of their faces a last time. "Tonight, you must go, each to his own cell, and in silence and Our Lord's sweet darkness, make your choice: take up this holy quest, or let it pass. As," he smiled gently, "any wise man would."

CHAPTER EIGHT

Gil closed the wicker door of his cell and firmly fastened the bentwood latch. Then he dragged a wooden kist across the floor and jammed it across the doorway. The sea wind rattled the open shutters and he jumped to the window and closed them, too, shutting out the last dim light. Darkness swallowed the room and he stumbled blindly to his bed, wormed his feet out of his sneakers and slipped his father's bone-handled knife from his belt. Aidan had given it to him as he left the church, wrapped in a make-shift leather sheath.

Still clutching it in his hand, and still wearing all of his clothes, Gil burrowed beneath his rough covers. The blackness pressed against his face like a smothering blanket. Something barked, sharply, beyond the shore. Gil pulled a sheepskin over his head. He thought of his own bed with such homesick yearning he could smell his Spiderman bedspread.

Chaotic images of the day filled his mind. The black night of the Turnip Head Tomb, Rachel's cell phone fading to dust, the dragon-headed longship looming from the mist, Aidan in the flickering shadows of the church. *Take up this holy quest...take up....* And then a flash of steel before his face: Magnus. Closing his eyes and clutching the leather-wrapped knife in both hands, he whispered, "Please. Just let me go home," and sank into sleep.

He jerked awake, what seemed scant moments later, and sat up, still holding the knife. He heard a scratching at the shuttered window and then a whisper of sea wind touched his face. A weight pressed down on the foot of his mattress. He felt a low, rumbling, vibration at his side. He turned, terrified, and bristly whiskers scraped his trembling chin.

"Shony!" He flailed out with both hands, and his fingers touched fur. Not sleek and sea-wet, but warm, dry and plushy. The rumbling grew louder. Then he giggled wildly. "It's purring! It's just the cat!" He reached out and grasped the warm, soft animal and pulled it gratefully onto his chest. It purred more vigorously still, and licked his nose with its raspy tongue.

"Oh, cat," he said happily. "Oh, Noble Cat. Don't ever do that to me again. I thought you were that thing!" He pulled the cat closer, curled around it, and dragged the rough blanket up over them both.

But sleep, before so overwhelming, had vanished and his mind was racing with urgency. Giving the cat a last pat, he got quickly from his bed, wrapped himself in his blue cloak, and unlatched the wicker door.

Outside, the mist had cleared and stars shone in such profusion that by their light, alone, he found Danni's cell. He tapped softly on her door and waited uneasily in the darkness. She took a lot longer to answer than he liked. "Danni," he whispered and tapped harder. "We have to talk."

"In the morning," she mumbled sleepily.

"No. Now. All of us. We're in this together." When she didn't answer, he said, "We can't just let him send us off like some kind of Gandalf. We have to...."

"You're doing it!" She flung open the door, sleep vanquished and eyes alight with excitement.

"I don't *know*, Danni. That's why I want to talk."

But her face broke into the adventuresome grin he remembered from home. "I'll get the others." She paused, quickly wrapping a shawl around her shoulders, "Go to the church," she said. "There's more room there." She gave him a little urgent shove down the path and ran to Rachel's cell.

The church was as black inside as the Turnip Head Tomb. Straining his eyes, he made out a small point of light at the far end; the flickering oil lamp that burned there always. Fingers tracing the damp stone above one bench, he felt his way toward it.

Gradually, his eyes adjusted to the starlight drifting through the narrow windows, revealing the two tables and the glimmer of precious metal in the niches in the wall. Then something brushed like spider webs against his face and he yelped in alarm. A small chirrup answered. "Cat?" he peered at the shadowy silhouette on a window sill. "Is that you?" He reached a shaky hand out until he felt soft fur. Laughing, he lifted the animal down from the ledge. "What did I tell you about *not doing that again?*" He hugged the cat, glad of living company, and set it back on its ledge.

He followed the stone wall as far as the reading table and the lamp hanging above from its black chain, and explored the inside of the little bowl with his fingers. There was oil and a wick. All he needed...fire-things. Spark-things. He stopped and scratched his head. But no image came. Abruptly he gave up and, wrapping his cloak tighter, he settled on the bench beneath the window while the cat began a small cat game, jumping from the window ledge to Aidan's book table and back to the ledge.

The door scuffed open and Gil jumped to his feet. A bobbing, bright red spark appeared in the doorway, and behind it, Danni's face aglow with excitement. A long, narrow, cloth-wrapped bundle was clutched awkwardly against her chest. With her free hand she held up a burning brand of knotty pine wood.

"Where'd you get that?" Gil cried, as she entered.

"From the longhouse fire," she said. "It never goes out."

Ismail appeared in the dark of the doorway, with Rachel behind him, and shyly followed Danni into the church. Danni lit the oil lamp at the reading table with her brand and when the church filled with its soft, fluttery glow, she stubbed the brand out on the stone floor. Then she laid the long bundle down beside it, and stripped away the cloth, exposing two battered, double-edged swords.

She lifted one, with a grunt of effort, and raised the blade high. With the side of her foot, she kicked the other toward Gil. "To arms!" She turned her blade and pointed it menacingly at his chest.

"Don't be stupid," he muttered. But she kept her stance, advancing toward him, so he crouched and reluctantly clasped the hilt of the other sword, staggered erect on trembling legs, and raised the blade. Immediately, Danni whacked it out of his hands. The sword clattered to the floor, missing Rachel's foot by inches. Gil raised his empty hands in protest. Danni aligned her sword point again with his chest.

Furious, Gil leapt for his own fallen weapon. This time he was ready for the weight and for Danni. When she swung at him, he slid aside, and her blade slammed down on a bench, beside Ismail who had perched there. Ismail smiled his broad white smile, but did not move.

"This is crazy, Danni!" Gil shouted. "There's no room in here. You'll kill someone."

"To arms!" she said again. She whirled, catching him again by surprise, and thrust her blade upward. Metal clashed, ringing, on metal and again his sword was on the floor. Danni slid the sharp tip of hers up to his chin. He raised his hands again in defeat.

Danni stepped back and lowered her sword. She eyed him and his fallen weapon critically. "You're going to have to work hard," she said. "Once we leave Cille Aidan everyone we meet will be armed. There'll be Northmen and knights and robbers. And that's before we even get to Alba. We'll have to know how to defend ourselves just to find Percy. And then...."

"This is stupid, Danni," Gil cut her off. "We can't fight Northmen and knights. We're just kids."

Danni regarded him solemnly for a long while. Then she said, "I've waited months and months for this. When I got here, the first thing I wanted to do was go after the raiders who took Percy. Aidan said I couldn't. He said I couldn't go alone. I had to wait for you. That's why I got Magnus to give me these. So I could practice."

A gust of wind from the sea rattled the wicker door and blew it open, as if some night thing was trying to join them. Gil hurriedly pulled the door shut and searched vainly for a latch. He looked up and met Danni's mystified gaze. Leaning close, he whispered brusquely, "Look, there's a Northman out there who tried to kill me, and a woman who turns into a seal."

"Oh, why are you always scared of everything!?" Danni cried. "She's just a selkie. Anyhow, they're back at Einar's Holm,

now. They only came to Cille Aidan because it was a feast day."
Gil sat down heavily on a bench. "You could have told me."
"I did tell you. I told you it was Lady Day in Harvest."
"So how am I supposed to know what that means?"
"I know," said Rachel.
"You know everything," Gil said fiercely.
Rachel looked him right in the eye. "Look. I've spent my whole life in old monasteries and churches. Medieval church history is Dad's big thing. He used to quiz me on Hebrew and Greek over breakfast!"
Danni stared with a mix of awe and pity. "Didn't you mind?" she asked.
Rachel shrugged. "Who else could he talk to?" She looked away. "If I could unlearn all this stuff, I would, you know."
"No!" Ismail shook his head vigorously. "Don't unlearn!" Rachel looked up, curious. "Is not accident you are here," Ismail said. "You have purpose. You are guide. We all have purpose. See, I am soldier. No accident. You, guide. We have purpose for quest."
Intrigued, but uncertain, Danni said, "What's my purpose?"
"You are sister," Ismail said, as if that was explanation enough. "You are same blood."
"And me?" Gil raised a deliberately cynical eyebrow. "Why am I here?"
"You are leader," Ismail said at once.
"Leader?" Gil raised both eyebrows. "I'm the scared one, remember?"
Ismail smiled. He tapped his brown forehead, and then his chest. "All heart, no head, sees no danger. All head, no heart, sees danger everywhere. Leader is head *and* heart. You are leader."
The little church went quiet as Rachel and Danni looked solemnly at Gil, then at Ismail, then back at Gil. Gil struggled between a warm rush of pride and a sinking feeling of total inadequacy. Raising his eyes to meet Rachel's, he said, with as much good nature as he could muster, "What *is* Lady Day in Harvest?"
Her face broke at once into a willing smile, reminding Gil

that it was a very pretty face. "Well, it's really a very old term," she said. "You wouldn't ever have heard it, unless you did a lot of history." She smiled again, kindly. "It's a church festival. A feast day. Sometimes it was called Marymas. The medieval world used church festivals like we use days and months. Candlemas. Pentecost. Marymas was the fifteenth of August."

"The fifteenth of August?" Gil cried. She nodded. "Then, today's the sixteenth!"

She gave him a puzzled look. "So?"

But Gil was already on his feet. He searched the floor eagerly, until he found Danni's discarded pine brand; then leapt on it with a cry of satisfaction, and thrust it in his pocket.

"What's that for?" Danni asked.

"For writing the days on my wall."

She shrugged. "Aidan keeps the days in his prayer book. We can just ask him."

"I don't want to know what medieval festival it is," Gil said angrily. "I want real days. And real months. I'm not some medieval person. I'm a twenty-first century person and I'm going back to the twenty-first century!"

He saw the shadow cross her face the instant he spoke and wanted to grab the words out of the air and stuff them back into his mouth. "And you are, too," he said desperately. But she was already turning away. Gil lunged forward and grabbed Danni's arm, pulling her back to face him. "Don't listen to him! What does he know about us and where we come from?"

"He sees the future," Danni said simply.

"No, he doesn't!" Gil returned fiercely. He paused and said more softly, "Okay, maybe he reads minds, a little. I accept that. But he can't tell the future. Nobody can tell the future."

But then Rachel interrupted. "Yes," she said. "People can. We can." She looked around the little stone building. "We could tell these people here the future ahead for a thousand years!" Her eyes grew wide at the thought and lit with a sparkle of amazed excitement. "We could make such a difference!"

Ismail shook his head slowly. "No difference. If we change one thing, everything will change. We must change nothing! Like Star Trek!"

"The Prime Directive!" Gil said. "Cool." He turned to the African boy. Then with sudden panic, he said, "But we're doing it! We're here! We're changing things by just being here. Even the air we breathe out. In a thousand years it could make hurricanes! We're changing all history and we don't know what way!"

Danni sat down on a bench. Wrapping her arms around her knees, her long dress gathered gracefully around her bare feet, she rocked gently back and forth. "But this is history," she said. "Us being here is part of the past. We've always been here. We're part of history."

Gil shook his head warily. "Before we were born?"

Danni nodded. "What is, is. We are here. So what is, was."

"You mean, when we were going to school and playing by the river, this had all happened already?" She nodded. "But how did it end?" Gil cried. "Did we do the quest?"

"Do we?" said Rachel quietly.

Danni toyed with the hilt of her sword and then looked up with a bold smile. "I do," she said. "I have to. Percy started it, and he's my brother. But no one else has to. I'll get Magnus to ask Floki to come with me. He loves fighting." She looked straight at Gil and then shrugged. "You can go home." She grasped the sword firmly and held it up to the flickering light. Her smile faded. "None of you have to do this. Only me."

Rachel shook her head. "Ismail's right. No one is here by accident. We all have a purpose. Not just you. I'll go with you, Danni." She leaned forward from her refuge by the wall and tentatively lifted the hilt of Gil's sword. "I'll learn this stuff," she said.

But Ismail looked quietly around the church and said, "Gil is right. Children should not be soldiers." He stood up and, stepping into the center of the little building, beckoned to Gil. "Come."

Uncertainly, Gil obeyed. Ismail crouched and lifted the sword from the floor. His skinny arms handled it with unlikely ease. He held it upright and then placed the hilt in Gil's hands. Then, stepping behind him, he reached around Gil's waist and clasped the sword again, his fingers just beneath Gil's. Shifting his weight, he guided Gil's hands with his own, swinging the sword left and right, lowering it and raising it.

"See," he said. "It has balance. Find balance." He slipped his hands free for a moment so Gil could feel the change, himself. At once the sword felt both light and alive. Ismail returned his hands to their place and together they did three more practice swings.

"Now," Ismail nodded to Danni, "Please?"

Warily, she raised her sword. Ismail tightened his grip, his arms locked against Gil's, and the blade leapt to meet Danni's, just above the hilt. She cried out, shocked, as hers flew from her hands. It crashed to the floor and she stood rubbing her wrists and staring at Gil. Ismail stepped back, watching her. "You are hurt?" he said gently.

"No, no, I'm fine." Danni's eyes were wide with new respect.

Ismail turned to Gil. "You see," he said, "If you must, you can." His fingers met Gil's in another high-five and his white smile lit up the church.

Gil grinned, holding the weapon up with new confidence. His eyes fell on the treasure-filled niches in the wall and his grin broadened. "Plunder!" he shouted gleefully. He swung the sword boldly, "Pillage! Loot!"

Danni's face blanched. "Don't, Gil!"

"I'm a Viking!" He laughed, charging past her.

"Don't touch them!" she cried desperately. But his hand had closed already on the gold cross.

The thing that hit him came from behind. He heard a horrible roar, and something slammed into his shoulder blades, sending him sprawling, face down on the stone floor. He tried to scream but the weight of the thing on his back crushed the breath from his lungs. Hot air steamed the back of his neck. He turned his head and glimpsed black and golden fur, black feline lips, and enormous gleaming fangs. The thing roared again, right in his ear. *Tiger*, his mind cried insanely. "Tiger!" he croaked aloud, and with a strangled last breath gasped, "Run!"

And then it was gone. The weight was gone. The roaring was gone. The heavy, hot breath was gone. All that remained was something soft, brushing his ear, and a distant soft hum. A purr. Cautiously, he raised his head. Danni was looking down on him, still white-faced, and the Noble Cat was gently licking his ear.

Slowly, Gil sat up. His back felt like he'd been run over by a train. Grimacing, he stretched his arms out, feeling his shoulders creak. He looked around. The little church was still and silent. Rachel and Ismail stared at him; she in shocked disbelief, he in wondering amazement. Nothing moved, but the little cat, which had found a loose thread trailing from Danni's hem and was tumbling sweetly around it.

"What was that?" Gil whispered.

"Him," Danni said. She pointed at the playful animal, which was lying, now, on its back, curling its paws and blinking wide green eyes.

Gil looked from the cat to her innocent face. "Like, real funny. That thing was enormous! It knocked me over. It felt like a truck and it looked like a tiger. Whatever it was, it wasn't a cat."

Ismail nodded gravely. "Was tiger. Bigger than lion."

"It was him being a tiger," Danni said. "He shape-changes." Gil stared at the cat. "Like Shony."

Gil felt his legs go weak. He remembered the soft purr in the night, and himself pulling the covers over the cat on his chest. "He slept in my bed," he whispered.

"That's okay," Danni smiled encouragingly. She picked up the little cat and rubbed under its chin. She held him out to Gil. "See? He's purring." She looked up suddenly. "Shhh. What was that?"

Gil heard a distant caw. "It's just the bird."

Danni set the cat down on a bench and sprang to a window. "Aidan's out there!"

"It's the middle of the night."

"He prays in the middle of the night. Quick, hide the swords." She knelt on the floor, wrapping hers in the cloth and reaching for his.

"Why?" Gil demanded.

"Because Aidan doesn't know I have them. This is holy ground! It's a sanctuary! No one's allowed to keep weapons here." She stood up, clutching the bundled swords.

"You idiot!" Gil's eyes darted around the room. "Give them to me." He thrust the bundle behind his back. Rachel and Ismail jumped to stand in front of him.

The door swung softly open. Head shrouded by the cowl of his robe, Aidan stepped inside. *"Benedictio."*

"Deo Gratias," Danni murmured hopelessly. Aidan lowered the cowl and his eyes swept them all.

"I saw a light on my way to church, and I thought, 'Ah, these holy children sing Vigils. I must join this saintly choir.'" He smiled and beckoned them closer. Flanked by Ismail and Rachel, Gil shuffled an awkward couple of steps. The swords slipped free from the bundle and clattered to the floor. Danni made a little moan of dismay. Still smiling, Aidan leaned down and lifted one weapon and stood sighting down its length. He turned it, one way and another, the steel catching the flickering light.

"I know this blade," he said mildly. "I have seen it in the hand of Magnus Redbeard, years past, having sport with his young son." He paused. "A son who has gone on to mightier things." He looked down then at Danni and his smile vanished. "How came it here? To this sanctuary where no weapons may be held?"

She met his eyes miserably. "I asked Magnus for them." She bit her lip.

Aidan studied the blade again. "Redbeard," he said quietly, "It is you, my friend, who sail the risky course."

"It's not Magnus' fault," Danni blurted. "I begged for them."

"And you, so big and fierce. And he so small and timid; he could not refuse." Aidan bent, lifted the second blade, and tucked both under his arm. Then he surveyed them all, his eyes, usually so gentle, suddenly dark and piercing. "This, then is your answer to the call?"

Solemnly they nodded.

"I welcome your courage," he said. "But I would welcome obedience more. Still," his face softened, "It is not as pilgrims you are called, to go armed with a wooden staff; but as warriors." He rested his hand on the hilt of one of the swords. "You will learn the warrior's trade. But you will take no weapon from Cille Aidan but a blessing." He smiled slightly, again. "Come," he beckoned. "You will have that now."

Outside, the brief summer night was already fading into dawn. Carrying the heavy swords easily, Aidan led them up the hill to the wood of white trees. Gil stumbled through the shadows, struggling to keep up with the Ab's long strides. Feannag flew from tree to tree ahead of them, cawing.

When they came out of the trees and looked down on the stone circle, Gil saw in its center, shining silvery in the grey light and as perfectly placed as the hub of a wheel, the little Wandering Pool. Aidan strode through the stones to its edge. He laid down the swords beside it, crouched, and cupped water in his hands. Then he rose and sprinkled each of them with it, speaking softly in his church Latin as he did.

"Kneel now," he beckoned them to the edge of the pool, "And reach, with one hand, into the water, as deep as your shoulder, and grasp the first thing your fingers touch. Danni will be first." Danni looked at the water and then up at Aidan, her forehead wrinkled. "Aidan! The water's an inch deep here!"

"With one hand," Aidan repeated. "One hand, only."

Danni resignedly dipped one hand into the silvery shallows. At once, the water swallowed it. "I've gone through the bottom!"

Aidan leapt forward and caught her around the waist. "Grasp it!" he cried, "The first thing you touch!"

"I am! I am!" Danni pulled hard back onto her heels, fighting to withdraw her arm. Aidan struggled to hold her, his face lined with effort. Then Danni's arm burst from the water, and she flung her hand triumphantly in the air, clutching something grey and soft between her fingers.

"A feather?" Rachel cried. "All that for a feather?"

Danni stared at it and shook it. "It's not wet," she said wonderingly. She tentatively touched the sleeve of her dress. "Neither am I."

Aidan smiled. "A gift from the grey goose, for Danni. Guard it well," He turned and summoned Ismail.

Warily, the African boy crouched by the pool. He braced his feet against two thick tufts of grass and took a firm grip of a heather root with his right hand, before plunging his left deep into the silver water. Even so, he needed all Aidan's help to resist the power of the pool.

"It's an antler!" Danni cried, when Ismail's fist emerged from the pool, clutching his prize. They all clustered around to admire the grey and white deer horn; its branching tines held aloft like a proud little tree.

"*Caberfeidh*," said Aidan, "The wood of the deer for Ismail! Guard it well." The African boy cradled it carefully against his chest.

Aidan beckoned Rachel. Gil offered her his hand to hold, as she knelt fearfully by the pool. Gratefully, she grasped it, extended her other hand to the shallow, shimmering water and plunged her arm in up to the shoulder. Her hand in Gil's lost its grip, as the pool dragged her downward. Then Aidan was beside him, and together they wrestled Rachel from the water's fierce grip.

Safe on the grassy bank, she held up her hand with wry disappointment. She, too, clutched only a feather, and hers was even smaller than Danni's, narrow and dark brown, striped with grey. "As fierce as she is bonny, the hen sparrow hawk," Aidan murmured. "A noble gift. Guard it well."

Rachel accepted the feather back, more pleased with it, and rolled down her sleeve over a perfectly dry arm.

"Now, Gil," Aidan said.

Gil put one hand on Ismail's heather root, and braced his feet on the tufts of grass. Ismail laid his antler down and locked his arms around Gil's waist. Gil reached his hand steadily toward the bewilderingly shallow water. But the instant his fingers dipped below the surface his mind filled with hideous circling bones. He gasped and pulled back his hand. "I can't!"

"You must," Aidan answered. "Now! To the shoulder! Grasp the first thing you touch!"

"Bones!" Gil cried. "It'll just be bones!" Closing his eyes, he plunged his hand into the awful water, grasping desperately for what he feared to touch. His hand closed on nothingness. And then he was jerked downward, his arm wrenched almost from the socket, his face dipping into the blackness. He heard Ismail shout, "Hold on!"

Aidan's powerful arms gripped him. The pull of the water tore at his arm, his elbow, his wrist, and then just his clenched hand, as he was hauled back onto dry land by Aidan and Ismail together.

"What have you got?" the girls cried.

Gil sat back heavily on the grass. He clutched his empty, battered fist against his chest and shook his head. Tears stung his eyes. "Nothing," he said. "I got scared, so it gave me nothing." Then he opened his hand to show them, and there, on his dry palm, lay a single, stiff white hair, too tiny even to feel.

"A hair?" he said, with an uncertain shrug.

Aidan's eyes lit with unconcealed delight. His long fingers delicately lifted Gil's odd prize and held it for all to see. "A whisker," he corrected, "A whisker from that most honorable of animals, the bold and noble tabby cat!" He handed it back to Gil with the same solemn admonition, "Guard it well." Gil stared at him angrily, but Aidan only smiled.

He leaned down, then and lifted the two swords, holding them high in the strengthening light. Then he whirled and flung them with two great splashes, into the still waters of the pool. "Seek them there, Redbeard," he said softly, "Before you defile my sanctuary again." Then he beckoned the children and led them away.

Still resentfully clutching the whisker, Gil followed the others back through the brightening dawn. The sky above Cille Aidan was rosy pink, the sea glimmering green and gold. Gulls cried and swooped over the white sand beach, when Aidan left them and re-entered the church. Gil leaned close to Danni. "So where do we learn," he asked, "If we can't have weapons here?"

She looked startled. "Einar's Holm," she held up her grey feather to the rising sun, "Of course."

"Of course," he murmured dully. A fist of fear tightened in his chest as he returned warily to his cell, burrowed under his blankets and pulled the sheepskin back over his head.

When he awoke, the fist had clenched into a black knot of despair. Grey clouds had betrayed the bright dawn and rain tapped against his shutters. Shivering, he rose from his bed wondering if he'd be alive to sleep in it that night. He reached for his father's knife, and then stopped, staring at it in the grey light. Memories buzzed like mosquitoes around Gil's brain: his father's smile the Christmas morning when he unwrapped the knife; the knife, itself, on Aidan's workbench, illogically worn and aged; the circling yellow kayak in the Indian Kettle pool. Had his father survived, just as he had survived? And, if so, was it only to meet a worse fate at the hands of Magnus Einarsson? The same Magnus Einarsson that he himself was to face, sword in hand, this day? He pushed the knife aside, and then angrily took it up and slipped it through his belt. He found the charred brand and carefully drew a black mark on his wall, and wrote beside it, 'August 16th.'

Outside, showers of rain blew on a cold, grey wind. The sea was sullen and rain-splattered. The stone buildings glistened like dark-scaled animals. Two sodden sheep huddled beneath the dripping eaves of the longhouse. Gil wrapped his cloak tighter, and ran to the church.

After breakfast Aidan sat on the end of a bench, with Feannag on his shoulder and the Noble Cat at his feet. Four small leather pouches were spread out on the folds of his habit, each strung with a braided leather cord.

He took from them the feathers and antler and the whisker and with a small knife carefully sliced a tiny piece from the goose feather, placed it inside a leather pouch, and tied the braided cord around Danni's neck.

Aidan took up the hawk's feather and did the same with it, for Rachel. He removed a thin slice of the antler for Ismail, and rolled the cat's whisker into a neat circle and slipped it into the last leather pouch, for Gil. He stood, then, gathered the remnants of their hard-won treasures and threw them all into the ever-burning fire.

By the time they started out on the walk to Einar's Holm, the sun was shining brightly, and except for the wind, it seemed almost summer again. Gil looked back at the longhouse as they climbed the hill, and said, "Okay, can somebody enlighten me? What was the point of all that?"

Rachel fingered the necklace at her throat and said, "It's a talisman. It's supposed to protect us."

"Two bits of feather, some antler, and a cat's whisker?"

"It's a superstition, Gil. We wear them and we symbolically gain the animal's traits. It's called sympathetic magic."

"I have seen this," Ismail said suddenly. "In Africa. Not Islam. Not Christian."

"No," Rachel said. "It's animism. Pagan." She shrugged. "Things are a little mixed up here, I guess."

Abruptly, Gil reached up to untie the leather cord. "I'm not wearing mine," he said.

"Don't take it off!" Danni said.

"Why not? It's just superstition. Rachel said so."

Rachel shrugged. "I can live with it. Aidan has been good to us."

"Maybe to you," Gil said grumpily. "You get hawks and wild geese and stags. I get a house cat."

Danni giggled. But Ismail said, "Sometimes small gift is best."

Gil's hand tightened on the cord. Then he shrugged and released it. "Fine," he said wearily. Then he grinned. "Hey, it'll be cool. Picture it: A hundred knights and Northmen surround us. My sword is dashed from my hand. But I whip out my trusty cat's whisker, and the day is won!" He grinned more broadly, and felt his spirits lift with his own rueful laughter.

They crossed the wood of white trees and passed the standing stones and then went inland, up the little valley of the bright stream until they reached its beginning in a rocky hollow.

Beyond, the ground rose higher and they stumbled, thigh-deep, through the thick wiry bushes. The sun, which had vanished in a sleety squall, came out again, and the whole land lit up, bright green and soft lavender. Rachel pulled clumps of the tiny purple flowers and wove them into her braid. "My mum loved this," she said quietly. "The heather blooming. My dad kept promising her, all winter, he'd take her back when the heather bloomed."

"Did he?" Danni asked in a small voice.

Rachel's chin trembled. "He said a lot of dumb stuff." She quickened her pace and left them behind. When Danni caught up again, she overtook the English girl in a wide, respectful arc. Gil's legs were burning and he was breathing hard trying to keep up with Danni. Soon Rachel was flagging, too, her cheeks red and her forehead sweaty. Ismail stayed a few feet behind them all, but his bare, brown feet kept an easy pace. From time to time he scanned the skyline, as if keeping guard.

The clouds blew in again and the wind rose sharply. A grey squall line shaded the hills and sea like a mist. Danni covered her head with her blue shawl and hurried on, cresting a final rise. "There!" she called back to them with satisfaction. She pointed ahead from the top of the little hill, as Gil joined her. "Einar's Holm!"

Below, lay a whole new landscape. Cultivated fields ran down to a new white sand bay. Some were dotted with neat, round haystacks. In others, ripening grain rippled, silver and gold. Amidst the fields were animal pens and a cluster of square stone buildings with roofs of thatch or green turf; the smallest, bigger than anything at Cille Aidan. At their center stood an impressive longhouse with painted, decorated roof beams, each ending in a carved dragon's head. Smoke rose through a hole in its turf roof, drifting over the farmyard.

On the curve of white beach, the longship *Silver Dragon* rested in the sand, shorn of its mast and with black cloth shrouding its deck. Two men worked beneath the dragon figurehead. The scrape of metal on wood rose to Gil's ears. Black long-horned cattle grazed the green fields. In a pen beside the longhouse, sheep, like Aidan's, milled, bleating. The cattle lowed. Chickens and ducks clucked and quacked. Men working in the farmyard shouted in the alien tongue of the Northmen. Somewhere, a dog barked.

"It's a real place," Gil murmured.

"Of course it's a real place. What did you expect?"

He smiled wryly and thought for a long while. "I thought we'd fall off the edge of the world." He looked down again at the Northman's longhouse, and said quietly, "Maybe we have."

Suddenly, a mighty roar of greeting broke from the hillside. The earth shook with thunderous hoof beats. Over the horizon came Magnus, riding a shaggy brown pony and leading three more behind. Cream, tan, and buff, they had dark crosses of black hairs on their shoulders and backs, thick, bristly manes, and tails that brushed the ground.

Magnus pulled hard on his pony's reins and it sat back on its haunches and skidded to a halt, its eyes white-rimmed and wild. The three others stumbled and wheeled, bumping into each other, rearing and biting and shaking their shaggy manes. Clutching his reins in one hand, he held out his arm to Danni and she flung herself into its mighty curve. He swung her up behind him on the brown pony's bare back, and they proceeded down the hill, with Danni riding, proud as a queen, and Gil and Ismail following warily in the animals' muddy hoof prints.

But Rachel ran quickly to catch up with the ponies and by the time they reached the longhouse she had detached one, the prettiest, a pale cream color with black mane and tail, and was leading it as confidently as if it were her own.

The longhouse was even grander close up; far broader and taller than the one at Cille Aidan; the eaves, with their dragon finials, painted green, black, red, and blue. It even had windows, their shutters thrown open to the sun and wind. Magnus herded his ponies toward a stonewalled enclosure beside the building. Rachel untied hers and released it to run, leaping and kicking, free to its companions. Danni led Magnus' pony into the enclosure, too. They came back to Gil with that aloof look girls always got around horses.

In the sheep pen, three young men got quickly to their feet and stood clutching their metal shears and staring as the girls passed. Startled, Gil recognized them from the longship crew at Cille Aidan. Nudging each other and grinning, they returned to their work, wrestling the baa-ing animals for their hot, greasy fleeces.

Then, the longhouse door swung open, and standing just within it, the sunlight dappling her strange grey hair, was Shony. She was dressed as Gil had seen her last, a braid-trimmed blue sleeveless tunic over her plain dress. But around her waist, now, was buckled a heavy-hilted sword in a richly ornamented scabbard, and over one arm she held a small, round leather shield, studded with dark metal.

The smooth, brown skin of her face and bare arms was adorned everywhere with bold patterns, circles and spirals drawn in vivid blue. Two blue snakes with winding, intertwined tails rose from her cheeks to her forehead, meeting above her dark brows. Beneath them, the eyes Gil had seen in the face of a sea beast looked him up and down. Then, like lightening, she drew the sword, the polished blade flashing sunlight. "To arms!" she whispered, in her sea-soft voice. "Warriors of Cille Aidan! To arms!"

CHAPTER NINE

"Shony's going to teach us?" Gil whispered. Danni nodded. "But she's a woman!" he blurted stupidly.

Magnus' big hand clamped onto his shoulder. "Warriors have crossed winter seas for this honor," he growled. He spun Gil around and clasped the hilt of his sword. "I show you how well she teaches."

Shony stepped quickly between them. "Leave him, Redbeard," she said. "He is young. He does not know our ways."

Magnus released Gil with a shove. "Then he should be silent and learn them." Shony sheathed her sword and smiled at Gil. Her smile, sudden and bright through her strands of grey hair, was like sun breaking through cloud.

"Come, Redbeard, show them Floki's gift."

Danni's eyes lit. "Did Floki bring us swords? He promised…."

Shony put her fingers to Danni's lips. "Warriors do not chatter." But she smiled again, and beckoned them toward the open longhouse door. Steeling himself against an image of sea-wet fins, Gil slipped by her and stepped beneath the lintel of Magnus Redbeard's Hall.

Within, one cavernous room stretched from gable wall to gable wall, and rose to high, blackened beams beneath a shadowy roof. There was an open upper loft room at one end, reached by a ladder formed from a driftwood tree trunk, its hewn-off branches serving as steps. Beneath the gallery there was a loom, like Aidan's, and kists and cupboards built into the wall, holding pottery and stoneware.

In the center of the longhouse a fire burned in a long pit beneath the smoke-hole in the roof. An immense, shaggy grey dog slept by the hearth, and over the fire the carcass of a whole animal was impaled on the crossbar of a wooden frame. The smell of roasting meat filled the hall.

Beyond, the room was empty but for a great table stretching the width of the end wall, with crude benches along its length. At each end stood a magnificent chair, padded in leather and carved with lions' heads. Pairs of many-tined deer antlers adorned the walls, and aligned amongst them, shields like the one Shony held, and swords and scabbards, and long lances, and huge, unstrung bows.

Magnus stood by the hearth, holding four sets of swords and scabbards in his arms. A stack of small round shields rested at his feet. He laid the swords down on the floor between Shony and the children, splayed out, points together and hilts spread, like a fan.

The hilts of each bore a flowing, entwined design of an animal; one, a stooping hawk, another, an antlered stag, the third, a flying bird, and the last, a pouncing cat. The leather-bound wood of the scabbards was adorned with silver on which the same animals were portrayed.

Shony went to the white tree-ladder, climbed, fleet as a girl, to the loft room above, and came down again, carrying a small, dark wooden box fastened with a silver latch. She brought the box to the fireside and beckoned Gil, Rachel, Ismail, and Danni. "Let Odin choose your weapons."

She raised the little box high over the fire, shook it back and forth, and began to sing; her voice as soft as a distant surf. Abruptly, she lowered the box, and raised the lid revealing four smooth oblong green stones, marked with rows of carved lines, some long, some broken, some branched like little trees.

She took the green stones from their box, laid them in a row on the beaten earth hearth, then lifted them in her two hands, crooning a verse in a language as baffling to Gil as Aidan's church Latin. With a shout, she cast the stones clattering onto the hearth and leaned forward studying them with deep concentration. Then, looking up, she smiled and beckoned Rachel.

The English girl looked from side to side at her companions

before getting to her feet. Shony stood, also, lifting one sword from the group fanned out on the earth. Solemnly, she extended it to Rachel. "Courage and love protect the nest—for you, Odin chooses the Hawk."

Gil felt a twinge of disappointment. Of the four designs, the Hawk had seemed the most noble, and he had secretly coveted it. But he could not deny that the Hawk suited Rachel, who had fought flames with her bare hands. Rachel took the sword and wonderingly traced the outstretched wings of the stooping bird of prey on the embossed hilt.

Shony knelt again by the hearth, chanted, once more, her song to Odin, and flung the stones. This time they scattered far apart. She stood and went from stone to stone, crouching to read them better. Then she took up the sword with the Stag, and presented it to Ismail. "Fleet as the stag, gentle as the hind; Odin sees a true warrior."

Shony looked from Gil to Danni and crooned her song and cast the runes a third time. They scattered in an arc before the fire. Shony crouched over them in silence. Her gaze ran over both their faces, but settled on Danni's. She said, very quietly, "Born for the sky, earth will not hold her. The Grey Goose for Danni." Danni looked almost fearful as she accepted the sword, as if she was hearing, as Gil was, an echo of Aidan's prophecy.

The remaining sword, with its playful, childish motif, was Gil's by default, but Shony still cast her runes as seriously as before and took as long to read them. When she looked up, she laughed softly. "Even the smallest cat has a tiger's heart," she said, awarding Gil the Pouncing Cat.

She bent then, and lifted one of the round shields, displaying its decorative face. Bold on a white ground, a mighty stag leapt around the central boss, its antlered head and supple body painted in red, green and yellow.

Slipping her hand through the leather straps, she slung the shield over her arm and mocked defense. "Lime wood!" She said proudly, "As light as it is strong. Here!" She tossed the shield to Ismail.

Ismail caught it and tried its weight on his own arm, then turned it to admire his Stag. Shony presented shields to Rachel and Danni; the design of each matching that of their swords. On Gil's, the Pouncing Cat chased his green and yellow tail around the polished boss. Gil stroked the length of the curling tail, with rueful affection, and touched the green painted eye.

Shony scooped up her rune stones, replaced them in the wooden box, and climbed the tree-ladder to return them to their hiding place. Ismail quietly drew his sword and shifted it from hand to hand, judging its weight and balance. Gil copied him, trying to remember what the African boy had taught him. Suddenly a brawny arm snaked around his throat, jerking back against his windpipe. Gil's hands flew up to fend it off, and his sword clattered on the ground.

"Ready for battle, little bride?" Magnus laughed. Gil gasped for breath until the Northman, still chuckling to himself, let him go.

"Pick up your sword, Gil," Shony said. "A warrior never releases his sword." Gil lifted the weapon and slid it clumsily into its scabbard, his eyes stinging from the choking, and from humiliation. But Shony laid her hand on his shoulder and he felt a cool calm flow from it.

Then she released him, spun around, and drew her sword. Firelight flashed from the blade as she set the tip beneath Magnus' bearded chin. "Affright my bairns once more," she whispered, "and I'll have your head." Then she lowered the sword and turned her back with a disdainful toss of her hair.

"Come," she said, and though Magnus glowered angrily, he followed her and the children outside. Shony lined them up along the wall of the longhouse. Danni pushed to the front, but it was Gil Shony called. Warily, he left the shadow of the eaves and stepped into the open farmyard.

"Here, beside me," Shony directed. She flung her small shield over her back and placed Gil on her left side, clasping him around the waist. "Now," she said, "You are my shadow. My shadow never leaves me." She side-stepped quickly, and stumbling slightly, Gil stepped in tandem.

"Good," she smiled, "Again." She leapt the other way. Gil followed. "Now, around with the sun." She spun, guiding him like a dancer. Quickly, he spun, too. "Against the sun." She spun the other way. Gil followed, giggling as he tripped dizzily and found his footing.

"Yes, it is fun. But it is fun that saves your life." She pointed at the open hill. "Calm eyes look far." Gil fixed his gaze on the horizon and the dizziness faded. He glimpsed the others watching and smiled.

Then Shony turned him again until they were facing Magnus. "Now," she said to Gil, "We fight Redbeard."

Gil flinched away, but she tightened her grip around his waist. "My shadow never leaves me," she said, as Magnus Redbeard drew his sword. Then, turning so Gil was slightly behind her, she drew her own blade. Magnus leapt forward, slicing down with the fearsome weapon. But Shony danced to the left, taking Gil with her, and the tip of her own sword turned Magnus's aside.

With a grunt, Magnus charged again. Shony slid once more to the side and this time ducked almost to her knees, pulling Gil down and up again at her side. He felt her arm lifting him almost off his feet and marveled that anything so slight could be so strong.

Magnus laughed and swung again and Shony spun in a circle, catching his blade above the hilt and forcing him back. Gil gasped, breathless and dizzy, but staggered to keep with her again. Magnus stepped back, catching his own breath.

"He is big," Shony said softly. "But a warrior need not be big, if he is swift. Go now," she released him, moving him aside with an urgent shove. "Stay clear."

Gil stumbled back to the others and turned to watch. Shony stood very still, her eyes locked with her husband's. Magnus smiled slightly. He charged forward, swinging his mighty sword. Laughing, Shony danced aside, then ran a few steps and leapt up onto the wall of the pony pen, playfully swiping at Magnus from above. He clambered up and chased her down the wall, both of them laughing and he balancing as delicately as she.

She jumped down onto the stone cattle trough set into the little stream that crossed the farmyard. Magnus followed, battling her over the water. Shony feigned a charge and as he rushed to meet it, leapt lightly aside while Magnus's momentum carried him forward, headfirst, into the brimming trough.

Danni shouted with laughter and as the big Northman wallowed upright and staggered, dripping, to his feet, Gil fought a treacherous twitch at the corners of his mouth. He saw Shony regarding him solemnly. "Do not smile," she said. "He is a mighty warrior. My best student, but one. Respect any man in his defeat."

By day's end, Gil had matched swords with Ismail, with Danni, with Rachel, and with Magnus himself, all under Shony's watchful eye. His ears were ringing with the clashing of steel, his arms aching and his thighs burning from the weight of sword and shield. The knees of his jeans were sodden from retrieving his weapon from the mud.

Released at last, Rachel and Danni retreated to the longhouse, rubbing blistered hands. Gil battled on with Ismail, sweating and stumbling, until a thunder of approaching hoof beats brought both of them to a halt. He looked up and saw two riders descending the hill at a wild gallop. In the lead, on a sturdy tan pony, was Magnus' son, Floki, yellow hair flying in the wind. Behind, hunched over the neck of his enormous black horse, rode the Saracen knight, Palamedes.

Raucous cheering broke out among the sheep-shearers watching the racing riders. On the flat fields surrounding the longhouse, the knight's black charger gained ground. But Floki suddenly reined his pony aside. Short-cutting between two low barns, he charged straight at the stone-walled pony pen, leapt the outer wall, scattering the grazing beasts in a neighing frenzy, and to gasps of alarm from his audience, cleared the nearer wall by inches.

He pulled his mount to a panting halt in front of the longhouse, and raised a triumphant fist, as, huge hooves shaking the ground, the black charger galloped around the side of the farther barn. His rider, with a great bow slung over his shoulder, and the carcass of a small deer tied in front of his saddle, lifted innocent hands in dismay. "Alas! You play false!"

"Of course!" Floki swung down from his pony. He, too, carried a bow, and a string of bloodied rabbits dangled around his neck. "And I win!"

Palamedes lifted his deer carcass to the ground. Then, as the sheep shearers returned to their work, and Gil and Ismail, to their lesson, the two men rubbed their mounts down with fistfuls of hay and watered them at the trough. Oblivious of the sword fight in their midst, they led the beasts to the stone-walled enclosure.

Freed, the charger cantered in a joyful circle, kicking up its huge, feathered heels, while the tan pony trotted, whickering, to its mates. Palamedes heaved the deer carcass onto his shoulder and strode off behind the longhouse.

Floki leaned his bow against the wall; then unbuckled his sword belt and hung it over a post of the sheep pen. Vaulting the fence, he landed among the bleating animals, took up shears, and flipped one woolly beast onto its back. Sitting cross-legged on the ground, he set to work clipping its fleece.

Gil lowered his sword and stared, fascinated by the transformation from lordly huntsman to dust-smeared shepherd. Shony tapped his face lightly and pointed at Ismail. "Here is the man you battle. Not there."

"Sorry." Gil turned again, and, shoulders aching, lifted the heavy weapon. Ismail grinned cheerfully. Skinny and slight, he had stamina Gil could only dream of, and balance and grace to match. Again and again, his sword swing made its perfect arc and Gil's blade lay in the dust. At last, when Gil had barely strength to close his fingers on the hilt, Shony called a halt. Sagging against the wall of the longhouse, Gil accepted Ismail's warm-hearted high-five, and turned to follow him inside.

But Floki rose suddenly from his place in the sheep pen. He laid down his shears and set the sheep on its feet. Shorn of its heavy fleece, it frisked away as the Northman vaulted the fence again and slipped his sword belt from the post.

He stepped to an open space in the farmyard, and without speaking, beckoned Gil. Gil tapped his chest uneasily. "Me?" he croaked. Floki nodded gravely, though a small smile briefly softened his lean features. Then he drew his sword and the smile vanished. Graciously, he held out his free hand; an invitation to combat.

Stomach lurching, Gil looked wildly around as if someone

else might appear to take his place. But the farmyard was empty. Even the sheep shearers were gone, and an early evening chill had drawn in from the sea. Gil drew the Pouncing Cat sword and stepped cautiously forward.

Floki did not move. His eyes were remote and peaceful, his blade lightly held, the point nearly on the ground. Gil stepped closer, again without response. He raised his shield, hunched behind it, and then, baffled by the other's stillness, jumped forward and swung with all his strength.

Steel met steel with a clash that came from nowhere. The sword spun from his bruised hand. Still unmoving, Floki smiled again, and nodded to the fallen weapon. With sinking heart, Gil retrieved it and approached his adversary again. Again, Floki stood utterly still and seemingly undefended, and again Gil's blade met solid steel. This time, he held his grip, though the shock buzzed the length of his arm. Floki beckoned him forward.

Exhaustion and frustration warred in Gil's spinning head. Five times he advanced. Five times Floki remained, still and silent as a statue, but for the deadly lightening of his sword arm. At last, Gil lowered his blade tip to the ground and shook his head in surrender. When he looked up, the Northman was watching him with a wry smile. He, too, shook his head. He raised his shining blade for the first time, and stepped forward.

Feebly, Gil parried, stepping quickly back. Again, Floki advanced. Again, Gil parried, retreating. Again, steel struck steel and Gil stumbled. Floki strode forward and Gil scuttled back, staggering, and swinging wildly in defense. Then suddenly his calves hit the edge of the water trough. Trapped, he turned to run, tripped, and felt himself falling. He hit the ground with a solid thud, the sword flying from his grasp.

Suddenly, everything was still. Even the sheep were silent. The sea wind, softened to a breeze, flicked the ends of Floki's hair as he raised the long blade and aligned the tip with the base of Gil's throat. Gil looked up the length of the shining steel into the Northman's grey eyes. They were without expression, the eyes of a man performing a small, insignificant task. For the first time in his fourteen years, Gil knew that life could end, suddenly and pointlessly, at another's will.

The Northman smiled. He swung the sword aside and sheathed it. Leaning forward, he reached out his hand. Gil lay frozen on the ground. Floki smiled again and beckoned. Numbly, Gil took the offered hand and the Northman pulled him up onto his feet. "Good," he said. "You will be good." His smile was suddenly warm and he laid an arm lightly on Gil's shoulders and extended his other to the longhouse. "Come," he said. "Feast with me in my father's house." He turned and walked calmly away. Gil collected his fallen weapon and staggered after him, torn crazily between cold terror and bewildered pride.

The great hall of the longhouse was already packed with men and more tramped in behind Gil; coming down from the fields and up from the shore. Again, he saw faces familiar from the crew of *Silver Dragon*, bold seamen transformed, now, like Floki, into shepherds or carpenters, cowherds or fishermen.

Divesting themselves of their cloaks and weapons they crammed the benches. Those left over squatted beside the walls where their swords and shields hung high above their heads. Others crowded around the fire, pulling bits of roasted meat from the spit with their hands and stuffing them into greasy, bearded mouths.

Shony, Rachel, and Danni wove in and out of the crowd, bringing platters of food to the table, and whole, carved cattle horns, filled with Magnus' ale. The Northmen fell on the ale horns with shouts of glee, throwing back their heads and swallowing the contents, in one. Soon scuffling and brawling broke out, but it was tempered by laughter and seemed more about winning the attention of the girls, than intending each other any harm.

Immediately embraced by a young and drunken crewman, Gil grinned awkwardly and patted the Northman's swaying back. An ale horn was thrust at his own lips and tipped. Coughing and spluttering, he swallowed and gasped for air. "Thanks," he grinned weakly, shoving the horn away.

Platters of food passed by, their contents vanishing in a blur of hairy hands. Gil grabbed futilely at a passing sausage, lost out again on a rapidly diminishing cheese. Then Rachel appeared carrying a whole smoked ham and he waved and pointed at himself and Ismail. She swept by and presented her prize to a big smiling Northman with bright blue eyes and a huge, bushy beard. "What's that walking bird's nest got that we haven't?" Gil muttered to Ismail, gnawing a husk of barley bread.

When the platters had been replenished three times and the last was finally empty, Floki stood up. Accepting a full jug from his mother, he walked around the room and refilled the drinking horns. Then he filled his own and raised it high. "Now, let Einar's Holm see our spoil! Bring us the treasure of the Golden Knight!"

Two of Floki's crewmen got up and strode to the door, returning carrying a huge, metal bound, wooden trunk. They set it on the floor before the fire and with a flourish, Floki sprang the latch and raised the heavy lid. Shony's eyes widened at the glittering splendor within. The girls crowded around, their faces mirroring hers.

Gold and silver plates and goblets, candlesticks and covered dishes, rich velvets and satins, furs and jewels, ivory and ebony; the looted treasures were reverently lifted from the trunk, held up, and passed back and forth. When Danni swept close to Gil, trailing an ermine trimmed cloak, he caught her arm, closing his fingers on her flesh till she winced. "They're pirates!" he whispered. "Thieves! How can you be part of this?"

She jerked her arm free and surveyed him coolly. "These things were meant for the Golden Knight! He's plundered all of Alba! Floki's a hero!" she declared, loud enough for all to hear.

Floki smiled down on her. "The next time the Knight demands a dowry, he will see it is sent on a sturdier ship."

"The lady's dowry?" Shony's eyes widened further.

"Wait," said Floki, "I have saved the best for last." Reaching into his rough shirt, he drew out a small roll of deep red velvet. Holding it in one hand, he swung himself up onto the great table, and settling cross-legged there, he unrolled the velvet package on his knee.

Cushioned on the blood red velvet, lay a magnificent necklace of gold, jewels, and beads, joined with a rich golden clasp and ending in a beautiful cross set with a honey-colored stone. A gasp of admiration went around the great hall. Floki lifted the necklace, draping it across his tough, scarred hands. "Amber from the Baltic, gold from the hills of Wales. Golden treasure for the Golden Knight's bride. Only," he smiled, "Now it will grace the throat of mine."

He looked boldly around the room and let his eyes fall, teasingly, on Rachel, and then on Danni. Danni lowered her lashes and tossed her hair as if she couldn't be bothered with him or his prize. But Rachel just stared at the necklace in Floki's hand. Her face was white, her lips trembling, and her eyes wide with horror. When Floki handed it proudly to his mother, Rachel turned away with a visible shudder.

"Is it really Lady Janetta's?" Shony breathed, stroking the amber cross.

"She was to wear it on her wedding day," said Floki.

Then Shony laughed. "He will have to find her, before he can wed her!" She raised the necklace, fingering each golden bead with awe. "And the Good Sisters have hidden her safely away."

"True," Floki said, "But she left their care to ride her pretty palfrey into the forest. And into the hands of his fiercest knights. For a mouthful of raspberries, she will be a bride."

Gil froze. For an instant he was back within the darkness of the Tomb, peering through the white stone. The image of the girl with her sparkling eyes and berry-stained fingers leapt unbidden to his mind. He saw the rough hand tear away her modest veil.... "What does she look like?" he cried.

Floki shrugged. "I have not seen her, but they say she is fair."

"Oh, fairest of the fair!" Shony cried. She smiled and closed her eyes as she recited, "*Eyes like the dawn-lit sea, Hair like the raven's wing.*"

Floki shrugged again. "Any lady can be fair if her father hires the right bard." He stood up on the table, then jumped down to the floor. Still holding the necklace, he sauntered through his cheering crew until he was standing beside Danni. "I like eyes dark," he said with a smile, "And brown as a hazel-nut."

"I've seen her," said Gil. Floki half-turned, staring at him, eyebrows arching. "Green eyes and black hair. Fairest of the fair.

I've seen her," Gil whispered. "I've seen her through the stone."

"You?" Floki's brows arched higher. "Why would you see her?"

"Because I'm meant to save her," Gil said. He was more certain of it than anything in his life.

"Well, Heaven help her, then," said Floki, with a gentle laugh.

But Gil turned away, his mind racing. His girl, his green-eyed girl. Now he knew her name: *Janetta. Lady Janetta*. But in the hands of the despised Golden Knight! He remembered the dark place where she crept with her candle to Percy.

Suddenly, he was fiercely impatient with the merriment around him. Floki, and his proud preening; his crew and their ale. All he wanted was his sword and the skill to use it. He looked toward Danni. But Floki was again teasing her with the necklace, lifting up her silky hair so he might drape the golden links around her throat. She giggled again and pushed him away.

Pretending grief at her rejection, he turned to Rachel with his prize. His arm was around her neck, the jewels at her throat, before he saw the stricken terror on her face. He froze, and in that instant, she pulled free of him, covering her bare throat with her hand, as if it had been burned. Looking wildly around, she caught sight of a stack of greasy platters, snatched them up, and fled the hall.

Floki still stood there, his necklace held out yet in his hand. He shook his head slowly. "Am I that fearsome?" he whispered. He turned, then, abruptly, and called for music and more ale and stories. A harp was brought forth and Gil imagined every house had one, like houses at home had...he stopped, his thoughts tangled...music thing, music thing...he sighed and surrendered and even took a swig from his eager friend's ale horn. The future was falling away from him, like leaves from winter trees. He had no power to hold it anymore.

Shony took the harp and sat by the fire and played a beautiful soft melody. Then Magnus rose to his feet, facing Palamedes, and addressed the knight. "A tale to brighten our hearth, honored guest."

"Tell of the Questing Beast," Shony cried at once and Floki raised his ale horn and said good-naturedly, "Even a phantom makes a good tale."

Palamedes stood, bowed to Magnus and Shony and cast Floki a warning look. Then he gazed all around the room, his dark eyes searching the shadows as if indeed the great beast he sought might lurk among them. "Alas," he began, "but for an evil meeting a bare fortnight past, I would recount this very day a tale of triumph. The Beast would be mine! My long quest ended!"

An expectant murmur swept the room. The Saracen leaned back, fingertips pressed together as in prayer, "It was upon the feast day of Saint James, and I was well upon my way, many days into my journey to the great *muinntir* of Hy, where I would meet with my noble escort." At this he bowed graciously to Floki, extending both arms to embrace all his crew who pounded the table with fists and ale horns.

"Alone, I travelled," Palamedes continued. "But for my great warhorse, Doombearer, deep within the wild dark forest of Caledon. It was a day of great beauty, but suddenly a mighty storm arose and I sought shelter beside a mountain torrent, a mighty linn thundering down to a haunted pool.

"I had not been there but for the blink of an eye when suddenly I heard it." Palamedes cupped his ear, as if listening. The Northmen all sat open-mouthed, eyes upon the great knight. "First faint and far away and then nearer and nearer and nearer." He covered both ears, grimacing in remembrance. "Until it was right above me, drowning the mighty waterfall itself with its cry, as if an entire pack of hounds were lodged in its very stomach! And so, at last," declared Palamedes, "I knew my hour had come. That creature that had eluded my father all his days and his father before him, the Questing Beast was within my hands."

He fell silent. The room was silent, too, every eye on the Saracen, drinking horns forgotten. "And then he came. That master of evil, curse of that once-happy land, and enemy of all good-hearted men." Palamedes paused and then whispered, "The Golden Knight. Glittering like a king's ransom of treasure, as indeed his golden armor might well be; treasure trove of ransacked Camelot."

"You fought the Golden Knight?" Floki cried. Until that moment he had lounged, unimpressed, beside one of the great roof pillars of the longhouse. But now his cold, alert eyes were fixed on the Saracen's face. "This I doubt."

Palamedes drew himself up tall and his brows lowered. "You question my word?" he said, both pained and angry.

Floki rolled his eyes heavenward. "No, no, no," he said. "Of course I do not question your word. I never question your word or your honor, both of which shine like the morning star," he said with another heavenward glance. "I am only surprised, and with no disrespect to your prowess, that you fought the Golden Knight and lived to tell the tale. And without even a scar to show for it?" Floki added smiling.

"Ah, said Palamedes, "There is more to the story."

Floki raised one cynical eyebrow, and Palamedes continued. "At first, when I saw him, I thought little of him, because he came there in disguise. A dark cloak covered his shining armor and his snow-white warhorse was draped in dingy trappings. I thought I had come upon yet one more of those roving, ill-fed knights who infest that unhappy land. 'Begone!' he ordered me.

"'Begone yourself,' said I. 'Leave me in peace to pursue my quarry.'

"'Any road but this,' says he and with that, he lowers his fewtered lance.

"'Bold fool,' says I, and do the same. But as he charges towards me, the wind, howling almost as loud as the Beast above us, lifts his cloak and rips the tawdry coverings from his charger, and I face him in all his splendor. And in that moment, I prepare, *Inshallah*, to die." He bowed dramatically. The Great Hall fell silent but for the crackling and hissing of the driftwood fire.

"Tell! Tell!" Magnus roared. "You did not die! Tell how you lived!"

Palamedes pressed his hands together, again, as in prayer. "By the grace of God," he said, "And the shelter of a tree."

But Floki shouted, "What tree can hide you?" He swigged ale and leaned back, laughing loudly.

"His lance struck my shield with the force of two lions pouncing! My own splintered against his unearthly armor. His mount clashed shoulders with mine and Doombearer shuddered beneath me, plunging to his knees. Even as I, in all my armor, was flung backwards to the ground!

"Instantly, I leapt to my feet and drew my sword! But already he was dismounted, and his blade, cast of some metal of the devil's working, sliced mine in two. And so, I was disarmed. Behind me was the thundering pool, above the howling Beast, before me, the fearsome adversary.

"Turning in one last desperate search for refuge, I saw, gleaming above the black waters of the pool, drenched in the foaming spray of the linn, a solitary branch." He breathed deeply. "A lace of green leaves and berries, red as blood. The rowan. The holy tree. For every evil on this earth, Allah places an equal good." Palamedes looked once around the room at his waiting audience, then reached up and out into empty air, grasping the remembered branch. "And it was mine! Clutched in my hand, I held it high, between me and the advancing foe. Halted in his tracks, the evil one stood, motionless. Beneath his shadowing helm, I saw the glint of eyes, blue as the ocean, magnificent and cruel.

"Above me the questing of the great Beast fell still, the roar of the waterfall faded, the dark clouds parted. And I saw it! Rising as clear as the smoke from that fire!" he pointed to the longhouse hearth. "Shining and splendid in the purest of colors, arching into the sky...."

"The Rainbow Bridge?" Floki laughed and waved a dismissive hand. "It is a myth. A tale I heard at my grandmother's hearth. And this tale is a myth, too. And a fine one!" he raised his ale horn in appreciation.

"No myth!" Palamedes declared, his face darkening. "Merlin himself crossed upon it, before the enchantress won him away, and Merlin himself fashioned its key."

Floki laughed again. "Merlin is a fool for a lass a third his age. There is no need of enchantresses where old men's hearts are concerned." He winked at the gathered Northmen and they punched each other and laughed.

Palamedes gave Floki a black look, but continued, "And more! I saw the knight fling himself upon his charger, leap out above me, mount the knife-edge arc, and ride the rainbow into the sky. Into the sky and beyond," he whispered solemnly.

"In an instant, my foe vanished from my sight. And then," his voice dropped wonderingly. "It was as if I fell into the deepest sleep a man can sleep, this side of death. And when I awoke, all around me was calm. The storm itself had vanished. The waterfall sparkled in the sun and the haunted pool shone smooth as silk and innocent as the day."

At once, the hall erupted with shouts of amazement and Gil could barely hear his own voice when he spoke, "Beyond? Where beyond?"

Palamedes turned, his burning gaze falling on Gil's face. "Where else?" he said, "But to Tir nan Og, beyond the Western Sea?"

"It's a Crossing!" Gil cried. "Like the Underwater Bridge!"

"Ah, no!" Palamedes answered. He crouched down beside Gil. "It is more; much more," he said. "The Sun and Stars themselves guard the Underwater Bridge. None of Fallen Man may cross without their willing. But the Rainbow Bridge lies open to any who hold Merlin's key. Even the Evil One may travel at will." He sighed. "Nor can the guardians of Arthur close it. Though he sleeps in Tir nan Og, he is not safe."

"He is safe," said Floki. He smiled wryly. "Arthur sleeps where all dead men sleep. He is worm food in the ground. No Golden Knight will joust with him there." He bowed then to Palamedes and his voice softened and became respectful. "Still, a fine tale, finely told, and I am humbled to follow such a bard."

He smiled innocently but Palamedes looked more angry than flattered as Floki stepped forward to take his turn. Shony took up her harp again and played softly as her son stood, firelight flickering on his yellow hair, and told his tale.

Though other men might hire bards to praise their daughters, it was clear Floki would have no such need. He told his story of longships and treasure so vividly that swords and shields and battling Vikings rose before Gil's eyes like the smoke of the fire. The words wove repeated patterns, like the refrain of a song, and he found himself swaying along with Floki's crewmen with each repeated phrase.

But the ale horn filled the fastest was Floki's own, and he, too, swayed, slurring his graceful words. Magnus watched, his broad face wistful. "Ripe barley and fat cattle are fine things," he said, raising his ale horn, "But they bring no battle light to the eyes."

Floki grinned and slapped him on the back. "Come with me! I sail to Dublin this Feast of Holy Rood. Come!"

"Aye," said Magnus, "when harvest is done, Odin be pleased."

Floki shrugged, wiping ale from his beard. "When Magnus Redbeard ploughs sea-furrows, then Odin will be pleased." He turned and snatched a sword from the wall and staggered drunkenly to the tree-ladder beneath the loft.

Sword in hand, he leapt high up its branches and swung around, hanging dizzily above their heads. "Odin climbs the World-Tree of Magnus Redbeard!" Roars of laughter filled the hall and then there was a great crash and a huge hiss of steam rose from the fire. The laughter died. As the steam cleared, Gil saw Shony, standing above the broken ale-jug she had flung on the flames.

"Enough!" she said fiercely. "Do not bring the curse of Odin on this house!"

Floki lowered his sword arm, but still hung, swaying from the tree. "I did not know you cared so for Odin's curses, my Christian mother," he said. "So, would you prefer Yesu's Tree?" He dropped the sword, and flung out his arms in mockery of a crucifix.

Shony made a gesture as of thrusting the vision away, and, signing the cross over her forehead and breast, closed her eyes. Magnus staggered again to his feet. "Get down from there," he said quietly. "Respect your mother, if not her god."

Floki shrugged. "But which god?" he said defiantly. He lowered his arms and climbed down from the tree. Then, turning towards Shony, he said, "You fear every god, and I, none. Are we really so different?" He smiled, but the laughter had gone out of him, and out of all the Great Hall. The mood grew as heavy as the stench of ale.

And then, a high, thin scream cut through the sullen air. A dozen heads came up. The scream came again, muffled and distant, from without the great stone walls.

"Where's Rachel?" Ismail said. Gil shook his head.

"Where's Bird's Nest?" he said urgently. Ismail looked around, then back at Gil. They both jumped up, as one, and dashed for the doorway. Behind them, the drunken Northmen belatedly began to stir. Gil grabbed his sword and jerked the door open with his other hand. With Ismail a step behind, he burst out into the evening sun.

A flurry of movement beside the water trough caught his eye. He turned and saw Bird's Nest, ale-sodden and staggering, with Rachel clamped to his huge chest as he strove to align his eager mouth with hers. Rachel bent her slim body backwards like a sapling, her face turned away and screwed up in tearful disgust.

Gil unsheathed his sword, threw the scabbard on the ground and charged. Ismail, sword in hand, was right at his side. Bird's Nest released Rachel, and stepped back with horrified eyes. Unarmed, he reached yet instinctively for his sword, then raised his empty hands, palms outward.

"I pay!" he cried. "Good bride-fee! Gold!" Gil slowly lowered his sword, astounded that the Northman watched his every move as if he was a real warrior. "Much gold!" Bird's Nest's eyes crinkled hopefully, his hands cupped. Gil struggled not to laugh.

Bird's Nest looked up then, over Gil's head, with renewed terror, and Gil turned to see Floki, very sober, bearing down on them all. His eyes fell on Gil, standing yet with his sword and he halted, then nodded. "So, the pup bares his teeth," he said, with a little smile.

Then Shony swept between himself and Floki, brushing them both aside. Her sword was in her hand and her strange eyes alight with a fearsome fire. "You will lay no hands on my bairns!" she hissed, and without pause, raised her sword and brought it flashing across the Northman's throat.

Gil cried aloud and closed his eyes in horror, then forced them open, braced to see streaming blood. But there was no blood, and indeed, the Northman's head sat yet on his shoulders. His eyes were wide, his features frozen in shock, and his chin bare, but for the forlorn remnant of his mighty beard. The rest lay at his feet, like a small, hairy animal, newly dead. He raised a shaking hand and felt the bristly remains.

Shony stepped close, and with the razor edge of her sword, shaved him clean. She stroked his cheek with her slender hand, and announced to his watching crewmates, "Fairest of the Fair! A bride for the Golden Knight!"

Roars of laughter greeted that, but Bird's Nest, happy to have his life, only smiled sheepishly when Floki cried, "No woman for Erling 'til he grows a man's beard!" He scooped up the fallen hair. "Away to your spindle, Fairest of the Fair!"

Shony laid a hand on Gil's shoulder and another on Ismail's. "Do not run before you can walk. I may not be there next time." She looked up at the sky and watched something there, and then, as Danni and Rachel joined them, she turned back to Gil. "Put your swords to their places, it is time you return."

Gil nodded, and then, as she turned away, looked up to the sky, too. A black speck circled high above. Feannag, calling them home. For the first time, the sight of the strange bird filled him with joy. "Magnus," Shony shouted to her husband, "Bring the ponies."

"Ponies?" Rachel and Danni looked at each other like it was Christmas morning. "Do we get the ponies?" Gil watched with alarmingly mixed feelings as, one by one, bridles were slipped over furry ears by Magnus, and then also, Rachel, who was now ecstatically stroking the shining black mane of her favorite.

Gil gulped. "Can you, like, ride him?" he asked.

Rachel looked pained. "Her," she said. "The answer's 'yes.'"

Danni finished adjusting the tan pony's leather and braided wool bridle and hauled herself aboard its bare back. Ismail was already astride the big brown animal that Magnus had ridden. He looked slim and small up there, but his legs gripped the pony's flanks with easy confidence, and he swayed gently with the creature's every move.

One pony remained. It was slimmer than the others and buff colored with brown legs and a brown mane and tail. The cross on its back was the color of chocolate. It looked at him and its eye rolled, white-rimmed and wild. When he touched its bridle with a wary hand, it jumped a foot in the air.

"Ah," said Magnus. "He's a young beauty. Barely away from his mother. Full of the fire of youth." He grabbed Gil and flung him unceremoniously onto the buff pony's back and gave its haunch a resounding slap.

Gil grabbed the flapping reins with one hand, and a chunk of mane with the other, as the pony leaped free. Snorting and puffing, it took off at once across the flat ground in front of the longhouse to the resounding cheers of Floki and his crew. Gil's legs flew up and his butt lost contact. He slid halfway off one side, bounced back, slid to the other. He lost the reins entirely and for a moment was so far off that his foot touched the ground.

Peals of laughter followed him as the pony whirled around, fleeing in a panic back to its stone pen. But Magnus waved it away and it spun again, kicking and dancing, with Gil, hands clutching fistfuls of mane, clinging miraculously, still, to its back.

Ahead he could see the girls and Ismail already mounting the hill to home. Gritting his teeth, he wrapped his arms around the pony's neck. Somehow, he retrieved the reins, and as the pony climbed the hill and slowed a little from the effort, found his seat. But then the creature's back formed a steeper and steeper slope, and Gil struggled frantically to keep from sliding over its tail.

Beyond, the others were just dots approaching the top of the hill. His pony slowed more, looking back now, over its shoulder, and then forward, shaking its mane. "It's okay," Gil said in a small voice. He leaned closer to the pony's head and it turned again and looked at him out of the side of one wild eye.

He heard fear, somewhere, deep inside himself, a wordless frightened voice. "It's okay," he said again, and felt stupid. It didn't speak words, and if it did, they probably wouldn't be English. He thought suddenly of Percy's donkey, calling for help through the silence of the stone. He must answer. No. He must listen.

Calming himself, he straightened his back and let his legs

hang loose. He closed his eyes. In the darkness, he heard fear and the fear made itself into words.

I'm alone. They've gone ahead without me. But they're leaving my field. What will I do without my field? How will I eat? Where will my tree be, where I rest at night? Gil felt a pain inside himself, grief for another's grief. It was homesick.

"It's okay," he said again, aloud. Then, in the dark inside of himself, he pictured the green fields of Cille Aidan. And Aidan himself, with armfuls of grass. *There will be a field. And a tree!* He pictured the white trees of the little wood. Beneath his hands, he felt the pony calm. Resolutely, it raised its shaggy head and stepped forward, and, seated on its dark-crossed back, Gil rode on, up the hill.

Halfway up, he even managed to turn and look over his shoulder. The fields and buildings of Einar's Holm lay spread out below, smoke still rising from the hole in the longhouse roof. Beyond, the great longship lay beached on the shore. Northmen gathered around it, some aboard already, gathering under the black tent that sheltered its deck.

He recognized Floki from his blond head, where he stood in the shallows of the sea, and, beside him; her long hair glinting like metal in the lowering sun; Shony. The pony stumbled, and he turned quickly to regain his balance. When he turned back, the place in the sea where Floki and Shony had stood was empty. Around it, ripples spread outwards in a widening ring. Gil fixed his gaze firmly on the pony's brown mane.

When he reached the top of the ridge, he found the others sitting on their mounts, with the assurance of people who've done something so often they can't remember when it was ever a challenge. "Good ride?" Rachel said pleasantly.

"Yeah," Gil said, because, for some pretty weird reasons, it was. Even now, he could feel the pony's shy happiness, being back among its friends and its quiet bravery as it faced the empty hill ahead.

He turned back to Rachel. "I've got to know something. What was it about the necklace?" Rachel closed her eyes and shook her head.

"You don't have to say," Danni offered.

Rachel nodded. "It's okay. Now that it's down there and not...." she touched her throat and shuddered. "It was grave goods."

"What?" Gil said.

"In the museum. It was grave goods. I told you."

"That," he whispered. "That necklace?"

"It's the one I saw."

Gil shook his head slowly. "Couldn't you maybe have gotten confused...I mean, one necklace is pretty much like any other necklace."

"You knew your father's knife. And, anyhow, you're not a girl."

"When it's jewelry, girls remember," Danni said.

"But what did it matter?" Gil said, then. "You looked terrified."

"It was grave goods," she repeated. "It came out of a grave."

"That's a thousand years from now," Gil said. "It hasn't been in a grave now; it's just a beautiful necklace."

"Who will be buried in it?" Rachel said. She looked from Gil, to Danni, who looked back with dawning horror, her hand brushing her own brown throat, where Floki had held his prize. But something deeper clutched Gil's heart.

It's hers. It's Lady Janetta's. Will it go back to her? Will it lie at her throat on her wedding day? Will it lie there in her grave? Will it lie there as she turns to bones, and bones, to dust?

And then he realized it didn't matter. Whoever the necklace graced, whoever was wed in it, whoever was buried in it, all of them, all; Shony and Magnus and Floki...and fair Lady Janetta, his green-eyed girl; every person here would be bones and dust when, at last and if ever, he returned to his home.

Then he heard the sweet sound he'd heard in the Tomb, ringing softly over the evening hill. He turned his pony's head and rode on, as fast as the beast would take him, to the sanctuary of Cille Aidan by the sea.

CHAPTER TEN

On the morning of All Saint's Eve, Gil rose before dawn. Only the Noble Cat awaited him in the dark church. Its tail made a question mark around his leg as he slipped into his place on the bench. He lifted it onto his knee and sat in silence, his eyes on the single point of light that burned always by the altar.

The days of damp, dawn rides to Einar's Holm, and battered, bone-weary returns were nearly over. Summer had turned to autumn and autumn was now fading into winter. The days were growing shorter; the evenings dim and the weather cold. Soon, they must leave Cille Aidan.

Gil's hands were tough and calloused and his body, grown stronger and more muscular, seemed at times one big aching bruise. Falls from horseback were routine, misplaced sword swings, a daily hazard. His shield arm seemed cramped into a permanent curve. At night, when he closed his eyes, he could feel his fingers twitching, gripping imaginary bowstrings, and he fell asleep, mentally parrying Ismail's ever-inventive blows. And still there was more to learn.

Outside, the bell chimed. Danni, Rachel, and Ismail trooped through the door. Gil rose to his feet as Aidan lit the candles and knelt to pray.

After mass and breakfast, he went alone in the grey dawn to gather the ponies. Feannag soared over his head as he walked. Gil watched until the crow was a black speck in the grey sky. In his mind's eye, he saw what the bird would see: the green field shrinking to a patch on the hillside, the wood of white trees, the Stone Circle, the grass mound of the Turnip-Head Tomb. And beyond, the heather hill brooding above the grey autumn sea, and Einar's Holm, its fields bare, the harvest gathered in.

His pony, Lionheart, dozed yet beneath the yellowing rowan at the edge of his field. Lionheart had befriended the tree his first night at Cille Aidan. Gil named him, that next morning, when he trotted so bravely from its shelter, his eyes full of terror, but his pretty head held high. *See? I'm still here. Nothing ate me in the night.* They all christened their ponies that first day. Danni and Rachel called theirs, Frosti and Freya, who Rachel said were a god and goddess of the Northmen. Ismail, whose brown pony was the biggest and wildest of them all, named his Chocolate.

Lionheart trotted down the hill to him, the others following in their don't-leave-me-behind pony way. Gil looked up again at the sky and again envisioned the bird's view from above. *I've seen this.* The thought came out of a well of lost remembrance. *Riding into the sky, the land falling away below, fields, houses, roads growing small.* How could he have seen what only a bird could see?

He greeted Lionheart with a distracted pat, clutched a hank of mane, and scrambled up onto his back. Lionheart rippled his skin, a pony shrug, and turned, without direction, towards Cille Aidan below. Frosti and Freya trotted to join them, and Chocolate came, cantering like an afterthought, behind. *How do I remember like a bird?*

Danni was waiting in front of the longhouse with their four bridles and the four new saddles that Floki had bought in an Irish market. Gil slid to the ground and slipped Lionheart's bridle over his head. Then he lifted the saddle from the ground and heaved it over the pony's back. Lionheart shuddered and jumped. *We need the saddle,* Gil said with the voice inside himself that the pony could hear.

I don't like the saddle.

You don't like anything new. You're just like me. But I can't joust bareback. Anyhow, I'm getting too big to bounce up and down on your backbone. He glanced down at his worn, patched jeans, ending two inches short of his anklebone. He'd grown a whole year's worth in a season and nothing fit. The girls were making him and Ismail new clothes. Since the summer shearing of the little sheep, neither was ever without her distaff and spindle, spinning with Shony while they talked and sang and told stories around the longhouse fire. Gil reached under the pony to fasten the saddle girth. *Hey. Don't puff up. I'll just have to get off and tighten it later. I can't help it. It feels funny. Whoop-de-do.* Gil paused and waited until Lionheart couldn't hold his breath any longer. *Thank you.* He smiled to himself as he tightened the girth. He had tried to tell the others about talking to Lionheart, but the girls, secure in their superior pony knowledge, only laughed. Even Ismail struggled to believe him. Secretly proud to have a skill no one else possessed, he hadn't tried again. Straightening up, he clasped mane and pommel, jumped, and hauled himself aboard.

"You've got stirrups," Rachel reminded him.

See? You don't need a saddle. You don't even know how to use one.

Gil flicked the reins at Lionheart's ears. Lionheart tensed his bucking muscles. Gil jammed his feet into the stirrups and wrapped his legs tight. He felt solid as a rock after the weeks of clinging to Lionheart's slippery sides with nothing but the strength of his legs. *Just try.* But the pony only rippled its mane and trotted, all innocence, after the rest. When Gil suddenly pulled back on the reins and slid from his saddle, Lionheart looked wildly at the three others, going on ahead. *Has anybody ever really abandoned you? Like trust me, okay?* Gil hurried back to his cell.

Inside, he found his worn charcoal brand and went to the wall over his unmade bed. Long rows of stubby black lines marched across the flat stone. Each six were crossed with a seventh; the date at the week's end written below. Gil crossed the last six through and wrote 'October 31' beneath. Halloween. All Saint's Eve. But it was in Aidan's book. Why write it down? He shook his head, dropped the brand, and ran from the cell. Outside, he mounted Lionheart in one jump, and shoved his heels into the pony's ribs.

Lionheart leapt into a gallop, but skidded to a shying halt beside Aidan's scriptorium. The Wandering Pool sat outside its door, like a stray cat looking for a home. Gil nudged the pony past, with a guilty glance at the shuttered windows. Within, their manuscript lay as forgotten as the things it was meant to recall. When Gil looked at it now, it was like reading in a language he barely knew.

When they came out of the woods, Feannag had returned, soaring, wing feathers spread like black fingertips, above their heads. Gil turned to Danni, riding blithely beside him; leaning back on the pony's rump, her face turned up to the autumn sun. "I remember seeing what Feannag sees." he said. Danni's eyes narrowed to a squint. "I remember going up, like that, into the sky…the way things looked, getting smaller and smaller below."

Danni stared at him. Then she said softly, "Were you a bird?"

"How could I be a bird?" he said. "I'm me!"

She shrugged and looked away, and then he thought all at once of Shony and Floki. "Danni. We're not like them." He could see from her face she knew exactly who he meant. "We're human."

"Aren't they?"

Gil shook his head. "I don't know. I don't know anything anymore. I don't know how I looked down from the sky, but I did." He paused and then it came all at once. "I was in a bird," he said triumphantly.

Danni raised her eyebrows and tossed her long hair back. "Well, that's crazy," she said.

On the ridge above Einar's Holm, the girls reined in their ponies and waited for Gil and Ismail to catch up. Before them, the sullen sea stretched out from the sandy curve of beach and where its grey touched the grey of the sky, a distant sail made a patch of sunlit color. "Floki's back," said Danni happily.

Throughout the late summer and the fall, Floki and his crew had come and gone, sailing out for days or weeks, and returning, bearing all kinds of goods. There were pots and pans, the Irish saddles, metal tools. Once, a little herd of sheep was clustered under the canopy amidships. But twice again they brought treasure; jewelry and silver cups and rich velvet; and once, a golden cross like the one in Aidan's church; though Shony drove her son from the house with it and he slept that night on his ship.

Between sailings, the Northmen tramped tamely out with

Magnus to bring in the harvest of oats and barley. Deprived of their swords and their swagger, they were just farmers. Even Floki could look harmless, running barefoot to the shore to take his little skiff out for a day's fishing. But he never left his sword behind, wherever he went. And when he sailed his longship, *Silver Dragon*, even to a neighboring island with grain to grind at the mill, he went surrounded by warriors, with all their arms.

The ship heaved about and turned shoreward, and by the time they reached the lower fields, *Silver Dragon* was already beached. A line of crewmen clambered up from the strand, each shouldering a heavy ale cask. In the sandy hollow where they practiced archery, the knight, Palamedes, was cantering his great horse in a circle. From head to toe, the Saracen was decked in glittering mail and Doombearer was armored, too. White and gold trappings fluttered around his mighty knees, and even his prancing hooves seemed to shine.

The knight lowered his steel-tipped lance and set the warhorse into a thunderous charge at the hapless archery target. At the last moment, he whipped the lance aside, sparing the painted stag, and turning Doombearer, cantered away to the longhouse. Palamedes dismounted and beckoned, as Gil approached leading Lionheart. "Good lad. Tend my horse, I beg you." He tossed Gil Doombearer's reins. Gil slipped around Lionheart, his eyes on the enormous warhorse.

He'll probably kill you.

Thank you, Lionheart. When I need your opinion, I'll ask for it. Gil stretched a wary hand up for the animal's silver-trimmed bridle, struggling on tiptoes to reach. The beast snorted once and tossed its head and lifted Gil half off his feet. Lionheart hung back, flattening his ears.

I'm afraid of him. His feet are hairy. And they're too big.

He needs big feet. If he had your feet, he'd fall over. Gil tightened his grip on both sets of reins, and watched the knight examining the helmets of wood and breastplates of straw-padded leather which were spread out beneath the longhouse eaves. Palamedes poked one set with the butt of his lance and whacked a helm with the side of his sword. Then he called Gil and Ismail to arm themselves and their mounts.

Gil gathered his own from the heap and donned it carefully. Then he turned to Lionheart, heaved the heavy pony armor over his back, and tied the padding firmly in place. Lionheart stood shivering unhappily like a misfit turtle in an outsize shell.

It's making a noise.

It's the straw rustling and you are not afraid of straw. You eat straw.

Can I eat it now?

No! Laden with his own armor, Gil hauled himself clumsily up into the saddle. He looked with awed respect at mighty Palamedes preparing to don his burden of chain and steel.

When Ismail was mounted, too, Palamedes swung himself up onto his armored horse. Raising his lance high, he shouted, "To the Field of Tournament!" galloped Doombearer in a ring, and came to a halt in front of the longhouse where Shony and Magnus and Floki's rough crew were gathered expectantly.

"The Joust!" he proclaimed. "Most noble of the Arts of War! "He trotted forward. "Armored, the knight enters the list, his lance aloft, his helm displaying the colors of his most adored lady." He beckoned Rachel, "I beg you, the ribbon in your hair."

Smiling, Rachel undid the blue ribbon that bound her long braid and gave it to the knight, who fastened it to his helm. "He pays homage to the Lord and Lady of the Tourney," Palamedes bowed to Shony and Magnus, "And rides to face the foe; most fearsome, but unfortunately," he looked across the empty space before him, "Imaginary."

Then a shout went up from the Northmen and around the corner of the longhouse galloped Floki, astride a shaggy half-tame pony, fresh from the hill. Riding bareback, he clutched the reins of the bridle in his shield hand, and, with the other, held aloft a hastily fashioned lance, a few green leaves clinging yet to its base.

Palamedes lowered his own lance, his dark eyes widening with surprise. "You enter the list? But sir, you have no armor!"

"Armor enough for all you'll touch me!" Floki returned, brandishing his battered shield.

Palamedes looked sorrowful "It would grieve my soul were I to run you through with this lance."

Floki laughed. "It would grieve my body more, I assure you." Still laughing, he trotted to the waiting crowd, turning his pony to left and right so that they all might admire him. His eyes fell on Danni. "My lady!" he cried, bowing deeply, "I beg a token of your favor." He gestured to the blue ribbon adorning Palamedes's helm.

A bright smile crossed Danni's face and she dug into the pocket that hung around her waist, bringing out a polishing cloth, marked with the stain of tarnished metal. Giggling, she held it out to Floki who swooped on it, and clasped it in his hand and bent down to kiss hers, as he did. With no helm to decorate, he tied the cloth around his wrist and galloped away as far as the pony enclosure; then turned, and, facing Palamedes, lowered his lance with a menacing glower.

"Desist, sir," Palamedes called, unhappily. "I dishonor myself to slay you in this way."

"You flatter yourself to think you may!" Floki shouted back. He jabbed his heels into his pony's flanks and charged. With a sorrowful shake of his head that set Rachel's ribbon fluttering, Palamedes lowered his lance and raised his shield.

He gave the tiniest flick of his reins, and Doombearer sprang forward into a thundering gallop. The ground shook as they passed and Gil winced as the distance between warhorse and pony narrowed. He held tight to Lionheart's reins. *Watch!* He ordered. *We have to learn this!*

But Lionheart had taken up an inward chant, *Run! Run! Run!* And turned his head away, his white-rimmed eyes on the hill above.

Floki sat bolt upright, lance braced and shield raised; then, at the last moment, he ducked flat on the pony's mane; lance lowered to one side and shield the other. Palamedes's lance met empty air and his momentum carried him forward over Doombearer's head. The crewmen roared and Magnus pounded his ale horn against his chest in glee. But Palamedes stayed aboard and found his seat again with swift and surprising grace.

"Villain!" he shouted, outraged. "Play fair!"

Floki sat up again, and waved his lance and shield gaily, and shouted, "And be skewered like roasting meat, just to please you?" He whirled his pony and charged again, whooping and pummeling the beast with his heels. And, again, Palamedes only flicked his reins and Doombearer leapt into his thunderous gallop.

The two riders closed upon each other, half obscured by rising dust. Floki sat as resolute as the armored Saracen, until they were upon each other. Then, under the very shadow of the enormous warhorse, he flung himself backwards, and lay flat; his blond head resting on his pony's rump, his feet hooked around its straining neck, shield and lance lowered to the ground.

"Scoundrel!" Palamedes cried as he hurtled forward in stunned amazement. With extraordinary skill he withstood the momentum and clung on, though one foot was out of its stirrup and the reins flew from his hand. But Doombearer came smoothly to a halt while his armor-laden master hauled himself back into his saddle. Behind him, Floki was galloping in an insolent ring, shouting insults in the language of the Northmen.

"You jest too far," Palamedes said. His brows lowered, his genial face hardened, and his eyes went cold. This time it was he who led the return to the list. "Fight like a man of honor or I will skewer you, villain," he roared.

Floki tilted his head and grinned, weighing up the choice. "But you will skewer me, too, if I do!"

"So, face death like a man! Your lady will honor your grave!"

"But if I live," Floki looked slyly at Danni, "Perhaps, one day she will honor my bed?"

"Enough!" Palamedes lowered his lance. But there was a hesitance about this charge and he swayed from side to side, warily watching his adversary. Floki sat boldly upright, as the horses met and both lances struck at once. Floki's greenwood shaft bent against Palamedes's shield, and sprang free. But Palamedes's steel lance tip split his own in half, flinging the Northman backwards over his horse's tail.

A groan went up from his crew and a cry of dismay from Danni. But Floki reached out, as he fell, caught the trappings of the warhorse and the high back of Palamedes's saddle, and hauled himself up behind his foe. Doombearer shimmied in outrage and an astounded Palamedes turned in his saddle and dropped his lance and shield. "Be off! What kind of fight is this?"

"My kind!" Floki cried, wrapping his legs around Doombearer and reaching for his sword. "A Northman's fight!"

Palamedes galloped in a furious circle, levering his huge arm between himself and Floki, and with a mighty shove, unseated the laughing Northman. But Floki hooked his own arm through the knight's and dragged him down as well. Palamedes landed with a ground-shaking thud, but he was on his feet, sword in hand, while Floki was still on his knees.

The Saracen lunged, caught the Northman by his long, blond hair, and held his head up, sword tip to his throat. The dusty farmyard fell deathly still. Palamedes turned slowly to Rachel, his face grim. "My lady?"

Confusion, and then horror, crossed Rachel's face. "No!" she cried. "Not for me! No! No!"

Palamedes bowed to her, released his hold, and graciously helped Floki to his feet. Then he laid his arm over his adversary's shoulders and said quietly, "Do not play with my honor, friend." He smiled his white smile, let the young Northman go, and called Gil and Ismail onto the field.

Gil rode forward, watching Ismail working hard to control his temperamental pony. Chocolate was bigger and tougher and meaner than Lionheart could even think of being. And Ismail was twice the rider Gil was.

"Behold the foe!" Palamedes declared.

"I see him," Gil muttered. But Palamedes wasn't looking at Ismail. Instead, he gestured grandly toward the longhouse door. From it, came Floki and Magnus, and between them, a massive, armored warrior. Gil stared at the warrior and then suddenly he laughed. The figure's legs ended, not in boots, but in clumps of dry straw, and neither leg reached the ground at all. "He's stuffed!" he cried. "He's stuffed with straw!"

Magnus and Floki carried their straw knight to the list. Behind them came Erling; the blue-eyed Northman who had lost his beard for love of Rachel; with a great, stuffed horse's head which he placed atop a horse-shaped frame of driftwood logs. Then Floki and Magnus heaved their knight aboard his mount, and Magnus hung a shield around his straw neck.

Floki dropped a winsome curtsy to the straw man. "Oh, mighty Sir Palamedes! I beg you; carry my favor into the tournament!" He kicked off one of his boots, pulled off a sock, and fastened it to the straw knight's helm.

Palamedes glowered. "Be gone, before I finish you properly." He waved his sword ominously.

Then, standing majestically in front of Gil and Ismail, he recited the names for each part of his armor, from the helm on his head, to the hauberk protecting his chest, the chain chausses guarding his legs, and the gauntlets shielding his mighty hands. He displayed his shield, revealing the sturdy crosspieces of oak, at the back, and the twin leather loops for his arm; then turned it toward them.

The shining white surface was decorated with a fierce dragon, black but for two red, burning eyes. "By this device you know the warrior, though his face be hidden by his helm." He drew his own down low over his forehead and linked the chain face-piece, like a scarf, over his cheeks.

He slung the shield over his shoulder and laid his hand on a round, felt-lined leather socket attached to his saddle, "This," he proclaimed, "Is the fewter." He swung himself up onto the horse, lance in hand, then settled the base of the lance into the socket, the long shaft held vertical. "Behold. I have fewtered my lance."

Palamedes cantered in a circle, with the lance resting upright. Then he lifted it free of the socket and lowered it, holding it diagonally, right to left, across Doombearer's back, the shaft resting on his shield arm.

"This," he said, "Is for the Tourney."

Then he set the base firmly in the fewter and tipped the lance horizontal. "And this," he said, "Is for war. Now, not only I, but mighty Doombearer thrusts the lance. And woe betide the foe who meets it." He lifted the lance free again, holding it lightly. "In the tournament, we are at play."

Floki appeared from behind the longhouse, carrying a

lumpy, laden sack, which he upended, spilling the contents on the ground. A dozen fat turnips tumbled into the dirt.

"Saxon warrior's heads!" cried Palamedes.

He galloped into their midst, lowered his lance and speared one, holding it high. "Thus end the enemies of Arthur!" Palamedes shook off the skewered turnip, backed Doombearer out of the field of play, and bowed to Ismail and Gil.

Ismail trotted Chocolate forward, circled once, and charged the scattered turnips, aligning his lance with the biggest. But Chocolate picked up frightened feet and danced sideways and Ismail's lance glanced off-target, gouging a bright orange scar in the purple skin as the "head" rolled free.

Lionheart pranced around like a demented spider as Gil rode out to take his turn. Gil tightened his reins, patiently. *They're just turnips. Cows eat them. You might if you were hungry enough.*

Chocolate was afraid.

Think for yourself. But ponies weren't supposed to think for themselves. Thinking together kept ponies safe. *Think with me,* he said then, and Lionheart considered, then slipped into a cooperative canter in response.

Gil's first pass was useless, the point of the lance waving wildly as he jounced on the pony's undulating back. *Slow down,* he demanded. *You're too fast.*

No.

No? Gil pulled back sharply on the reins. *I don't do 'no,' thank you.*

Lionheart threw his head up and leapt into a gallop. Gil jerked harder on the reins, but the bitless bridle was as useful as chewing gum if Lionheart really wanted to run. *My back is flat when I gallop.*

Oh! Secure in Lionheart's smoother gait, Gil lined up his lance. It splatted into the big, scarred turnip and he whooped with glee. Kicking his legs free from the stirrups, he galloped in a victory ring, holding his speared turnip-head high.

"Way to go!" shouted Ismail. He offered a high five as Gil galloped triumphantly past.

They took turns then for the rest of the turnips. Ismail picked a more careful path and put Chocolate into a smooth gallop, too. But Gil kept his lead until they'd conquered the fattest of their quarry. Left with smaller targets, Gil lost out to Ismail's spear skills. They ended exactly even, which felt exactly right.

Palamedes granted them a few minutes rest and a chance to water their ponies, while Floki strode into the list with a stack of rough rings, fashioned from twisted willow. Holding one boldly, at arm's length, Palamedes commanded Gil to capture it with his lance. He looked casually over his shoulder as Gil prepared to charge.

The lance, held at shoulder height, was heavy and hard to master. And, aiming at a person was a lot more alarming than targeting vegetables. His first charge went three feet wide. Palamedes covered his mouth in a false yawn.

Ismail lined up for his turn, bearing down on his human target with unflinching intent. But the lance tip skidded off the nearside of the willow ring and clanged; steel on steel; against Palamedes's gauntlet. Knocked back by the force, Palamedes dropped the ring and clutched his armored hand.

"Splendid! A knightly thrust! And, as fortune has blessed me with two hands, I may yet tourney again. Come! To the game!" he signaled Gil to charge. Gingerly, Gil lined up again, seeking a course between a humiliating miss-by-miles, and a bloody end to their jousting master.

Make your lance shorter. Let me take you close.

Gil listened carefully, his eyes on the distant ring. Then he choked up on the lance like he would on a baseball bat, drawing it closer and holding its base further back. The shortened tip was steady and sure. *Go for it,* he said.

In two strides, Lionheart hit his swift gallop. Then, four strides from the waiting knight, the pony swerved sharply to the left, and Gil, swinging his body with him, lunged the lance tip at the willow circle. It swept through the airy center, snatching the ring from Palamedes's hand. "Yes!" Gil shouted aloud. *Thank you, Lionheart. You are ace!*

When they'd collected three rings each, the straw knight was carried out into the center of the list and armed with a steel-tipped spear. It sat bold and threatening, now, on its driftwood horse. For the first time, Gil looked down his lance at the point of another. Beneath him Lionheart had begun to shiver.

When Gil tried to turn the pony toward the target, Lionheart reared and backed. Gil tightened the grip of his thighs and moved easily with the frightened animal, balancing lance and shield. *It isn't real. It's straw.*

It wasn't there before. It's new.

I know. Just being new doesn't make it dangerous. Lionheart, please trust me. But what if he got this wrong? The straw knight's lance point glinted. Lionheart's eyes rolled, showing their whites. Gil fiercely shut his mind to his own fears, trusting himself so the pony could trust him.

He made his first charge. His thrust was wide, glancing so lightly off the straw knight's shield that his stuffed adversary barely trembled. Ismail's lance struck the shield with a solid thump, tossing the straw dummy askew. Palamedes straightened the sagging figure as Gil shifted his position slightly and tried again.

Intent on the target of the shield, he forgot the knight's lance, until the last moment; then jerked wildly on the reins. Lionheart jumped heroically aside and then galloped away in terror. *I want my field! I want my tree!*

Gil trotted the pony to the side of the list. Lionheart stood with his head low and his ears flat. Gil stroked his neck. *Give me one more chance. I'll get it right.*

Home. Home.

Okay, Gil said. *Fine.* Pointedly he picked up the reins and just as pointedly dropped them on Lionheart's mane. Lionheart blew air through his nose, then shook his mane, raised his head, and without direction, turned back to the list.

Cool dude! Gil said. He looked down the list at the waiting knight, a bit bedraggled now from Ismail's attentions, and then, with reins yet lying on his pony's neck, squeezed his knees together, gently, and said, *Go for it.*

Lionheart tossed his head, and then gave a feisty snort and broke, unbidden, into his gallop. Reins flapping free, he charged their mutual foe. Gil set his lance. A stride from the target, Lionheart leapt forward, throwing all his weight into the charge. Gil struck the knight square in the center of his shield, his lance splintering the wood and slamming into the chain hauberk behind. The straw knight flew from his mount and landed like a metal-clad rag doll, in the dirt.

Lionheart snorted and threw his head back and galloped in a victory ring. The crowd shouted and cheered. In the distance, among the cheers, Gil suddenly heard Danni's voice proudly shouting his name.

Palamedes called for silence. He turned again to Ismail and Gil, and he looked very serious. "The joust is a war," he said, "A war in miniature. The knight is an army in one man, and the Cause he fights for rests on his shoulders, alone. Therefore, no man enters the list without a clean heart and a soul intent on the triumph of the good. Good knights," he addressed them directly, his voiced ringing across the list, "to your arms and to your places; the joust begins."

Gil and Ismail looked at each other. "You and me?" Ismail whispered. He gestured from himself to Gil.

Gil nodded. He reached across Lionheart's neck and offered Ismail his hand. "Good luck." Ismail shook hands and grinned a little weakly. Then, they turned their ponies, tail-to-tail, and trotted resolutely to the far ends of the list.

Shouts and raucous argument arose from the watching Northmen. But all Gil really heard were the voices of Danni and Rachel, chanting together with deliberate fairness, "Go, Ismail! Go, Gil!"

When he turned at the end of the list, Ismail's mount, Chocolate, loomed rangy and tall. Lionheart was clearly the underdog. *Underpony*, he thought, before he could stop himself.

I'm too small! I'm too small!

We'll use it, Gil said, thinking fast. *We'll come at him from underneath.*

I've got to go underneath him? Lionheart bristled his mane and flicked his tail in a panic.

No! You just keep your head down and I'll go underneath his lance arm.

Lionheart's ears were still horizontal, but Ismail had

Chocolate lined up, ready, at the start. Hastily, Gil arranged himself and his pony the same.

"The Field!" cried Palamedes. Gil and Ismail stared at each other; then, as one, lowered their lances and roused their mounts to the charge. Gil clutched his steel-tipped lance in horror. This was no dummy-knight, but his own best friend, galloping toward him in armor made of straw! *I'll kill him!*

Kill him! Kill him! Lionheart chanted helpfully.

He's my friend! Gil slapped the pony's neck with his reins and Lionheart snorted and missed a stride. Gil focused on Ismail's homemade shield. *I won't hurt him if I hit the shield.*

Chocolate and his rider became just a blur. Lionheart ducked his head low beneath Gil's lance. Chocolate's brown head and neck snaked out and there was a dim flash of something white. Lionheart exploded beneath Gil, leaping sideways, with all four feet. Gil's lance passed a yard wide of its target. Ismail's flailed uselessly at empty space. Lionheart, head down, galloped for the open hill.

The list was far behind them, when Gil finally negotiated a halt. The pony stood, panting, and looking with wild eyes over his shoulder. *He was going to bite me!*

Gil remembered the snake-neck and the flash of white. *He's a bully!* he said, exasperated. *Bite him!* Plastering a good-sport grin on his face, Gil trotted Lionheart back toward the list. Ismail was so busy averting kind eyes, that he didn't notice Chocolate sidling into Lionheart's path.

Gil grabbed the reins, but then Lionheart curled back his furry lips showing his white teeth, and did the snake-neck thing himself. Chocolate half-reared and shied away. Lionheart pranced and flattened his ears meanly.

Don't overdo it. He is still bigger than you. Gil lined up for the second pass. *Go low, choke up just a little on the lance; focus on the shield....*

"The Field!" shouted Palamedes.

Chocolate and Lionheart leapt forward, like twin springs. Gil sunk deep into his saddle, bracing himself, his mind still racing; lance, shield, the pony beneath him. Then Ismail loomed in front of him, huge on the brown pony's back.

Gil grasped the reins, jerking back hard. Lionheart stumbled and Gil's lance grazed over Ismail's shield. Then there was an enormous crashing thud and Gil's shield flew from his arm. The force shook his whole body; his neck snapped back and his teeth clacked together. He saw a flash of stars on blackness, reeled, and dropped his lance.

Lionheart slowed his gait, unbidden, to a smooth, running walk, keeping his back absolutely flat. Shakily, Gil straightened up in the saddle and found his stirrups once more.

In the distance he heard shouts of Ismail's name. He turned and glimpsed the African boy galloping away, the lance that had struck Gil's shield held in the air. But for Lionheart's pace change, Gil would have been sprawled, like the straw knight, on the ground. *Thank you. You are one smart pony.* Lionheart's ears twitched happily forward.

Floki came into the list and stooped to pick up Gil's fallen shield and lance. Returning them, he suddenly shrugged a shoulder toward Palamedes. "I've seen him arse over heels in the dust," he said, with a quick grin.

Gil slipped the shield onto his arm, lifted the lance and turned Lionheart to the start. He lowered the lance to face Ismail, and when Palamedes shouted "The Field!" he dropped the reins resolutely on Lionheart's neck.

Immediately the pony leapt forward, ears pricked and head high. Gil gauged the distance, and shortened the lance as much as he dared. He wrapped his thighs tightly around Lionheart's flanks, but kept his upper body loose, flowing with the pony's rhythmic charge. Chocolate and Ismail closed, in a cloud of dust.

Five strides from target, Gil tilted his own shield upward and ducked beneath. Focus. No Chocolate. No Ismail. No lance. Just the shield. Lionheart leapt forward and Gil lunged with the lance. The crack of contact flung him backwards, but he kept his seat, even as Ismail's lance flashed by his ear. He had a glimpse of Ismail's surprised face and then a flurry of pin-wheeling arms and legs. A great cheer arose from the Northmen, shouting Gil's name. Lionheart, his head still free, carried him in a proud, snorting ring of victory.

Gil lowered his lance and his shield and caught up the reins, turning the pony back to the center of the list, where Ismail was sprawled on the ground. His heart sank with horrified remorse, but then the African boy sat up, grinning and laughing, and ruefully rubbing one shoulder, jumped to his feet.

Gil slipped down from Lionheart and reached out to his friend. Still rubbing his shoulder, Ismail held up a valiant high-five. "You are champion!" he said with awed respect.

Gil's fingers slapped against his friend's and he opened his mouth to correct him. It wasn't him. It was Lionheart! But a strange feeling came over him, a kind of greedy secrecy, and he merely shrugged as the Northmen surrounded him then, and hoisted him up onto shoulders. Gil laughed and struggled to get down and back to Ismail and to Lionheart. But the Northmen carried him away, chanting his name.

At the door of the longhouse, they set him down, and with more back pounding and hair tousling, trooped past him into Magnus's Great Hall. Gil still felt like his feet were yet somewhere above the ground when he turned belatedly to his pony and his friends.

Danni was rubbing the saddle-sweat off Lionheart's back with a handful of dried bracken. He reached to help, but then Erling appeared at the doorway, waving an ale horn and thumping his chest. "Hail! Warrior!" he shouted, and blundered back inside. Gil turned toward the door, but something stopped him.

The dusk that fell earlier and earlier each day, was falling now. The air had gone still, and in that still moment, he had heard a sound. It seemed to come from another place and another life. "It's Aidan's bell," Danni said. "When the wind falls, you can hear it from here. We should go."

Gil looked wistfully back at the door. The good smell of roasting meat drifted out. He was hungry, for food, and for something as intoxicating as Magnus's ale: the adulation he had only just tasted. It was so soon to have it snatched away. It felt like leaving his own birthday party early.

A huge hand descended on his shoulder. He looked up into the piercing dark eyes of Palamedes. Doombearer's jeweled bridle was draped across his arm and he balanced his silver-studded saddle on his shoulder.

Palamedes smiled gently down on him. "You are small and you are fearful," he said. "But fear is the companion of every wise knight. And a good companion, too, as long as he rides at his heels." His mighty voice softened. "You will make a worthy knight." He clapped Gil's shoulder, and disappeared beneath the lintel of Einar's Holm.

Gil felt a rush of confused emotion: pride, at the praise, humiliation at the barb within the praise, and resentment, aimed illogically at Aidan for dragging him away from the best moment of his life. He balled his hand up into a fist.

"I'm not going," he said.

"You're not going back to Cille Aidan?" Danni stared at him. The last chiming of the bell hung on the air and then the darkening dusk was still.

"We'll go back after supper," Gil hunched his shoulder toward the longhouse. "Smells better than cabbage soup."

"We always go back to Cille Aidan for supper," Danni said.

"So, this time we'll do something different. Like it won't kill us to have one supper here."

"It'll be dark."

"We'll take torches," he said. "Like you did, when you came to the Pool to find me. Come on. It'll be fun!" He gave her shoulder a playful teasing punch. She shrugged it off.

"We really should go home," Rachel said. "Aidan called us."

Gil raised his palms and looked heavenwards. "What is he, our mother?"

"I think we should vote," said Ismail.

"Right. You're the one who says I'm supposed to be the leader. So, when I try to lead, you over-rule me. Great!"

"No one over-rules you. I said we should vote."

To Gil's surprise, first Ismail, then Rachel, then Danni, herself, raised hands for "we stay." Gil raised his own, feeling foolish. "Well, if you all agreed with me, what was the argument about?"

"I don't agree with you," Danni said bluntly. "But you want this a lot."

Ismail put a firm hand on his shoulder and turned him toward the Hall. "Enough. We have agreed. We do it."

Gil felt more foolish. But then he stepped through the door and was met by a cheering wall of Northmen. Floki thrust an ale horn into his hand and mimed a toast. Grinning shyly, Gil raised the ale, foaming and cool, to his lips.

"You're not going to drink it, are you?" Danni hissed, right in his ear.

Gil grimaced, "Just a sip. It's good manners." Ignoring her look of outrage, he swallowed a mouthful of the ale, and then another. He hadn't realized how thirsty he was or how refreshing the honey-colored liquid would be. He swallowed a third gulp, and then conscientiously thrust the horn aside.

But he couldn't put it down, without rudely spilling it, because the primitive vessel wouldn't rest, upright, unsupported. So, he swallowed the rest. When Magnus passed again with the ale jug, he found himself holding out the empty horn like all his boisterous companions.

Danni had gone with Rachel to join Shony beside the cooking fire. Rachel had tightly braided her hair again and wrapped it around her head. Danni had veiled hers with her shawl, like she did in church. They busied themselves with kitchen work, and when the Northmen called out to them, they ignored them. Gil looked with sudden distaste at the half-full ale horn in his hand. He searched the room for somewhere to lose it; then tried to edge toward the door. But the Great Hall was packed with sweating, jostling bodies blocking his way.

Then, Magnus appeared behind his big carved chair and Shony and the girls swept through the eagerly parting crowd bearing laden, steaming platters. A stampede to the table swept Gil back into the room and he was picked up bodily by two hulking Northmen and plonked down in the other great chair, facing Magnus down the length of the mighty board.

"No!" he protested. He struggled to his feet, but big hands pushed him back down. He just glimpsed Floki and his ale jug passing and when he looked down his drinking horn was again full to the brim.

His head felt thick and sounds seemed to come from far

away. His hands, still clutching the miserable drinking horn, felt clumsy, like he'd grown extra fingers. He was more than glad to be sitting down, even in this outrageous place, and his stomach was churning with hunger and with sloshing ale.

He searched his meagre fund of drinking lore picked up from older kids in the playground. *Eat.* But he needed two hands to eat. With a sigh of dismay, he lifted the ale horn and in six huge gulps, drained it dry, and then flung the horn itself over his shoulder and fell upon the first platter of meat, clutched two handfuls of roasted venison, and stuffed them into his mouth.

He ate heroically, as fast as he could, but the ale out-paced him, swallowing his sense and his will. Suddenly, he was talking and laughing and shouting like the worst of Floki's unruly crew.

Erling lurched to a place beside him, engaged him in a one-sided bout of arm-wrestling, and then dragged him up on his unsteady feet. He thrust an ale horn into Gil's face and poured more of the golden liquid down his throat. Gil braced one leg against the table to keep from falling. "The warrior tells his tale!" Erling declared and pounded the table. The Hall fell instantly silent.

Gil looked blearily around at the expectant faces. And then, all at once he understood. This was what life was about! Fighting and drinking and eating, and stories. Warrior's stories. They were warriors, and he was a warrior, too.

Inspired, he staggered across the room and grabbed his sword from the wall. Unsheathing it, he swung it in a flashing arc, glittering like the rows of shields above. Turning back, he shouted, "For Arthur!" Cheers and shouting echoed his ringing words. "For Camelot!" he cried, to more cheers, though someone also laughed. He swung the sword again. "For Janetta!"

Raucous table thumping greeted that. When the noise at last stilled, he heard Rachel's weary murmur, "Nice one, Gil." He staggered, briefly disconcerted. But Erling slapped his back.

"Arthur can wait. Let's have the woman!"

And suddenly Gil wanted nothing more than to ride at the head of an army to rescue his green-eyed girl. "So, what are we waiting for?" he shouted, striding down the center of the Hall beside the glowing fire. "Let's go! Now!"

The cheering died away and with it the laughter that had grown like weeds amidst it. Palamedes rose to his feet. There was no ale horn in his hand and no ale light in his eyes. "Restrain your knightly eagerness," he said gently. "Your time is coming, sooner than the winter winds. Only the saints hurry to greet death."

Gil squinted at Palamedes uncertainly, and the Hall remained silent.

"Before you lies a perilous journey," Palamedes continued softly. "Fierce seas stretch between this far Northland and your next sanctuary at Hy. Beyond the holy island, are great mountains, and beyond them, the Forest of Caledon—now, alas, a lawless land, blighted by war, harried by dishonored knights.

"Chapels lie abandoned. The great *muinntirs* stand roofless to the rain. There is neither solace, nor shelter, in all that forsaken land. And you must challenge the Golden Knight's very holdings to recapture the Holy Fool."

"Please, sir," Shony reproved softly, "Do not insult the child. He is their kin."

Floki, slouching lazily against a roof post, straightened up and laughed. "So where is the insult?" he said, grinning. "In his holiness or in his foolishness?" He drank from his ale horn and leaned back against his post, "And are they not two strands of the same cord?"

"I mean no insult!" Palamedes said fervently. "Indeed, we honor the child; for only guided by his innocent heart can you seek out the Holy Chapel in the Forest of Pentecost. There, within its briar tangled walls, lies hidden the blessed relic that is your goal.

"But, there, too, the Guardian of the Chapel awaits. Approach the relic bearing a single evil thought and you will perish, flung into the thorny maze out with the walls." He paused and lowered his voice. "Bones of warriors, mounted yet on steeds of bone, hang trapped within its thickets to this day!"

He smiled gently, bowing his great head so the black curls tumbled over his face. Looking up, he whispered wistfully, "Do you wonder that only the young are called? Souls grown old, like mine, can only watch from afar."

The room fell silent once more. Gil looked around, struggling to focus. Even Floki's Vikings looked wary and one, an enormous giant with hair and beard as black as the Saracen's, shook his head.

"What?" Gil cried. "Are you afraid?" He staggered into the center of the Hall, again, and raised his sword high. "Of what? Some ghost story about bones? Come with me! Now!" He swung the sword in a wildly wavering arc and three Northmen prudently ducked.

"I would wait for dawn," Floki said amiably, over his shoulder. "And the tide. Ale floats few ships, but sinks many. And," he paused, "I take that now, before you cut yourself." His fingers closed gently on Gil's wrist and then the grip slowly tightened until Gil shouted in pain and dropped the sword. Floki released him. He stooped gracefully, lifted the weapon from the floor, and laid it on the table.

Rubbing his wrist, Gil turned furiously on the Northman. "You still don't think I'm good enough?"

Floki looked down on him in silence, his eyes sparkling with amusement. Then he leaned forward and ruffled Gil's hair with a gentle hand. "We talk in the morning, warrior," he said. "When Redbeard's ale has less to say. This night, I sleep."

Dismissing Gil, he bowed to his father and his Saracen guest, and turned toward the tree ladder and the loft. Gil stared after him and then red rage filled him, and with his eyes still on the Northman, he reached back for the sword. Before his fingers gained the hilt, Floki stopped and stood absolutely still, his back yet to Gil.

"Touch that, warrior," he said, "And I will kill you."

Gil froze. His vision came suddenly into vivid focus and as his hand drew back from the sword, he saw his own movement reflected in the shields on the distant wall, and Floki's distorted image, watching him. Without turning or speaking, Floki walked to the tree ladder and mounted to his bed.

A deep, collective sigh swept the room and Palamedes said gravely, "It is time all do the same. The night grows long."

And then, suddenly and without the slightest sound, the

mighty door of Einar's Holm swung slowly inwards, revealing a sliver of pitch-black night. The sliver broadened and a gust of wind burst in. The fire flared, scattering ash and sparks up to the black beams.

"Who goes?" Magnus roared but his huge voice held a tremor of fear. Palamedes leapt to his feet and drew his sword. Shony's was already in her hand.

Gil glimpsed a shadowy movement beyond the door. Giddy and sick, he clasped a roof-post tightly. Visions of skeletal knights rose grimly in his befuddled mind. Then, to his horror, just such a figure stepped from the darkness into the flickering gloom of the hall; dark-robed, bearing a bent staff as tall as his hooded head and shadowed by a fluttering of half-glimpsed wings.

The figure rested the staff against the doorframe, reached up, and lowered its dark hood. Gil flinched, but the face was very human, if a little stern. "The night is long indeed," said a gentle voice. "And the way is dark."

"Mo'Aidan!" Shony gasped. She dropped her drawn sword to the table and rushed forward, pushing past her astonished guests. "Forgive us!" she cried, clasping both of the Ab's hands, "We have kept the children far too long."

Aidan smiled. With a rustle of wings, Feannag settled on his shoulder. "No doubt they struggled very hard to be released." Aidan raised his gaze to Gil and his companions. Then he held out one arm as an invitation that was also a command.

Danni got up at once and hurried head down, to his side. Ismail crossed the room after her. But Gil remained, stubbornly in his place. Something thumped hard into his back, taking his breath away. "Who?" he sputtered, turning angrily. Rachel was standing right behind him, her small hand still balled into a fist.

"You've made enough of an arse of yourself, already," she hissed and gave him a fierce shove. Staggering for balance, he had no choice but to stumble ignominiously into Aidan's grasp. The Ab caught his shirt collar and hauled him upright. "Tomorrow is the Holy Feast of All Saints," Aidan said mildly. "And, so, tonight, it is time for bed."

Outside, gale-blown clouds raced past a rising moon.

The ponies whickered and snorted in the stone enclosure. Doombearer was a huge, sleeping shadow in one corner. The fresh air that was supposed to clear his head, made Gil instantly nauseous. He clapped a hand over his mouth and staggered to the enclosure wall and puked until his eyes watered. Aidan stood patiently beside him until he finished. Then he pointed to the dim stone water-trough. Gil washed his face. With all of his dinner, and most of the ale on the outside, he felt a little better.

"I'll do that," he called weakly, as Danni struggled to lead both her pony and his from the enclosure. She ignored him, but he reached and grabbed Lionheart's bridle and jerked the pony toward him. Lionheart snorted and reared.

Hey!

Leave me alone. I don't know you.

It's me, dummy.

You smell funny. I'm afraid.

You're always afraid. I'm sick of afraid.

Gil pulled hard on the bridle and Lionheart reared higher, dragging him off his feet. He stumbled, regained his footing, but lost the bridle. Freed of restraint, Lionheart skittered sideways. Gil lunged, caught the reins again, and jerked the pony's head down close to his. *Stop it! Stupid, useless pony. What good are you going to be, afraid of everything?* Lionheart reared again. Gil raised his fist.

He had a glimpse of Lionheart's wild, rolling eyes, flashing in the moonlight, and then Aidan's strong hands grabbed him from behind, clutching his shirt and the seat of his pants. Lifted right off his feet, he was swung up into the air and landed with a thud, spread-eagled on Lionheart's back. The pony shuddered, but stood still. Aidan gently stroked its neck.

Gil pulled himself shakily upright and let his legs fall into place around Lionheart's belly. He looked at the Ab with new respect. "I wasn't going to hurt him," he muttered. "Just show him I meant business."

Aidan said nothing. As Gil's words hung stupidly in the starry silence, he accepted the beautiful carved *bachall*, from Ismail, who had held it while he dealt with Gil. Then, turning once to be sure they were all following, he set off up the hill with long, steady strides. Feannag soared ahead, a black ghost. They rode on, each in silence. Gil was glad of the darkness hiding his shame.

At Cille Aidan, they released the ponies into the field above the church. Gil stroked Lionheart's neck and felt the skin tense beneath his hand. *I'd never hurt you. You know I'd never hurt you. I want my tree.*

Reluctantly, Gil slipped the bridle over the pony's head. Instantly, Lionheart shied away and then trotted with sad determination to the shelter of his rowan. The last Gil saw of him was a hunched back and a lowered head, pressed up against the comfort of its little trunk.

Gil walked slowly down the hill, clutching the bridle. He brought it in with him, into his little cell and laid it on the floor. Then he curled up in the dark on his bed and cried until he fell asleep.

CHAPTER ELEVEN

A moment later, Gil was awake again. Aidan's bell was ringing. Ismail's voice called, "Gil! It is prayers. You very late." Gil sat up, holding his pounding head and staggered erect in the pitch-black cell.

His feet tangled with something on the floor and he sprawled on top of a ropy bundle. Lionheart's bridle. He got to his feet with a leaden heart, tucked his shirt into his rumpled jeans, and stumbled out to the church. A huge, black silhouette shadowed the doorway. Gil grabbed Ismail's cloak. "Who?"

"Palamedes stands guard."

"Is Floki here?

"All here. It is All Saints. Big Feast." Gil turned to run. "Hey! Where you go?"

"Not in there," Gil whispered grimly. "And you wouldn't either if he was as mad at you as he is at me!"

"He is not angry," said Ismail. His white grin flashed in the faint light.

"He was going to kill me. Like, six hours ago?"

"Yes," Ismail agreed cheerfully. "But he is not angry. He is warrior. You, silly, drunk boy, challenge. But others, not silly, not drunk, watch. You touch sword, he must kill you." He grinned and patted Gil's back, "Come. He is in church now. Very holy."

"Yeah, right." Gil slunk past Palamedes into the dimly lit building, huddled in a corner while Aidan sang Mass, and, scuttled out afterward in the Ab's safe shadow. Inside the longhouse, Gil's empty stomach lurched at the smell of food and he bolted for the door. Hunched over a rock, retching up nothing, he felt a light hand tap his shoulder. Ismail handed him a bunch of dried grass. Gil wiped his mouth with it and straightened up. "If you ever see me go near an ale horn again...." he began.

"I punch you," said Ismail, with a grin.

Gil walked alone to the pony field. Rain was slashing down, driven inland by a fierce sea wind. His cloak was sodden and his feet, in threadbare sneakers, squelched in the black mud as he looked out over the mist-shrouded field. *Lionheart!* he called with his silent, inner voice, and then, when he heard no answer, he shouted, "Lionheart! Come!" aloud.

Freya, Rachel's ever-hungry little mare, came, with Frosti and Chocolate pushing in beside her, eager for a treat. Drenched and miserable, Gil waited; his fingers clutching the piece of dried apple in his pocket; until the ponies drifted away.

The girls joined him after breakfast. "No Lionheart?" Danni asked. Gil shook his head.

Rachel nodded wisely. "Ponies have long memories. But they do get over things."

"Not Lionheart. He didn't know me anymore because I smelled funny. He wanted his tree! That's, like, total misery, for Lionheart."

Danni looked at him oddly. "How do you know?"

"Because he told me!" Gil burst out. "Lionheart talks to me," he said quietly.

Rachel folded her arms. "He's a pony, Gil. You can talk to him all you want, but he understands three words: Stop. Go. And food."

Gil shook his head. "Look," he said grimly, "How else did you think I beat Ismail at jousting? Lionheart really talks to me. He told me what to do."

Danni thought about that, and then slowly nodded. Rachel's eyes lit up with humiliating certainty. "He's right! Didn't I say it was weird? Like Gil and his pony were sort of one. I mean, maybe Ismail...he's like such a horseman...but Gil?"

"Yeah," Danni breathed. "It didn't make a lot of sense, did it? Hey, not fair, you and Lionheart ganging up on Ismail!"

"Well, since we all agree I'm hopeless, maybe it is fair."

"You're not hopeless," Rachel said in her fair-minded way

that was somehow worse for being so honest. "You're just not usually as good as Ismail." She smiled kindly, but Danni was studying Gil, her eyes flicking from him to the little group of ponies and beyond, to the mist that hid Lionheart and his tree. "How long have you been doing this?" she asked.

He shrugged awkwardly. "From the beginning. When you all left me behind, when I didn't know how to ride at all." They both lowered their heads and looked guilty. "I was so scared, and then I heard him, even more scared. Scared to leave his field, and scared to be left behind. So, I spoke to him in my head. And he heard me, in his."

"You could have told us," Danni said.

"I tried. You didn't listen." He paused, knowing he could leave it like that and get away with it. But then he said honestly, "I didn't tell you because I didn't want to. I wanted you to think I was brilliant at jousting, all by myself. For once I wanted to be best at something."

Rachel surveyed him critically and then suddenly smiled. "You will be," she said encouragingly. "You just haven't found it yet. Come on." She held out her hand. "Lionheart will stop sulking soon enough. Just leave him."

Four times in the day, Gil trudged through the wind and the rain to the pony field. But he never saw Lionheart, though the others emerged, like shaggy ghosts, from the mist, each time he came.

In the longhouse there was soup and meat, oatcakes and honey and warm milk from the little sheep. Gil nibbled squeamishly while Shony played the harp and Magnus told a story of a great sea battle of his youth, when a hundred longships clashed off the High Isle and the men of the islands defeated a great North king.

Floki followed, with an adventure in the snowy regions far to the North, where even the bears were white and men froze to death if they stood still for a moment. Then he took the harp from his mother and sang a love song for the girls, so sweetly, that Gil struggled to remember he was the same man who would have killed him the night before for a single false move.

Night was falling when he made a final weary trek to the

field. He stared hopelessly into the darkening mist, and saw at
last an unmistakable pony shape, coming toward him through
the slanting rain. Uncertain head lowered, Lionheart stepped
warily over the sodden grass to where he stood.
Gil dug in his pocket for the half apple. Lionheart reached
furry lips and wrapped them around it. Gil reached out very
carefully and patted the warm place under the pony's thick
mane. Lionheart stepped closer and pressed his nose against
Gil's chest. *You smell better.*
Well, you don't. Gil flung his arm around the pony's neck,
and hung on, crying for happiness. Joyfully, he strode down the
hill, oblivious of his soaking cloak and dripping hair. When he
reached the longhouse, Aidan was bidding his guests farewell.
As they rode away, he turned to Gil, his face solemn.
"Saint Martin's Mass, on the morning tide, Floki sails for
Ireland. He will take you with him, as far as Hy." Aidan raised
his eyes to the young Northman, mounting the hill on his half-
wild pony. "He is proud and he is ruthless, but no man will
keep you safer. Sail with him and obey him. But never forget
who he is."

They rode to Einar's Holm the next morning, hunched beneath
a rain-swept sky. The sea wind battered their faces with sleet.
In the Wood of White Trees, the ponies' hooves scuffed sodden
yellow leaves. Ten days remained 'til Martinmass and the mood
in the longhouse was as wintry as the hill.
Floki and Palamedes greeted the boys without humor and
drove them without mercy. Every sword swing was criticized,
every lance thrust derided. Their horsemanship was ruled
hopeless. The morning passed in a blur of armed clashes,
splintered lances, and bone-shaking falls. At midday, bruised
and aching and drenched to the skin, they fled to the warmth
of the longhouse and stood wringing out their clothes in front
of the blazing fire.
Shony watched gravely, and then beckoned the girls. "Bring
down your summer's work." Danni scrambled up the tree-
ladder to the sleeping loft and tossed two bundles down to
Rachel. Together, they unrolled them, revealing braid-trimmed

tunics, trousers of heavy grey wool, chunky knitted socks, and shaggy woolen cloaks.

From a kist by the loom, Shony brought boots, thick and sturdy and lined with plush sheepskin. Gil stroked one, admiring the beautiful stitching. "This must have taken forever."

Danni smiled and shrugged, but Shony nodded proudly. "In winter in the Northlands, the spindle wins as many battles as the sword." She thrust the garments toward them. "Go. Dress. And come back Northmen!"

Warm and dry in their new clothing, they returned to the field in better spirits and battled on until dusk. By the week's end, Gil felt as if he had lived his entire life on Lionheart's back, a lance or a sword in his hand. He barely noticed when Palamedes lost his expression of perplexed concern and Floki stopped looking heavenward in despair. But when he held his ground for a precious few sword swings against Magnus himself, he knew a kind of miracle had occurred.

Floki gripped his shoulders in a triumphant bear hug. "Good! A good day, warrior!" Then he raised his eyes to the sea and exclaimed, "And a good ending to it!" He pointed to a green striped sail brightening the horizon and called to his father, "Redbeard! This fair wind brings your fosterling!"

Already Floki's men were coming down from the fields. Shony and the girls ran from the longhouse, looking eagerly out to sea. Floki slapped Gil's arm. "Come. Meet my closest kin!"

He ran to the pony pen, vaulted the gate, and jumped on the bare back of a startled beast. Clasping a hunk of mane, he kicked the pony into a gallop, sent it soaring over the stone wall, snatched Danni up before him, and thundered off to the shore, with all of Einar's Holm following behind.

Sail lowered, the longship rode in under oars, beaching beside *Silver Dragon*; their fierce prows bent close like the heads of friendly ponies. Floki galloped to the rail, as the gangplank was lowered, and lifted Danni up to a dark-bearded man on the deck. Then he stood on the pony's back and stepped aboard himself. Enfolding the dark man in a laughing embrace, he spun him around to face Gil and his friends.

"Behold the warriors of Tir nan Og!" Floki pronounced

boldly. The dark Northman studied them with intense eyes under slanting black brows, his solemnity belying his obvious youth.

"They are small," he said finally.

"Small, you say?" Floki looked astonished. "Among their own, they are giants! In Tir nan Og, grown men are three feet tall."

The Northman stared down, his eyes widening. "Is this true?"

Floki grinned and cuffed the dark man's head. The other smiled uncertainly. "This," said Floki, beckoning them up the gangplank, "Is my cousin, Hakon Sea-Friend. Redbeard's sister's son. Raised with me as my foster-brother and renowned through all the Shetland Isles for his great humor and wit."

Hakon smiled again. "I am renowned indeed, but only for being the poor shadow of my cousin Floki Magnusson." He shrugged good-naturedly.

Floki shook his head. "Perhaps not, then, for wit, but his seamanship is praised by every man who sets hand to oar, or sail to wind. My warriors will be glad of it, when the white horses of Pentland come to play."

"Is Hakon sailing with us?" Danni asked.

Floki laughed, "How else am I to transport four ponies and four warriors and that monstrous pagan and his horse? For him, alone, I cast five good barrels of meal to the sea, to keep myself afloat. Hakon sails with us to Hy, and then he and I sail on. We pay a visit to Irish shores before the snows." He slapped Hakon's shoulder and grinned. "It is not fair that only the Saxons enjoy your company. What have you brought us, Cousin?"

Hakon called to two of his crewmen in the Northmen's language and they brought forward a large, metal-bound trunk from among the plundered goods stacked amidships. They set it at Hakon's feet and he raised the heavy, creaking lid.

Floki grinned again and lifted out a gleaming knight's helm. "Well done, Cousin!" Turning to Gil, he set the helm upon his head. It fit perfectly, and when Gil lifted it off to admire it, he found the interior of the polished metal was lined with a soft padding of red silk.

Floki plucked another helm from the trunk and presented it to an awed Ismail. Two chain mail hauberks followed from the trunk and chausses as well. The twin, padded undercoats for the hauberks were of quilted red silk.

"No humble squire's armor, this!" Floki exulted. "Two Saxon princelings will go bare-arsed to battle, this winter!" His eyes twinkled and he punched his cousin.

"But wait," Hakon said. "There is still more." He clambered down among the barrels and chests and returned carrying two lances; fine and steel-tipped and just the right length for Gil and Ismail. Palamedes mounted the gangplank and helped them into their armor, adjusting the chausses beneath their knees and lowering the hauberks and chainmail over their heads. Jingling shyly, Gil pulled on his gauntlets and followed Palamedes off the ship.

Floki seized Lionheart's reins and led him to Gil and before Gil could get his foot in the stirrup, heaved him aboard and slapped the new lance into his gloved right hand. When Gil twisted around to see Ismail, mounted on Chocolate, the chain mail moved so supplely over the padded undercoat that its weight was no more hindrance than the cloth.

Floki clasped Lionheart's bridle again and ran with him up the white strand. Hakon caught up Chocolate's reins and followed. "All hail the Warriors of Tir nan Og!" Floki cried. The watching crowd thumped fists on shields to the rhythm of the ponies cantering feet, as they returned in triumph to the longhouse. Then, for the last time, Gil and Ismail put away the tools of war, and rode home, with the girls beside them, to Cille Aidan. Dusk was falling, though the afternoon was yet young.

At the crest of the hill, Gil turned and looked back. The lighted windows of the longhouse glowed amidst the darkening fields. A fire burned on the beach, casting a flickering red glow over the sea. Shadows of dragon prows moved like sea beasts over the sand. Gil fingered the leather necklace at his throat. When next he saw Einar's Holm, the two longships would be readying their sails.

CHAPTER TWELVE

There was neither moon nor stars when Gil rose on Saint Martin's Eve, and as he stumbled blindly toward the ringing bell, his feet splashed into water. "That Pool!" cried Rachel's indignant voice, as another splash sounded in the blackness. "What's it doing here?"

"Maybe we're getting another blessing," Gil muttered warily.

When he and Ismail returned from carrying hay up to the ponies, the little pool shone in the soft, grey morning, reflecting the sky and the hill and the church through a thin layer of mist. Beyond he saw Aidan working on the shore.

While Feannag flapped in circles around him, and Danni and Rachel watched, Aidan laid an armful of yellowing rowan boughs on the white sand and arranged them into a wide ring. Feannag flew down with more branches in his beak. "It's a nest!" Danni cried.

Ismail studied the circle of branches. "No. A snare. There is, underneath, a trap?"

Aidan stood up, looking down on his rowan branch ring. "The eagle's nest is a trap for the hare," he said. "Is it not?" Then he smiled and lifted a piece of tattered rope from the sand. "And, see, Lord Yesu's mice line their nest with my fishing net. So, a nest is a snare, and a snare is a nest." He stood again and said suddenly, "What do you see, Gil?"

"Me?" Gil looked down at the branches on the sand. "A circle?" he said, feeling really stupid.

"Very good," said Aidan. "Find me another. Find me a circle."

Gil looked around. It seemed an easy request until he thought about it. He stared out over the flat sea, the straight horizon, the open curve of white sand. Did nature make circles? The Indian Kettle, he thought suddenly. Water could make circles. He ran to the sea's edge and picked among the pebbles washed by the little waves, and found a white shell with a circular hole worn into its ribbed curve.

"Here!" he cried. He held it up for Aidan to see.

"Very good!" Aidan said, again, taking the shell in his hand, as if it were some rare treasure. "And now," his eyes crinkled at Gil's mystified stare, "Another?"

Gil looked around blankly, finding nothing. But Aidan had built his circle. He scooped up a handful of wet pebbles and quickly arranged them in a ring. Then he raised his eyes to the cluster of stone cells in which they lived. "And there's a bunch of circles! There, there, and there...." He strode up the beach, eagerly hunting more. Behind him he heard Aidan laughing.

"It's like an Easter egg hunt!" Danni exclaimed. She joined in and they chased each other in and out of the longhouse, the scriptorium, the cells and the church. When they'd used up all the easy circles, like the circle on the altar cross, and the rim of the black cooking pot, they got more inventive.

Ismail took a scrap of vellum from the scriptorium and caught the sun shining through the yellow leaves of the apple tree and a whole cluster of sun circles appeared. Then Danni tied a long rope to Frosti's bridle and set him to cantering in a ring until a circle of beaten, muddy earth marked the field.

Gil tried for the Noble Cat, curled in a ball by the longhouse fire. But Danni and Rachel made a rule against live circles; though the fire itself, a circle of glowing peats, was allowed.

Still, the best were the simplest: a curled tuft of grass sparkling with dew, five feathers laid out in a ring, Rachel grinning through a perfect circle of her own luxuriant braid, Danni biting a round hole in her bannock, at lunch.

While they played, Aidan worked, tilling his garden with a curved piece of driftwood. When they found a particularly good circle, he looked up and watched and smiled. Sometimes, Gil felt he was watching, too. As if, even as he ran and played, a part of him stood back, like an older brother, too old for games.

He looked up. The others were standing in a row, down on the beach, beside Aidan. He had left his garden and instead of his driftwood foot-plough, he held his carved *bachall*. At his feet was the rowan branch ring.

"Come, Gil," he called. "The day is passing." Gil ran down onto the sand. Aidan studied him in silence. "The gift of the Pool," he said, "It is with you?"

Gil drew the leather pouch from within his tunic, secretly thanking Rachel for convincing him to keep it. Aidan touched it lightly. "Always have it with you. Always, always, always."

He reached out and took Gil's hand and led him to the rowan ring. "Stand within," he said and stepped back. Danni came forward, eagerly, to join him. Aidan caught her and held her back. "Just Gil."

Still holding her gently, he raised his *bachall* high and struck its curved head three times against the empty air as if knocking on an invisible door. A ringing clear sound echoed, three times, over the shore, the wind itself ringing like a bell. Aidan lowered the *bachall* to the ground.

"Three times I will do this," he said. "The three of the Holy Triune; and you will hear. Wherever you are, you will hear; be that beyond the farthest star."

Gil nodded and whispered, "Yes."

"And when you hear it—"

"I seek a circle," Gil whispered.

Aidan's smiled flashed, "Yes! At once, and without delay, seek a circle, and, through it, come."

Gil nodded, suddenly breathless with excitement, because at last he understood. He understood it all; not just the circle game, but the talisman as well. It was a key. Like Aidan's seeing stone. And the rowan ring was another door. Like the Indian Kettle and the Wandering Pool. He was going home.

"Remember, then," Aidan repeated. "The three of the Triune, then seek a circle, and come."

"I will," he nodded eagerly. "I'll come back. I promise."

"Very well," Aidan said with a little smile. Then he bowed his head and spoke so softly that his words seemed just an echo of the soft sea wind.

"Bless to me my sister,
Bless to me my brother.
Bless to me, O Changeless One,
My Change-Thing, my Other."

Aidan raised his eyes, and met Gil's again. "Now, you," he said. Gil nodded, breathed deeply and whispered the same words back. He held tight to the talisman and closed his eyes, eager to meet what he knew lay ahead. At once, he felt something tugging at him, softly and urgently, like the first breath of a rising wind. He braced himself for the fierce whirling power of the Underwater Bridge.

But it didn't come. Instead, he felt a lightening and loosening of each of his limbs, as if something had taken hold of them and now was pulling them, utterly painlessly, out of their sockets. Something squeezed his body, pulling and pummeling it like modelling clay, and he felt the first pang of fear. Then the Thing took hold in all its fearsome force. Gil's eyes snapped open.

He saw the world grow huge and alien, rising higher and higher above him. An eerie intensity came over all his senses. The wind tickled the sides of his face and he smelled a mass of scents: ponies, fish, smoke, hen feathers, birds flying...which smelled weirdly delicious. His vision sharpened. The distant roof of the longhouse revealed a prickly outline of heather twigs. Grass blades rustled like clashing swords.

Then his body was sucked into itself, shrinking down, as if the ground would swallow it. His spine bent so much it must surely break. Then part of it did break, coming free, waving loose into the air. And yet, through all of it, he felt no pain. But for the deepening horror on his friends' faces, he might not even have been afraid.

Rachel screamed, her voice rising to a crescendo of hysteria, until Aidan, watching Gil from higher and higher above, closed his palm over her mouth.

Fear enveloped Gil, and then immense fury; all of it directed upward at the remote smile of the grey-robed Ab. *Why did I trust you? You had my father's knife. You killed him, and now you're killing me.* His anger rose into his strangely supple throat; a deep growl rumbled within him, then exploded into a yowling hiss. Even Ismail shouted in horror, but Aidan only laughed.

Then, suddenly, something caught Gil's eye, a flicker of movement in the grass by the church. Instantly, nothing else mattered. He turned his head, narrowing his eyes, sharpening his vision even further. There it was, again. The Ab vanished from his consciousness. He raised one hand, in brief hesitation. Then his nose caught the musty, furry scent. He gathered himself onto his hips, swishing his free-flowing spine, and sprang.

Gil crossed the sand like an arrow and was into the grass. His hand came down on the furry thing and his stubby fingers, with their fierce, curling nails, closed on its narrow tail. He felt the tail snake through his finger pads, and vanish.

Disappointed, he drew in his nails and sat up straight. He glanced over his shoulder. They were watching, so he pretended he didn't care. It was just a game he played with Lord Yesu's mouse, was it not?

He raised his hand and began to wash, carefully licking his fingers clean. He looked down on his hand, as he did, and saw a fur-covered paw. A brief, stunned amazement gave way, at once, to a feeling of rightness. Of course, a paw. What else should complete his beautiful furry forearm?

He stretched his fingers out and chewed each splendid, white claw clean, then carefully licked every beige hair into place, right up to the first, rust-colored stripe. He admired the stripe, basking in the soothing comfort of washing. Then he sat back, wrapped the curving end of his spine around his toes, and yawned, contemplating a nap. But he heard a shout, then, and remembered the others.

"Where's Gil?" Rachel sobbed. "Where is he?"

Gil blinked. Girls could be stupid, but that was stupid even for a girl. He stood up and walked purposefully back to his friends. When he got near, he let his spine float upwards in a friendly curve.

Rachel shrieked, "Get it away from me!" She shrank back, clutching Danni's arm and trying to hide herself behind her friend.

Danni looked mystified. "It's just a cat," she said.

"Where's Gil?" Rachel cried, louder. "What has it done to Gil?"

Then Ismail, with a wondering smile, squatted down and looked eye to eye with Gil. He extended his brown hand, fearless as always. "It's not just a cat," he said clearly. "It *is* Gil."

Gil swished his tail-spine in a mental high-five, and, as it seemed the obvious thing to do, rubbed his head against Ismail's hand. Lazily, he stretched down low with his supple fore-arms extended, paused, came up, and stretched his legs, one by one, then proceeded walking toward Rachel and Danni with deliberately soft steps.

They both jumped back and shrieked, and behind him Aidan laughed with delight. Gil's anger towards the Ab had vanished, replaced by an overwhelming desire to be close to him. He stopped walking and looked backwards over his shoulder blades, which was surprisingly easy to do.

Aidan crouched down beside Ismail and laid his big hand over Gil's head, pressing down hard and flattening Gil's ears. Gil did the rubbing thing again and his delight in the sensation released an inner sound, a rumbling of happiness that vibrated his whole being.

"It's purring!" Danni cried. She let go of Rachel's hand and stepped cautiously closer. "Will it bite me?" she asked Aidan warily.

Gil's tail-spine began to swish. *Call me "it" again and I definitely will.* He sank down low and narrowed his eyes. But then a new scent joined the blur of smells all around him. He sprang up and stood, alert and wary, one paw raised and his tail-spine horizontal and still.

The scent came again, stronger. He flared his nostrils and flattened his ears. The sound of soft paw steps trembled the grass. Gil swiveled his head. A low growl rose in his throat. He felt every hair on his body prickle and rise, bristling upward from the back of his neck to the tip of his spine. And then the Noble Cat emerged from behind Aidan's beached fishing boat; huge and striped and magnificent. The scent of feline masculinity preceded him like heralds before a king.

With a yowl of despair, Gil leapt four feet in the air, scattering his stunned friends, and streaked for the longhouse roof. He didn't stop until he'd reached the summit of the smoking heather thatch. But then he turned, and his heart fell. The mighty beast was sauntering up the beach, huge green eyes fixed on Gil in his foolish sanctuary.

But then, with a clumsy rustle, Lord Yesu's mouse blundered to his rescue. The Noble Cat sprang sideways, all his attention focused on the movement in the grass. With two quick slaps of his savage paws, he flipped the mouse from its refuge. Squeaking, it met its end in a cavern of gleaming teeth. Gil heard the bones crunching in his rival's mouth and felt a flow of envious saliva in his own. He sniffed hungrily at the smell of fresh blood, and then, since the mouse was not going to be his, forgot it.

He sat down, regarding his new situation. It was nicely high and pleasantly warm, and the spot he had chosen had almost no smoke. If he had to be stuck on a roof, he could have done worse.

The thought of a nap returned. When he woke up, the problem might have vanished. He scratched aside a few stiff twigs, then turned around in a circle and curled himself up in a ball. Far below, he heard anxious voices shouting, but couldn't be bothered to uncurl. Wrapping his tail-spine over his nose, he purred a couple of contented rumbles, and went confidently to sleep.

When the knocking sound came, Gil tried to ignore it. But even with his head burrowed into his paws and his tail cinched in around them, he heard it. *You will hear it...beyond the farthest star.* Aidan! He snapped awake, from snug, furry ball to alert all fours in a second. The third knock was fading from his ears. *Come. Come at once. Find a circle, and come!*

Gil's fur rose all over and his tail stood straight up. He felt his back arch, involuntarily, in fear. A circle! Find a circle. It had been easy, before, but he hadn't been a cat before. Everything looked different now.

He ran down the ridge of the roof, nimbly balancing on the rough tufts of thatch, his head flicking left, right, ahead, down; searching, searching...and then, suddenly, it was there. Like a gift from heaven, a perfect, black circle, safe as a burrow, lay before him. Haunches coiled, tail swishing, he paused just a moment; then leapt joyfully into its smoky mouth. He was already falling, tumbling, head over paws, when he remembered the fire beneath the hole in the longhouse roof.

With a screech of horror, he fought to break his fall. His fore-claws caught in the huge sooty links of the pot chain, and he clenched himself to it in an instant, scrabbling with his powerful hind legs. The links were shrinking beneath his paws, and then his claws lost their hold, flattening back against his toes. But his paws were huge, the toes grown long and supple, wrapping themselves right around the chain. Then his foot clanged into the cooking pot, and with a frantic effort, he swung. Gil, chain, and pot cleared the fire, and sooty, safe, and human, he dropped to his feet on the solid floor.

The door was flung open, and Aidan burst in, followed by Ismail, Rachel and Danni. Wide-eyed and breathing hard, his three friends stared at him as if he had indeed come from the farthest star. Aidan came closer and brushed soot from Gil's sleeve. Then his eyes crinkled into a smile. "Very good. But, next time, choose your circle with a little more care."

Gil nodded soberly, looking back at the fire. "I will. He will." He paused; the magnitude of what he had just undergone rocking his very human brain. "Is he...is he me?"

"He is you. Had our Good Lord fashioned you other."

Ismail was next. The girls had forgotten their fear completely and were urging the African boy into the rowan ring, eager to see his transformation. Standing calmly in the circle of branches, he whispered along with Aidan,

"Bless to me my sister.
Bless to me my brother.
Bless to me, O Changeless One,
My Change-Thing, my Other."

Before Gil's eyes Ismail's body began to swell. His shoulders grew huge, his head expanded and lengthened. His back pitched forward as his arms shot downward, to the ground. His hands blackened, fingers melding, till just two remained, thickening further and encasing themselves in horny cleft shells. Hooves. Horrible images arose from dark stories, dimly remembered, as cleft hooves appeared on Ismail's feet as well.

The hoofed feet began to stamp. Ismail's head was covered in short, brown fur, his ears were tall and pointed, and, between them, two great horns suddenly sprouted. Gil heard a moan of fear from his own lips. Beside him, Rachel covered her eyes and Danni flinched and backed away. The horns on Ismail's head lengthened and branched and branched again sprouting glistening sharp points.

"The stag!" Rachel shouted. "The leaping stag!" And, as if to answer, the Ismail-Stag leapt gloriously from the rowan ring, his great rack of antlers raking the air. The stag pranced, turned, stared straight at them with eyes as black as Ismail's own. Then he made another mighty leap that took him nearly to the church, and galloped away scattering the sheep and ponies in his flight for the hills, and vanished beyond the ponies' field.

Then Aidan raised his *bachall* and knocked three times against the clear air, and the ringing sound echoed over Cille Aidan. Gil peered nervously at the skyline. Aidan stood silently. His eyes were also on the far hill, but his face was peaceful and untroubled. Suddenly, he smiled. He pointed up to the misty heavens. Feannag appeared, circling, and suddenly beneath his outstretched wings, the stag was there on the horizon, antlers silhouetted against the sky.

"Ismail!" Danni shouted. "Come! Come back! Find a circle and come!" She jumped up and down, waving. Aidan laid a quiet hand on her shoulder.

"He must come freely," he said quietly. "As must each one."

The stag trotted to the center of the pony field; then stopped, looking left and right, sniffing the air. He pawed with one hoof, then flung up his head and galloped across the field, one way, and then another, scattering the worried ponies. He looked afraid, and the idea of Ismail afraid was like a physical pain in Gil's chest.

"Can't we help him," he begged, looking up at Aidan. The

Ab shook his head, not taking his eyes from the stag. Then suddenly it leapt one huge bound that sent Lionheart into a fearful gallop of his own.

The stag landed, reared up on hind legs, and then shrank down, drawing inwards, his antlers fading, translucent as the misty sky, his fore-legs shortening, hooves flowering into two brown hands. He raised his head and Ismail's white smile flashed as he bounded on fleet, but human, legs, down to the beach.

Gil greeted him with a joyful high-five.

Ismail turned to Aidan, and said, "Thank you," in a soft voice. Aidan nodded acknowledgement, his eyes warm.

"But where was the circle?" Danni looked back at the field, where the ponies were still prancing around in leftover excitement. "How did you come back without a circle?"

Ismail laughed. "Mushrooms!" he said. "They grow in big circle. I know I see them in the pony field," Ismail said. He mimed his frantic search, "But where are they?" He grinned, looking down at his hands, his body, his legs, then reached up to touch his head as if he might yet find antlers there. "He is inside me, still," he tapped his chest. "I have him always?"

Aidan nodded gravely. "As long," he said, "As this is with you." He touched his hand against his own throat, at the place where Ismail wore his leather necklace.

Aidan called Rachel into the ring. Danni's face fell. Danni, who had been here longest, and had learned the most, and was three times as brave as Gil, was left to be last. It seemed unfair, and yet Gil was certain that if Aidan had a favorite among them, it was Danni. He caught her eye and shrugged in solidarity and she grinned bravely back.

Rachel stood in the center of the rowan ring. She bowed her head, her long braid falling forward over one shoulder, tense, but happy, as Aidan began the blessing. It was easier now, for all of them, but when it happened, it took Gil's breath away.

Rachel's arms, folded across her chest, fuzzed over with white down. Then soft grey feathers covered the down, then longer feathers, deeper grey. She opened her arms and they had become wings. Half girl and half bird, she stood before him, like an angel. But when she turned her face to his, it was the hook-billed face of a hawk.

She shrank down, dwindling as if she would vanish. The hawk's head flicked sideways, lightning fast, and a glittering eye met Gil's. With a rustle of wings, she sprang from the rowan ring, into the sky.

Gil's stomach lurched, as from a night of ale horns, as Rachel's Sparrow Hawk mounted higher and higher into the dizzying air. He shaded his eyes as she spiraled upward. Another dark bird shape appeared, circling around her.

"It's Feannag," Danni said. "Hawks don't eat crows, do they?" she asked worriedly.

Aidan laughed and shook his head. "Nor crows, hawks." There was a brief flutter of wings and a few irate squawks, high above. Two feathers floated down as the two birds soared off, north and south. "Nor," said Aidan, "Do they choose to share. But watch," he said. The hawk had resumed her circling, above them; then suddenly plummeted from the sky, wings folded tight.

"She's falling," Gil cried.

"Stooping," Aidan corrected. "She's seen her dinner." He pointed to a tiny, chirping bird innocently fluttering above the turf roof of the church. The Rachel-Hawk swooped after it, darting low over the turf, fierce talons outstretched.

Danni covered her eyes. "Tell me when it's over."

"It's okay," Gil breathed. "She missed." He thought of his mouse and how he'd envied the Noble Cat the taste of fresh blood. The ale horn feeling returned and he covered his mouth and gulped. "Are we going to eat like that?" he winced.

"Yes," Ismail said quietly. "And we will not go hungry."

Then Gil suddenly understood the weapon within Cille Aidan's blessing. All the swordplay and archery and jousting in the world could not change the simple fact that they were children, sent to challenge warriors whom even mighty Palamedes had cause to fear.

But now, they were more. More than children, more even than grown men and women. More than any but Shony and her selkie son. They were Others. Change-Things. They could run and fly; shelter and hide. They could vanish and change, disappear and reappear, pass at will in and out of the world of ordinary men.

What forest should a stag fear? What castle walls stymie a hawk? What dungeon would be closed to a cat? For the first time Gil really believed they could defeat the Golden Knight. He grinned at Ismail and Ismail grinned back, his eyes reflecting the same revelation.

Aidan leaned on the curved handle of the *bachall*, watching the soaring hawk, calm and confident. When he raised it and knocked three times against the ringing air, the distant hawk responded in a flash, plummeting out of the sky, straight for Cille Aidan. Swooping low over the church roof, she whisked above their heads and then flew to the cluster of stone buildings, found an open window and with one quick flutter of grey wings, vanished into her own circular cell.

Moments later, the door was flung open, and Rachel, face flushed with joy, stumbled out to greet them. "I flew!" she cried. "I flew! I flew!" She held out her arms as if they were yet wings. "Aidan!" she cried. "Let me go again! One more time. Please. Please!"

They all laughed and Gil thought Aidan would laugh, too, but instead he was suddenly solemn. "This is not play," he said. He sounded sterner than ever before. Rachel looked crestfallen.

"I'm sorry," she said politely. "It's just that it felt so wonderful...."

"We do not live for feelings," he answered. Then he raised his grey cowl and turned his back, and walked away to the strand. The children trailed after, uncertainly. He prodded the rowan ring with the tip of the *bachall*, as if considering its destruction.

"Aidan?" Danni asked fearfully. "Can I go now?" He didn't answer.

Rachel said, "I'm sorry, Aidan. I didn't understand. Please let Danni go."

"Danni didn't do anything wrong," Gil said.

Aidan turned to him. "And you are her friend and you want what is right for her?"

Puzzled, Gil shrugged and said, "Of course."

"And what if what is right for her is to remain safely here, bound in bonds of love?"

"It's not love if it won't let her be free," Gil answered stubbornly.

Aidan smiled, "Oh, Gil. When you've lived as long as I have, come back and tell me what is love." Then he shook the hood back from his head and raised his *bachall*. "Come," he said gently to Danni. "You will fly, too."

Danni leapt into the circle, her eyes fixed on Aidan as if she feared he would yet change his mind. She clutched the leather necklace with both hands and closed her eyes. Softly, she whispered the blessing after Aidan. Then her eyes opened and met Gil's and for one instant she looked utterly terrified.

Gil reached out to her, but it was too late. The hand she stretched out to his was feathered, already, the arm transformed into a wing. He shook his head and whispered "I'm sorry," as Danni shrank before him. Her slender neck grew longer and more slender. Her mouth expanded into a huge and comical grin. She swayed her neck left and right, ruffled her feathers, and ducked her head. When she raised it, again, it was the head of a yellow-billed bird.

It was not a small bird, like Rachel's fierce and graceful sparrow hawk, but a solid, grey-feathered chunky creature with webbed yellow feet; the grey goose whose feather she wore. It looked up at Gil with one dark eye, turned its head, and surveyed him with the other. Then it opened its bill and made a loud, croaking cry that was both endearing and comical.

Ismail smiled and Rachel giggled. Gil tilted his head and studied the creature. It seemed wrong somehow for lithe, slender Danni; a timid, clumsy beast that waddled to the edge of the rowan ring as if flying hadn't crossed its mind. But then suddenly, it spread its wings. They were long and powerful, the feathers reaching for the air.

"Let her go," Ismail said, as the goose came toward them, neck outstretched. They all scattered and the bird took three running strides, flapped her great wings, and with one loud cry, mounted the air. Her flappy yellow feet tucked in neatly beneath her, her long neck stretched like an arrow, and her great, ringing wing beats carried her higher and higher. With one magnificent circle over their heads, she set out over the sea, as if she would fly forever.

Gil watched and knew at once what Aidan had feared. "Call her back!" he cried. "She's going too far!"

Aidan shook his head. "She has not even stretched her wings." He stood, resolute, his *bachall* resting on the sand. A distant vee of flying birds passed over, wings beating in rhythm with their faint, faraway cries. Wild geese, flying south.

"Aidan, look...." Gil began, but Aidan had already seen them, and so had Feannag. With a mighty caw, the grey and black crow sprang into the air and flew up, straight and fast, toward Danni. Aidan raised his *bachall* high and struck three times against the air. The paths of the lone goose and the noisy vee-flock grew closer and closer.

The Danni-Goose faltered, her wing beats briefly slowing, but they renewed then, stronger and more certain. Even when Feannag flew round and round her in cawing circles, she held her course. "She didn't hear you!" Gil cried. "Do it again!"

"She heard." Aidan did not move. A space had opened in one side of the vee, as if the wild strangers were welcoming Danni in. "She must come freely. As must you all." His voice was very calm, but his eyes, fixed on Danni, were filled with anguish.

I will raise my bachall and call...but you will fly from me. Gil remembered the eerie prophecy that had frightened Danni months before.

"Do something!" he shouted. He flung himself at the Ab, pummeling him with his fists. "Don't tell me you can't. You're the magician. You make these things happen. Do something!"

Aidan absorbed his punches as if they were nothing, then wrapped his arm around Gil and held him gently, still looking up the while. Then suddenly he smiled. "Look, Gil."

Danni was still flying, almost parallel to the vee of wild geese, their course set southerly, over the sea. Feannag, a black dot high above, circled and cawed. But then, slowly, Danni's flight veered and curved inland, east, and then north, and turned homeward to Cille Aidan.

Gil buried his face in Aidan's tattered robes, his anger lost in relief. Danni flew nearer and nearer, great wings beating effortlessly, until they could see the flashes of white on her body and tail. Happiness sparkled from her grey feathers, the long, glorious glides between wing beats; the still comical honking beak. She swept over them, soaring above the field. Extending her bright, silly feet, she swooped playfully down over Frosti's head.

"My mushrooms!" Ismail cried. With a solid thud, Danni landed within the unseen ring. Bowing her long neck and folding her wings, she sank down to the ground and then rose up, graceful and laughing and human.

She trotted toward them, pushing the curious ponies aside. But then she stopped and stared toward the Wood of White Trees. A rider cantered from their shelter, his yellow hair flying. A roll of brilliant red cloth fluttered across the withers of his snorting hill pony like the trappings of a charger. Holding the wild-eyed beast with one firm hand, he rode toward them, blithely unaware of the extraordinary thing that had just happened on the shore of Cille Aidan.

"Floki!" Danni cried, "You won't believe...."

With a frantic glance at Aidan, Gil willed her to silence, but Floki wasn't listening anyhow. He brought the nervous pony to a skidding halt in the sand, leapt down, and swept the fluttering burden from its back. "Plunder for a winter sailing," he proclaimed, and shaking out the heavy cloth, revealed two fur-lined cloaks, one red, one green, rolled within each other.

He bowed before Rachel, presenting her with the green cloak, and then, with his own hands, draped the red one around Danni's shoulders, raising the fur-lined hood over her head and linking the silver clasp at her throat. He stepped back. "No queen would suit it better," he said with a little smile.

Danni's eyes widened. She paraded an awed few steps along the sand, swirling the supple fur around herself. "Was it really a queen's?" she cried. "Did you win it in a battle?"

He grinned. "Shall I show you my scars?"

"You really fought for it?" she gasped.

He shrugged innocently. "No. I bargained for it, meek as a merchant, with a trader in Norway." He grinned again and brushed her chin with his fingers, turning her face up to him. "Would you like it better, little Viking, if it were stained with blood?"

Danni looked briefly shocked and shook her head. Floki turned away and said softly, "Good. Blood enough was spilled for the silver that bought it." He laughed, then, and turned to Rachel. "This one, at least, does not demand swordplay."

Danni didn't hear him. Her eyes flicked to the sand beach and suddenly she flung off the cloak, thrust it into Gil's arms, and ran to the rowan ring.

"Danni!" Gil cried. "No!"

She looked up from the circle of branches and shouted, "Floki! Floki! Look at me!" She closed her eyes to say the blessing. Aidan turned and saw her then, but it was too late. Her Other self was upon her and her wings were reaching for the sky.

She soared up, out over the sea, climbing until she was but a wavering speck. Then she circled and came gliding back, sinking lower and lower, until she swept once more over their heads. Laughing, Floki leapt for her, as if he would pluck her out of the sky. His face was alight with enchantment and as she soared away again, his eyes fell on Aidan.

"You?" he whispered.

Aidan shook his head. He raised his *bachall*, as he had done to call each of them home and struck it against the sky. All heard, but Danni kept flying as if she had loosed every tie to the earth. When at last she turned back to them, it was so clearly only to please herself that Gil felt an eerie chill.

"The field!" Rachel pointed and waved. But Danni had found her circle. Straight and true, she plunged toward it, where it lay yet before Cille Aidan's church; the perfect shining circle of the Wandering Pool.

"No!" Aidan shouted. A look of horror crossed his face and was mirrored on Floki's. Grasping the *bachall*, Aidan pushed through the watching children and ran up the beach. Floki reached the grass slope before him, but not before Danni. Fast as they ran, they could not outrun her flight. Aidan turned at the last moment, raised the *bachall* high, and stretched out his other hand.

"No, lass! No!" Floki leapt for her with all his young strength.

But she soared over his head and then down, feet outstretched, tail feathers splayed, broad wings braking against the air. She hit the silken water with a joyful splash, soaking them in spray, and then, as softly as a feather floating from heaven, she slipped beneath the surface and vanished from their sight. Floki plunged into the pool an instant after, and stood in shocked defeat, the water splashing innocently about his knees and his crossed arms clasping empty air.

CHAPTER THIRTEEN

Gil crouched, alone, in the black morning beside the Wandering Pool. The sun was still not up and the damp sea mist wrapped everything in silence. He peered into the silken waters, willing them to release Danni back into their world. Aidan rang the morning bell and as the notes died away, walked to the pool's edge and knelt beside Gil. "She will return no sooner for you shivering in the cold."

"Why did you listen to me?" Gil whispered. "Why did you let her go?"

"Because you were right." Aidan stood, and leaning down, pulled Gil to his feet as well. "Come."

Rachel and Ismail were waiting already inside the church. Gil joined them, listlessly mouthing the responses. When Aidan closed his book, Gil looked up into his eyes and said, "She's been gone a whole month."

Aidan smiled gently. "The blinking of an eye." He laid the book aside and stood up. Untying the worn rope belt of his habit, he held it by one knotted, frayed end, crouched down, and flicked the rope twice, extending its length across the stone floor. The Noble Cat jumped up and crouched, too, its narrowed eyes on the twitching rope end. Something stirred, deep down, in Gil, tugging his attention to the same frayed fibers.

"This is the Bridge," Aidan said. "I hold fast my end, and the other moves." He pointed to the frayed knot worried by the playful cat. Then he dropped his end of the rope. The Noble Cat rolled over, taking the knot with it. Aidan's end of the rope slid back and forth across the stone. "Here," he said, "Is the Wandering Pool. There, in Tir nan Og, is the place through which you came."

Gil wrenched his mind from the fascinating twitching of the rope. "Africa. America. England. She could be anywhere."

"No," Aidan answered. "Not anywhere. The rope moves, but only so far." He caught up his end, and wrestled the other from the claws of the clinging cat. "Here, there," he flicked the rope back and forth, "But not there, or there," he pointed to the altar and to the window. "It is bounded by gates, but they are far apart."

"It moves much further in Tir nan Og," Ismail said. "Here, it is never farther than a thousand paces from the Great Stones."

"But here," said Aidan, "It moves through time."

"So, time passes faster here," Gil said, suddenly understanding. "I went through the Indian Kettle, like, that far behind Danni," he held up his two hands, palms almost touching, "but weeks passed for her, here, before I got here. And the second time, it was a day, there, and here it was months and months."

"It does not match," Ismail said. "A few seconds was weeks? Then a day should have been years. Many, many years."

"You said your father was gone a year," Rachel added. But it's just twenty years since Magnus found the knife. Ismail's right. It doesn't work."

Aidan bent to retrieve his belt from the playful cat. Tying it again around his waist, he went to the first niche in the stone wall and took down the jewel-encrusted gold cup. He carried it to the reading lamp, and beckoned them to his side.

Raising the cup, he turned it slowly. One clear crystal in the stem of the cup captured the lamplight. A blood-red shimmering band appeared on the floor.

"Watch," said Aidan. He turned the cup, realigning the crystal. The band of light on the floor broadened, turned from red to orange, then yellow, sparkling at the edges with points of blue and green. Aidan turned the cup again and the light band narrowed, thinner and thinner, till nothing remained but an intense ruddy point. He spun the cup and the light spread out a whole rainbow on the floor.

"Oh!" Rachel gasped. She stepped forward and reached out her hands. Aidan handed her the cup, smiled, and stepped back. Rachel moved to the altar and held the cup up beside one of the two wax candles burning there. The candlelight pierced the crystal and a new rainbow formed on the floor. She moved the cup back and forth, broadening and narrowing the band.

"The jewel," she said, "Is the pool. The light is time. When the pool moves, time bends. It gets broader or narrower. Look!" She turned the jeweled cup until only a point of light remained, like a drop of gold on the floor. "An hour, a day," she began turning the cup, "A week, a month," the light spread out, spilling across the floor. "Years."

"But she didn't have the key," said Gil, "The white stone that Feannag brought. It's the key, isn't it?"

"It is indeed a key," Aidan said. "But, if that were all, anyone who possessed it could cross at any time. All who sought power or plunder would make use of it. It would be a causeway for evil."

Aidan turned the jeweled cup onto its side and held it out with the rim facing Gil. Running his forefinger around the golden lip, he said, "Here is Our Lord's year; ploughing, planting, harvest and fallow." With each word he touched one of the four jewels, red, green, purple, and white, set at quarter points around the rim.

Aidan returned his fingers to the white jewel. "Here, in the Dark Time, when night is strongest; at the Feast of the Nativity, the Bridge lies open."

He turned the cup in his hand and rested his fingers on the red jewel. "And here, in the Light Time, when the day is longest, at the Feast of the Holy Baptist, so, too, all may cross."

Aidan spun the cup a quarter turn and rested his fingers on the green jewel and the purple. "When Light and Dark are equal, at Lady Day in Lentron, and at Saint Matthew's Mass, then, too, a man may cross."

"And only then?" Gil cried. "Four times a year? Just four days?"

"Three days at each Crossing Time. Twelve days each year."

Gil reached for the cup and Aidan gave it willingly. Gil held it, turning it, studying the jewels and the silver banding. "But it wasn't any of those days, and Danni crossed anyhow."

"But not as herself, Gil," Aidan took the cup from Gil's hands. "Only as her animal Other. There is no guard set for animals. Animals can do no evil in any world. She crossed in her animal form and so, too, she must remain, until she returns, for Change-Things are gone from that world. None can change there any longer."

"She'll never be human…just a bird forever? But that's awful," Rachel cried.

"Is it?" Aidan smiled. "Do we alone rejoice in our Lord's creation? Does not even a sparrow delight in his life? And, if the sparrow, then what of the cat? Or the stag? Or the hawk or the wild goose, high in the Northern skies? What of the grey seal, at home in the grey seas?"

Rachel nodded solemnly. "This is why you were angry with me, when I wanted to be hawk again. It's not that we won't be able to come back, but that we won't want to."

"Being Other brings great power, but also, great danger," Aidan said. "Each time you change, it will be harder. The longer you stay, the less you will wish to return."

"But, if animals and birds can always cross," Rachel said, "You can send Feannag to bring Danni back!"

Aidan shook his head. Gil gave a weary shrug. "I know," he murmured bitterly. "You can't send what's not your servant."

Aidan rose, and restored the cup to its niche in the stone wall. He turned and faced them, arms folded, hands tucked within the sleeves of his robe. "Gil, Gil," he said. "How angry you are that I cannot control the world. But I cannot. I am not a magician. There is no magic. Only the Lord's beautiful world, full of wonders. 'Things that no eye has seen, no ear has heard. Things beyond the mind of man.'"

He stepped away from the altar, bowing once. "She must come freely," he said. A sudden whinnying and a thud of hoof beats broke the dawn silence. "Ah, the Angel Erling." Aidan smiled. "Bearing tidings of little joy."

Each day since Danni vanished, Erling had ridden from Einar's Holm for news of her and ridden reluctantly back with none. Saint Martin's Mass was long passed. The cold days dwindled, until the sun barely scraped above the horizon before falling beneath it again. The Northmen, eager for the sea and wary of winter gales, drank ale and argued. But the longships rested yet on the winter strand. Danni had not returned and Floki would not sail without her.

Outside the church, Erling hunched on the bare back of a shaggy grey pony. His fur cloak was wrapped close and his cheeks were red with cold. "She is come?" he asked, as always, his blue eyes briefly hopeful. When Aidan shook his head, he shrugged resignedly and dismounted, handing the pony's reins to Gil.

Gil released the beast into the field behind the church and returned to the longhouse. Erling was seated beside the fire, awaiting breakfast and looking happy to be away from Einar's Holm. "There is no peace in that house, day or night," he said wearily.

"When wolves fight, wolf cubs squabble," said Aidan.

Erling laughed. "Well spoken, good father. Indeed, a dark wolf and a fair wolf growl across Redbeard's fire!" His laughter faded. "The seal-wife begs you come and make peace, before growls are forsaken for swords between her son and her fosterling."

Aidan stared into his own fire for a long while. When he looked up, his face was grave. "Bid them come here," he said, "To Our Lord's sanctuary, to make this peace."

Late that afternoon, seven riders appeared from the Wood of White Trees and descended to the longhouse door. At the front was Shony, her beautiful face solemn. Behind rode Magnus on a big, black hill pony, his son and his nephew on either side. Each of the young Northmen was joined by his longship helmsman; Erling riding behind Floki, and Thorbjorn, a grey-bearded man who rarely spoke, shadowing Hakon.

Magnus' fiery features blazed with annoyance. Hakon looked quietly angry, the two helmsmen wary. The Saracen knight, Palamedes, shepherding them all from the rear, seemed gently perplexed. Only Floki appeared untroubled, and even smiled at Rachel in her new fur cloak.

Magnus' eyes swept past Gil, Rachel, and Ismail with ill-humor. "Aidan!" he roared. "We are here in your holy sanctuary!"

Aidan appeared from the church, then, and in no great hurry crossed to the gathering by the longhouse door. He touched Gil's shoulder as he passed and said, "See to the ponies and then go to your cells and remain there."

"But the meeting's about us," Gil protested. "And Danni...."

"It is about things beyond you and beyond your control. I will call you when a decision is made."

Gil stared after as the door closed behind the last of the Northmen. Then he collected pony reins in a messy clump and stamped angrily to the field. "He treats us like little kids," he grumbled, shoving the last equine rump through the wicker gate, and tossing his cluster of bridles on the ground.

Ismail picked them up and said, "Perhaps because you act like one?" Gil balled his hand into a fist.

"Oh, great," Rachel said wearily. "Big boys fighting in the longhouse and little boys fighting out here. Holy Cille Aidan." Gil glared at her, and then, in spite of himself, he laughed.

"Okay. Guilty. But we should know what's going on. It is about us. And Danni. He stared sullenly at the longhouse. "We could listen at the door."

"Oh, that will look grown up when they catch us," Rachel said.

Gil looked again at the building under its wreath of smoke. Then a slow, wary grin crossed his face. "No," he said, "Not the door. The roof."

Ismail scratched his head. "Roof very thin. They hear us."

"They won't hear me," Gil whispered, and triumphantly he ran for the beach and the remnants of the rowan ring. The tide was lapping at its edge when he reached it. He heard Rachel and Ismail shouting in dismay as he leapt within. He rested trembling fingers on the leather necklace, shutting out their voices, concentrating. His throat felt dry and his voice croaked when he spoke aloud:

Bless to me my sister,
Bless to me my brother...

Aidan's stern warning echoed in his mind: *This is not play.*

But it was too late. Already, the stretching and shrinking and pummeling of his body had begun. His spine bowed and his hands dropped to the ground, furred and clawed. His tail whipped free, swishing excitedly in the cold air.

Scents and sounds overwhelmed him, rich and raw. The world was alive with rustlings and chirps, snorts and snuffles, and spiced with living smells. Mouse, bird, earth, grass, fish, moth, pony, sheep. Sensation trembled at the sides of his face, rushing in from the tips of his whiskers.

Behind him the sea splashed and gurgled on the shore, pungent with salt and seaweed. He heard each pebble turn beneath a receding wave, then turn again as the water rolled back in. The rowan branches crackled, as the next wave broke right below them, splashing Gil with spray.

Each hair on his back recoiled in disgust. Gathering his powerful hind legs beneath him, he leapt over the branches to the dry refuge of the beach. Immediately, he sat down and carefully licked each droplet from his beautiful fur until every hair was dry. Then he stood and stretched, head down, then head up, reaching out one hind leg and then the other. Then he sat down again.

Ismail and Rachel waved and pointed at the longhouse, but he ignored them. There was nothing chasing him, and nothing he was chasing, so why should he run? He stood up again and walked with soft, quiet steps past the church.

At the bell frame, he halted, his fur rising. A fierce smell of cat clung possessively to its wooden leg. He sniffed, his nose twitching, then opened his mouth and drew in more air. A low growl rose in his throat. With stiff, slow steps he made a wide arc around the offending wood and approached the longhouse.

At the door, he stretched and sat down to think things over. His nose did a lot of the thinking. *Smoke. Fire. Warm. Good.* But also, *mouse, bird-asleep, old fish-bones. Interesting.* Then another, sharper smell raised his fur and flattened his ears in alarm. Cat. Big, fierce, and near. He heard a growl from the shadows beside the scriptorium and he streaked for the longhouse roof.

He gained the smoking thatch with a battle raging between his human mind—*Look! What does it take to get you to understand?*

He can climb!—and his cat mind—*It worked last time.* But his cat mind seemed to be right. Neither growl nor scent had followed him, and he scrambled to the height of the ridge unmolested, and paused.

Hearing angry voices through the thatch, he trotted down the ridge to where they were loudest. Then he crouched down again at the edge of the smoke hole, wrinkling his nose at the stinging blue haze. Argument rose to his ears, hot as the smoke.

He wormed closer, peering down with slitted eyes, claws clinging to the rough heather thatch. He glimpsed Magnus' red head and beard and the huge, velvet-clad shoulder of Palamedes. Hakon and Floki were seated on opposite sides of the fire, with Shony watching closely. In the shadows, the two helmsmen huddled uneasily, half hidden by Aidan's cooking pot. Aidan himself sat at the end of one bench, with one of his little four-horned sheep on either side.

"Who brings complaint?" he asked mildly.

"I bring complaint," Hakon pointed across the fire. "Against my foster-brother who breaks his pledge." There was a flurry of movement below, and Gil's ears flattened as Floki lunged forward. Magnus' big arm shot out, blocking him.

"Hakon Sea-Friend will speak," Aidan said calmly.

Hakon rose to his feet. Gil's fore-claws twitched as the Northman's black head bobbed to and fro, three paws lengths below. "All here know my circumstance," Hakon said quietly. "I pledge to sail to Ireland upon Saint Martin's Mass, and bear four warriors to Hy along the way. But Saint Martin's Mass passes with the last full moon. This night, the moon is full again. Tomorrow brings Lady Day in Fallow. The good father makes his winter fast! And yet we do not sail!"

He looked aggrievedly around. "My oarsmen are promised trading in Dublin. Tools and seeds for the spring ploughing and planting."

"And silver for the spring courting," said Floki from across the fire. "It is raiding, not trading, on your mind, Sea-Friend." Floki folded his arms and met his cousin's eyes. "I pledge to bear four warriors to Hy. No more. No less. I sail when the lass returns." Hakon looked to Aidan, shrugged despairingly, and sat down.

"No one returns from Freya's Pool," said Magnus grimly. He, too, looked to Aidan. "You play like a child with things beyond your kenning," he said. "The pool and the stones are older than your god."

"Then they are very old indeed, Magnus," said Aidan. He turned to Floki, but Thorbjorn, Hakon's grey-bearded helmsman suddenly laughed.

"Grandmother's tales. The girl is some Viking plunderer's prize. She is in Norway. Where slave masters are harsh and husbands harsher." He laughed again at Magnus's black glower.

"The girl is in no man's thrall," said Aidan.

Magnus turned on him, his face darkening further. "If you know that, you know where she is. So read the runes, or the stars, or that witches' stone, and bring her back and end this strife!"

"I end it," Hakon said. He stood up again and set his gaze on Floki. "I sail tomorrow. South, with you, to Hy, or north again to Shetland. It is your choice." He sat down and also folded his arms.

Floki smiled. "How generously you break your promise, Sea-Friend."

Hakon's dark eyes smoldered. "Let this company judge who has kept his pledge and who has not."

Floki grinned in reply but Magnus cut in sharply. "Clever words do not make wisdom," he growled at Floki. "Nor do you sail a longship alone. Your oarsmen expect reward as much as Hakon's, and care as little who you wish to bed. However prettily you tell the tale."

Hakon laughed aloud. Floki was on his feet in an instant, lunging across the fire. Hakon leapt up, reaching for his sword. Magnus barged between them, flinging out both huge arms, and shoved each roughly back onto his seat. "You bring this mockery on yourself," he muttered to his son, "as if you could not find another woman."

The knight Palamedes shook his head sadly and looked up from his place directly below Gil. "Might I speak, good father?"

Aidan nodded and the knight rose and bowed respectfully

to Floki. "The girl is a grievous loss to all and all desire her swift return. But the fate of others rests now on the remaining three. And they do have great virtue. The young Saracen is the equal of men. And the boy, Gil, shows much promise."

"The lass is worth three of him," Floki said. "She has the courage, the daring." He waved a dismissive hand, "He is timid."

"Obedience is also a virtue," said Aidan. "Even in a warrior."

Floki laughed, "Then I leave him with you, good father, obedient in holy vows!"

A growl rose in Gil's throat. His tail swished harder and his toes tingled at the thought of sinking claws into Floki's arrogant blond head. Then he heard another growl, as loud as if it, too, arose in his own throat, but it came from the darkness behind him. He sprang sideways, twisting his head around, his body low, forepaws flattened against the thatch. A furry weight thudded onto his back. The Noble Cat's teeth sank into the loose skin at the nape of his neck and two powerful paws pinned his shoulders and forelegs.

Instinct clamored in his feline brain: *Give up. Run!* But his prideful human self rebelled against defeat. So he fought on, scrabbling with his hind legs, twisting and snarling, till his enraged adversary lost patience and sunk his teeth in hard.

With a hopeless kitten wail and the strength of desperation, Gil wrenched himself free and leapt into the only empty space in sight: the smoke-hole of the longhouse roof.

Instantly, he was falling. His Cat-self twisted mid-air, claws seeking the black pot chain. But already claws were nails and paws were hands. Then his hands lost their grip, and, boy-heavy, he hurtled downward toward the fire. Eyes squeezed shut, he braced for the flames, but, with an enormous thud, collided with something hairy and soft, instead.

"Begone!" roared the hairy thing. Great hands clutched Gil's body and hurled it sideways. He crashed to the floor, scattering onlookers left and right. Bruised and stunned, he opened his eyes. Above him loomed the face of the great knight, Palamedes, his black eyes flashing something akin to fear.

"Tis a demon!" he cried, and drawing his sword, raised

it high above Gil's head. "Back to the Hell from whence you came!"

Gil flung futile hands before his face. Then the door burst open on a blast of cold air. A flash of color passed between him and the sword, deep green and flaming red, as Rachel, long hair flying loose, flung herself between his body and the Saracen. Ismail ran past her shouting, "No, Sir Palamedes! Is not demon! Is Gil!"

Gil struggled up, half sitting. The still-wary Palamedes lowered his mighty sword. "It's just me," croaked Gil.

"Welcome, obedient warrior," said Floki with a cheerful grin.

A mutter of astonishment swept the room, growing louder and more animated.

"Do I behold a Change-Thing?" Palamedes whispered. The knight's black eyes bored into Gil's; then turned quickly to Aidan, sitting quietly by the fire. Aidan nodded gently.

Extending a suddenly tentative hand, Palamedes gently touched Gil's shoulder. "That such wonders should befall me and such companions be mine!"

Behind him, Erling and grey-bearded Thorbjorn stared in awe. Palamedes raised his eyes to Ismail and Rachel. "They, too?" he whispered. Gil nodded.

"Let the Golden Knight beware!" Palamedes proclaimed. "One Change-Thing is worth an army of Self-Bound men! But three! Or," he paused wonderingly, "Four?"

But Hakon looked from Gil to Floki. "You do not tell me this," he said gravely.

Floki shrugged, "I spare your fears. Whether she crosses Freya's Pool on her two brown feet, or the wings of the grey goose, she is still in Tir nan Og, as I say."

Hakon regarded him coldly. "I have no fear of Change-Things. I know one well. One foot in each world, and no head in either. So, this is your gift, cousin?"

Floki laughed delightedly and shook his head, "I would give her sleek fins to swim with me to the skerries." Then he nodded to the Ab, sitting by the fire. "Who gives this gift, Aidan?"

Aidan acknowledged the Northman with courtesy. "The

Giver of all gifts," he answered, stroking one of the sheep.

"To Whom be all honor," Floki said quietly. "But are you not, gentle Ab, His servant?"

Aidan nodded solemnly. "A servant whose only treasure is his Master."

Floki laughed. "Humility is a graceful mask, Mo'Aidan."

Aidan rubbed the horned forehead of the little sheep as if it was all that interested him. "I have no mask," he said, "nor any sorcery. I gave only a blessing." He rose to his feet, looking eye to eye with the young Northman. "You read the world in the mirror of your own soul, Floki Magnusson. It shows you little truth."

Magnus let out a gleeful rumble of laughter. He gave Floki a friendly punch. "Do not cross words with the Ab, my golden-tongued son. He is better armed." Gil smiled uncertainly, as Floki ducked his blond head in response. Then suddenly there was a flash of movement and Floki's shining blade was in his hand.

"I read the world in the mirror of a Northman's sword, Mo'Aidan. And one day, for all your wisdom, you will do the same."

An unearthly screech echoed above them. Gil's eyes flew to the rafters. The Noble Cat sprang through the smoke-hole onto a sooty beam, then soared over the sparking fire, and landed beside the Ab. With a rasping caw, Feannag swept out of the darkness and took his place at Aidan's other side.

Floki's voice rose above the tumult of surprised cries, "And on that day," he continued, "no man, no woman, nor any Change-Thing, will save you!"

"Silence!" Magnus roared, and Shony threw herself between her son and Aidan.

Then, quiet Hakon rose to his feet and put a firm hand on Floki's arm. "Save your threats for warriors, cousin. This is a holy man and we are in a holy place." Angry muttering swept the room, affirming his words.

Floki's eyes followed the sound, surveying the ring of fierce faces. He looked confused. "I do not threaten," he muttered.

Hakon smiled wryly. "You speak such words in affection, then?"

"They were not my words," Floki whispered. "They came to my tongue, but they were not mine." Hakon waved him away, but Gil understood. They were words like Aidan's to Danni, of how she would fly from him; words of prophecy. A chill settled in his heart, the same chill he had felt that day for Danni. But this was worse. For, if the Ab and his little church were not safe, then what, in all this strange world, was?

Solemnity fell on the longhouse, as if the same dread had lodged itself in every heart, even that of Floki, whose words had caused it. He sat down quietly and Hakon did the same. Aidan gave his little sheep a final pat and rose to his feet as if nothing had happened. Looking from one young Northman to the other, he said, "The sea is your friend, Hakon, as men have named you, and to you," he turned to Floki, "it is even more. Let the sea decide your dispute." He waited until both nodded wary acceptances.

"Five days hence, we keep Saint Lucy's Feast. The first fair wind before that day, bears both ships south, as Hakon wishes. With, or without, the girl. But should Saint Lucy's Day pass with sand beneath your keels, Floki's wish prevails, and all remain."

Hakon nodded his head uncertainly, but Floki jumped up and caught his cousin's hand in an iron grip. "Yes. I make this pledge!" His cold eyes swept the company. "And may never a fair wind cross these isles, until the lass returns!"

A fearful murmuring swept the company and the two helmsmen cast each other looks of dismay. "Guard your tongue," Shony whispered.

But Magnus laughed, "To tame the woman, he will tame the wind!" He caught Floki's shoulders in his bear-fighter's grasp, embraced him gleefully, and turned to Aidan, "Go to your prayers, good father," he chortled, "That your god may tame him!"

CHAPTER FOURTEEN

A blast of sea wind burst open Gil's shutters, scattering hailstones on his bed. He stumbled to the window, stubbing his bare toes against his oil lamp, torn loose and lying on the floor, and fought the flapping shutters closed. Outside an eerie howling rose and fell around his stone dwelling. A low rumble accompanied the wind, the thunder of the sea crashing against the island shore.

Wrapping himself in his cloak and stuffing his feet into warm boots, he felt his way to the door and opened it a cautious crack. The wind caught the frail wicker, flinging the door wide and tumbling Gil out into the storm. The force of the gale sent him sprawling, his cloak flapping like wings. Pulling it closer, he staggered to his feet.

In the dim light of a wild dawn, he saw Aidan struggling to save his little fishing boat from the sea. Waves crashed over its stern, engulfing the Ab in rolling foam. Gil ran to his side. Stumbling through the surf, he gripped the drenched wood of the bow, and together they hauled the little craft over the sand and up onto the grass in front of the church. Gil clutched the bow rope in both hands, and, bent almost double against the wind, staggered to the bell frame, where the heavy bell trembled like a leaf in the wind. He wrapped the rope three times around the sturdy frame and tied it fast with a knot his father had taught him.

Aidan grabbed his sleeve and pointed to the longhouse roof. The thatch was lifting and shredding along the eaves. They gathered armfuls of fishing net from the boat and dragged the sodden weight of it to the longhouse. Ismail appeared from his cell, gripped the net, and clambered onto the thatch. Gil followed, pulling more net with him.

Up on the roof, the wind was like a wild animal, clawing their faces and snatching at their clothes. They fell to their knees and crawled to the peak, and, lying flat, spread the net out, dropping it down the back, to Aidan, below. Rachel joined them, then, gathering stones and tying them into the net's ragged ends. With the roof secure, Gil slid down the thatch to the ground. Looking up, he saw that the sea, in the grey dawn, was a solid froth of white.

A frantic, panicky neighing rose above the constant roaring of the wind. Gil turned and ran, with Ismail and Rachel, to the pony field. Frosti, Freya, and Chocolate were huddled together in the bottom corner, backs to the wind, heads low, tails and manes streaming around them. Far away, Lionheart's pale, wind-tossed shape galloped frantically in circles. Behind him lay the wreckage of his tree, toppled by the gale.

Gil climbed over the low stone wall and ran up the hill, staggering in the wind, and calling silently, *Lionheart! I'm here!* until, at last, the pony saw him. His ears pricked forward and he shook his thick wet mane, and then, still wild-eyed, he galloped down the hill, stumbled to a halt, and thrust his dripping muzzle against Gil's chest.

My tree hit me!

It fell. The wind blew it over.

It hit me. It hit me.

Gil put his arms around the pony's wet neck. *It won't hit you anymore.*

*I want...I want...*Lionheart looked over his shoulder and shuddered in despair. Gil caught a hank of his forelock and led him by it, down the hill.

The others followed, Rachel leading the ponies and Ismail driving them from the rear. They gathered the animals safely behind the Long House; then fought through the gale to the church, where, with the sea drowning his words and the wind battering the door, Aidan chanted his morning prayer.

When they emerged, Gil saw the approaching figure of a storm-drenched Northman on the back of a sodden pony.

Cloak-wrapped, the horseman rode to within feet of them before he saw that it was not Erling, but Floki. Floki lowered the hood of his cloak and let the wind whip his rain-drenched hair. "Good father," he said, bowing his head humbly, "I seek your judgement. Is this wind fair? Shall I turn my dragon's head to the south?"

Aidan smiled amiably. "I am but a scholar and a priest, Floki Magnusson, and these great seas frighten me. But if they please you better, so be it."

"Don't dare him," Gil murmured, "He'll do it." But Floki only laughed and reined his wild-eyed pony in a ring, and cantered back up the hill.

Inside the shelter of the longhouse, Aidan also laughed. "Do not fear," he said. "He will risk his life for a jest, but never his ship."

The next morning, the gale had only increased its strength and they struggled to keep their feet between the longhouse and the church. The messenger waiting in the brutal wind that day was Erling, who gratefully accepted Aidan's welcome into the longhouse. Gil, Ismail and Rachel shuffled in after, shaking water from their clothes.

Inside, the fire burned bright, drawn up by the roof-shaking gale. Sheep and hens nestled in the hay. Feannag clung to a sooty rafter and the Noble Cat basked in the ruddy glow of the hearth. The Northman wrung out clumps of his thick blond hair and brushed water from the tufts of his new-growing beard.

"Do you sail?" Aidan asked innocently.

Erling shook his head vigorously. "Hakon Sea-Friend polishes his sword. The Saracen reads his Holy Book. And Floki Magnusson walks the strand, praising Odin and Lord Yesu for the storm."

After breakfast, Gil brought in baskets of peats for the fire, and fresh bedding for the animals. He fed the ponies with Rachel and checked the netting on the longhouse roof, then struggled with Ismail out past the rain-drenched standing stones, to the old tomb for sacks of turnips for the sheep. But the storm did not relent and Gil woke the next day to another wind-lashed dawn.

When Erling, arrived, he told how the Northmen drank ale and squabbled over board games and muttered in the shadows of the fire that Odin's wrath would never cool because Floki Magnusson had cursed the wind.

Gil and Ismail and Rachel laughed uneasily after he had gone, but when, the next morning, the gale was still blowing and even the surface of the Wandering Pool was a white froth, Gil hung back after prayers and confronted Aidan. "Is it true? Could he really change the wind?"

Aidan smiled. "Not without calling upon powers beyond him, and Floki is far too vain to share his glory, even with the Evil One." He laid a gentle hand on Gil's shoulder. "It is the Dark Time. Winds blow. Even without Floki Magnusson."

Then, at last, on the afternoon of the fourth day, the wind dropped and the sky cleared. Gil walked the strand with Aidan, collecting the bounty of driftwood cast up by the storm. The calming sea was grey and the sun low.

A gnarled, whitened tree trunk lay washed up at the place where Gil had foolishly watched Shony on the shore. He remembered the joyful barking of the seal folk all around and their shining black heads in the sea. He stared out at the emptiness of water.

"Why does Shony stay?" he asked suddenly. Aidan raised a quizzical eyebrow. "She's a selkie," Gil said. "Danni told me. She was born Other. She doesn't even need a circle to change."

"No," Aidan said. "Only the sea."

"And it must be beautiful to swim with the seals, under the sea. As beautiful as flying. So why does she stay human?"

Aidan smiled. "For the sake of Magnus Redbeard," he said, "Whom she loves more than any human woman ever loved any man. Which is not to say that she will not yet murder him." Aidan smiled again, and shouldered one end of the whitened tree trunk. Gil took up the other end.

"Why does Floki stay?" he asked.

Aidan's smile faded. After a long pause he said very quietly, "Because Floki seeks power. And that is only to be sought in the world of men."

When they returned to the longhouse, Floki was waiting

beside the door, sitting on his pony, his bare head bowed. "The storm ends, Mo'Aidan," he said. "I keep my pledge."

Aidan looked out at the surf tumbling yet on the shore. "A day remains to Santa Lucia," he said. "The winds may return."

"I know the sea," Floki answered calmly. "White horses seek their stable. Longships ride tomorrow's tide." He dismounted, handed his pony's reins to Gil and joined Aidan stacking the driftwood against the longhouse wall.

Gil released the pony with their own, where it ran in wild circles, stirring them to do the same. Soon all would leave Cille Aidan's field. Except for Danni's Frosti. Sorrow tinged Gil's relief at the end of the eerie storm. He shut the wicker gate and returned to the shore, imagining Danni returning some day and finding them all gone.

He looked around at the cluster of stone buildings clinging to the rocky shore, where Aidan and the Northman worked side by side, and remembered Floki's prophecy. His mind conjured the thud of axes, the clash of swords, flames sweeping the heather thatch. He heard the squawking of hens, the bleating of frightened sheep, the shouts of triumph over the plundered treasures of the church. Gil turned away and closed his eyes. In the darkness, he saw Danni, huddled in the charred ruins of the longhouse, bewildered and lost.

He took Rachel with him to the scriptorium. She helped him arrange inks and a quill and a scrap of parchment on Aidan's desk, and then sat down herself at the other, while he worked. Drawing his father's knife from its sheath, he trimmed the curled edges of the parchment until it lay flat. Then, taking up the quill he wrote:

Danni
Saint Lucy's Feast
We Sail for Hy
Follow if you can
Gil

He crowded out of his mind the hugeness of the sea and the smallness of the ships and how she would ever find her way alone, and carefully slipped the vellum inside his shirt.

He looked up and saw Rachel bent over a discarded piece of Aidan's work, writing with a swift sure hand in the bare margin. She smiled. "Marginalia," she said. "It's where we find history. The unimportant things people scribbled in the margins." She held up her finished work.

Gil read, "*And all will be well.*" He paused. "That's history?"

"It will be." She smiled again. "In a few hundred years. '*And all will be well. And all will be well. And all manner of things will be well.*' It's Julian of Norwich. She's a medieval Christian mystic. She will be a medieval Christian mystic," Rachel corrected herself. "Dad's written stacks on her. It's a message for my father," she said.

Gil raised a wary eyebrow. "Do you think he's going to find it?" he said cautiously. "Like, here?"

She shrugged and smiled, putting away her inks and dropping the parchment back on the floor. "Who knows where it will be in a thousand years?"

Outside the scriptorium they skirted the Wandering Pool, which had come to rest there. The wind had fallen utterly still. The surface of the water was smooth as grey silk. Beyond the buildings of Cille Aidan, the sea, too, was pearly and calm.

Gil strode down the hill toward his own cell. He reached his door just as the bell began to ring for prayers, and slipped quickly within. He laid the vellum on his reading desk, weighting it with two round pebbles from the shore.

Except for the parchment and the pebbles, the cell was as empty and bare as the day he had come. The spare clothes that Danni had made him; an extra shirt, a pair of socks, and two pretty itchy pairs of wool underpants, along with the wooden spoon and bowl Aidan had given each of them, were wrapped already in a sheepskin bedroll to be tied behind his saddle. The old-fashioned metal compass his father had given him was in his pocket. His sword and armor awaited him at Einar's Holm.

The blackened metal lamp that the storm had blown down hung again from its chain. He'd even filled it with fresh oil. He went out of the cell, just as the last peal of Aidan's vespers bell died to silence.

When he heard the call, it seemed at first to be only an echo of the bell, so sweet and musical did it sound on the winter air. But then he heard it again. He turned and looked up, scanning the darkening sky. He heard it a third time. Still, there was nothing in sight, not over the wood, or the hill, or the sea, nowhere at all.

Then suddenly he remembered the day Rachel arrived and how he'd heard a cry for help out of empty air. "The Pool!" he gasped, and in the same moment, he saw Aidan and Floki running from the church.

Gil ran as well. They reached the scriptorium in the moment she rose from the Pool, wings outstretched, long neck thrusting, just as she'd entered it weeks before. But this was not the Danni-goose of shining feathers and sparkling joyful eye, but a weary, battered, dirty creature, struggling even to fly. One wing flopped awkwardly, a circlet of waterweeds surrounded her graceful neck, and her webbed feet were caked with mud. She wobbled in flight and wheeled above them, calling and calling, as if still lost.

"Danni!" Gil cried. He waved his arms over his head. "We're here! It's Cille Aidan. You're home!"

She turned, flapping wearily, and sank lower, as if she would simply fall from the sky. Aidan loosened the rope that bound his robes, and turned it, once, into a circular loop. Leaping skyward, he cast it around her. Floki leapt beside him and caught her, even as she fell, into the circle of his arms.

Together they crashed to the wet grass. Gil ran to them, afraid of what he would see. But Danni, released from the Northman's strong arms, was already sitting up. She was thin and dirty, her lip was cut, her slender throat still tangled in weeds, and her bare feet muddy and bruised. But her eyes were bright and her grin stretched from ear to ear. She hugged Floki happily; then grinned at Aidan. "I flew to Heaven!" she said.

CHAPTER FIFTEEN

"Not Heaven, little daughter," Aidan said, as Danni filled her porridge bowl for a third time. "Nor Hell either, for all the Northmen sometimes say. It is the Land of Ice and Fire, far to the north and west. Magnus Redbeard has sailed there."

"It looked like Heaven," she said.

"And how would you know, my disobedient daughter, what Heaven looks like?"

Danni locked eyes with the Ab. "But it was so beautiful! Fields and fields of flowers and black, black rocks. And whole rivers made of ice! And the ice mountains in the sea! All blue and green...and fountains and plumes of white smoke and a huge waterfall, a hundred feet high, covered in rainbows!" She folded her arms. "If Heaven doesn't look like that, it should!"

"First you fly over my head into the Pool. Then you cause greatest difficulty for all, while you amuse yourself on your pretty wings. And now you tell the Most High what to do." Aidan folded his arms, too, and looked at her fondly, "What am I to do with you?" He walked to the door. "Come, finish quickly," he said. "The day comes already and you must be in Pentland before its end."

Gil and Ismail brought the ponies down from the hill. The sky was starry and the ground was white; the end of the gale had brought snow. Rachel was waiting with the pony tack. Lionheart's ears went flat. *The saddle's there.*

Surprise, surprise. Gil lifted it, flung it on the pony's back and slipped the girth under his belly in one quick movement. Lionheart stamped his feet, puffed up like a hairy balloon and held his breath. *You'll turn blue and fall over.* Gil yanked the girth tight, left the pony and went to his cell for the rolled sheepskins that held his clothes.

Aidan was waiting for him outside the longhouse. Rachel took Gil's bedroll to tie behind Lionheart's saddle and Gil followed the Ab indoors. Aidan went to a tall kist by the back wall and lifted out a square satchel, slung on a broad leather strap. He undid the ties that held it closed and withdrew a book, encased in silver banded wood. Releasing a delicate gold latch, he opened it, and laid it before Gil.

The vellum pages were adorned with Latin script in black and red. Animals and birds, men and ships, dragons and fabulous beasts, entwined around each other in the margins. Each page began with one huge letter, itself filled with pictures. Gil reached out hesitantly and then drew back his hand.

"You can touch it," Aidan said. "It is a book. Its purpose is to be read."

"It's the most beautiful thing I've ever seen," Gil whispered.

Aidan smiled, "But you are young and you have seen little." He closed the book and returned it to its leather casing, "This is my gift to the Ab of the *muinntir* of Hy. I ask that you bear it to him, and with it, my gratitude for the shelter he offers on your way."

Gil shook his head, even as he took up the leather satchel and its glorious contents. "For us? We're not worth this!" he cried.

Aidan laughed softly. "It is for the Lord to judge your worth, not I," he said. "But the risk the Ab takes in offering you sanctuary is worth a very great deal indeed. The Golden Knight has laid castles to waste in search of the good king's friends. A *muinntir* of humble monks would be a morning's work."

He slipped the leather strap over Gil's shoulder. "But," he said, "Though you are a danger to them, this itself," he touched the hidden book gently, "Is a danger to you. Show it to no man."

Gil nodded. "It must be worth a fortune," he whispered.

Aidan shook his head gently. "Only the words within are worth anything, Gil, and they are recorded elsewhere. But the world has a different reckoning." Feeling the weight of his responsibility more than the weight of the book, Gil followed the Ab back outside to his friends.

It was not yet light when they left Cille Aidan. Aidan walked with them, past the Wandering Pool, and through the Wood of White Trees, striding ahead of the ponies, *bachall* in hand. The Noble Cat trotted at his side and Feannag wheeled overhead. Aidan led them past the Standing Stones as far as the snow-bent rowans, by the little stream.

There, as the ponies jostled around him, he reached up and marked each of their foreheads with Lord Yesu's sign and did the same to each pony. Lionheart nuzzled against his robes pathetically. "Be brave, little brother," he said, patting the pony's neck. He looked up at the children and his eyes settled on Rachel.

"Who shall climb the mountain of the Lord?
Who shall stand in his holy place?"

She smiled,

"The man with clean hands and pure heart,
Who desires not worthless things."

Aidan laughed softly. "Ah, little scholar. What I would make of you, were you mine! Look, now," he said to Gil. "The wisdom of the Fathers at your right, and the Man of Pure Heart on your left," he nodded his head to Ismail. "Was ever a knight better companioned?"

"What about me?" Danni said. She sat on her pony, a little at a distance, looking hurt to be left out. Aidan stepped closer and stood by her stirrup, resting both hands on the curved head of the *bachall*. "So," he said, "I find you again only long enough to say goodbye." He smiled up at her. "Farewell, little daughter. I will see you in Heaven, if not before."

"Aidan!" Danni cried, "You can't go to Heaven!"

"Do you decide that, too, now?" he said, laughing.

"But you'll have to die! You can't die."

He inclined his head solemnly, but his eyes were still merry. "I can, and so shall you. One gets there no other way." He stepped back and slapped Frosti's furry rump. The startled pony leapt in the air, then lunged forward so fast that Danni had to grasp his mane to keep her seat. "Ride, little daughter!" Aidan shouted, as Frosti galloped for Einar's Holm. "Godspeed!"

The others galloped after, Freya at Frosti's heels, Chocolate thundering behind, and last, Lionheart, tossing his head and rolling his eyes, fearful of leaving, fearful of being left behind. Feannag soared above them, circling grandly, but when Gil turned to look back, Aidan stood yet, in the grey light by the Standing Stones, leaning on his *bachall*, the Noble Cat, still as a statue, at his side.

When Gil caught up with Danni, she was telling anyone who would listen about the wonderful time she'd had in the Land of Ice and Fire, while they'd all been frantically worrying about her. "I'd go back in a second," she declared, boldly enough, now that Aidan was far behind them.

"I can't believe you were home at the Indian Kettle," Gil said, "And all you could think of was flying off with a bunch of wild geese."

"Didn't you even think about us?" Rachel said.

"I meant to come right back," Danni said. "But they kept saying, 'Fly a little further and you'll see the great Pine Woods, and fly a little further and you'll see the frozen sea.' And then they said we'd gone too far to turn back to our river and the Indian Kettle, but they'd show me a new way, in the Land of Ice and Fire. And they did. They showed me a whole other Bridge!

"I can't believe you trusted them," Gil said. "They take you to this weird place and tell you to dive into a boiling geyser."

"It wasn't boiling then."

"Whoop-de-do. You didn't even know them," Gil said, feeling like he was her parent or something.

"But I did know them," she protested. "Flying in the Vee is like you're one great bird. I was part of them and they were part of me." She gave him a pitying look. "You're just the same," she said resignedly. "You may look different. And you've learned a lot of stuff. But you're still Gil. Scaredy-Cat Gil." Her eyes lit with sour delight. "Hey. Scaredy-*Cat*!" she cried.

"Stop!" Gil and Danni both turned, startled. Ismail barged his big brown pony between Frosti and Lionheart. "That is enough," he said. He looked hard at Danni, and then equally forcefully at Gil. "We all have fears. We all make mistakes. Both of you. Stop."

Chastened, Gil and Danni hung their heads. Each gave the

other a grudging nod, since no one was quite ready to shake hands, and they rode on in silence, if not exactly peace, to the hill above Einar's Holm.

Below, the snow-covered sands of the bay were covered with men and beasts. Baskets and sacks of supplies lay piled on the shore. A line of seamen trailed back to the longhouse, carrying more. The two beached longships, lying like sleeping dragons in the sheltered cove, were urged now to wakefulness. Men and ponies strove with ropes on every side to drag them free of the sand and into the rising tide.

Magnus stood knee-deep in the water, bellowing orders in the Northmen's tongue, his huge voice carrying even to where they sat. Gil spotted Floki, and then Hakon, both up to their waists in the water, directing the oarsmen already aboard. Shouts rose on the still air, and whinnying, which was answered by their ponies. Gil felt his spirits rise, and looking around, saw grins spread across the faces of his companions.

Danni thudded her heels against Frosti's sides, and, in a moment, they were careening in a crazy gallop down the hill. Laughing and shouting, the others followed, cantering down the last grassy slope and pulling up at the edge of the sea.

Immediately, a rope was tossed from the nearest ship to Ismail and another to Gil. They secured the lines to the square pommels of their jousting saddles, and rode into the sea. Chocolate plunged ahead confidently, but Lionheart shied at the first splash around his knees. Gil coaxed and pleaded, but the pony flattened his ears and whinnied in dismay at the cold water, lapping up to his belly, and the dark, sea-smelling hull of the ship grinding against the sand.

Men and ponies grunted and strained, but the ship held firm. Then Doombearer plunged through the waves, his huge shoulders adorned with the humble harness of a plough horse. Palamedes strode behind him, directing his great charger by voice alone. The ropes of the harness grew taut, and the heavy hull groaned and creaked. Then Doombearer gave a mighty leap, and the ship broke free.

Instantly, the ropes all slackened and the ponies plunged forward. Gil clutched at Lionheart's neck, lest he pitch over his head, into the sea, and in that moment, he remembered the leather satchel slung across his back. Aidan's book! He tossed the rope free, and clutching the strap of the satchel against his chest, urged Lionheart back to dry land.

Amidst the creels of salted fish and sacks of meal, he saw the Saxon kist that held his and Ismail's armor. He turned and surveyed the beach. A couple of straggling Northmen were on the path to the longhouse, their backs to Gil. Quickly, he jumped down from Lionheart's back and raised the lid of the kist. There was just room, beneath their swords and shields, their chain mail hauberks and *chausses*, steel gloves and silk-lined helms, for the leather pouch. Rejoicing in the watertight solidity of the kist, he laid it within. Then he arranged the hauberks and the thick, padded undercoats over the top and replaced the helms, as before.

Lowering the lid, he straightened up, and turned back to the sea. Hakon's ship was afloat, too, now, and standing high on its moving deck, one hand on its dragon prow, was Floki Magnusson, his eyes intent on Gil. Quickly, Gil turned away from the kist. Floki watched him more closely. Striving to look casual, Gil strolled up the beach and mounted Lionheart again.

Ismail trotted Chocolate to his side. "Danni calls us." Gil saw both girls with their ponies in the sandy hollow that held the archery target. Frosti and Freya shuffled and stamped. Beside them, Shony held the bridle of a third pony. Danni grinned at Gil. "Meet Midnight," she announced. She gave Rachel a quick, sly look.

"Meet Star," Rachel said at once.

"Midnight is going to be our pack pony," Danni said.

"Star," Rachel replied, "Is going to carry all our extra stuff." Her eyes flashed angrily when she looked at Danni, but her face softened when she turned back to the new pony. "Isn't she gorgeous," she murmured.

The pony was black all over, with a single white diamond on her forehead. Danni stroked her shining black neck. "She is just so Midnight. And so not Star. Half the time you can't even see the white...."

"Midnight just sounds dumb," Rachel snapped. Danni

turned her back. Gil looked at Ismail. Ismail raised his forefinger and drew it solemnly across his throat. Gil nodded, very aware that this was less about names than about who took charge of the new pony. But, even more, it was about Rachel's hurt at Danni's desertion, and Danni's refusal to be sorry.

"Okay," Gil said. "Her name's Lucy."

"Lucy?!" Both girls stared at him, appalled.

"We're sailing on Saint Lucy's Day, so we're naming her for Saint Lucy."

Shony smiled. "Mo'Aidan will be pleased!" She stroked the pony's face. "Lucy," she murmured. "May the good saint smile on you and keep you safe."

Gil ducked his head to hide his grin from the girls. "And," he continued quickly, "Since each of us already has a pony, this pony will belong to us all. One quarter share each. Right, Ismail?" He turned and gave Ismail an agree-or-die look.

Both girls looked at the sky and the snow and anything but Gil, but eventually each of them sighed and said, "Right."

Magnus shouted from the shore. The longships had turned their dragon prows seaward. Floki's oarsmen were holding *Silver Dragon* steady while a ramp of battered wood was positioned against her rail.

"Quickly," Shony said, "They must load the ponies now." She led the way, her hand still gripping the black pony's bridle. "Hurry. The sea does not wait."

Lionheart shied and flattened his ears. *Why is that pony there?*

That's Lucy. She's coming with us. Gil's eyes were on Floki's ship and his mind on how exactly he was going to get Lionheart up that precarious ramp. He pressed his knees tight.

Lionheart balked, legs straight. *I don't like her.*

Gil sighed. *You will like her. You never like anything new.* He squeezed his knees hard and gave Lionheart a sharp nudge with his heels. Lionheart shied and then started forward in a stiff-legged belligerent walk. He caught up and passed Freya and Frosti and shadowed Lucy, ears still flat against his head.

I thought I was your pony.

You are my pony. Look, she isn't really even mine. I just have a part of her.

Which part?

Who knows...a leg. The closer Gil got to the beach, the more daunting Floki's ramp appeared, just two halved tree trunks bound together with fraying ropes.

Which leg?

Floki was calling him, beckoning from the water. Gil slapped Lionheart's neck to get his attention and pointed at Lucy's left foreleg. *Okay?*

Lionheart's head snaked sidewise. Lucy squealed and bucked. "Your stupid pony!" Danni shouted. Both girls jumped down and crowded around Lucy's left foreleg. "He bit her!" Rachel cried. "Look! There's teeth marks!"

Shony led Lucy aside. "They kick, they bite; they chase each other around the hill. They are ponies." She smiled.

"Of all people," Danni hissed at Gil. "You should be able to control your pony!"

"Oh, don't bother," Rachel comforted her. "He's just useless."

Ismail rode up and gave him a gleeful high five. "See!" He pointed at Rachel and Danni, standing side by side, guarding Lucy. "You make them friends again!"

Shony came between the girls. She slid an arm around Danni's waist, then caught Rachel with the other. She looked up at Floki's oarsmen aboard the ship and turned, taking in any left on the shore. When she spoke, her voice rang, clear and sweet, over the frosty air. "These are my daughters," she said. "Should any man lay one unlawful finger upon them, that man shall die. Neither land nor sea will hide him from my sword." A murmuring and a shuffling swept round the crew, and Gil shivered, imagining Shony rising with the seal folk from the dark sea, set on vengeance.

"My word is enough to rule this ship," Floki said quietly. He waved an impatient arm and called for the first pony. Ismail stepped forward, leading Chocolate. Talking softly, he walked backwards up the slippery wet wood until the pony clattered the last few feet onto the ship and into the straw bedded enclosure awaiting him.

Danni was next, leading Frosti, and Rachel followed with Freya. They both returned to coax Lucy toward the ship, but she danced and shied, rearing up and trying to turn. "What's with her?" Danni cried.

Gil looked suddenly at Lionheart. The pony's ears flattened and his lips curled back. Lucy shied away behind Doombearer, in terror. "Will you stop him doing that?" Rachel demanded.

Palamedes strode forward and took the reins from Rachel. "She may sail with Doombearer and return to you on land."

"Good," Floki said. "Take her. Enough time has been wasted on the honor of women and the tempers of beasts." He stalked away.

"You and that useless pony!" Rachel snapped. Then she bowed dramatically toward the ramp and said, "This should be good," before running up it to join Danni on board.

Gil gathered up Lionheart's reins. He took a step forward and the reins grew taut, another, and they reached their limit. Lionheart's feet were splayed in front of him, his weight firmly on his haunches. He looked ready to stay there until spring.

Lionheart. Please. Just do one thing for me, today.

I'm scared.

Lucy was scared. Did you care?

I hate her.

Gil stood staring at the immobile pony while around him, the Northmen grumbled and yawned. Then he dropped the reins and walked away. Lionheart looked over his furry shoulder.

Where are you going?

To get Lucy. I have to have something to ride. He turned his back and strode up the beach. Behind him there was a sudden drumming of hoof beats on wood and a loud cheer. He turned just in time to see Lionheart leap like a foal off the top of the ramp and onto the straw covered deck. Gil ran up after him and then the ramp was hauled up, grating and rumbling across the rail.

Floki and Hakon waited by their steersmen. The wide, curving strand fell still. Magnus' eyes were dreamy as the oars dipped deep. "So come, Redbeard!" Floki shouted. "Sail with me!" Magnus smiled, but, shaking his head, he turned back to the fields of Einar's Holm. Only Shony stayed on the strand.

Even as they left the shelter of the bay, and the dragon prow bowed to the waves, she stood watching, alone. Floki shouted to his crewmen in the Northman's tongue, and two left their oars and grasped the ropes that raised the sail.

The broad square of blue-striped cloth mounted the mast, jerking higher with each mighty pull, until it bellied out with the winter wind. All oars were stowed, and the longship surged out into the open sea. Gil's heart leapt with it, filled with the rush of wind and water, the snapping of the heavy sail and the splash of icy spray. A cheer rose to his throat, unbidden, and was joined by the voices of his friends. When he turned to look back, Einar's Holm was already small and faraway, the figure of Shony a tiny dark smudge on the snow-covered shore.

Beyond, the receding coast spread out, revealing headlands and cliffs and foaming surf. White hills rose up behind. The landscape that had grown so familiar showed itself new and strange from the sea. Far to the north, the rough shoreline faded into blue mist, while to the south, a great headland loomed. Surf churned on black rocks at its foot, tumbling foam marked hidden outcrops beneath the waves.

Above, amid the noise of sea and wind and the cries of following sea birds, Gil heard a harsh, familiar cawing. He looked up and saw Feannag, black among the white of the angry gulls, circling the racing ship. As they rounded the rocky headland and came into the next bay, Danni pointed toward the shore.

He made out the snow-covered turf roof of the church, and the huddle of round cells, looking so small; barely buildings at all. But for the haze of blue smoke that marked the longhouse, it was easy to imagine there was no human dwelling there; only a trick of light, playing briefly on some natural formation, fading as quickly into sand and grass and stone. The chime of the bell came, as far away and sweet as when Gil first heard it, within the Turnip-Head Tomb. Feannag circled once more and then set out on sure wings for home.

"Goodbye," Gil whispered. His heart yearned to fly with the bird, but he turned his face seaward. When next he looked back, there was nothing to be seen but dark, empty shore.

Somehow, then, it was easier. His spirits lifted, stirred by the grandeur of the sea and the rocky coast to which the longships clung close. He wondered then, for the first time, how the Northmen found their way. His fingers found his compass in his pocket, but Floki sailed without help of one, his untroubled eyes on the southern horizon.

They had moved out now, farther from the shore and the sea was choppy. Gil balanced easily, rocking from foot to foot, as if the ship was a cantering pony. But, beside him, Ismail sat down, heavily, on the crude deck. He pointed unhappily to his head and made a gesture of a circle, looking sick and miserable. "Never am I on boat so big, water so big."

Rachel settled on the edge of their armor kist, looking green. But Danni was standing up beside Floki, taking a turn at the steering oar, a big, happy grin on her face. Gil could have guessed she would be immune. But, happily, so was he. In fact, he felt wonderful, like sailing on a Northman's longship was what he'd been born for.

He heard a sad little whicker from the cluster of ponies in their straw-filled enclosure. Lionheart was standing at the end of the row, feet braced, head down, back hunched. His unhappy ears barely twitched when Gil climbed into the enclosure beside him. Gently, he patted the pony's neck, feeling his whole, warm body trembling under his thick winter coat.

It's okay, Lionheart, he comforted.

Lionheart raised his head and snorted. *There's water everywhere.*

That's why we're on a boat.

The boat will break and a fish will eat me.

You're too big. Gil stroked the pony's neck and straightened his damp mane.

Many fish will eat me.

Gil put his arms around the pony and hugged him and returned to his place, by Ismail. The African boy was on his feet again, struggling gamely against the motion of the ship. He pointed past the dragon tail stern and said, "Hakon falls behind." His brown forehead creased with concern.

Gil saw that Hakon's vessel was many ship-lengths to the

rear. Floki had taken the steering oar back from Danni, and was shouting instructions to Svein and Erling, who pulled on ropes, turning the big square sail. It billowed and snapped, gathering more wind. The dragon prow rose higher, skimming the waves. The wind flattened Gil's long, tangled hair, and Danni, standing by Floki, cheered and shouted, clutching his arm and urging him on.

"They're racing," Gil said.

Ismail shook his head. "*He* is racing," he said, nodding towards Floki. "He is good sailor. Bad soldier."

"Bad soldier?"

"Before, we are two," Ismail said. He pointed to the wide sea behind their snowy wake, where Hakon's sail was but a bright splash of white and green on the horizon. "Now," he added simply, "we are one."

Gil nodded slowly, "We're pretty close to home, still." But he remembered, even as he said it, Aidan hiding them in the church at the sight of a sail, for fear of Vikings.

What he had no doubt about, though, was Floki's skill. His longship streaked ahead, and as they followed the rocky curve of the coast, Hakon's sail disappeared behind one headland, then another, and soon they had lost him completely.

Gil stood up and waved to Danni. She ignored him at first, but he beckoned more vigorously, and, with obvious reluctance, she left Floki's side. "What is it?" she demanded when she reached them.

"Look," he pointed to the empty sea behind them. "We've lost Hakon."

She grinned. "*Silver Dragon* is three times faster than any other ship. *Storm-Serpent* hadn't got a chance!"

Gil gestured toward Floki and whispered, "Get him to slow down."

Danni gave an exasperated shrug. "You are *so* boring," she said. She started to turn away, but suddenly her eyes opened wide and she raised her arm, pointing over his shoulder. Gil turned. To their left, the land had risen to high, dark cliffs, hundreds of feet tall. Surf fringed them in fierce white lace, and standing free of them, soaring above their ship, was a great pillar of sea-carved stone, cut off completely from the land.

"Fantastic," he murmured.

"No!" she shouted, pointing again, urgently. "There!"

Then he saw the ship; long, dark, and dragon-prowed, emerging from behind the rock pillar like a beast from its lair. Oars splashed, churning white froth. A red-checked sail rode up the mast, billowing out as the longship gave chase. Erling shouted a warning, and in the same instant, Gil saw, along the rail of the approaching raider, the flash of steel.

CHAPTER SIXTEEN

Floki shouted an order and every man of the crew leapt to his place. The oarsmen hunched over oars on the sea kists that served as rowing benches. Beside each man, another stood, armed with shield and sword. Archers took places at bow and stern. Steel-spiked javelins were raised until the ship bristled like an angry boar. Warriors waved swords at the distant raider. Taunts and laughter rang out on the salty air. Snaggle-Toothed Svein and the huge, silent man they called Bjorn Break-Neck stood by the stepped mast, ready to lower it and make room for combat.

"We're not going to fight them, are we?" Gil whispered to Ismail. "We're the fastest thing around. We can just run!"

Ismail said, "We change course." Instead of fleeing to open sea, they were making a wide half-circle that would bring them closer to the raider's path. Floki held the steering oar firm, his eyes intent on the other ship.

Erling barged through the shouting warriors to the girls. "Come!" He pulled them to the center of the ship, just behind the pony pen. While the ponies snorted and stamped in fright, he hauled a heavy, black, woolen cloth over a wooden frame, making a tent. "For you. Hide."

Danni shoved him aside, and raced to join Gil and Ismail at their armor kist. Gil raised the heavy lid. Inside, the hauberks and helms he had neatly replaced were jumbled in a heap; swords and shields thrown carelessly on top. "Aidan's book!" he whispered. He searched frantically and found the leather pouch, half un-tied, but safe. Relieved, he covered the book again, retrieved his sword and shield, and strapped the scabbard around his waist.

Danni did the same. Rachel took up her own sword and the Stooping Hawk shield. "Would Shony hide?" she said. Gil shook his head as Erling shouted at one side and the girls glared at the other.

Then suddenly Ismail was there. "In," he said, his arms gently shepherding both girls, his voice soft, but firm. "This is not game. Men fight for prize. You are prize. They not see you, maybe no battle. Who faces sword for no reason?"

"I am not a prize!" Danni shouted. "I am a warrior!"

Ismail shook his head gently and his smile made him look as old and wise as Aidan. "No," he said softly. "You will be warrior. You are not warrior yet. Do not hurry to that day. It will come, too soon, and you will not be the same again."

Danni shrugged angrily, but she moved to the entrance of Erling's makeshift tent. Ismail smiled, and smiled again when Rachel followed her. "Good," he said. "If warriors come, find you, you fight like Shony. But first, hide. No battle is better than battle. Always."

The approaching ship was much closer now. Gil saw blurred faces and sword arms and the bright colors of painted shields. *Silver Dragon's* sail sagged and fluttered overhead. The bow settled heavily into its own white necklace of foam. The sail lost more wind and the longship wallowed clumsily on the choppy sea.

Floki was smiling, one hand on the steering oar and the other raised to the other ship in salute. Distant bellowed insults sounded across the narrowing wedge of water between the two ships. Gil grabbed Erling's sleeve. "Why are we slowing down?"

Erling shrugged. "They will talk."

"Talk?" Gil cried. "They're waving swords!"

"We wave swords," Erling shrugged again.

When the raiders' ship was near enough that Gil could make out the devices—eagle or bear, snake or dragon—on each shield, Floki shouted again to his crew. Bjorn Break-Neck and Svein turned the sail, and catching the wind, the longship rode forward again 'til both sailed side by side as companionably as they had sailed with Hakon, except for the torrent of insults hurled back and forth. Floki left Erling at the steering oar and climbed up on the dragon's tail. On the opposing ship, his counterpart struck a heroic pose, waved his sword and shouted, in the Northmen's tongue. Floki bowed meekly as he answered.

"What are they saying?" Gil whispered to Erling.

"He asks who sails. And Floki says, 'But a humble oarsman, making passage to the *muinntir* at Hy.'"

"Humble?" Gil muttered to Ismail.

Ismail said, "It is not wise to give our course."

As the two ships rode side by side, barely two oars lengths apart, Gil saw behind the armor and the swagger that their opponents were all young; some even boys, his and Ismail's age. "He asks if we be holy men!" Erling crowed. He slapped his belly and laughed, but Floki answered in the same meek voice.

"'Alas, we are not,'" Erling translated, struggling to control his laughter. "'But,'" he says, "'we have with us a holy book, which, alas, he cannot read! A very pretty book, much adorned with silver and gold!'" Erling wiped away tears of laughter from his red cheeks.

Gil stared at Floki, in horrified silence, knowing too well who had ransacked their armor kist. On the other ship a great cry went up and Gil knew without a translator that the word they were shouting meant "Gold!"

Floki spoke again, with an air of total innocence, matching it with a blank-eyed village idiot grin. "He says," Erling struggled amid fits of laughter, "Very pretty gold!" A roar went up from the strangers' ship, but on their own a wave of laughter echoed it. Floki looked about with the village idiot smile and his crewmen collapsed, laughing, on each other's shoulders.

"This is game?" Ismail asked.

Gil shook his head. Game or not, the prize was Aidan's beautiful book which he had promised to guard. The master of the opposing ship climbed up again on the rail. He grinned cockily and swaggered as he spoke. At the end of his speech, he made a magnanimous bow that brought hisses and roars of outrage from Gil's shipmates. Erling raised a fist and spat out of the corner of his mouth. "He says," he translated disdainfully; "He shall let us pass free for the mere prize of the book."

Floki stepped down from the stern and made his way with

bowed head through the ranks of his amazed crew. The game, if it were a game, had gone too far for them and they plucked at his tunic and argued. But Floki ignored them, proceeding in his humble way toward the armor kist, and Aidan's book. Like a man walking in a dream, he clambered past the pony pen, bumping clumsily into a railing. In the same sleepwalking way, he brushed by the side of the girls' black tent. And then suddenly he tripped, and sprawled right across it.

With a crack of splitting wood, the tent collapsed and tumbled onto the deck. The black cloth parted, revealing Rachel and Danni, huddled together, open-mouthed with astonishment. The winter sun lit the rich colors of their costumes and shone on their long, loose hair. Amidst the battered interior of the ship, and the rough garments of its crew, they appeared as rare and splendid as a pair of tropical birds.

There was a moment's utter silence in which only wind and wave could be heard, and then thirty loud and raucous voices shouted at once. The young captain leapt to his steering oar and thrust it hard to the left. The ship responded swiftly, swinging sharply to the right. "He's going to ram us!" Gil cried to Ismail, as the dragon prow ploughed toward him, the fearsome wooden beast aimed directly at the place where he stood.

"Hold on!" Ismail returned. Gil flung himself backwards, grasping a heavy kist. Bracing for the impact, he looked over his shoulder at the terrified girls. Beside them, Floki sat like a fool on his own deck, his handsome features set in an expression of shocked dismay, but his eyes alight with excitement.

The thud of the impact shook the whole ship. The kist Gil gripped slid sideways, as *Silver Dragon* tilted ominously. The ponies whinnied in panic and Gil cried out, despite himself, in fear. But the ship settled back and instead of splintered wood and spouting water, he saw an eager rush of his comrades to the side.

Bellowing threats, they pushed and shoved to be first to greet their counterparts with a sword-swinging welcome. Bjorn and another man swung heavy, three-pronged hooks like lassos around their heads, and hurled them across the other ship's rail. Tightening their ropes, they dragged her closer; the intention on both sides to engage battle. Gil drew his own sword and took up his shield, and Ismail did the same. Danni and Rachel drew theirs as well, and took firm stances.

The Northmen on the raiding ship hung back behind their shields, shouting fiercely and clashing swords only at cautious arm's length. There was a lot of shouting and shield ducking on their side, too. But then, suddenly, Floki was at the front. He called to his young counterpart, pointing the tip of his shining blade at the other's chest.

"Look!" Erling cried, "He is a Christian! And Floki asks, has he said his prayers?" Laughter swept the ship. The boy captain, who wore a silver necklace bearing a rough-shaped cross looked scared and his voice trembled when he spoke.

"Ah, but he is a true Northman," Svein cried, "He says his sword speaks his prayers!" Floki grinned, his eyes flashing, and shouted his answer. "'Let it speak, then!'" Erling translated gleefully, "'for my name is Floki Magnusson, and today, you die!'"

Gil saw the boy captain's face turn white. He took a step backwards and looked wildly around at his crew. Panic flashed across all their faces and one tall sailor attempted to fend *Silver Dragon* off with the base of his javelin. But Floki leapt from his ship to theirs, in the same instant, and with a hearty kick, tipped boy and javelin into the sea.

Cries of alarm swept the raiders' ship, answered by shouts of triumph from Floki's. Bjorn and Svein jumped after their captain, and in moments the strangers' deck was a battleground. Ismail leapt the gap between the two ships, sword held high, and with a wild thought of the prayerful peace of Cille Aidan, Gil leapt, too.

At once, he was in the midst of the melee, surrounded at every side by struggling men and flashing steel. His heart pounded and words chanted unbidden in his brain: *This is real. This is real.*

It was not Ismail facing him, but a skinny, blond boy with snot dripping from his nose and spittle on his chin. Eyes screwed up with fear, he shouted words Gil didn't know and swung wildly at him with his sword. Gil swung back. The swords clashed and the stranger's flew from his unsteady hand. The boy flinched away behind his shield, his chin crumpling. Then he turned and ran to the safety of two larger crewmates, babbling and pointing at Gil. The two men joined ranks, shoulder-to-shoulder, and advanced. Gil braced himself grimly on the rocking deck, and raised sword and shield.

But before the avengers could reach him, Bjorn Break-Neck stormed in between. With one sword swing, he knocked both their weapons to the deck. Sheathing his blade, he grabbed each man by his tunic, spun both around, and hurled them across the ship. They slammed into their axe-wielding colleagues, bringing them down like felled trees. Then Svein slashed the ropes that held the strangers' sail, and it tumbled to the deck, engulfing half the raider's warriors. They bumbled around beneath it like kittens beneath a blanket, as Floki's crew poured onto their ship.

Floki, himself, cut through the cowering ranks of the raiders, like a longship through the sea. They backed away, clambering over each other in desperation to escape. Only the boy captain still put up a fight, and Floki pursued him, laughing, around his own mast. But his blows were light and playful. And for all the noise and the clamor, the shouting and the fearsome weaponry, no one had actually drawn blood.

Ismail sheathed his sword and shrugged. "I do not fight rabbits," he said. Gil nodded and sheathed his sword as well. He turned back to *Silver Dragon*. There, too, the battle had become a comedy. One hapless raider remained on the ship, and while Erling held the steering oar steady, the rest of Floki's crew lounged against their oars, pointing and laughing, as Danni battled the man fiercely across the deck.

Ismail watched, too. "She is good!" he cried. "He is not bad, but she, so much better!" Gil smiled, enjoying the show. The months of practice shone in her speed and agility and in her laughing confidence.

Rachel, standing by the pony pen, stroking and calming the frightened animals, cheered. The boy stumbled and fell backwards over a kist. His sword flew from his hand and he sprawled on a heap of meal sacks, holding up empty hands in a plea for mercy. The Northmen howled with laughter. Danni smiled coolly and sheathed her sword. "Tell him," she called to Erling, "He has lost the prize."

There was more laughter, then, and cheering for Danni, but in the midst of it, Gil heard Lionheart whinny. He turned to the sound; then froze. A hand, wet and dripping, had appeared on the rail behind Rachel. Another joined it, and a lean figure, hair and beard sodden, clothes plastered to his body, climbed up out of the sea. With a soft grunt, he heaved himself aboard and staggered to his feet.

Gil's mind flashed to Shony and the seal folk in the water by Cille Aidan. *A selkie!* he thought wildly. But more laughter arose behind him and Erling cried, "Hey! Floki! We land your big fish!" The sodden figure before him was only the boy with the javelin who Floki had kicked into the sea. He seemed befuddled by his swim in the icy water, and shook his head. Then his eyes fell on Rachel and a strange smile lit his face. Reaching out one hand, he stepped toward her. Busy with the rearing ponies, she neither heard, nor saw.

"Rachel!" Gil cried, "Watch out!" She looked up. The boy stepped closer, still reaching out his hand. He spoke a word Gil did not know, and nodded and smiled again. Rachel shrank back from the sea-borne apparition, but she drew her sword, and quickly took up her shield from the deck.

Laughter and cheering arose from the oarsmen, again, and they gathered around, expecting more sport. Rachel raised her sword, but she stepped back, retreating. The man followed, repeating the same phrase, and his intent, unarmed pursuit was more frightening, somehow, than the chaotic swordplay of Danni's opponent.

"Go away!" Rachel cried. "I'm armed. I'll hurt you." But he stepped closer and stretched his arm towards her. "Please!" she cried. "I don't want…."

"Get him!" Gil shouted. "Now!" But in that instant, the boy lunged, and caught her reluctant sword arm, deflecting the blade, even as he reached to draw her closer. Gil leapt forward, but Danni was quicker.

She crossed the deck between them, her blade flashing

before her. There was a hideous splash of red and a shriek of anguish from Rachel. The raider released her then in a kind of slow motion, and stood staring at the blood pouring from his outstretched forearm. He whispered his word again, and then slumped down to the deck, sitting in a heap, clutching his wounded arm, his face white with pain. With a clumsy shuffling of feet, *Silver Dragon*'s oarsmen gathered around. The boy on the deck looked up and half-smiled at Rachel and said his word again.

"What is it?" she cried miserably. "What do you want?"

"Your hair," Erling said. "He says 'Fire-Hair.' He wants to touch your hair."

"My hair?" Rachel whispered, incredulous. "It was just about my hair?" She stared down at the wounded boy in a mixture of horror and pity.

"Surely, it is very beautiful," Erling said solemnly. Then he pointed at the boy's bloody arm and cried, "See! He, too, feels the Selkie's wrath!" And touching his own half-grown beard, he took two careful steps back. A murmuring of agreement swept the deck and Floki's rough crew of Northmen shrank away from Rachel as if her flaming hair were real fire.

"'Neither land nor sea will hide him from her sword,'" Erling recited.

"But it was my sword," Danni said. "It wasn't Shony's fault."

In that moment, Floki leapt, with a shout of triumph, across from the raiders' ship. Standing once more on his own deck, he sheathed his sword, punched Erling's shoulder and looked around, grinning, at his crew. They were all still huddled in a wary clump, staring fearfully at the fallen raider. Floki turned to Erling, "What? You have not seen blood before?"

Danni's voice cut across the cold air. "There!" she cried, indignantly, "There's whose fault it is!" She pointed, outraged, at Floki's chest with the tip of her still bloody sword.

Gil shrank back, expecting a burst of fury. But the Northman's grin widened into a delighted white smile. He pointed at the sword, and the bloodied boy on the deck. "She?" he looked around at his nervous crew. "She vanquishes the champion?" They nodded uneasily. "She spills the only blood of the day?"

There were more nods, and, this time, another shuffling retreat, as if they, too, expected the wrath of their captain. But Floki raised his gaze to the winter sky and shouted, "Odin be praised!" He punched the air and then looked back at Danni, his face aglow with pride.

She strode forward until the point of her blade was touching his tunic. "You made me do that!" she declared. He looked a little baffled, but nodded happily.

"Good!" Floki announced. "You learn well!"

"He's just a boy!" Danni cried. She looked across to the other ship where their opponents cowered. "They're all just boys. And you knew it."

Floki shook his head. "Boys play with women's spindles," he said. "Men go a' viking."

But Danni waved her sword and shouted, "You tricked them." She lowered the blade and imitated Floki's holy man charade. "'Oh, I'm just a humble oarsman, sailing to Hy,'" she simpered.

Erling laughed and slapped Floki's shoulder. Floki laughed, too, and joined Danni, giving a repeat performance of his act. Then suddenly he leaned forward, grasped Danni's sword, and ran his fingers down it, wetting them with the wounded boy's blood. His eyes shone as he raised his dripping hand. "First blood," he said to Danni, proudly. Then he reached forward and solemnly touched his reddened fingers to her forehead, leaving a bloody mark across her smooth brown skin. She reached trembling fingers to the mark and brought them away, blood-stained. "Hail!" Floki cried, "Viking's woman!"

A roar of salutations drowned out Danni's cry of disgust. Glaring at Floki, she flung her bloody sword, clattering, at his feet. "I hate you!" she cried. "You made me hurt that boy. I almost cut his arm off!" She looked down at the wounded sailor who was rocking and moaning in a widening pool of blood. "Can't anyone do anything?" she cried.

Ismail ran forward, unwinding the strip of undyed wool that had replaced his red headband, and knelt by the boy. But Rachel was there before him. She pressed the fingers of her right hand against the bloody wound, holding it firm, while with her left, she searched within the woven pocket that hung about her waist. Gil saw her withdraw a thick wad of bog cotton, like Danni had gathered the day he came.

Her face reddened, and she averted her eyes from the watching men, who surely knew why she, like all girls and women, carried it. Raising her fingers, she slipped the thick, white wad beneath them, pressing hard. The stream of red eased a little, and then, slowed to a trickle.

The young sailor looked up at Rachel, bleary-eyed with cold and loss of blood, but still enthralled. He reached out the fingers of his good hand and whispered his word again, in wonderment. She stayed utterly still, her hand pressing the bloodied bog cotton, her eyes downcast as the shaking fingers touched and softly stroked her windswept, flame-colored hair. A blissful smile crossed the boy's face, and he closed his eyes, content.

That was all, Gil thought. He looked at the bloody deck, the injured boy, the silent, watching Northmen, and Danni, in her heart-wrenching remorse. *All for that*. A shout broke the spell. Svein Snaggle-Tooth pointed and the Northmen looked up and out to sea. Across the white-flecked blue, a ship was fast approaching. Gil reached for his sword, but Ismail's face broke into a smile. "Hakon!" he whispered. "Now we have peace."

Hakon's sail came down and his oarsmen brought *Storm Serpent* smoothly alongside. *Silver Dragon* barely trembled as Hakon nudged his craft expertly into place. His own crew threw grappling irons and tightened the ropes until the three longships lay bound together like a raft, bobbing on the choppy sea; Hakon and the strangers' on either side, Floki's in the middle.

Hakon's crew eyed the vanquished raiders with suspicion while the young Vikings shrank in renewed terror from the sight of Palamedes and his huge warhorse, aboard the new ship. "So," Hakon said, stepping across onto *Silver Dragon*'s deck, "Your swift sail has borne you into trouble."

"None that we could not handle," Floki replied.

Hakon looked around at the defeated raiders and then down at Rachel and the boy at Floki's feet. "No," he said dryly, "I think not." He turned and shouted in the Northmen's tongue to one of his crew and the man leapt quickly to join him. He carried with him a leather sack from which Hakon withdrew two small glass jars and a neat roll of linen cloth. He knelt then beside the boy and gently lifted Rachel's fingers from the wound.

He nodded and smiled at Rachel, then called for water. Another leather sack, bulging with liquid, was brought forward, and removing its wooden stopper, he poured the contents over the wounded arm. The boy shrieked with pain and cried out again when Hakon dabbed the cleansed wound with the contents of each of his glass jars, but all the while he watched the dark Northman with pathetic trust.

Hakon bound the wound tightly with a length of his linen cloth. Then he made the boy sit up, gave him water from the leather sack to drink, and helped him onto his feet. The boy stood, shakily, and managed a grateful smile before he staggered, with helping hands from Gil and Ismail, back toward his own ship. He was hoisted across by the arms of two of his own shipmates, who inclined their heads humbly toward Gil and Ismail. The boy looked back then, and smiled at Rachel and shouted something. A wave of wry laughter swept both ships.

Rachel shook her head, but Danni cried, "What was it?"

Erling smiled. "He says, 'Wait for me, Fire-Hair! I come again, one day, with gold!'"

"He means to wed her," Hakon said. He shook his head. "Youth lives in hope." He laughed and then released the grappling hooks that held the raiders' ship to Floki's. "Go home to your mothers until you grow men's beards!" he shouted, and thrust the ship free with a shove of his boot.

The young Vikings leapt willingly to their oars. Hakon turned to Floki. "Enough play," he said, looking out to the winter sea. "It is not bare-chinned boys who splinter timbers, but early dusk and the black rocks of Pentland. Now, cousin," he said, "We sail." He jumped across to his own ship, and released her from her bonds. Floki called orders to his crew and stepped back toward his steering oar like a man in a trance. All the while, his eyes rested in troubled uncertainty on Danni. Only when the sail rode up the mast and the longship bowed to the wind, did he turn, reluctantly, away.

Ismail crouched down on the deck and lifted Danni's discarded sword. Carefully, he washed the blood from it with the remnants of the water in the leather sack. Then, drying it on the sleeve of his tunic, he offered it to Danni. She thrust it away. "I don't want it. I hate it."

"No. Take," he said. "You are warrior now."

She shook her head and brushed tears away with the back of her hand. "I don't want to be a warrior," she whimpered. "I want to go home."

Ismail nodded solemnly. "So does every warrior, in his heart." He thrust the sword back into her hands and closed her fingers over the hilt. Then, slowly, and with a bitter glance at Floki, Danni slid the blade back into its sheath.

They sailed on, then, and saw no other ships, nor any sign of human life at all, for the rest of that day. Once, Gil thought he glimpsed a curl of blue smoke above a small bay, but all else was snow and rock and sea. Birds flew by, but they were stranger birds, with stranger's voices. He yearned for Feannag's raucous cry. And when he saw the dark glistening heads of seals bobbing in the water, he wished that Shony would appear among them. But they were strangers, too. The land, for all its beauty, was without comfort or friendship.

Then, at mid-afternoon, with the sun already low in the sky, they came to the end of the coast they had followed from Einar's Holm. Beyond lay open sea, thick with frothy waves and, barely visible across it, a low dark line.

"Pentland!" cried Erling, pointing a stubby finger, "And here," he swept his hand from side to side, "Here, the White Horses play." In the fading light, the great, breaking waves did look like galloping warhorses, with curving dark necks, like Doombearer's, and manes of white foam. Aboard *Silver Dragon*, the real ponies neighed in fear as the ship rode out from the last shelter into the full strength of wind and tide.

The deck beneath Gil's feet rose and fell violently, until he was forced to crouch low, clinging to their armor kist to keep his balance. Ismail curled up in a ball and groaned, while Rachel covered her mouth and closed her eyes. Lionheart whinnied and stamped. Gil stumbled across the spray-soaked deck to the pony pen and wormed in beside him, speaking comforting words in his heart. Danni joined him, calming Freya and Frosti, and even reaching to stroke wild, fierce Chocolate, who reared and snorted in reply.

She was calm and unafraid, either of the staggering ponies or the sea. But the joyful delight with which she had begun the journey was gone, and she never looked at Floki where he stood, bracing all his weight against the steering oar, fighting to hold his course. A ship's length away, Hakon, too, struggled against the ferocity of the current and the waves.

Side by side, the two longships plunged onward until they were in the very center of the crossing; with the land they had left as far away, now, as the land to which they sailed. Gil imagined the two ships as if he could see them from afar, two fragile chips of wood in the hugeness of the sea. Again, he had the feeling that he had found the place he was always meant to be.

In the fading light, the coast of Pentland was only a charcoal smudge against the darkening sky. A low rumble reached their ears, and Gil could see the froth of a fierce surf, glowing in the dusk, the only sign of the black cliffs toward which they sailed.

Hakon reefed his sail, shortening it until only a sliver remained to catch the wind, and *Storm Serpent* proceeded under cautious oars. But Floki's ship plunged past, his mast creaking with the force of the bellying cloth. Floki's face and beard were drenched with spray and his eyes were aglow with pure joy as *Silver Dragon* raced on toward an unbroken wall of rock.

Then suddenly a gap appeared in the cliffs, and in an opening between the lines of surf, Gil saw a small bay, sheltered behind a stark headland. Floki leaned hard on his steering oar, swinging the dragon prow toward the narrow gap. Gil's heart caught in his throat as the longship slipped between fierce pillars of rock, and under full, magnificent sail, swept into the refuge of the bay.

At once, the prow settled into calmer seas and the wind dropped. The crashing breakers fell behind them, and, lordly as a queen, *Silver Dragon* rode through the quiet waters up onto the white sand beach. As the keel thudded to rest in the sand, a cheer swept across her deck. Gil heard his own voice, loudest of all.

He looked back and saw Hakon's oarsmen carefully maneuvering *Storm Serpent* through the gap. They rowed the ship to a quiet rest beside Floki's. Taunts and laughter greeted them, but Hakon bowed to his cousin with a smile. "I beg leave, oh noble earl of this splendid harbor, to ground my humble keel beside your own?"

Floki bowed in return and offered the beach as if he was indeed its lord. Then both captains shouted orders to their crews and Northmen poured off the ships into the icy sea. Hauling ropes after them, they struggled ashore, dragging the heavy hulls up the sand. Palamedes mounted Doombearer, and they leapt with a mighty splash into the shallows and thundered up the beach. Wrapping a rope around the pommel of his saddle, the knight bent the strength of the great warhorse to the task.

Gil mounted the rail and Ismail staggered to his feet, grinned weakly and joined him. Together, they jumped, landing thigh deep in the freezing water, and, gasping for breath, struggled up onto dry land. Ismail joined Erling on a rope, and Gil grasped another, with Bjorn. He scrabbled gamely up the sand, hauling on the line. But then Bjorn wrapped it around his burly shoulder and pulled, and Gil rose up off the ground like a tee-shirt hung out to dry. Dropping uselessly back to earth, he went to join Svein dragging the split log ramp over the rail.

The ponies reared and backed, sliding and stumbling, wild-eyed, to the beach. Even Chocolate whinnied in fear and Lionheart, all four feet braced, tail brushing the ramp, skidded down the wet wood on his haunches and landed in a heap on the sand. Scrambling to his feet, he galloped in frantic circles around Gil.

Where's my field? Where's my field?

With an unnerving lurch of homesickness for Cille Aidan, Gil looked at the rough shore vanishing into darkness. *There's a field here,* he said. *Well, sort of a field.*

Lionheart peered into the dusk and snorted. *There might be a wolf.*

Gil stared at the black landscape. *Who said there wasn't a wolf?* He gave Lionheart a reassuring pat. *Wolves don't eat people.* Somebody, somewhere, had told him that.

Wolves eat ponies.

Gil winced. He spotted the other ponies standing together, and the bigger bulk of Doombearer, nearby. *Doombearer will kill the wolves. He's killed hundreds of wolves,* he lied. Gil led Lionheart over to stand by the big warhorse. But Lucy had got there first, snugged up against her new friend's shoulder like she was pasted on. Lionheart's ears went back. But then his eyes gleamed and he shook his head, snorting happily.

Maybe a wolf will eat Lucy.

Gil sighed. *Sometimes I'd like you better if I didn't know what you were thinking.* With a less than genuine pat, he left the pony and joined his friends gathering driftwood along the shore.

The smell of wood smoke from the newly lit cooking fire reminded Gil how really long it had been since they'd eaten. It was colder than it had been at Einar's Holm. The grass was thick with frost, crunching beneath his boots. His sea sodden trousers were stiffening. Alone at the dark edge of the encampment, he stopped, slapping his legs hard to warm them up.

Something rustled in the grass. He leapt back, his mind full of wolves, but then he laughed. A small, brown tail disappeared into a hollow in the frozen grass...a mouse. Suddenly, his mouth twitched and his body trembled, as if an invisible tail of his own was swishing behind him. *I don't eat mice,* he told himself. But then the answer came at once: *I could eat mice.*

He looked down at his armful of driftwood, and then up to the distant flickering campfire. Danni, Rachel, and Ismail were already making their way back. No one could even see him out here. How long would it take him to lay the driftwood in a circle? He could be in and out in a minute. With a fat mouse filling his empty stomach.

The mouse rustled again and his stomach growled as if it were already cat. He thought guiltily of Aidan and his warnings. But Aidan was far away. He crouched and laid the first branch of driftwood down.

"Gil!" Danni's voice cut through the dusk. "Where are

you?" Gil leapt up, heart pounding. He snatched up his piece of driftwood, and turned back to the camp, filled with remorse. And yet, along with the remorse was a tug of regret, as if part of him had just been waiting, all along, for the chance to again be Cat.

"You'll get your chance," he muttered to himself. "Probably sooner than you want. Like Danni becoming a warrior." He broke into a run.

In the light of the campfire Palamedes stood within a circle of puzzled Northmen, staring morosely at the sky. Erling, too, peered upward, as did Ismail and Rachel. "There!" Erling said, and pointed, but the others shook their heads.

Danni shrugged. "It's no use. It's all clouds." She saw Gil and cried, "About time! Have you still got your compass?"

Floki suddenly joined them, laughing, "The Saracen has lost his god!"

Rachel cast him a withering look, and said to Gil, "Palamedes prays facing east to Mecca. But it's too cloudy to read the stars."

Gil dug the compass out of his pocket, checked it in the flickering firelight and then pointed. "North," he said, and then, pointing at right angles, "East." He started to slide the compass back into his pocket, but was suddenly aware that a stunned silence had come over his watching audience. It was broken, at last, by a soft sigh from Palamedes.

"Ah, there, truly is a treasure. How came you by this gift of Allah?" He stared at it, from afar, as if the old metal compass were one of Cille Aidan's golden vessels.

But Bjorn Break-Neck lunged at Gil, pointing a shaking finger. "Throw it away! It is witchcraft! It will bring doom!"

Then Floki strode forward, and, brushing the big man aside, took the compass from Gil. Several of his crew gasped in alarm. "Everything is witchcraft to Bjorn," he said. He brought the compass close to his face and turned it in a circle, his eyes intent on the moving needle. "I have heard of this thing. But I have not seen it." He studied the compass hungrily and Hakon joined him, peering at it over his cousin's shoulder.

"My father sailed once with an earl who possessed one," Hakon murmured. "He said it was a piece of Odin's sword."

"No," Floki said. "I hear it said it is a piece of a falling star. It flies always to the North Star, seeking its home. That seems right to me." He turned it this way and that, his eyes full of wonderment.

Bjorn reached for the compass with his great, hairy hand. "Give it to me and I will throw it into the sea. It is witchcraft! Witchcraft from Tir nan Og!" He looked ominously at Gil as he spoke. "It will bring disaster." There was a rumbling of discontent among the Northmen.

Floki smiled and pushed Bjorn away. "Too many ale nights addle the mind. It is but a clever tool, forged by men, I think, not Odin." He turned it again and looked out to sea, as if imagining where it might take him. He shrugged. "I would not throw it away. No more, would I seek it. A man who knows the stars, knows the winds and the coast, needs no witchcraft. No falling stars or swords of Odin."

"All very well," Hakon said, and he reached out and took the compass from Floki's hand. "But clouds hide the stars, and mist the coast, and the winds are full of trickery. Still, it is not ours to keep or throw away, but the boy's." He pressed the compass firmly back into Gil's hand. Gil slipped it into his pocket, with relief.

The gathered Northmen seemed relieved, too, to be done with the compass. With wary backward glances at Gil, they went away to their tasks. Some tended the cooking fire. Two men turned two haunches of venison, a parting gift from Magnus, on a spit over the flames. Others hung black woolen cloth over the lowered masts of the ships, making their rough shelters. Two more, each, from Floki's and Hakon's crews, mounted a silent guard at either end of the camp.

It made Gil think of the shadows beyond in a new, unsettling way. He watched as Ismail and Palamedes knelt and bowed their heads to the snowy ground, then turned back to the fire, drying his wet trouser legs by its welcome heat. He thought of Cille Aidan's bell, bringing each day to an end; and his small stone cell across a day's length of icy sea. Loneliness enveloped him, as black and cold as the winter night on this first, alien shore.

Then the good smell of sizzling meat began to rise from the fire. Rachel and Danni joined him, and then Ismail; and Gil's spirits rose, too. He wolfed down his portion of hot, charred venison, dripping with bloody juices, glad again to be a boy and not a mouse-eating cat.

After supper, with his stomach full and his body aching from the long day at sea, Gil felt ready to curl up and sleep, right there by the fire. Some of the Northmen were already cloak wrapped mounds beside it, though others were singing and drinking ale. But Svein Snaggle-Tooth beckoned him to board the ship, its black tents being the privilege of guests. Erling reconstructed the girls' shelter and then stepped respectfully back, as did every man of the crew.

Gil watched until the two girls disappeared safely inside their tent. Then he went to check the ponies a last time before bed. He found them just beyond the light of the fire. Lucy was still pasted to Doombearer, but Lionheart had secured a place, one warhorse width away, at his other side. Gil patted the dozing pony. Then he turned away, and suddenly froze. The shadowy figure of a man loomed between himself and the campfire. With a cry of alarm, he drew his sword.

"A good, quick hand," said a quiet voice. "But you may sheath your blade. Battle is done for today."

"Floki?" Gil said. The young Northman stood waiting with a look that in anyone else would pass for shyness. For a brief moment Gil suspected he was play-acting again.

But then he said, with odd formality, "I would speak with you, if I may."

Gil nodded slowly. "Sure." He sheathed the sword.

"I am grateful," Floki said. He sat down on a smooth boulder and Gil sat too. Floki looked at him gravely in the flickering firelight; then smiled. "You wield your sword well, today. But, watch, always for the man behind. Battle has no rules."

"I saw that," Gil said. His heart swelled at the praise, in spite of himself.

Floki clasped his hands and looked down at them for a long while. When he looked up, he smiled again, and so openly, that Gil couldn't help but smile back. "Women," Floki said. "They are a great mystery." He inclined his head soberly, and again studied his hands. "You know Danni well," Floki said. "Perhaps you see what I do not see." He looked up with his forehead furrowed with doubt. "Today, she is angry with me. And I do not understand."

Gil rocked back on his boulder and clasped his hands around his knees. "Today. The battle."

"Did I not fight well?" Floki said hesitantly.

"You?" Gil cried, "Nobody fought like you!"

"Yes! Of course! I am Floki Magnusson, Feaster of Ravens! At twelve winters, I blooded my sword! I have killed more men than I have years." He shook his head. "So why is she angry?"

Gil paused, "Floki, will you promise me something, before I say anything?"

"Is there a price to your wisdom?"

"No, of course not," Gil shook his head. "Just promise you won't cut my head off if you don't like my answer. Swear on something. Odin, or...."

Floki nodded vigorously and reached within his tunic. He brought out a leather pouch, hung from a cord around his neck, and withdrew from within a thing that glowed golden and lustrous in the light of the flames; the beautiful amber necklace that had filled Rachel with terror. Gil stared, surprised that Floki carried it with him even here. Floki held up the amber-inlaid cross that hung from the rich beads. "I swear on Lord Yesu's sign, honored by the holy Ab, Aidan!" he said solemnly.

Gil took a deep breath. "Okay. Here goes. Sure. You fought fabulously. But the whole battle only happened because you let those kids catch us. Then you tricked them by pretending you were harmless, and you bragged about Aidan's book—which you had no right to even know was there!" Floki glowered. "You promised, right?" Gil reminded him quickly. "And then you pushed that tent over. I saw you. You put the girls in danger just so you could get them out of it!"

"In danger?" Floki cried. "From those fluff-chinned fools? I could have slain them all, single-handed, had I chosen."

"Well, the girls didn't know that, did they? All they saw was that you used them as bait. That's, like, pretty insulting, you know. And then," he continued, "You were so busy showing off, you never even saw that idiot climb out of the sea."

"What of him?" Floki muttered sullenly. "A Viking who couldn't defend himself against a girl? Where was the danger? And Danni herself fought like a Viking!" He smiled, remembering. "Ah, there is a woman!"

"She hates herself," Gil said bitterly. "She nearly killed that boy. She nearly cut his arm off."

"It will heal," Floki shrugged. "I have had worse. And then, he will have a scar to tell of around the winter fire."

"A scar given to him by a girl? Will he tell of that?"

"Ah, but the story will grow!" Floki said happily. "She will become a fire-maiden! A daughter of Freya! And, indeed," he paused and finished dreamily, "Perhaps she is."

He leaned forward, then, speaking eagerly. "The earls give me good land, for the feats of my sword. Hrolf's Isle. A share of the Horse Isle, as well. Soon, I will have silver enough, and I will build a longhouse. Twice, thrice, the size of Einar's Holm. Fit for a king's son. Then, I will wed her." He held up the necklace, catching the firelight, "And she will wear this on our marriage day."

Gil sat a long while, studying the young Northman in silence. Then he shook his head slowly. "Danni can't get married," he said. "She's just a girl."

"A girl? She has seen fifteen winters! My mother bore me a full year before her age!"

Gil gave an awkward shrug. "There's more to it than that, where we come from."

Floki looked appalled. "What? In Tir nan Og they do *that* thing differently?"

"No!" Gil felt his face go red. "I mean…I think…look, at our age in Tir nan Og, we're still children. We have to go to school. Study. For years."

"What is there to learn in so many years? She lays a fine fire. She roasts meat and makes porridge. She spins and weaves and plays harp by the fireside. Look!" he touched Gil's cloak, "Who could dress her man better than that? And she can ride like a king's daughter and wield a Viking sword! What more is there?"

"Other things," Gil murmured. He thought wildly, shaking the murk from his memories. "History!" he cried. *You. Like a thousand years after you're dead.* He looked hard at the young Northman, then. "Floki," he asked cautiously. "What is Tir nan Og? Do you know?"

"Of course," Floki said. "It is a land. A kingdom."

"Where the guardians keep Arthur?" Gil prompted.

Floki shook his head. "I do not believe in the guardians. Arthur is dead. But Tir nan Og; that is real."

"Okay," Gil tried again, "Where is it?"

"Across the Western Sea. Past the Land of Ice and Fire, I think." Gil shook his head slightly. "Am I wrong?" Floki asked. "Does your Falling Star tell you other?"

Gil leaned back on the boulder and looked up at the sky. It had cleared a little and he glimpsed high, icy stars, between patches of cloud. There was no moon. "No," he said. "You're right. But it isn't as easy as that. You can't just sail there."

Floki grinned. "Show me the tide I cannot sail!"

Gil paused. He felt older and wiser and even protective of the young Northman. "This tide," he said, "You cannot sail. No man can. Not even you."

But I have, he thought wonderingly. He looked back to where the ship lay waiting on the strand, and beyond, to the black starlit sea. He saw the face of his green-eyed girl, framed in starlight as in the white stone. *And I'll sail it again, one day, and take her home with me.*

EPILOGUE

The night was black. There was no moon. Gil glimpsed high, icy stars between patches of cloud, but when he opened the curtains as far as they would go, their frail light barely penetrated the darkened room. Behind him he heard a muffled sob. He turned to face the darkness. "Hey, roomie. It's okay."

"Put the light back on. Please," Aaron whimpered.

"I can't," Gil said. Even when he hung a blanket over the door, the nurses saw it. "You know what will happen."

"It's dark," Aaron said hopelessly.

"I know," Gil murmured. The dark was just one of the things that freaked Aaron. Aaron was a really weird kid, and Gil could see why he was in a place like Safe Haven. If Safe Haven was a little nicer, and–big "if"– if Dr. Fairchild wasn't there, it might be the best place for him. Except that was what Gil's mother was always saying about Gil. "It's the best place for you. And as soon as you're better, you'll come back home."

"Come on," he said then, "No Man's Land."

He heard Aaron's little gasp of relief as he scrambled out of his bed, to the place in the middle of the room where Gil told his stories. Gil felt his way through the blackness until they bumped into each other. Aaron giggled, and they sat down, cross-legged on the linoleum. "Hey, you don't know what dark is!" Gil punched his roommate gently and Aaron giggled again. "Remember when I got locked in the Tomb? *That* was dark."

"But you got out and the bones were just turnips. Right?"

Gil said, "See? Most of what we're scared of isn't real."

"The dragon was real."

"Yeah, well. That was real."

"Tell me a story," Aaron said.

"Sure. But no noise, whatever." Gil glanced at the closed door. He paused a moment. "How about the hounds in the Forest of Pentecost?"

"When you were the cat?"

"Yeah," Gil nodded in the darkness.

"I had a cat once," Aaron sounded a hundred years old. "But they took it away." Gil wished he could be Cat, here, just once, for Aaron. Then Aaron said, "Tell me about Merlin's Tower."

Gil's hands clenched on his knees. "No," he whispered. "Not that. I don't want to tell that again." He shook his head, feeling another, colder darkness closing in. "Something else," he said.

He thought Aaron would ask for the dragon, then. Or maybe the battle in the Forest of Caledon. But instead, he said, "Tell me about meeting the girl."

Oh, yes. Even just saying her name brought her back to him, alive and laughing and beautiful. So he could believe again, and shut far away the truth: that she was bones and dust in a grave. Unless, unless he could return.... "Janetta," he whispered. "My green-eyed girl...."

"Wait!" Aaron's hand gripped his arm, and then he, too heard the footsteps. They both plunged into their beds and in seconds Aaron was convincingly snoring. When the door clicked open and light flooded down, it was Gil's fast breathing that gave them away.

"No talking after lights out, boys. You know the rules." Dr. Fairchild was using his jolly scoutmaster voice. "No late-night feasts. No witches' covens." Gil knew he was meant to laugh, but he clung steadfastly to the pretense of sleep. "Gil?"

"It was me, Dr. Fairchild," Aaron burst out. "I talk in my sleep."

"It was Gil." The voice was suddenly cold.

Gil sat up and shoved the covers aside. "Look," he said, "He's scared of the dark. So, I was telling him a story." He paused and angrily met Fairchild's brilliant blue gaze.

Fairchild ignored him and turned to Aaron. "Do you want to sleep in Room 10, so Gil won't disturb you anymore?" He smiled like he was being kind. Room 10 was solitary where they put kids who were maybe going to off themselves. It didn't even have a window. "No. Please," Aaron whispered.

Gil balled his hand into a fist and punched the metal bedframe. "Would the world end if you gave him a night light?" "Aaron needs to face his fears," Fairchild said. "Just like you. Even if you won't help yourself, you could still help him." "So, put me in Room 10, you bastard," Gil shouted, "Not *him*."

Fairchild nodded briefly, "Goodnight, boys," and turned off the light.

Gil lay awake trying to blot out the small whimpers until he couldn't stand it any longer. Then he slid out of bed and crept, silent as Cat, across the floor. "Hey, dude," he murmured. "I'm back." Aaron made a big choking sob and grabbed his hand. "It was the day we came to Camelot...." Gil began.

About the Author

Alison Scott, the daughter of two writers, Alexander Leslie Scott, master of the western detective novel, and artist turned short story writer, Lily Kay Scott, was born in Manhattan. Her brother, Justin Scott, is a master of thrillers, mysteries, and sea stories, including the Isaac Bell Adventures. A Junior Year Abroad from her American university took her to Scotland, where she met her future husband, Clement Skelton- -an actor, playwright, film cameraman, Battle of Britain Spitfire pilot, and monster hunter. She had her first baby while living on the shores of Loch Ness.

From an apprenticeship in Gothic romances, she went on to publish her first hardcover novel, A World Full of Secrets, writing as Alison Scott, while her husband became C.L. Skelton, writing successful family sagas. After she was widowed, she continued writing while raising their two sons, Professor Alasdair Skelton, geologist researching in climate change, and actor and gardener Justin Skelton.

As Alison Scott Skelton, she has published several works of contemporary and historical fiction in the US and Britain; among them, *Different Families, A Murderous Innocence, Saving Grace, An Older Woman,* and *Family Story.*

The Warriors of Tir nan Og, the six-book series that opens with *The Underwater Bridge,* is her first work for a young adult audience.

Curious about other Crossroad Press books?
Stop by our site:
http://store.crossroadpress.com
We offer quality writing
in digital, audio, and print formats.

Printed in Great Britain
by Amazon

23272120R00148